Angelica Selby

In the Sunlight

A Tale of Mentone

Angelica Selby

In the Sunlight
A Tale of Mentone

ISBN/EAN: 9783337122188

Printed in Europe, USA, Canada, Australia, Japan

Cover: Foto ©Andreas Hilbeck / pixelio.de

More available books at **www.hansebooks.com**

IN THE SUNLIGHT.

A TALE OF MENTONE.

BY

ANGELICA SELBY,

AUTHOR OF "ON DUTY."

" To love is the great glory, the last culture, the highest happiness ;
to be loved is little in comparison."

LONDON AND NEW YORK:

FREDERICK WARNE AND CO.
1892.

To

G R A C E.

" All things come round to him who will but wait."

CONTENTS.

CONTENTS.

IN THE SUNLIGHT.

CHAPTER I.

"Woman's at best a contradiction still."—Pope.

"My dear Puff, I am extremely sorry to disturb you, but I really *must* have a blaze—burn up, do!" and the speaker attacks a cheerless pile of coal vigorously The prodding proves successful, and the tiny tongues of yellow light lick the dark patches with ever-increasing volume, until they join forces, rising together in the ruddy glory of a steady blaze.

The room looks picturesque in the firelight, which touches with beautifying tenderness all the dear old, *very old* furniture. What matter that the carpet is threadbare, heavy curtains and old satin chairs well-worn, when in the red glow all is blended into harmonious equality, and the "high lights" are picked out with such sweet consideration, that even well-kicked piano legs and scratched tables are all the fairer for its kindly illumination?

The flames leap and laugh as they note how old Dick, the privileged bull terrier, hugs himself against the brass fender, squeezing into a tighter knot of joy as the comforting wave of warmth surges over him. They croon and crackle a cheery greeting to that recumbent figure in the big arm-chair, but she takes no notice whatever, excepting that the little feet are poked as near as possible to the bars, and the heavy gown is tweaked each moment a wee bit higher. Suddenly the "chair-back" is twisted over her head, and two strong hands hold it firmly there, while with a rapid in-drawing of the scorching ankles, and a kick that sends Puff flying in disgust, the girl ejaculates, " Teddy, don't! O Teddy, my hair! don't be an idiot—do let go; as if I didn't know it was you!"

"I like that. I believe you were asleep, and a precious sell it would have been for you if it had been—Billy, for instance! Neat ankles are all very well; but, you know "——

"Stuff! look out! don't sit on Puff. Here, give him to me; he was so comfortably curled up on my lap until you frightened him off. There, darling," stroking the sleek black cat fondly as he settled himself with slow deliberation (after a feeble lick or two) to the luxury of sleep.

"Where's mother?"

"Writing. Oh! did you get the letters? Were there any? Has father come in yet?"

"Yes, I went on while father went to the gorse end; there were two for mother, none for you. Get out, Dick, you brute! I believe you're qualified for the best foie gras on record. Been out, Ivy?"

"Too cold and detestable. What letters, Teddy?"

"Only Aunt Amy, and some circulars. Why?"

"Oh, I don't know; I always hope something will happen. Nothing ever *does!* but still every post *might* bring something new, something to break the dead level of such absolute monotony. How I wish to goodness I were a man!"

Teddy's sleepy grey eyes glance amusedly at the

little pretty mignon figure, the tumbled small brown head, and meeting the petulant glance of the brown eyes smiles blandly, and slowly closing his own, preserves silence.

"If there's one maddening thing on earth it's having any one smile at you and say nothing. It means either you're not worth arguing with, or I shan't take the trouble—*which*, Teddy?"

"My dear child, I was merely seeking a solution for your present state of mind. I am rather afraid it must be caused by liver, though I'd give a good deal to know it is due to *love.*"

"Teddy! you *wouldn't!* I can't think (with a little impatient wriggle extremely discomposing to Puff) what you all mean by harp, harp, harping about Billy! It's hardly flattering to see how you are longing to get rid of me, simply *throwing me* at the head of the first stranger who will have me."

"Considering that you have ridden Billy's horses for the last three years, that he's been almost living in the house ever since he's been here, I don't quite see how you can round on him now and call him *a stranger;* and there's another thing I take exception to, even allowing for a slight inaccuracy in your statement (don't fidget, it's particularly distressing to Puff), by no possible line of argument can you back up that assertion that this is the *first* who will have you, though I don't for a moment deny the advisability of 'throwing you at his head,' as you so aptly term it."

Half turning in her chair, resting her elbow on the arm of it that is nearest her brother, Ivy leans towards him and breaks out impatiently—"It *is* the first—the first *man*, I mean! Would you have had me marry Tommy Ponsonby, a boy of twenty, six feet long by one broad, nothing inside him, and crowned with a straw-coloured tuft like a cockatoo! Would you?" (viciously).

Teddy's lazy reply is barely audible, "I didn't specify Tommy."

"Who, then—old Mr. Jamieson, father's friend? All outside neatness and inside fussiness, with his two thousand a year and one eye! No, thank you; he'd drive me mad in a week. He *measures* himself into the centre of every chair he sits on; he'd never let me have a flower askew or anything trimmed on one side. Why is he bald? he *counts* his hairs daily and pulls out the uneven ones! He'd have the cats in pairs, and each on its cushion, an exact match! Ugh! I wouldn't have him if he could arrange his possessions differently, and instead of two thousand and one eye, have two eyes and one thousand!"

"I should think not—more fool you if you would! But how about Barker? he's right enough to look at, and *good* enough in all conscience—a hard-working, unselfish parson, just the sort of fellow for you!"

"Teddy, you know I *reverence* parsons—that is, a few, a very few, like father, for instance. I quite agree with you about Mr. Barker, he's a very fine fellow, and a very good man, and all that, but you know he could hardly have expected any one to accept him, except a humble-minded saint of the Middle Ages" ("or a middle aged saint," murmured Teddy *sotto voce*), "when he proposed as he did. I am not *really* very vain, I think, Ted, but when he just remarked placidly as we came back from choir practice, 'I'll send you that chant of Bridge's as soon as I return to Twynham. Suppress those altos if they roar so,—it is chiefly Sammy I am coming to help your father next Sunday, but I think I may as well tell you now how I agree with Solomon, that a man that findeth a wife findeth a good thing ; and, my dear Miss Peyton, favour is deceitful and beauty is vain, but a virtuous woman is far above rubies ; therefore, may I trust, Ivy, *may* I trust, that the heart of her husband may safely trust in her ?' and he made a grab at my hand, and upset all the Psalters in the mud ! So I had a rare excuse for a laugh, for I must say I thought it was rather qualifying the compliment (if it is a compliment to be asked to be any man's wife) by letting me know I was selected simply because I wasn't beautiful or likely to find favour elsewhere !"

A smile flits across Teddy's brown face for a moment, but it dies as he gnaws at his tiny moustache, and his eyes lose their usual expression of amused indifference and become a degree graver as they darken and contract with some intenser thought. He is such a fine-looking fellow in his old shooting suit that Ivy watches him with undisguised satisfaction, not that he is really so handsome—not nearly as handsome as Fane, the next brother—but there is about him a charm in manner, voice, and expression that far outweighs the advantage mere physical beauty bestows upon the younger brother. Just now, as the grey eyes look wistfully into the fire, and the big fellow turns with a little smothered sigh for the *Times*, Ivy's heart smites her with sudden contrition, and she whispers, as she pulls at the coat sleeve near her—

"Oh, I know what you're thinking of, Teddy. Do you suppose *I* haven't thought and thought till I feel ill—positively *ill!* But I don't see how, supposing I were to marry Billy, it would make things any better. It is not you or I, or Archie's schooling, or Cyril's future, that makes father look years and years older from anxiety, and brings that look into mother's eyes. I know, Ted; no, I won't stop! I feel sometimes I almost hate Fane! Teddy, listen; I know it's wrong to feel *mad* as I do, but I can't tell mother. It seems to make things worse to put them into words, but why should he be so different? His intolerable selfishness, his calm appreciation of himself and utter disregard of every one else, and his conviction that he is alone the one deserving of success, and *naturally* a favourite of Fortune's, drives me perfectly wild "——

"Father says I've did them all right, mother."

"I am so glad, my darling; it is so nice to have tried hard and conquered. Ah! take care of Paul."

"I'll carry him."

Ivy and Teddy push back their chairs and rise to rearrange the firelit circle, as their mother enters the room followed by a little boy of about seven years old. Tall, stately, regal looking, a noble type of woman, of gracious mien, with a look of depth and power about the calm grand brow, of tenderness in the sweet firm mouth, and wide penetration in the clear hazel eyes, which in their directness of expression are an index to the purity of soul which shines through them—a face it rests one to look at, lined though it is by sorrow's touch, leaving there no bitterness, but only an additional depth of patience.

"Sit here, mother." Teddy pushes a chair forward.

"Thank you, my boy; take care, Cyril, darling!"

" Cyril !   Mother, *do* look at the way he's carrying Paul !"

The child advances into the light clasping a large
tawny Persian cat with one arm ; its head and fore-
paws protrude comically above his little elbow, and
the poor thing's huge fat body, contracted hind-legs,
and bushy tail, hang down, oscillating ponderously
as he walks.

" *Really*, Cyril," Ivy begins again, " how can you be
so cruel ? squeezing up his head like that, with all
his poor dear heavy body hanging down and wobbling
about—you *really* might think ! How'd you like it
yourself ? "

Teddy's " *Well*, Ivy!" is lost in his mother's smiling " Bring him here, Cyril darling,—no, he won't
interfere with my work, Ivy,—there, poor puss !
You must think of his feelings, my boy, another
time !"

" Yes, mother."

Lamps, afternoon tea, and t.e appearance of the
Vicar, a squarely built man, with kindly brown eyes
and a profusion of grey hair, introduces scattering
elements to the hearthrug coterie.

" Well, Ted, my boy, I am sorry they won't give
you more leave, but soldiers cannot expect a roseleaf
existence, I am glad to say, any more than we can.
Thanks to Billy, you have had some good hunting,
for poor old ' Rat-trap wouldn't have carried you
for an hour. By the way, didn't you meet Billy ?
I thought I saw him coming up the lane on that
new big bay of his. How does he like him ? "

" Pretty well—too big and heavy to be fast. He
thinks he'll just use him for riding about the farms.
Such a vile mouth, you have to pull him in like

anything. I advised him to call him 'Staylace,' Teddy adds, with a quiet smile.

"You didn't ask him in?"

"N—no, I didn't."

In the pause that follows Ivy feels distinctly uncomfortable. That it is no longer possible to invite Billy—more properly speaking, Mr. William Dare— to come in at any hour, and at all times, is certainly due to her. All the old sociable intercourse and familiar visions of Billy "dropping in," generally twice, *always* once a day, are over and done with now, and the knowledge that it is so is very annoying, quite depressing, in weather like this, when there is so faint a chance of any one else interesting appearing upon the scene! It is rather a relief when her father departs for another trudge to some far cottage in his scattered parish, and Teddy accompanies him, vowing he has not had half enough exercise that day. Cyril vanishes to the study for his hour of "preparation," and Ivy and her mother are alone.

For some moments there is silence between them; then Ivy, resting her head against her mother's knee, while she sits gazing into the fire, begins in rather an uncertain sort of voice, " Mother, I've been thinking perhaps I am putting self first ; it seems to have spoilt so many things my not caring for Billy, —that—that—I think I'll tell him, if he really does care so much about it, I *will* marry him whenever he likes ! "

For all answer one of her mother's hands quits the knitting and smooths soothingly the little brown head.

" Why, my child, what reason have you for con- templating such a thing ? "

" I haven't any reason, only everything is so

horrid now! and it used to be so different. I never thought of Billy like *that!* he seemed just Teddy's best friend, perfectly devoted to father, and with any number of horses longing to be exercised. When he first came here you remember how fond he was of you and father *at once!* I thought he just loved coming because there was some one to talk to, and Horston was so lonely for him all alone. Now he has spoilt *everything!* I don't mean only that I can't ride his horses with Teddy any more, but everything was so nice and comfortable, and *now*, I think him downright stupid, mother, really I do!"

"I do not agree with you in thinking him 'stupid' because he likes my little girl. I think in so many ways he would have suited you, my child; but it is a matter I would have you decide entirely for yourself, only remembering that respect and esteem must be only the foundation for a love that must be absolute and entire, to ensure the probability of happiness."

"Mine's not *that*. When I don't see him I like him so much, I can almost imagine I love him a little, but it goes the moment he comes!"

"Then, my child has yet to learn what love means. And I think the opportune invitation I have may be the best thing for you, hard though it will be to lose you. I think certainly it will be as well both for you and poor Mr. Dare that you should go away for a time"——

"Leave the schools, you and father, the choir and cats! Indeed, no, mother! he will get over it soon enough. He is only a man, and of course, like the rest, proverbially fickle!" and Ivy smiles at the quiet face above her.

"So you do not care in the least to go to the Riviera with Aunt Amy and the girls?"

"Mother! when? how? what? why? *really!* Oh, mother, what does she say? *me* to go to the Riviera! How I've longed and pined and hoped some day I'd see something really *foreign*—something absolutely unlike dull, brown, unpoetic Mudsbury! Hot white houses, Berlin blue skies, palms, wicked, handsome Russians, and dark-eyed Italians. Oh, mother!" with a look of delight, "oh! say when and why?"

"Next week, my child," and Mrs. Peyton looks somewhat wistfully at the sparkling eager face at her knee. At the first opportunity how willingly does this child rise with glad enthusiasm to leave the shelter of her tender care, to risk alone the perplexing possibilities of the unknown! Is it always so that the mother's love is absolute and that of the children but partial? that each child is a limb, a part of the whole to the one, an offshoot capable of separating itself from the parent stem to grow and flourish elsewhere, to the other? If one member suffer all the members suffer with it, is undoubtedly true of a mother's participation in aught that affects the outermost limit of her children's interest, but are the children's sensations equally reciprocal? Ivy's eyes are lifted in glad questioning to her mother's face, where no shadow reflects upon it one glimmering of regret. She smiles as she continues—

"It is rather sudden this determination of your aunt's to go abroad, but her anxiety about Gwendoline, and the doctor's decision that spring in England would be a risk for her, have quite settled the question. You must join them in London as soon as possible, for there are several things you will want, my child, and on Wednesday next they leave."

But there is no answering gladness now; all the keen delight has died from the parted lips, the brown eyes overflow with sudden tears, and clinging to her mother with a little convulsive clutch, Ivy sobs.

"Next Wednesday! I won't go! Nothing on earth shall induce me to go! I should *die* without you, mother darling; I should get into fearful trouble by myself; no, I won't go! I feel I should *hate* it! I'll stay at home quietly and marry Billy, I feel *much* more inclined for that," with a little sob.

It was never intended by a merciful Providence that the amphibious duckling should vex with anxious fears its agonised hen foster mother. The nature of each child, however diverse or antagonistic one from the other, finds its keynote only in its mother's chord of perfect sympathy, and hence that wonderful comprehension that needs no explanation, to throb with answering conformity to every sensation —a knowledge attained by intuition not analysis.

Through her tears Ivy could feel perfectly secure in the conviction that her mother knew every turn and double of her impetuous desires, and indeed smiled a rainy little smile to herself at the grotesque alternative she had suggested! One thing she did *not* know, and that was that the untenableness of her position had been realised by her mother, and this invitation was the outcome of her correspondence with her sister on the subject.

Mrs. Peyton and Mrs. Lestrange were sisters, bound to each other by a devotion that deepened as the years rolled by. Meeting as often as the affairs of their married lives permitted, they kept up the keenest interest in each other's concerns, and in the welfare of their children. Their father and mother were both dead; their only brother, too, having been killed by a fall out hunting, and leaving only one son, Percy Mainwaring, they had perhaps unconsciously permitted their interest to concentrate round the fortunes of their children. Mrs. Peyton, the elder sister, had five—four boys and Ivy, who had been up to the present, from various causes, one of the predominating anxieties. Her wayward impulsiveness and high spirits, blended with a certain fixedness of purpose approaching to obstinacy when thwarted or misjudged, combined with an airy flightiness in intention and action when not acted upon by outward influences, made her a difficult problem to many, needing an intimate knowledge of her complex character to judge its contradictions fairly. Realising the danger of her being hurried into a decision contrary to her inclinations, Mrs. Peyton had arranged with her sister for Ivy to visit her cousins for some time.

An alliance with Mr. Dare, viewed from the vantage ground of common sense, was entirely desirable. He was young, rich, well connected, and what counted far higher in the unworldly wisdom of Mrs. Peyton, high principled, and endowed with many lovable qualities. But to Ivy herself it was distasteful. As long as he had been merely a *friend*, there had appeared no adverse criticism, and their intercourse had always been most cordial and enjoyable; but at the first symptom of a desire for something more and deeper than this friendship, Ivy's feelings seemed to undergo a complete change. All that had pleased before was now ridiculous, his very virtues were represented as reflecting upon his intellect, and the girl's justice seemed to wither in some overpowering dread of being caught in the toils of his constancy and devotion. To free her from all disquieting influences had been her mother's desire—to let her find in unbiassed freedom the solution to the problem, Do I or do I not care? With tender words of advice and encouragement, Mrs. Peyton talked to her as she sat outlined in bold relief against the red glare of the firelight. And the petulance gave way to a deeper earnestness and gravity of expression until Ivy rose to attend the usual choir practice.

"Mother mine, I am going to be serious *always*. I feel it growing, the old husk of frivolity is cracking (don't smile, mother!), and I shall return as practical and philosophic as Sybil herself—there, darling. I can't say more! Good-bye. Oh!" (putting her head round the door), "I'll suppress Dawson's everlasting oboe stop, and hustle him over the Amens. Ta-ta," and she goes.

CHAPTER II.

"Oh! 'tis the curse of love and still approv'd
When women cannot love where they're beloved."
—*Two Gentlemen of Verona.*

EVERYTHING is ready! Boxes packed with her wardrobe enriched with "spoils" from mother. Delicate lace, and any jewellery Ivy pronounces modern enough to wear.

Few indeed are the trifles she chooses, a string of pearls and a thin gold chain being all she selects

from the store from which the cream has long ago
been skimmed.

Teddy has returned to his regiment, leaving her
his blessing, and expressing the hope that she will
have acquired a grain of common sense by the time
she returns.

"Now for my good-byes in the village and that's
all! I won't *hear* of your coming out, mother, it's
simply perishing. I have no fear of Billy, he can't
know I'm going, no one has seen him for the last
two days," and Ivy buttons her gloves contentedly.

Dragging the reluctant Dick from the fire, and
whistling to the other dogs, who scamper after her
joyously, she disappears behind the laurels.

The bitter wind on this raw January day, the
abominable state of the roads, ankle deep in mud, the
exasperating behaviour of the exuberant retriever pup
(who simply *wallows* in the gutters, and then bounds
up, splashing her Newmarket with reckless affection)
are trying in the extreme, particularly when the fund
of light-hearted good temper is at its lowest ebb.

"Oh! but it's nearly over now," when *again* that
pup —"Drop my boa! drop it, Rollick, you wretch!"
gyrating, while Rollick ambles round, his floppy
ears cocked, his knowing brown eyes full of mischief,
as he tugs merrily at the long waving end he has
sportively caught in his mouth. *He* is perfectly cool,
while Ivy is clearly furious. As she makes frantic
forward grabs, Rollick as promptly retires, splashing
up showers of grey slush in his retreating gambols.

"If I pull it in with a sudden jerk it will break,
and that little villain will keep his end: never!"—
Another bound, a despairing stumble, a wild totter
that brings Ivy to her knees, but oh! joy, the

careering puppy is caught! After the satisfaction
of banging him *well* (which he takes as a very good
joke), she surveys herself with disgust.

"Thank goodness, there's no one to see; I've only
the Millars to go to, and it's already dusk. Oh, you
beauty, I'll be revenged! you shall be *washed!* Do
you hear?" addressing the rampageous puppy, who is
eyeing her from the top of a bank with cool defiance! "The stable yard shall swim, and you shall be
half drowned ere this insult can be wiped out!" Then
suddenly breaking into a merry laugh she shakes
her muff at him, and runs down a lane leading to a
large farmhouse. One of the Miss Millars opens the
door herself: there are seven of them, all short, and
—well, plump, in gradation, from the pig-tailed ten-
year-old to the neatly plaited eldest. Although they
live in the parlour, read novels, and sing Tosti's
last, they are not too fine to be of great help in
the parish; indeed, Ivy has come to ask a favour
now before bidding them farewell. "You know you
promised you would take my class, Lucy, if I went
away. Well! will you do it now? Of course it is
asking a great favour, because I may be away *months,*
but you understand my boys so well. You know
Georgie Hobbs *can* only get through his collect at
railway speed—if you check him, he is done for; and
Sammy *can't* help rocking, he really must be allowed
to churn up his answers while he rolls, and if you
will only wait for a minute or two, and not hurry
or *look* at him, they are generally right." Ivy
finished eagerly.

"Yes, Miss Peyton, most certainly, Miss Peyton;
I shall be very glad to assist you in any way I can,
Miss Peyton."

"Ah! thank you so much.   No! I must not stay for tea"—to Mrs. Millar, who is the good farmer's "old woman," an authority on dairy and poultry matters, with none of the modern gentility of her daughters.

"Good-bye, my dear, good-bye; don't ye stay away too long.   We can't get on without ye, and leastways there is *one* as won't be happy till you're back."   She shakes Ivy's hand warmly, laughing at her own little joke, while the poor child hurries her adieux, feeling nervously conscious of her crimson cheeks, and dreading a further reference to poor Billy's well-known penchant.   With a long sigh of relief she clicks the little garden-gate and turns into the lane.

Between the high walls, behind which loom huge ricks outlined against a sullen sky, she espies—Billy! There is no escape, for she can turn neither to the right hand nor the left.   She would fain flee past him, but scorns an act that *might* convey a notion of fright.   With cold hands and a head that swims, she walks slowly forward.   A moment more and Billy stands before her.

"I couldn't let you go without saying good-bye."   His voice sounds far away, although undoubtedly those grey gaiters are not a yard off. Lifting her head with sudden resolve, Ivy encounters a pair of blue eyes gazing at her with such passionate longing, that her own fill with sudden tears.

"It's only for a little time," she murmurs.

"To you perhaps—to me!   Ivy, I will not bother you.   I suppose I can take ' No ' if you mean it, but *do* you mean it?   Do you think you know your own mind? I'm not such an ass that I don't know I'm not half good enough for you and all that, but you *do* like me a little. Can't you give me a *grain* of hope before you go? Of course you'll meet loads of fellows much more worthy of you than I am, but not *one* who could love you as I do."

How his voice shakes—his white face, fair hair, and blue eyes are a blur in the mist of Ivy's tears. "This will never do; I shall cry if he goes on much longer, and concede anything." With a little tug at her boa, she summons indifference successfully—

"Nonsense, Billy; I go down very well about here, because there is no one to 'cut me out,' but among a lot of 'smart' people I shall be nowhere; I shall return so crushed, I'd be grateful if you'd look at me." His lips are quivering with an odd smile. Ivy hurriedly continues, "But don't expect me to make any promises—I have a conviction I shall *adore* foreigners, they're *so* amusing!"

"I know I'm not amusing," Billy begins sorrowfully.

"Oh, yes, you are, often when you least mean it," Ivy replies magnanimously; "but I'm not thinking of you, I never do, I meant ordinary Englishmen; you're so different, so much more"——

"What?" he cries eagerly.

"Like Teddy, so you don't count."

A slight pause, then, "You're awfully fond of Teddy?" insinuatingly.

"Rather, he is my own particular brother."

"I am so thankful you think me like him then; I daresay I could get more like him in time," Billy continues meekly; "our tastes are the same, I have got, too, hair as short and stirrups as long, and I don't stoop so much now, do I, Ivy?"

"You don't; but for pity's sake give up moulding yourself after Teddy's model, you're very well as you are for a—for a friend, you know."

Poor humble Billy! Catching Ivy's outstretched hand as she jumps a puddle, he holds it with gentle deference. "I shall always be your friend, but can I *never* be anything more. I won't ask you to write, or anything, but will you—can you, just promise to think of me sometimes? How long will you remember me, Ivy?"

"That depends entirely on the foreigners!" she answers, with a cruel little laugh.

Oh! Billy, why don't you retaliate? Indifference would serve you so much better than devotion! But he only turns his head away for a minute, and when he next speaks his voice is as gentle as ever. "Here is the gate; but before you go will you—will you grant me one favour? It's nothing," he continues hurriedly, seeing a look of cool surprise in Ivy's eyes. "It's only—only this," producing a little case from his pocket, "you won't mind taking such a little thing from an old friend?"

"Indeed I shall! Girls *never* take presents from men!"

"Oh yes, they do."

"Not *nice* girls."

"It's not a ring," he cries quickly. "I knew you wouldn't take *that;* it's only a little brooch, any one would keep it."

"Would they? You argue from experience doubtless!" scornfully.

"Indeed, I don't! I've never—I don't—know anything about it—but—other fellows—Ivy, you *might*, it's nothing from an old friend like me," pushing the little case into her hand.

It is too dark to see distinctly, but a little sparkling butterfly flashes out whitely against its dark background.

"Diamonds!" Ivy whispers reluctantly. "It's quite *impossible!* I really can't, I wouldn't for worlds; it's too kind of you, Billy, but oh! I *couldn't* —what a lovely butterfly it is! Appropriate, of course, the bitter with the sweet. Billy, it was *dear* of you, but I can't indeed. Mother wouldn't let me, so there's no use asking," tendering back the case.

"Billy," clutching at his arm, "what *are* you going to do?"

"Chuck it into the pond; if you've no use for it, I haven't."

"Oh wait! can't you? Won't you, do—*keep* it, Billy, it will do for—Mrs. Billy, some day."

"You may as well take it now, then," with a smile.

"What d'you mean?" haughtily. "I suppose you will marry some one by-and-by."

"No one but you, Ivy. All right, then, in any case it is *yours* or *no one's*," slipping it into his pocket.

"Too dark to see the '*case*,' and not being mine it is—? How do you like the inference?"

"I'd rather be *no one* to you than *everything* to any one else," he replies weakly.

"Poor Billy," softly; "I must go. Look how dark it is."

"It is." The hollow lugubriousness of his tones

causes Ivy to hurry her farewell.　Putting her hand in his she says gaily—

"Ta-ta, Billy; I shall hear of you, of course. Good-bye."

He holds her hand tightly.

"Ivy! take *something* of mine, I want to feel you will be reminded of me; will you keep this old pin?" pulling at it with his disengaged hand.

"Is it the horse shoe?"

"Yes, *do* keep it, Ivy, it will make me so much happier if you will; it's such a *little* thing to ask you, my "——

"Yes, I will," hurriedly—a tight squeeze of her hand—"such a capital present—*to pass on*," she adds ruthlessly.

The glad light dies out of his blue eyes, and with a sudden quiver of his lips Billy turns to go.

"No! I can't let him go *so*." Hurriedly pulling from her coat a sprig of heliotrope Mrs. Millar had given her, Ivy lays her hand on Billy's sleeve. She lifts the little purple flowers to her lips and kisses them slowly, then holding them out to him whispers softly, "I'm sorry, Billy, for you *are* a dear!" then vanishes, leaving him standing in the winter's dusk with the sunshine of summer in his heart!

How the most trivial act becomes invested with solemnity, when it is done for *the last time*. Afternoon tea and feeding the cats on their separate newspapers is quite depressing; supper, at which Archie and Cyril do all the talking, is bad enough, but prayers reduces Ivy to tears. She buries her face in fat Puff's fur, and lays an affectionate toe on Dick's grilling back, with a longing for their sympathy, which they totally ignore.

Her father's kindly words, and her mother's long chat as she sits over the fire, for the last brush and comb conclave, are things to be remembered. Ivy recounts faithfully the minutest facts about her interview with Billy, and confesses to having hovered between "judicious coolness and kindly compunction" until she can't answer for the effect produced. "He's so radiant at the veriest *crumb*, mother! One has to 'snub' him rather unmercifully, to bring him back to common sense; it's coming down like the stick, but it's *honester*—eh, mother?"

"I would have you quite honest, my child; let us hope the pin and the flower will not prove misleading," with a smile at Ivy's pouting negative.

A night of troubled dreams brings her to the dawn of a sad, sour-looking day—her last at home.

Archie and Cyril haunt the passage prophesying all sorts of breakdowns unless she "hurries up," and flying like carrion at her luggage to convey it to the carriage. The good-byes are said, handkerchiefs are waved until the last bend in the road leaves the dear old grey gabled house lost to view.

The journey to town, under the care of a fussy old lady, is rather monotonous. As the train steams out of the station, leaving her father standing on the platform waving his hand, Ivy feels horribly forlorn, and longs with unreasoning intensity to give up the foreign tour, and rush back to the untroubled happiness of home! After the old lady has seen Ivy into a cab (she won't hear of a hansom), and taken the driver's name and number, she ejaculates fervently—

"There, I've done all I *can*. I hope you'll arrive

safely, my dear; but there's *no knowing!* what with fogs and Socialists, and all those Irish loose in London, one can't say what may happen! However, driver!—do you hear, driver?"—imperatively—"*I have your number*, so remember! Good-bye, my dear, I think it's all right," (in a loud aside) "he *looks* sober. Good-bye," with a reassuring nod, and then through an inky mist, studded with flaring gas-lamps, Ivy is driven with exasperating slowness to her uncle's house in Queen's Gate.

"Come up, Ivy, Morris will look after your things. I can't come down," and Ivy runs up the stairs to find Sybil in all the agonies of "trying on," while the dressmaker and Hammond, the maid, fuss about with their mouths full of pins in a state of excited satisfaction.

"Gwen has just gone off to dress; we have been *lambs* in the hands of these two for hours. Oh! look out, madame, that's me. Yes, *high*, I like the collar high," and Sybil lifts her chin, whilst casting a scrutinising glance at her reflection in the pier-glass.

The morning-room is in a state of wild disorder; half-packed trunks and card-board boxes, looking delightfully "shoppy," are lying about everywhere. Ivy regards Madame Bongoût with respectful admiration, and is so absorbed in watching her manipulations that Gwen's gentle touch made her jump.

"Standing, Ivy! Oh! what a shame! It's quite like the flight of the Midianites, isn't it?" indicating with a wave of the hand the surrounding litter. "Come and take off your hat. Hurry, Sib, there's the gong for luncheon," and linking her arm in her cousin's she walks her off.

The constant intercourse has made the cousins more like sisters than anything else, and Sybil hesitates no more in admonishing Ivy, who is her senior by a year, than in lecturing Gwen, who is barely eighteen, just two years her junior. In appearance there is a vast difference between them, Sybil and Gwendoline being both tall and fair, while Ivy is nearly a head shorter, and decidedly a brunette. In character the difference is as clearly marked—Sybil's quiet firmness and practical common sense, and Gwendoline's gentle plastic nature, being entirely dissimilar from the impulsive determination and flighty irresponsibility which appeared to be Ivy's strongest characteristics.

Looking at her aunt as she sits at the head of the table, Ivy notices (as she always does, in the scrutiny of the first few minutes) how wonderful is the resemblance to her mother. Mrs. Lestrange is some years younger than Mrs. Peyton, and both physically and mentally she reflects the strong individuality of her sister; but, in paler colours. Some priceless bronze may be faultlessly reproduced in brittle porcelain by the hand of the modeller, yet who would barter the original, scored deep with time's rough usage, for the fairer copy beautiful in its perfection ?

General Lestrange is a big good-tempered man, who takes life easily when the *Times* is punctual and his pipe draws, but who flashes out with a blaze of wrath at the smallest trifle with a vehemence truly alarming, until one realises the necessity for the most good-natured to find some safety valve for the irritation that never escapes in petty bickerings.

London is a great delight to Ivy, and the shopping a perpetual joy. In due course all the gowns are packed, and the thousand and one trifles crammed into the trays, swelling to such gigantic proportions that it necessitates one of the girls sitting on the covers of the trunks, while Hammond struggles with the hasps and eventually locks them.

"Fifteen inside parcels besides the heavy luggage! We have the carriage to ourselves, so I can have a smoke, if you don't mind, Amy? We're pretty heavily weighted, but, heaven be praised, we have no dog this time!" and General Lestrange gives a little grunt of satisfaction as the lights of Victoria Station are left behind, for at last they are really "off."

CHAPTER III.

"Fixed to no spot is happiness sincere,
'Tis nowhere to be found, or, everywhere."
—POPE.

LONDON in its gaslit darkness, Dover coldly grey, with the wide heaving sea and ruthless boisterous breeze, are behind them now. And in a deck cabin are gathered the three girls and their aunt. Ivy, whose experience of the sea has been limited to sailing in the Solent in an eighteen-ton cutter, announced her intention of walking about on deck, to watch the white cliffs fade from view, "And the swirl and swing of the waves, I *love* it so!"

Scorning advice from the others, who are wedged comfortably, with eyes closed, she airily prances along the deck. How beautiful it is! the low line of cliffs, the breadth of heaving sea, grey green and ribbed with foam—cool, though, rather cool. The countless eddies in the seething white track of the vessel, as she churns the channel, begin to lose their attraction after a time, and she turns to pace the deck, nursing the belief that she never felt so "thoroughly jolly" in her life!

It's very odd, but her legs feel *all* lengths! At one moment too long, as the vessel rises up aggressively to meet her advancing foot; at the next too short, as it is suspended in an incomprehensible vacuum, and then sinks down *yards*, as if on a flight of stairs! The up and down feeling, with the throb! throb! throb! of the paddles, is a monotonous sensation one *might* get accustomed to, but the unexpected lunges, and staggering reels, that bring one with an internal quiver to the pinnacle of glory but to be dragged in a burrowing plunge to the lowest abyss, reduces Ivy to a worm-like meekness, and in the faintest of whispers she announces that she "thinks she had better lie down!"

All are in that passive condition when nothing appears of the slightest consequence, and the overthrow of one's country, the sinking of the ship, or the loss of one's keys, are viewed with equal indifference—the calmness not of stoicism but of limp despair.

Calais — a swarm of blue-coated, vociferating porters—Hammond appearing from below, deathly, but determinedly grasping her mistress's bag, unmoved by the solicitous gesticulations of the officious Frenchmen. A slow procession to the train, where a reserved carriage receives them, fervently thankful for the luxury of privacy, and pitying all the crowd of passengers, who are separated from their party and poked in anywhere—here a maid and child, there the mother and irate husband—until every carriage is crammed, and then, after endless delay, on to Paris.

Dinner, blazing wood fires, and rest, restore the spirits of the party, and the next morning Ivy (to whom everything is delightfully novel) is sent with Sybil as cicerone and Hammond as chaperon to see as much as she can before dinner. She is too entranced to talk much, only her eyes grow rounder and rounder, until Sybil laughs and says, "Don't, Ivy, it looks dangerous, as if with the slightest tap they would fall out!"

To Englishmen foreign railway stations are a ceaseless annoyance. Being penned like sheep or helpless idiots, and then hustled along and dictated to by bustling officials who know more about you than you do yourself, is absolutely maddening. General Lestrange is in a condition that baffles description, purple with passion, and choking with disgust at having so few French expletives at command. "*Sacré! Beté—confound* that ass. No! not *that* carriage—no! *Here*, I say!" wrenching open a door and preparing to shoot in some of the thousand parcels. "Mais c'est *impossible*, Monsieur!" Round him swarm the smart officials and blue-bloused porters, talking with angry vehemence and gesticulating wildly

"I say, *here!*" the General shouts. "One carriage is as good as another; I engaged one and won't be dictated to by that grinning ape as to which it's to be!"

"He says, father," calls Sybil desperately, "this

one is a slip carriage, and we want to go through to Marseilles; and look! that one *has* 'reservé' on it."

By dint of much persuasion he at last gives way, and in nervous haste the party scramble into the compartment originally destined for them, while the irate General further harasses the perplexed guard by announcing his intention of going to the smoking carriage when the train next stops. He doesn't mean to do it, not in the least! but he considers that he has been worsted, and owes the guard *one!* He, poor man, can but blankly speculate upon what these "mad English" may or may not do. If, instead of sleeping the sleep of the just as his train ploughs southward through the darkness, that towering fury of an Englishman should take it into his head to leave his carriage, will not his blood be required at his hands? for stop—we don't stop! not for *hours!* and the fury may wax impatient! He locks and double locks the carriage door, fastening down the bolt at the bottom.

Silence reigns; all are asleep, or pretending to be so, but Ivy woos Somnus in vain, and idly watches the swing of a label on a parcel in the opposite rack. She is getting accustomed even to the screams of the engine, and no longer imagines they are driven by a madman, or on the verge of a crash, Sybil having informed her that the 8.30 is no worse than other trains, one being as bad as another. The guard's face at the window as he perambulates past ceases to excite curiosity, only producing hazy speculation as to *how* he comes there. Recollections of flies keeping up with her galloping horse, and the dawning grin of "Alice's" cat, grow mistily indistinct; up the Champs Elysées, under the Arc de Triomphe, into the darkness of an endless tunnel she is being hurried, while far ahead gleams like a pale star against the blackness of the night, the grand Venus of Milo.

"Ivy, Ivy, wake! here we are at Marseilles!"

Oh, the joy! After ablutions that get rid of the thick coating of dust, the party repair to the huge refreshment-room and revel in a delicious breakfast. How fresh they feel! and chatter merrily as they race eastward, leaving Toulon behind them, and whirling into a new land, where the stunted olives and cactus hedges are a revelation to Ivy. The snow-capped mountains, the blue blue sea, the wide clear sky bright with the glorious sunlight, elicit little squeals of rapture from the girls, which last intermittently all through the day; but later, when they race along by the shore where gleaming lights are studded in jewelled clusters on the rocky points of land, they grow curiously silent.

The moon now waxing to the full pours across the blue black sea a rippling pathway of silver, while the dark shore line stands out clear cut and distinct, with its little jagged promontories sharp silhouetted outlines against the foamy fringe of the sea. When nature bids us gaze upon her beauty she seals our lips, that in silence we may write it on our hearts.

At last Mentone is reached in safety, and all emerge from the omnibus into the hotel, where at the whisper of arrivals the domestic staff crowd assiduously into the hall.

The rooms, engaged beforehand, are ready for them, with none of the inevitable alterations usually found necessary to the "great regret and annoyance" of the proprietor. He knows the general of old, hence perhaps the reason!

Standing near the bureau are two gentlemen, one a young clergyman, evidently of "Anglican" tendencies, evinced by the cut of his coat and collar; the other a tall freckled youth, with green eyes (they look green) and red hair. As the girls mount the wide staircase in the wake of bowing garçons, and followed by a host of loaded porters, they are met by a lady and gentleman coming down. She is decidedly handsome, and eyes them with a cool indifference that borders on rudeness; he is so wrapped up in a huge plaid that little is to be seen of him but a pair of hollow eyes gleaming from under dark overhanging brows.

Ivy is very sleepy, and as she takes one long look at the wide sea, heaving in the moonlight, she murmurs drowsily, "The most pathetic eyes I ever saw." Kind child, thinking of Billy's, dim with the pain of their farewell!

The following morning is devoted to settling down.

"The advantages of having a salon of one's own is the sense of security it gives one," Sib is saying, as she dexterously twines some soft-toned "Liberty" silk round an execrable little picture.

"Lower the cord, Sib; bring the end of silk in a long uneven piece down to this easel—it looks more straggly and artistic," Gwen remarks, with her head critically on one side.

"I can't reach it from the chair."

"Get on the table, then."

"I shall scratch it so."

"Nonsense," calls out Ivy, coming up with her

arms full of books, which she deposits with a bang on another table. "Kick your shoes off, and get up."

Sybil complies, and is just crouching down for the other two to correct the "tilt," when the door is flung open, and a gentleman advances into the room. With one bound Sybil is on terra firma, or rather carpet, flushing scarlet at being caught in such an undignified position. Her usual calm self-possession fails her now, and in perplexed timidity she stands silent. Ivy, from the further corner of the room, grins mischievously, "For once Sib is nonplussed, she has no shoes!"

"I'm afraid I have come at rather an inopportune moment," begins the stranger; "but it was at the permission of your father. He allowed me to come up thus early to pay my respects to your mother, who is a very old friend indeed."

"Who can he be?" thinks Sybil. "Just like father, he *might* have thought;" then aloud to Gwen, "Tell mother, will you, Gwen."

"Will you sit down," Sybil remarks, coolly sinking herself with the greatest care upon the edge of a chair close at hand; she is preserving a Grecian-like bend, to conceal her shoeless state.

Here a little uncontrollable squeak from Ivy sends the hot blood surging in another wave to Sybil's forehead. Has she revealed a white-toed stocking? How mannerless of Ivy to go on choking like that. She watches her as she picks up a pile of books (conveniently overturned), and in some astonishment sees her cousin calmly seat herself on the sofa by the side of the unknown, and enter into conversation with him. "Where *are* those shoes?"

Furtively she glances round the room : not a sign

of them : cautiously her feet skirt round behind the safe screen of petticoats ; "That's a heel—no, the leg of the chair;" her eyes grow anxious, and the sweeping motion continues. Ivy's manners are certainly to be deplored; she jerks out little spasmodic questions, and returns monosyllabic answers, but she is evidently struggling with her laughter the whole time. She darts one look at Sybil, but the anxious blankness of her cousin's face appears quite too much for her, and biting her lips she digs her nails into the sofa cushion and remains silent.

Enter Mrs. Lestrange and Gwen. As the stranger rises to greet her aunt, Ivy, with a quick step, hurries across the room and flings down to Sybil the missing shoes. It dawns upon her then with ludicrous clearness. He has been *sitting on them !*

For a second or two both girls are shaking in an agony of suppressed laughter; then Sybil, having slipped on the much-desired articles, recovers her self-possession and advances in rejoiceful security to her mother's side.

"Sybil, dear, let me introduce Lord Egerton. I don't suppose either of you remember him. This," drawing Gwen forward, "is my youngest daughter. And Ivy, dear—Lord Egerton, my niece, Miss Peyton" turning to him.

He bows gravely, and not a quiver of a muscle betrays his consciousness of the byplay so recently enacted.

Sybil remembers him now as an M.P. for their division of the county years and years ago, when she was about ten, and he a grown-up important Tory, decked with blue ribbons, making speeches. She wore blue ribbons too ! Dear me, how very old he must be! He was only Mr. Percival then, and one of father's friends. So the girls listen, and hardly join in the conversation at all, while the visitor talks to Mrs. Lestrange of old times and new, of his old parliamentary struggles, and his new Irish experiences learnt with bitter heart-burning through the medium of " Castle " officialism.

" Tell it not in Gath, my dear Mrs. Lestrange, until I have proven my armour, but I am a convert to Home Rule!"

" A *pervert*, rather! Richard must win you back to the old faith," she answers kindly. Sybil looks at him with a touch of scorn about the curve of her lips. This man to have been exalted so high and to have fallen so low! Nothing has ever shaken the opinions of her youth; her loyalty owns but the home standard of orthodoxy, and her father, belonging to the old school of Tories, has strengthened the conviction that no good thing ever came from the opposite party!

Before the conversation has time to drift into another channel, General Lestrange enters the room with a tall dark man behind him. The stranger strides forward and shakes Mrs. Lestrange warmly by the hand with both his own, speaking rapidly the while. " I am glad, I am *real* glad to see you! I should have been round before, but I've been having a talk with the General. You look well, remarkably well—Miss Sybil! that *is* nice!"

" I daresay it is," thinks Ivy; " he has held her hands for *quite* five minutes—auntie's too, with both hands. There's Gwen, and then—oh! he's clearly perfectly mad!" as he is now going through the same proceeding with Gwendoline.

"Ivy, let me introduce Mr. Cleveland," and she bows smiling. This, then, is their American friend, Mr. Vyner Cleveland. Oh, *that* explains it. She has never met Americans before; perhaps this is the national method of shaking hands. Further knowledge of them leaves the question still undecided —for Ivy.

Mr. Cleveland knows everybody. He discusses all subjects amusingly ; criticises the visitor's list, sketching rapidly the chief "stars," giving their relative magnitude.

" One of the first degree is Count Enrico Contarini, a Russian-Italian, who is carrying all before him. He looks like a Swede, is a typical Italian Jehu, gambles royally, and is fairly English in speech and dress, wonderfully handsome, and the ladies pronounce him 'fascinating.' If you are going in to the concert this afternoon, you will be able to judge for yourselves," he adds, looking at the girls.

Sybil does not answer as freezingly as usual, but merely says, "We are going into the town, and then meant to look at the tennis."

"Then we'll go together," Mr. Cleveland answers eagerly. "Mrs. Cleveland hopes to come in and see you this afternoon, and might manage the tennis later, but she is rather poorly this morning."

Here Lord Egerton, who has been engaged in conversation with General L'Estrange, takes his departure. He regrets he cannot join them at the tennis courts, as he has promised to meet a friend in Monte Carlo, then shakes hands with all.

Sybil, who is standing apart talking to Mr. Cleveland, gives him the coolest of bows, and his is almost elaborately foreign in answer. Ivy just

wonders why he looked preternaturally grave, and
what the gleam in his eyes could mean, and then
the banging of the gong summons them all to
luncheon.

CHAPTER IV.

" All may be well, but if God
  Sort it so,
  'Tis more than we deserve or I expect."
                                        —*Richard III.*

As the girls follow their parents down the broad
flight of stairs to the salle-à-manger, they look
curiously at the people all converging to the same
spot. Ivy, to whom hotel life is a novelty, feels
deeply interested in the new phase of existence
opening before her. " Why does not Mrs. Cleveland come down?" she whispers to Gwen cautiously
behind Mr. Cleveland's back.

" She is delicate and always lunches in her own
room; she is very nice, and not a bit melancholy or
anything. I hope we are all going to sit together."
Apparently not. A few moments of indecision,
much bowing of waiters, and then Mr. Cleveland
says cheerily—

" Oh, that's it, is it? General, there are three
places for your party on this side next ours, and
two opposite, so we shall all be together nicely."

Sybil moves quietly round to the further side with
Ivy, who finds herself placed opposite Gwendoline
about half way down the table.

" I wonder who our neighbours are?" remarks Sybil
under her breath; " that is such an important point.
Mr. Cleveland generally manages to get us tolerable
ones. How would you like the people opposite, low

down on your left? Don't look yet." They are Germans; they are enjoying their dinner; and after mixing vegetables and every accompaniment imagined into a mash, proceed to convey it to their mouths with extraordinary rapidity of motion.

"Teddy said Verbeck's sleight-of-hand was wonderful, but this beats it hollow," Ivy whispers; then adds, "My fate, do you see? 'the Prawn!'" as the red-haired youth they had noticed the evening before takes the seat next her.

"Well, Hood, been having a 'knock up'? Ah! here's your partner," cries Mr. Cleveland, as a very pretty girl now comes up and takes a place beyond Sybil. "By the way, Miss Peyton, let me introduce your neighbour to you—Mr. Hood, Miss Peyton."

They both bow, the red-haired individual flushing a brick-dust hue, which he retains for some minutes. Ivy, with one keen glance at Gwendoline, enters into conversation, setting the poor youth at his ease before five minutes are over. He adores tennis, so does she. "She cannot play a bit, however, and dare not join good players, as she is so fearfully out of practice."

"I—I—er—should be only too awfully glad to practice with you, if that would be any use, whenever you like," he says quickly.

"Do you mean it? Oh, you are good; thank you so much," Ivy answers, with a grateful look at the green eyes.

"Will you come out now?" he says. "The court will be free directly after luncheon; the match does not begin till three."

She shakes her head sorrowfully. "We are just going into the town; but," with *impressement*, "tomorrow."

They are pushing back their chairs now, "the Prawn," as he moves Ivy's for her, flushing a violent red. She does not seem to notice it as she nods a pleasant little farewell.

"Cleveland, I leave you to manage the three girls," calls the General, as they come trooping out into the sunshine ready for a walk.

"Are you not coming, Uncle Dick?"

"Not I; your aunt and I will stroll up to the tennis by and by—that's about all I can manage," and he settles himself comfortably in a large cane chair, and rolls a cigarette in his fingers contentedly.

As the girls stroll along in the sunshine, drinking in with fresh delight the beauty all around them, the brightness and joyousness of the day seems to pour into their natures a strong flood of fresh vitality, filling them with an absolute content in being alive. Sybil is in quest of flowers for their sitting-room, and as she threads her way through the picturesque streets, gay with all the outspread wares of the little shops, she talks gaily to Mr. Cleveland, leaving Gwendoline to act as Ivy's guide. She has to be dragged past every shop in turn, Gwendoline desperately explaining to the congregating stall-holders, the young lady is not furnishing an hotel, is merely of an appreciative nature, but is coming to *buy* to-morrow. "Ivy," she gasps, "you will be mobbed for ever after! Why, mother's life is a burden to her, and she never started with half your enthusiasm. It's a mistake ever to look at anything; the shop people here simply force their goods on one, whether you will or no. Here! come, follow them up the parade, and with luck we can dodge the olive-wood men."

Along the broad esplanade they walk, thronged at

this hour with society taking its airing in carriages, bath-chairs, or doing the prescribed constitutional. Russians in long coats and low hats, fur-coated men and cloud-enveloped women, groups of animated foreigners sauntering along, solitary Englishmen speeding by at their usual five miles an hour, picturesquely clad nursemaids with white caps and long floating ribbons, with extravagantly dressed children, all enjoying the music of the town band, and even the most decrepit basking like flies upon a wall in the blissful idleness of true sun-worshippers.

"Who is she?" Ivy asks, as a tall handsome woman bows to Gwendoline. "Goodness, what a wind!" she continues, grabbing at her hat.

"Yes, another gust, and every one will clear off. Don't you know who that was, really, Ivy? Why, Miss Templeton; she sat beyond Sib, on your side of the table. They always go to the 'Bellevue.' Old Sir Noel has lungs or something. There is Lady Templeton walking by his bath-chair, and the pretty girl is their niece, Miss Bingham. She was 'the Prawn's' tennis partner—now you remember."

"Perfectly; and we met Miss Templeton on the stairs last night. Do you know who the man was who was with her?" Ivy asks quietly.

"No; Mr. Cleveland said she was engaged, perhaps that is the man; why, Ivy?—Oh! catch it, stop it!"

Gwendoline makes an ineffectual grab, and then, turning scarlet, feels she would like to sink into the earth.

Ivy's sailor hat, that has all through the walk been in a very shaky condition, has been freed by a sudden gust of wind, and is now being carried in spasmodic little rushes along the esplanade! Ivy,

with wide streaming boa, is frantically chasing the
spinning hat, aided by many interested pedestrians.
Some young Frenchmen are evidently enjoying the
proceeding intensely, and with many expressions of
concern have twice (accidently, of course) set it free,
and continued with fresh ardour to assist in its
capture. " If I had an umbrella," thinks Ivy, " I could
pin it to the earth," but with muff in one hand she
can only make sudden dives, and invariably, just as
she feels it almost within her grasp, away it bowls
again ! Her hair feels coming down, she jams in hairpins desperately, conscious that with tumbled fringe,
and scarlet with mortification, she must cut a truly
laughable figure. " That dog has it—no, he hasn't—it
is making for the sea ! Oh, thank goodness ! " as a tall
man, leaning on a stick, dexterously pins the whirling
truant to the ground, and stooping carefully grasps it.
" Thank you so much," Ivy gasps, " it's mine."
The utter idiotcy of the remark makes her cheeks
burn until it is absolute pain. As if any one else
would be likely to own it ! To whom could it
belong but to this demented, hatless damsel ? As he
hands it to her Ivy recognises in her benefactor
Miss Templeton's friend. Some incomprehensible
sensation makes her dumb with mortification, and
yet—how silly—*glad* that he should have caught it.
" These gusts are so sudden," he remarks, " and
must render it very difficult for ladies to secure
their hats, particularly when there appears to be no
means of attaching them." He speaks in a very
low voice, and Ivy wonders if he is laughing at her.
No, he is clearly just one of the " good " and " kind "
of this world.
Banging the dust from the hat, she sticks it on,

and pushing her halo of hair under it, tries to secure it with hairpins. With a little smile at its rescuer, she bows, and joins her cousins, who have at last appeared upon the scene.

"We were in the flower shop at the corner, or I should have been here earlier to render you some assistance, Miss Peyton," Mr. Cleveland begins.

"Ivy," Gwendoline whispers, "I am so sorry I can't run; and, besides, there were such crowds, I knew it would be of no use."

"Really, Ivy, you need not have flown after it yourself; some one would have been sure to catch it for you," says Sybil severely.

Poor Ivy! she feels too humiliated for explanations or defence. Gwendoline, however, continues kindly—"You see, Sib, Ivy can't have an elastic like mine, as she does her hair on the top of her head, and pins are not half so safe."

"I never have any difficulty with mine," Sybil answers, still in an annoyed tone. "I have no elastic, yet my hats keep on my head properly."

"Yes, Sib," Ivy's voice breaks in meekly, "we all know nothing ever goes wrong with your *head*, but I have known your feet bring you into trouble, not even leaving you a leg to stand on."

Here they all laugh, and Ivy feels that to rally from her humiliation may be possible. She experiences a sudden collapse as they pass the group of young Frenchmen, several of whom know Mr. Cleveland, and bow. Not a smile mars their ceremonious politeness, yet the consciousness that she has afforded them amusement dyes Ivy's cheeks carnation.

"I'm so thankful Miss Templeton wasn't there," she remarks, after a moment's pause.

Mr. Cleveland looks amused. "Don't you like her?" he asks.

"I don't know her," Ivy answers quickly; "only she looks as if she would always remember anything horrid, and bring it up against one at any time."

"By the way, wasn't that Talbot who caught the hat at last?" he asks again.

"What makes him think of the 'good and kind' in connection with Miss Templeton?" Ivy feels vaguely irritated. "I don't know at all," she answers shortly.

Mr. Cleveland is far too sweet-tempered and irrepressible to be affected by trifles of this sort. "Oh yes, it was," he goes on pleasantly. "Poor chap, he is such a nice fellow, pity he's such a melancholy beggar; but luck has been against him all the time. This is the first day I have seen him out for quite a while."

"Who is he?" Sybil asks.

"Well, he's cousin to the present Earl of Eyre. He was a colonel in one of your regiments of Guards, has done most things in his time, and been unlucky in all—his hardest hit being that his brother ran away with the girl he was engaged to. They say he has never been himself since."

"But—but, isn't he?—didn't you say, Gwen, he was engaged to—to Miss Templeton," Ivy breaks in hurriedly.

Mr. Cleveland laughs aloud. "My goodness! if there's one woman he could dislike, it would be Miss Templeton; but that is one of the nice things about Talbot, he never says or allows to be said, if he can help it, a word against any woman, and he hasn't much to thank them for."

" What a queer girl you are, Ivy," Gwen remarks, as they turn into their salon to give the flowers to Hammond's care, " I believe you loved chasing your hat, you've been in such frantic spirits ever since."

"It served to clear my brain, dear, and that's always a good thing. My patience (catching sight of herself in a glass), have I been like *that !*"

" Your hair is fruzzed about quite dreadful, miss," Hammond remarks in a horrified tone, and Ivy, with the gayest of laughs, rushes to her room to get it into better order before going to the tennis courts.

As the two girls make their way there, they find quite a crowd gathered to watch the match. Miss Templeton and the curate, whom they discover to be the Rev. Boniface Dalmatic-Cumin, are playing against pretty Miss Bingham and Mr. Hood (the Prawn). The play is good, the players well-matched, and the excitement sustained. As they join their own party, Gwendoline steps forward eagerly, say-ing, " Oh, there is Mrs. Cleveland ; she is such a dear !" Ivy, looking at her curiously, felt attracted at once, and when the introduction had been gone through, found herself shaking hands as with an old friend.

Mrs. Cleveland is tall and slight ; her hair, real Titian's auburn, is drawn up smoothly under her hat, all the curly ripples catching the light in little lines of gold ; her eyes are blue, or dark grey, with curling black lashes and arched eyebrows. A most imperti-nent little nose gives a piquancy to a face that a very expressive mouth renders extremely sweet.

" I know all about you," she says, with a little nod ; "you're a sad girl, never out of mischief, and the most accomplished coquette in Christendom, but" (with a delicious little pout) "who isn't? If girls aren't a little 'flirtatious,' believe me, my dear, it's because they're dull, poor dears, and can't help it! Now, come and sit down here, I want to verify your cousin's description of you."

"My cousin's! Whose—Sybil's?"

"No; Sybil is a dear, but she has no experience of unorthodox people like you and me. Vyner and your cousin Percy are my authority."

"Percy!"

"Yes, we met him in the early days of his scorched state, and I assure you I thought you a cruel little wretch; but of course with cousins it is an invariable phase they pass through. Vyner, of course, can't have much experience, he only saw you *at lunch,*" Mrs. Cleveland adds with a smile.

"I assure you "—— Ivy begins.

"Don't perjure yourself; let us admire him. I've often wondered," she continues, "what he would do best for. Stuck through with arrows, against a sage green background, he might do for a St. Sebastian. Tied into artistic knots, with his hair combed into a halo, he would make a personable saint for a stained window; left as he is now, he looks nothing more or less than an extremely ugly bulldog boiled to a startling brilliancy, but " (with a little gesture of contrition) "perhaps I offend! forgive me, he is, no doubt, adorable, dear, but you'll confess he does look—warm!"

While still laughing with Mrs. Cleveland at the peculiarities of the wildly animated "Prawn" who is, however, winning the set for his pretty partner, Ivy is honest enough to attempt a weak protest. "He looks good-natured, anyhow," she says.

"Don't! Invariably that is the last clause of a lame defence. Now here *is* a man, if you like, although I always feel utterly insignificant whenever I see him, and I don't like the sensation."

A moment later and Mrs. Cleveland is greeting Colonel Talbot. Ivy seeks to rejoin the others without appearing to be making any abrupt move. Stooping for her muff, she rises, and is about to flee, when Mrs. Cleveland's voice arrests her.

"If you don't know Colonel Talbot, Miss Peyton, let me introduce him to you," and Ivy bows, biting her lip nervously. Shyness, a very novel sensation, makes her feel strangely embarrassed, and, like a French girl, unable to raise her eyes above the level of his waistcoat.

"Are you not a player, Miss Peyton ?" he asks.

"No—yes; that is, I have played, but am a duffer at it, and have not patience to practise and persevere."

"Perseverance is doubtless necessary, but patience ?"

"Is a requisite my partners are more likely to require, you think," she suggests with a little returning confidence.

"Excuse me ! I never meant to imply anything of the kind. I was only surprised at discovering that tennis is qualified to teach us life's hardest lesson," he answers very quietly.

Ivy looks up quickly. He is watching the game absently. Her glance convinces her he is not cynical. What then ? " I don't think I understand," she remarks thoughtfully.

There is a kindly glance in the grey eyes as he answers, " We rarely learn life's hardest lesson at its outset, but" (with a little sigh) "we master a few of its rudiments before the final break-up of our school.'

If this man wore a turn-down collar and a soft hat, Ivy would have resented his remarks as evincing a desire to improve the occasion, for her flightiness was very prone to take offence at the faintest suspicion of "lecturing;" but there was a seriousness about him that ensured immediate respect, and a certain isolation that struck one as pathetic. For the first time in her life, Ivy found herself conversing with a man who in every way satisfied her somewhat extravagant demands, whose appearance was prepossessing (strictly military regarding moustache, and length of hair, so supremely important!), who in experience of life, in love of sport, equalled all Teddy's most enthusiastic friends, whose knowledge of politics and art brightened his conversation with the intense colour of decided convictions, and whose higher aspirations were the keynote of a character wrought into harmony by the slow labour of suffering and self-sacrifice.

I do not mean to imply that Ivy was possessed of sufficient divination to gauge this man's character in the course of an hour's conversation, but the perceptions which developed into certainty hereafter, were generated when she realised he was "good and kind" in securing her hat, if not in the very first moment when their eyes met as they paused upon the stair. The instinct of women is as remarkable as that of dogs, whose opinions are generally but developed "first impressions."

Some time later, but well before the dangerous hour of sunset, all wend their way back to the hotel. As Ivy passes Mrs. Cleveland, the gleam in her eyes is more mischievous than ever, and stepping forward, she taps her shoulder lightly, saying in an undertone, "Take care, coquette! The eagle soars to heights beyond the ken of lesser natures, and were the king of birds to carry up some little linnet with him, I almost think it would turn its poor little head, or send it fluttering earthward stunned and sorrowful. Beware, child! After electric light who cares for common gas?"

But Ivy only laughs and walks on with Nora Bingham, wondering perhaps, with a little smile, if "the light that never was on sea or land" was only electric light after all!

———

CHAPTER V

"As long as love continues the most imperious passion, and death the surest fact of our mingled and marvellous humanity, so long will the sweetest and truest music upon earth be ever in the minor key."—CICELY.

NATIONAL peculiarities are never more strikingly apparent than on a Sunday abroad. As the foreigners greet each other, there is an additional gaiety about them, born of the satisfaction that this is a "festa day." As the English file off soberly to the little church, there is about the majority of them an indescribable melancholy that surely cannot be the outcome of the faith that is in them. There still remain a certain number who consider cantankerous moroseness and morbid asceticism as a desirable compound for manufacturing the salt of the earth, but where should one look for optimism if not from those who are bound to regard all things as "working together for good"?

Thus soliloquised General Lestrange as he puffed reluctantly at a cigarette that must sustain him for the next hour and more, and watched with amused indolence the hotel disgorging its inmates to church.

Mrs. Lestrange and Mrs. Cleveland come down the broad stone steps together, followed by the girls. Sybil so often reminds one of a Tenniel's Britannia, with her calm, proud face, low, broad forehead, and rippling hair undisfigured by any manipulations of curling irons. To-day, as she stands with the sunlight shining down upon her, brightening the greyness of her coat and gown into silver, with her heavy black velvet hat and thick boa framing the sweet grave face, she excites quite unsabbatical sensations in the heart of Miss Templeton. Poor soul! nature gave her many good gifts, but disappointment had fostered a bitterness that dropped gall into the very essence of joy, and nothing was satisfactory because with her lost illusions of youth had not come acquiescence.

"Are you waiting for any one?" she questions tartly, looking up at the girls from the foot of the steps where she lingers for old Sir Noel.

"Yes," Ivy replies promptly. "Mr. Cumin must pilot us to the choir; we are much too shy to present ourselves, and Mr. Hood means to join the basses. Ah! there you are, Nora!" as Miss Bingham joins them; "that's right. Here's Mr. Hood, so I think we might move on."

They do; and some minutes later so does Miss Templeton, giving an arm to irascible Sir Noel, and speculating irritably upon the non-appearance of Colonel Talbot and Lord Egerton.

The English church is crowded, the service as

elaborate as four officiating clergy and a voluntary choir can make it, and on the whole a hearty one. Ivy feels her lips twitching once or twice when a sudden flash of the ludicrous wakes some dormant jibe; as, for instance, the prevailing fashion of reading amongst young curates. The Rev. Dalmatic Cumin is no exception to the rule, and his soft and gently modulated voice is forced up to the inevitable falsetto, where it clatters along in even monotony through the grandest passages of Holy Writ into "Here endeth the First Lesson," without any perceptible pause, only a faint hustle at the finish, pulling up dead short, with eyes closed and mouth open.

The reproachful pity of Sybil's eyes subdues the little touch of scorn about her lips, but the grave concern with which she regards the curate preening with satisfaction and wound up for the Second Lesson, is almost too much for Ivy's gravity. Looking up at her uncle, to whom this piping intonation is an abomination, she becomes aware of a pair of eyes whose influence affects her disagreeably. They are blue—bright blue, and were it not that they are hard and cold, would be as beautiful as the face to which they belong. The features are regular and of the purest Greek type. Excepting that the jawbone is rather squarer, the face might have been a model for Mercury; it is too keen for an Apollo. The fair hair curls low over the forehead, the moustache, of the same flaxen colour, is not suffered to conceal the exquisite curves of the mouth. The eyebrows and eyelashes are black, and give a rather theatrical effect; but so startling is the face that the peculiar colouring hardly excites especial attention.

Ivy, after one amazed glance, turns her eyes on the psalter in front of her, wondering who this striking-looking man can be. " A Swede perhaps ; they say they are so handsome. His hair is too long, but he looks like some ideal Viking, or a Wagnerian sun-god secretly scorning his black coat and Sunday. I don't like him ; his eyes are horrid, and give one the creeps," she concludes decidedly.

After the first sensation of surprise, she is conscious of an almost over-mastering impulse to look again. Conquering her curiosity by praise-worthy determination, she rivets her attention upon the service, which by some curious chain of associa-tions carries her beyond a crowd of home memories to a well-known pillar in her father's church, where, against the rough grey stone, Billy's head and shoulders are clearly outlined. A little smile hovers for a moment round Ivy's lips, and then with a sudden bitterness she murmurs, " It's no use, mother. I've no capacity for caring. I haven't a heart, though you always tell me I shall discover its existence some day. I *am* being good, mammy ; for instance, I'm not going to criticise this oration," and she proceeds to give her attention to the sermon with an intentness not due entirely to right-minded conscientiousness, but partly from her natural impulse to escape the thrusts of unsparing higher consciousness.

It was Ivy's method of eluding responsibility by shutting her eyes to all but the immediate present. Her experience led her to the conclusion that happi-ness was the one thing needful, and to bring glad-ness into the lives of others the highest good.

Surely there are many who in the confidence of

youth demand as their just right a pathway strewn with flowers.

"Billy is too serious. Every one can be happy if they will only not get too much in earnest about things," Ivy had often said; and certainly she was a capital illustration in favour of her argument. Brightly interested in others, making the best of the present, and never troubling about the future, she was the cheeriest companion imaginable, and deservedly popular. That she had thrown a shadow across the brightness of Billy's life was her one trouble, for hers was the thoughtlessness of impetuosity, not the selfishness of indifference. "Billy will forget, or I shall learn to care for him," she would say with a troubled little sigh. "Anyhow, I need not worry yet. I mean to be happy now."

And so a week had gone, and, with all the changes it had brought, it seemed more like a month to Ivy. Yet she was conscious of but one definite impression—to enjoy to-day and let to-morrow take care of itself. And to Billy, to whom the seven days already seemed like seven years, had come the comforting conviction that it was well to endure misery *now*, for it must lead to happiness by-and-by, or one would not have to endure it. An optimism by no means rare, and justifiable if one removes all limits to the "by-and-by."

Gwendoline is sitting in the garden. The warm afternoon sun pouring down upon the palms and cactus plants is hot enough to justify a parasol, and under its red shade she is reading and lazily watching the lizards darting in and out of the broken stonework of the terrace wall.

The Rev. Dalmatic Cumin, inspired with a laudable

desire to improve the occasion, and implant aspiring tendencies sandwiched between palatable commonplaces, joins her, and sitting down upon the garden bench, enters upon a long and somewhat exhausting conversation.

Gwendoline's highly sensitive mind and extreme self-distrust make her as wax in the hands of any one on the look-out for malleable material. She is a rare " find " to the eager little enthusiast, more interesting than a Hottentot, less captious than the purely illiterate.

After an hour's innings, in which he has had everything entirely his own way, there being no observant onlooker to catch him out, he has succeeded in shattering the happy fabric of hopeful confidence of which her citadel is built, and upon the ruins of her childlike faith is implanting with scrupulous nicety angles of dogma and blocks of doctrine with most praiseworthy but mistaken ardour.

Poor Gwen! now tortured by self-analysis that would question her most generous impulses, is conscious of but one way of escape. In self-abasement to acknowledge the presumption of individual judgment, and bow to the dictates of the Rev. Dalmatic Cumin and the guidance of the little " religious aids " he will lend her — those elegantly bound manuals so patronised by a section of Churchmen.

Forlornly tucking " Thomas à Kempis " under her arm, and viewing with vague apprehension the little volume that is to supersede it, she makes her way to her room, where she encounters Sybil.

To a strong-minded soul nothing is so purely aggravating as the want of self-reliance in others

The practical common-sense of the older sister had been an anchor to the younger through many a stormy hour when buffeted by some "wind of doctrine."

Lifting her eyes now from the letter she is writing, she sees at a glance that Gwen is at the lowest ebb, and before ten minutes are passed she is crying from sheer nervous exhaustion, and Sybil with soothing tenderness is quieting the troubled conscience, and restoring by her calm convictions the banished peace of her poor little sister's mind.

"Ivy," she says some time later, as she enters their sitting-room with a book in her hand, "what am I to do with *this?* Mr. Dalmatic Cumin has been exhausting his eloquence on Gwen; it has produced the most natural results, and she is horribly upset mentally and physically, and is lying down with a headache. You know Gwen; you know the enthusiastic type of which he is a fair specimen; you can perhaps realise to what condition an hour of his arguments have reduced her! Here is his book, a pot-pourri of traditions, humiliations, and penitential observances. What on earth am I to do with it? I dare not return it to him. It seems so hard on Gwen, treating her as such a child. *I* would not look at it, and don't want to bother mother about it."

"Give it to me," Ivy cries quickly with a little laugh. "I am quite willing to take him as my pilot over unknown country. Thirsting for instruction, I have borrowed this from Gwen. Will that do, Sib?"

"Don't laugh, Ivy. You forget how annoying it is."

"I know it is; but make the best of it. Leave it to me. I always fly into rages; but then father says we ought to remember the great mistake is youth and inexperience, and *that* they cannot help. I wish, as father says, none might be ordained as priests until they had proved themselves men. But don't worry your head any more about this. I think !"—mischievously—"I shall take it out into the garden to read now; perhaps he will come and explain it !"

They rise and move to the door, where Mrs. Cleveland meets them. " Come into the garden, girls. Vyner says it is simply perfect, and I am beginning to get pure fidgets from the flapping persiani instead of the clatter of your tongues, and she tilts her hat back comfortably and lays her hand on Sybil's arm.

" I can't," Sybil answers quietly. " I'm going to stay with Gwen ; but Ivy will go. Remember tea-time."

Mrs. Cleveland s one of those fascinating women who, without being harassed by the opinions of others, smilingly listens to all and retains her own. She has been engaged in a discussion with Colonel Talbot and Lord Egerton on a variety of subjects, and is now escaping dispute by reverting to the Jubilee. " Shall you return for it ?" she asks with animation. "No, don't fly the subject. Let us chatter now. Why should every one be so argumentative on a Sunday ? Do look at Ivy and Mr. Cumin; they are clearly exhausted after their last ' round.' What are you two fighting about ?" she called out, smiling.

" Nothing," Ivy answers, " only I am being enlightened upon many questions. Just now we are discussing the influence of art upon the masses !"

" Religious art, and its elevating influence upon the uneducated," supplements Mr. Cumin.

" Mr. Cumin believes we should have no wife-beating horrors and general ruffianism if our churches had altar-pieces by Fra Angelico or sermons in stones by Giotto," Ivy says gravely.

Colonel Talbot's glance is a keen one, and Ivy almost resents the scrutiny that seems to pierce through her habitual frivolity. With a smile in which there lurks a shade of defiance, she turns with pretty deference to Mr. Cumin, and looking at him with clear innocent eyes, continues in thoughtful gravity—

" It is a beautiful idea. I have not thought of the effect that might be produced in general by the influence of altar-pieces; but I *have* heard of a curious impression made by a print of the Madonna di San Sisto upon a poor illiterate woman in a country parish. You may have heard the story?" Ivy says, glancing up questioningly. Mrs. Cleveland, lowering the lace border of her parasol, telegraphs an appeal. Slightly closing her eyelids and raising her little nose a degree or two, Ivy smiles imperviously. In answer to, " No, never heard it. Pray do tell us, Miss Peyton. An illustration of the purifying and ennobling emotions engendered by the vision of that beautiful masterpiece would be indeed gratifying," she continues—" It was only a *print*, Mr. Cumin, a large print with ' *Ave Maria* ' written below—that was all. A new vicar came to the parish, a very Low Churchman. Visiting the cottages, he came to the one where this print hung. Horrified, he cried to the poor woman, ' My good woman, you must take that down ; that is a terrible picture, quite a Papist production—in fact, a shocking spectacle on a Christian woman's walls.' And then the woman answered," Ivy continues with fervour. " Yes, yes ! what ?" cries the curate. " She answered, ' Well now, lor, sir, you don't say so ! Why I allus thought as this genelman (pointing to Pope Sixtus) wanted to marry that sweet lady with the baby in her arms, at whose feet he's a kneeling, and she is a saying kind like to him, and her sister what's a kneeling too No, you can't 'ave me—'*ave Maria !*'"

As Ivy finishes, she looks up at the group in front of her. They all laugh ; even little Mr. Cumin has been betrayed into an amazed " Ha! ha !" and is now speculating upon the degree of guilt he has incurred thereby.

Colonel Talbot does not even smile, and Ivy is angrily conscious that she is flushing beneath his look of pitying regret.

" I don't care ; there's no harm in it ; it is *true*, and he is ridiculous to be so horrified ; I *don't* care," and, with characteristic obstinacy, she stills her compunction, and coolly addressing him, asks, " You have not said what you think of my story. Don't you think it portrays British religious sentiment rather accurately ?"

"As accurately as the recital betrays the *want* of it," he answers quietly, then raising his hat slightly leaves the group.

A glass of cold water dashed into the face of any one with hysterics invariably brings them round. And this calm disapproval, though it makes Ivy mentally stagger, clearly defines her words as not the outcome of thoughtlessness, but flippancy. Biting her lip nervously, she plunges with a little forced laugh into conversation with Mr. Cleveland, and delights him by the humorous recklessness of her remarks. Mrs. Cleveland attempts no interference, and is relieved that the outburst, which she attributes to feminine pique, should find its vent through such a safe channel.

Never has Ivy been in higher spirits, and her ringing laugh reaches Colonel Talbot as he sits reading in the warm sunshine.

Why does that angry piquant little face come between him and the pages of his book? He tries with laudable resolve to banish the vision, but the brown eyes blaze from the lettered background, and with a sigh he rises at last, and pocketing his book, walks away between the orange-trees with philosophical indifference that does him credit.

As long as that preoccupied man wrapped in the huge overcoat, and poring over the pages opened before him, had formed a background to the scene around her, Ivy's gaiety had been irrepressible, but when the bench is deserted, and only far away between the cactus and orange screen paces a solitary figure, the brightness seems to die out of her, the merriment is no more spontaneous, and Mrs. Cleveland fully realises that the petulant defiance is in danger of dissolving into tears. Sending Mr. Cumin for a glass of water and her husband for a shawl, she gives a little sigh of relief, and pulls Ivy down beside her, saying lightly, " What a chatterbox you are ! I've been dying to ask you something all the time, and you haven't given me a chance. Did you notice Count Contarini in church this morning? I ask you because I noticed him looking at you, and you seemed to me to be consciously unconscious. Were you ? "

"I don't know; I really forget." (What ages ago it seems!) "Oh, yes; a theatrical creature who stared horridly, I remember. Is *that* Count Contarini?" with a little reviving interest.

"Certainly; there never were *two* such men. Don't affect indifference, dear. You must be content to count yourself among his crowd of devotees . . no   Oh, wait; you will in time. *Every* woman is in love with him—so surpassingly handsome, so intensely fascinating, and such a flirt! His safeguard lies in his devotion to *all* women, and if he affects one more than another, it is only for a little time."

The supreme scorn of Ivy's face is superb, and Mrs. Cleveland, having excited another emotion, continues the conversation in a spirit of raillery that barely veils her sarcasm, and soon rouses sufficient indignation in Ivy's mind to act as a counter-irritant to her mortification. Then, in unsuspicious gentleness, Mrs. Cleveland insinuates herself into the girl's confidence, and paces arm in arm round the central oasis of palms and flowers that lies directly before the hotel steps.

When she has successfully banished Mr. Cumin and her husband, she flings herself down on a garden bench, and giving vent to a profound sigh, remarks with a yawn, "Ivy, I must have forty winks. I'm going to escape detection under my parasol. Just stay about here and keep off any perambulating bores," then relapses comfortably into silence.

And so the girl sits there musing with wide unseeing eyes, noting nothing of the exquisite picture of purple land and blue sea, framed in a fringe of jagged palm branches that formed a picturesque foreground.

She is distinctly in an irritable frame of mind, and

vindictively attacks any protruding little pebble with the point of her parasol, crunching it down to the level of its neighbouring atoms with communistic ferocity. Engaged in this pleasing pastime, she is unconscious of approaching footsteps until they are stayed close beside her. Instinctively she knows who stands there, and realises for the first time that the bench on which she is sitting commands the approach to the "orange-walk," and in a flash of resentment suspects the depths of her sleepy friend's tactics. To rise and leave her is her instant resolve, but a glance at the face beside her lulls the suspicion as unworthy; its babe-like innocence forbids the thought. Resting against the iron rods that should be covered with climbing creepers, but are not (it being too early for them yet), Mrs. Cleveland is sleeping like a tired child, the long dark curling lashes lying unflutteringly in dusky crescents against the delicate fairness of her cheeks.

Drawing away from the parasol that shields her, Ivy sits up stiffly, and turning to Colonel Talbot says severely—

"Mrs. Cleveland is asleep, and I am here to see that she is not disturbed."

"I would not disturb Mrs. Cleveland on any account," he replies in tones too soft to rouse even the proverbially watchful weasel, " but I owe you an apology, Miss Peyton, and shall not be satisfied until you accept it."

"An apology!" Ivy stammers. "Yes, I know. No, you don't ; certainly not—of course not. Why, you were quite right. You see "—— Then, peeping under the parasol, " Perhaps we had better move farther off; we can't talk properly here," and without a qualm

Ivy leaves her sleeping friend, and strolls away deliberately to the orange-walk. What has become of the raging antipathy she had felt for Colonel Talbot? It seems to have evaporated instantaneously, as with burning cheeks and downcast eyes she listens to his calm, restrained voice.

"I owe you an apology," he is saying, "because, no matter how disappointed I might be by the recital of what I deemed unworthy of you, I had no right to show my disapproval so plainly. I extremely regret having done so, and I trust I may be forgiven." He is smiling, but there is a shade of anxiety in his eyes.

"You were quite right," Ivy begins hurriedly. "I only did it to annoy Mr. Cumin. He" (laughing nervously) "thought I was agreeing with him, and I daresay it was wrong, but I *revelled* in the 'sell' I was preparing for him."

"Then it affords you pleasure to wound the feelings of others?" This is too much!

"It does *distinctly*. It affords me exquisite pleasure to rub people up the wrong way," in a tone of sharp conviction.

Colonel Talbot pulls up the collar of his coat, and looks down upon the little figure at his side with a glance preternaturally grave. "Indeed!" he answers quietly. "I should not have thought so."

"I daresay not. If so trivial an offence disappointed you, your notions about me must be singularly inaccurate, if" (with cool indifference) "you have any at all."

"I *have*," he replies slowly. "I have a notion that under the mask of frivolity it is your pleasure to adopt, you hide feelings of whose depths you are but dimly conscious."

Ivy is silent. "He thinks about me—thinks all that," she murmurs to herself proudly, and her heart bounds gladly, and the orange-walk seems a bypath into Paradise; so she keeps her eyes upon the ground to hide their tell-tale gladness.

Colonel Talbot continues, "What from a younger man would seem like an impertinence, you will pardon from an old fellow like myself. Yes, I am an old man now" (a quick, indignant glance from a pair of brown eyes), "and the result of my long experience teaches me the paramount importance of universal kindliness. In a moment of irritation I was guilty of discourtesy to you. Oh, yes, I was" (at a determined shake of her small head), "and you were justly annoyed; but perhaps you have forgiven me now" (endeavouring to get a better view of the face under the parasol). Here a little hand is held out quickly, and two suspiciously bright eyes are raised to his, as Ivy whispers rapidly—

"I'm glad you . you made me feel small. I oughtn't to have told that story. It's true, but" (remorsefully) "flippant, and it might make people think I didn't care   and   . I do . and   " (with a sigh of resignation) "I'll read the whole of Mr. Cumin's book—the Humiliations twice over—to make up."

Colonel Talbot does not laugh. He listens to the account of the curate's proselytising zeal calmly, and arrests Ivy's newly-roused indignation, as she recounts Gwendoline's troubles, with unbiassed coolness; finally launching into a defence of the poor little man, proving the kindliness of his nature and sincerity of his belief, though he by no means agrees with his present convictions, which he trusts will widen into a nobler creed. "I think," Colonel Talbot goes on, "if we would sink small differences, 'the light that lighteth *every* man that cometh into the world' would make existing unity clear to us."

"It is very easy, "Ivy replies, "to feel a bland love for humanity in general, but slightly different to allow that soured snappish scolds are one's sisters, and that some repulsive vulgarian or hypocritical pomposity is also 'a brother.' Of course, in this case it is only because the little outside mannerisms hid the honest 'real' that I misjudged. I will now go through life growling no more at the palpably silly, or distinctly odious, believing that at heart all are heroes, and it only wants a flood or fire to reveal the fact. Will that do ?" smiling.

"Yes! Never lose faith in humanity. The family likeness may be too faint for any but a Father's eye to trace, but it is there. Let each follow their highest ideal; then in loving reverence or unconscious homage every sacrifice offered on the altar of Right is accepted as purest incense by the Love that asks only truth."

And so they walk along the orange-avenue, the man of over forty and the girl of twenty-one, and talk of subjects that lie beneath the surface of the common-place with an openness that is novel to them both. Colonel Talbot finds his interest stretched beyond the bounds of mere courteous attentiveness; the variable moods and sudden flashes of earnestness or passion making the girl's impulsiveness an attractive study; while Ivy, feeling for the first time the power of a will greater than her own, and honouring the character of the man intensely, rides for a fall recklessly, pulling wide with joyous haste and a great throb of gladness, a gate that she will never more have strength to close.

The sun sinks behind the Cannes range of mountains, flushing the western heavens with a rosy flood of fire, against which the bluff headland stands out in purple softness, all the rest of the range silhouetted in inky distinctness against a pale primrose background. The palms wave darkly below the softly-tinted sky, and the wind comes sighing shorewards with its cool fresh breath heavy with the incense of the sea's thank-offering to the departing monarch of the day.

"How late!" Ivy cries suddenly. "I forgot all about time. Oh, look at the glow! Why, the sun must have set."

"It has; the first time I have been out of doors for the event for nearly a year," Colonel Talbot answers smiling.

"Come in, do!" she cries with sudden nervousness. "I forgot all about cold, and that it is bad for your cough, isn't it?"

"The doctors say so," he replies quietly. "I don't think it really matters very materially—in my case, I mean. Yes, let us go, and after tea you will sing?"

"Anything, only come." And under the heavy-scented orange-trees and graceful swaying palms they walk back slowly. All the world is ablaze with a beauty that brings a wondering glory into Ivy's eyes, and only far away on the horizon has crept a tiny cloudlet—one black speck in the wide heaven of happiness—one wee drop of anxiety in a cup brimful of bliss.

CHAPTER VI.

"The Prince of Darkness is a gentleman."
—Sir John Suckling.

"And that is the Casino! How do we get there?"

"Straight through the station and up those steps. Why, Ivy, you are as excited as if you expected to make your fortune. Come, girls;" and Mrs. Cleveland, closely following her husband, moves across the crowded station at Monte Carlo, with the three girls and Mr. Hood behind her.

Some days have passed since the Sunday conversation between Ivy and Colonel Talbot took place, which had established the friendliest relations between them. Indeed, it now seemed perfectly natural that the radiant, irrepressible girl should pace in sober intentness by the side of that grave, bowed-down man — a state of things that exasperated Mr. Cleveland by its incongruity. "He's the best fellow living," he had said to his wife, "but I do say it's enough to scare one blue to see those two together, and always puts me in mind of that lively ode, 'To a butterfly reposing upon a skull.' I wonder you don't keep her out of mischief, Dora, before she gets well started in, unless you think she is merely keeping her hand in with the poor old man."

"Poor old man, indeed! What next? You don't think I'm going to allow *you* to be old in another ten years, and you will be very near his age then, my dear boy. You will keep *me* in countenance as long as I can keep a waist, and haven't sunk to the comfortable stage of heel-less shoes with square toes! You conceited creatures! As if *any one* could

not see that it is simply out of pure kind-heartedness that Ivy talks to Colonel Talbot, cheering him
up from simple good-nature;" and Mrs. Cleveland
smiles with the satisfaction of superior intelligence
and adroitly turns the current of the conversation.

To-day she has inveigled Mrs. Lestrange into
letting the girls go under her chaperonage into
Monte Carlo for the afternoon. "Sybil and Gwennie
are athirst for the music, and Ivy must see the
tables. She won't have done the place properly
unless she does. Nora was coming too, but the cat
of a cousin has prevented her. Lady Templeton
had given way, but the daughter reversed the
decision out of pure spite," Mrs. Cleveland says.
"The 'Prawn' is coming, and Lord Egerton is to
meet us there. Vyner and I will take the greatest
care of the girls, and tear Ivy from temptation,
unless we see that she is likely to break the bank!"
So Mrs. Lestrange smiles and allows the expedition,
and in the wildest spirits they set out.

As they climb the steps that lead into the beautiful gardens, they meet Lord Egerton. He has the
programme for the afternoon's concert in his hand,
and giving it to Sybil, is soon deep in animated conversation as to the merits of the "Götterdämmerung."
They all press onward, hardly caring to linger and
look back on the brilliant beauty of the exquisite
scenery, so intent are they upon entering the Casino;
and when they do enter the huge Salle, where
crowds are already gathered round the roulette
tables placed at regular intervals on either side of
the room, Ivy feels curiously disappointed. All seem
idling away an afternoon in careless enjoyment.
Those sitting round the tables are calmly staking

to win or lose with equal equanimity. Others are watching the games with amused interest or cool indifference. There are no sudden gleams of misery, no tragic horrors, no gaunt victims of despair.

"That room at the end is the 'trente et quarante' room, Ivy, where the greatest gambling goes on. You see here at 'roulette' you can play with silver if you like; there they stake nothing but gold. Do you want to put down a five-franc piece—it's the lowest you may—to say you have afterwards? I did," continues Gwendoline, "but I lost."

"Yes," Ivy answers quickly, "I *do*; but I don't know where to put it. I will only try one, but I must see if I win."

"Don't try a number, Miss Peyton," Mr. Hood says critically; "take a dozen, or back the colour— say the middle dozen. Shall I?" holding her silver piece suspended.

"No, put it on the red," Ivy cries with the nervousness of a novice. He does. The croupier spins, the ball flies round, and slowly, slowly rolls into its number. The stakes are raked together, and Ivy finds herself minus five francs.

"I don't think it is so very amusing. Do you, Sib?" she says with a pout.

"I think it is decidedly wicked, that's what I think," Sybil replies gravely.

"Don't scold; I'm not going to play any more. Let us go to the other room. Can't we, Mrs. Cleveland?"

"Of course. Come, Vyner. What! all that?" as he shows his winnings.

"What's your secret, Mr. Cleveland? Do tell me," Ivy asks eagerly. "Not a system?"

"I should smile," he says comically. "When we get

into the other room I'll show you. Here! come to the left. Now, can you see?" making room for her until she stands the first row behind the seated players.

"1 can, beautifully. What is he doing with those cards? Oh, look at the rolls of gold and notes! Don't I wish I had this fat heap near me!"

"She needs it. She was pretty well cleared out yesterday, and is always here."

Ivy looks curiously at this player. She is an old woman, with grey hair and wrinkled, careworn face, untidy in dress, but unmistakably a lady. Her brown eyes are keen and restless, and the twitching lips and trembling hands betray an excited nervousness but ill suppressed.

"Now, look here! You see this card. Watch me prick down the results. I never try systems or any bosh of that sort. I merely follow the luck, and back the colour when I think it's in for a run. Now look! Red has won these last three times. Watch now! I back red." Mr. Cleveland pushes two Napoleons on to the table; in another moment his stake is doubled. Ivy watches the game with the keenest interest, and gradually grasps some idea of the scoring, and sees before long a reason for the detestation in which such games are held. The grey-haired lady has been winning largely—so much so, that others have begun to stake according to her play. Among these is a boy who hitherto had been losing heavily. Mr. Cleveland points him out to Ivy as a young Frenchman who had not been long in the place, but already had become an inveterate gambler. He is so young looking, it is ridiculous to call him anything but a boy. His dark hair is brushed back in a wave from the smooth forehead, the blue eyes look very eager, and the sensitive mouth trembles slightly under its shadow of a moustache. He must be just about as old as Fane. After winning for a few turns, following the old lady's lead, the luck suddenly changes, and both old and young player lose heavily.

"Why don't they stop? Oh, why don't they stop?" Ivy whispers to Mr. Cleveland.

"They are fools!" he answers shortly. He has stopped playing and is watching the game intently. Ivy is conscious of but one longing—to see that boy win. All he has gained has gone long ago. He left the table, but returned with more money, and is now staking more recklessly than ever. So absorbed is Ivy in his play, that she is unaware of the notice she is herself attracting. Her lips are parted and her breath is coming quickly. Her hands are locked tightly together, and her eyes are as piteous as a beaten dog's. As, after a bigger stake than usual, the boy again loses and the croupier rakes in the gold, Ivy's lips tremble with a sudden quiver and her eyes fill with tears. The boy, glancing up for the first time during the game, looks straight into her face. He flushes slightly, then with a quiet smile gathers up all the money remaining and pushes it on to the red. For a moment there is a long-drawn hush, and a tightness clutches Ivy's heart in a breathless grip; then—the croupier is raking in the money, and the boy, slightly bowing, rises and leaves the room.

Mr. Cleveland is guilty of an expression more forcible than polite, and turns to apologise to his companion. It is unnecessary. She has not heard him. With firmly-closed lips and eyes stretched wide, she stands gazing at the door by which the boy had vanished. Mr. Cleveland, in momentary dread of "a scene," whispers, as he touches her arm, "Had we not better join the others? Dora is with them in the concert-room. We may get places near the door. Come;" and without a word she goes.

"Will you do me the honour, Mr. Cleveland, to introduce me?" and dimly as in a dream Ivy hears, "Miss Peyton, will you let me present Count Contarini?" She bows but does not speak.

"You are interested in the play, but it is *bête*, such play as that. He is a fool, that boy, and deserves what his fate has brought him," Count Contarini remarks as they walk through the long rooms.

"And it has brought him—what?" Ivy asks softly.

"Ruin," he answers lightly. "Bah! it is a misfortune these young Frenchmen can never stop; they are as bad as Russians. What a pity we cannot all emulate your countrymen in that respect, Mr. Cleveland. You Americans are not gamblers."

"We are not," Mr. Cleveland replies. "We make our money with too much trouble to let it slip so easily. There is room here," he adds, turning from the door of the concert-hall, and making way for Ivy to an empty place, while he stands in the doorway to listen.

Ivy is fond of music. She cannot understand or appreciate what does not directly appeal to her. No education would ever make Bach's fugues a delight, but as Schubert's serenade is given in faultless harmony and expression by that most rare and perfect orchestra, the pathos of its reiterated melody seems to ring with answering directness through every nerve in her body.

Poor child! A longing so intense seizes her for the shelter of her mother's arms, there to sob out

her remorse for her gambling propensities! and
fears for that reckless boy, that it is all she can
do to restrain her tears. And then the sweet notes
rise and fall, and carry away from the folly, and
greed, and vice, the girl's troubled consciousness,
bearing her on trembling wings over the swelling
waves of sound out to the wide eternal silence.

With a prayer upon her lips for all the thought-
less, reckless ones who greet dishonour and remorse
with careless impetuosity, she commits Fane to
angelic guardianship with rekindled faith, and leans
back in reviving calmness, though feeling mentally
and physically tired out.

"It is impossible that you are entirely English,
since you have the fire of my country in your heart.
I can see," whispers a voice so close to her ear that
she starts violently.

It is Count Contarini! Ivy being in an outside
place, he can stand at her side in the passage, and
has bent down to whisper. A speechlessness born
of indignation keeps her mute. "To have observed
me intently is rude enough; to acquaint me with
the result of his investigation is simply intolerable,"
she reflects. "I shall not answer him."

"You do not answer. You wonder at me. Do
you not know you have not the power of conceal-
ment, like the rest of your sex, and all your thoughts
come quite plainly into your eyes, to show their
meaning to one who studies you?" he continues.

"Do they?" she retorts sharply, giving him a
glance of withering scorn. "I wish they *could!*"
leaning back with a bitter little smile.

A laugh—such an amused little laugh—and then,
"I will not spoil the music for you. I can wait;"

and Count Contarini draws himself up and remains silent.

"Of all the odious, conceited creatures prancing on this earth, he's the worst! Looking at me as if I were a rag-doll, and buzzing in my ear like an irritating midge! I won't stand it!" Ivy ejaculates mentally; "and I don't think he is a *bit* good-looking. I always did *hate* blue eyes, nasty cold, hard things, without any soul behind them! Oh, except—yes, of course—except Billy's," as in a wave of recollection his earnest piteous gaze comes before her.

Fingering a little pin that fastens the collar of her dress, she smiles a little regretful smile, and then in another minute the concert comes to an end.

"Mr. Cleveland, we ought to find the others, don't you think?" and Ivy whisks up to him and stands at his side almost before the people have risen from their seats.

"We had best remain here, I think," he answers, with his eyes on the stream of people, "unless—supposing you wait here with Contarini while I go to the other door."

"Please, no!" Ivy cries quickly in an undertone. "I mean—don't you think," as he looks at her, "we had better not get more mixed up. It is such a crowd."

"It does not matter; they know we are off for tea directly after this. Hood will bring them along, and I saw De Noisy with Dora, so they have men enough. We can clear;" and moving with the crowd, out they go.

"*There they are!*" A moment later Gwendoline lays her hand on Ivy's arm.

"Where were you? We were at the top. Wasn't

it splendid?   Only some of the people near us tried
to talk.   You should have seen Sib and Lord
Egerton!   They were perfectly rabid, and said
'Hush!' out loud.   Mrs. Cleveland and Vicomte de
Noisy were so amused.   And Mr. Hood nearly went
to sleep; he said the 'Götterdämmerung' was 'rot,'
the bass like fog-horns, and the treble like having
one's teeth drawn.   I'm afraid he can't have enjoyed
it *much*," Gwendoline concludes sympathetically.

"Ah! he must have very bad taste, then.   It was
a beautiful concert.   I have never enjoyed one so
much," exclaims Count Contarini fervently.

"Really?" Gwennie asks simply, and he answers,
"Yes, really," with a smile at Ivy which she will
not see.

"Wagner must be my excuse for some more tea:
he is so exhausting," and Mrs. Cleveland pours out
another cup and leans back in her chair lazily.

All are gathered in a group chattering through
the idle nothings that make the sum of ordinary
conversation.   Ivy feels her arm touched lightly.
"Look out for my tea!"

"Don't look, Ivy.   It is the girls who would talk.
Do you see who they are?   'Pop' and 'Flop'
Speedwell.   I suppose, as the drill season has not
commenced, they can be spared," Sybil supplements
with slow disdain.

Ivy laughs.   "Oh, for Teddy!   Those hussar
jackets are very 'fetching,' though."

"Horridly *outré*," Mrs. Cleveland remarks.   "Don't
whitewash girls like that, Ivy; they drive a tandem—
("Wish I could," from Ivy)—"go in for pigeon-shoot-
ing" (disdaining to notice her interruption), "sing
comic songs, and talk of nothing but the army.   They

make me perfectly ill. Listen to them now talking to those men, more ear-piercing than pea-hens their voices must have been moulded upon bugle-calls or the blare of trumpets."

"Teddy says they aren't bad," Ivy interposes.

"I don't say they are, and I hope"—here Mrs. Cleveland eyes the objects of the conversation critically—"as they say good Americans when they die go to Paris, that these girls may be appointed to some smart staff. I am sure they would be most efficient. And now, if every one has done frivolling, we ought to go, or, Vyner," with a mischievous smile, "we shall miss our train and have to remain for a late one."

"That would be best," Count Contarini joins in. "You should see the rooms at night; they are more imposing then. No? You are going? Then allow me," picking up Ivy's boa. "Can I not assist you?"

"You can hold one end and walk round, if you like," she answers without a smile.

"I would walk round for ever, if at the last it brought me nearer to you," he answers softly. Without a word she turns and follows the others.

"That woman will know us again," Mrs. Cleveland remarks with conviction as they establish themselves in the railway compartment. "Vyner, dear," with great sweetness, "is she some friend of yours?"

"What? Who? The Boronowsky! Don't I wish she were! She hardly notices any one but Contarini. Look, he is making it up for his absence now," as Count Contarini with every appearance of devoted attention stands talking to her.

Princess Tina Boronowsky, or, as she was generally called, "The Boronowsky," was a lovely woman.

Not very tall, but so perfectly proportioned that no worshipper of Amazons could sigh for another inch. With hair as black and glossy as a raven's wing, and eyes whose dusky depths shone in liquid darkness, like some deep pool shaded from the light, she could not fail to be uncommon. She is pale, and the brilliant crimson of her tiny lips enhances the whiteness of her skin. Dressed in bronze-green and sables, with a high French hat and hair stuck through with a long jewelled pin, it does not require the unusually large diamond buttons in her ears, and studded arrow at her throat, to pronounce her distinctly Russian. As the train slowly—so very slowly—leaves the station, Count Contarini raises his hat and smiles his farewell. His eyes are upon Ivy, but she is unconscious of all but the vivid beauty of the woman beside him.

"I think she is perfect," she ejaculates fervently, "like some stray goddess from a dead world, with all her soul's sadness shining in her eyes. Who is she, did you say?"

"Princess Boronowsky. Oh, don't distress yourself; she is not sad; she rules every one, even her husband. The Prince isn't here now; he has some official appointment in St. Petersburg, and had to return there a while ago; they don't give them much leave. She is delicate, or makes it her excuse for remaining here. I think she is a sort of cousin of Contarini's; his mother was a Russian. I believe in many ways he must take after her, he likes to call himself Italian, but under the veil of their quick passions I would not be much surprised to discover a considerable strata of Tartar," Mr. Cleveland concludes sagely.

Sybil is strangely absent. She has never noticed that Gwendoline is sitting near an open window, or that in the compartment lingers an aroma of tobacco, either cause being generally productive of considerable excitement.

Under cover of the general rattle Mrs. Cleveland murmurs into Ivy's attentive ear, "I admire Lord Egerton more than I can say. It is splendid the way he avoids all friction of ideas. The crudeness of dear Sybil's Toryism he has toned down by judicious applications of 'Besant and Rice,' until all the sympathy he can spare from himself is flowing in broadening volume towards his pet hobby, the People! Really, Englishmen amuse me; they go more mad over individual rights than we do ourselves. I am speaking as an American, you see; for as I married so young, I've lost all previous impressions. Look at them now with heads bent over that programme. Such nonsense! they know it by heart, and are holding it upside down, I expect! Do you know the stately Tory has even been guilty of giving the august Radical a rose? Believe me, dear, we are on the eve of an extraordinary coalition. wonderfully influencing Home affairs." She laughs softly, then continues, for she is rarely silent save when asleep, "And now tell me, for I am burning with curiosity, how did you get on with Count Contarini?"

"I don't like him at all," Ivy answers promptly. "I never do like handsome men."

"Really!" smiling. "How odd! You wait, my young friend. Oh, don't look so vindictive. Dear me, so excited already! Well, I won't say any more —only, wait and see!"

Here the train grates raspingly as it slowly stops. The chatter ceases, and all are rattled off together in the hotel omnibus.

* * *

CHAPTER VII.

"Every one can master a grief but he that has it."
—*Much Ado About Nothing.*

THE morning sunlight streams gladly into the little salon where Sybil is warbling "Tante Cose" in the most joyous mood. Gwendoline is doing her hour of "heavy" reading with praiseworthy diligence, though Alison's Epitome gets strangely mixed with the bright abandon of Pinsuti's music.

Near a window, reading a letter, sits Ivy. Something appears to perplex her, as she races through its clearly-written pages with eyebrows drawn together and lips pouting in evident annoyance.

Leaning back with a sigh, she runs her fingers through her hair and ejaculates, "It really is *too* riling! just as we are enjoying ourselves so much. What do you think?" with a tragic gesture to her startled cousins. "No, you will never guess. Fane, *Fane*," with slow scorn, "is coming here!"

"Nonsense, Ivy! Why, how can he?" Sybil cries quickly, crashing out a grand chord in protest. "Who says so?"

"Mother! No, he is coming, there's no doubt of *that*. He certainly does fall on his feet wonderfully. Teddy never gets such chances. A Mr. Philip de Trafford has met him somewhere, taken a fancy to him, and is bringing him cruising about here in his yacht. Luck for Fane, but how horrible for us!"

"Really, Ivy, I don't see why. I always think

you are rather hard upon Fane. He is only like you, dear" (with a smile), "irresponsible, but great fun."

"Fun to you, death to us! My recklessness is paid for by a week's remorse in sackcloth and ashes; *his* invariably means a fresh sale of household effects! Sib, dear, don't, as Archie says, talk about what you can't eat. *You* have not got brothers; for that be very thankful. Fane is effective, and 'takes' the public, but," with a comical grimace, "he is very expensive to keep."

"When is he coming, Ivy?" Gwen asks nervously.

"I haven't an idea. They never knew anything at home until he had started. He might be here to-day. Oh!" with a long sigh, "now I shall not be happy till he leaves. No, I know it! His theory is perpetual surprises, reserving for us the supreme one of 'squaring up on settling-day,' as Teddy calls it."

A hard look comes over Sybil's face as she says coldly, "I can't see what is the use of men."

"They do to bring one flowers, carry one's wraps, or—er—sing duets with," Ivy answers musingly.

"Ridiculous nonsense!" and Sybil stoops for a pile of music slipping flutteringly to the floor. To arrange it in her case takes some few minutes, and her cheeks are scarlet. Gwendoline is betrayed into a smile of comprehension, and then buries herself guiltily in her history. Ivy's eyes are fixed in amused contemplation upon the back of Sybil's head; now, as she turns abruptly and faces her cousin, she speaks quickly. "I dislike that sort of nonsense extremely, Ivy. I don't know what you mean about duets! He sang some simply because mother asked him, that was all!"

"*He!—duets!* my beautiful one! I fail, I entirely fail to grasp your meaning. I spoke in the abstract. I cannot   oh! good gracious! you cannot imagine for an instant I *could* have referred to Lord Egerton, or the fact of his singing duets with you!" and Ivy grasps Sybil's hands and looks up in her face pleadingly. Sybil struggles to maintain the coldly severe gravity by which she hopes to elude any jibes made at her expense, but in vain. Her lips twitch, bringing suspicious little dimples dancing in her cheeks, while conscious blushes send hot tears burning to her eyes. Struggling to free herself, she pulls Ivy to her feet. "Let go, Ivy! Ivy, take care! I'll put you flat if you don't stop."

Ivy clings on desperately. "Beautiful blind one! do you *still* say you cannot see of what use men are?" she pants.

"I say," Sybil laughs, "that you shall go *flat!*" calmly depositing Ivy full length on to the floor; "and be quiet, Ivy. As for men, as I never think about them at all, I'll say nothing."

"Oh, you story!"

"Mrs. Cleveland!" cry all the three girls, while Ivy scrambles hastily to her feet.

"Yes, if you are safe from an invasion, I will stay here. I had nothing to do this morning, and don't feel lazy. My rôle of invalid certainly is useful, and saves me being victimised, but it's dull at times. Where's your mother? Writing? Then I'll stay here. Another cushion, Gwen; thanks!" and settling herself comfortably on the sofa, she leans back luxuriously, just catching Sybil as she passes, to ask demurely, "What do you mean by such a story? As for the conversation I interrupted, I can pretty accurately gauge its drift. Any girls engaged in so animated a discussion are pretty sure to be airing their ignorance about the other sex. Odd, isn't it, the interest we take in them, eh, Sybil ?"

"I think"—the calm seriousness of Sybil's face is delicious—"we are bound to study the peculiarities and characteristics of the human race in the individuals thrown in our way, to comprehend the ramifications of thought and evolving process of opinion, that is—civilisation."

"Exactly! Therefore if one of the human race holds your hand a trifle longer than the rest, you say to yourself, ' Nineteenth century civilisation evolved from the germs of a dead chivalry.' If another less fortunate crushes the poor little fingers in passionate forgetfulness, you gasp in wounded disgust, ' A backward slide to Vandal barbarism.' Well, I think it's a charming way of studying the civilisation of the day. May I ask if among the modern-minded— whose radical divergence from the old school is strongly marked—you have found an embodied 'Thought' to your liking ?"

The sweet lips part in a bright smile, that lingers tremulously about the corners of her mouth, as Sybil twists a bangle round and round absently, and answers nothing.

"What! 'Thought' as approved by Miss Sybil still 'ramifies' disembodied, and refuses to locate in the individual ! The truth, Sybil ?"

" *Thought,*" with serious forgetfulness, "is too vague a term; rather say matured and definite *principles,* for they are certainly the motive power that governs his whole existence."

The universal roar of laughter that follows Sybil's unconscious disclosure, makes her snatch her gown from Mrs. Cleveland's hands and fly towards her mother's room as a desirable haven, until the glow that is staining her very ears and neck carnation can die away unchecked.

"How could she give herself away like that? Oh, it is simply delicious!" and Mrs. Cleveland's peals of laughter ripple on in spontaneous enjoyment, with the overflowing abandon of a happy child. "Oh, you girls, you girls! You are the rarest fun in the world. I could not get on without you. Next to having love affairs of one's own, I enjoy other people's; and to cover my stately Sybil with confusion sufficient to necessitate flight was indeed a triumph. And now, Ivy, for you!"

"Well?" looking up with sleepy indifference.

"Just so! *Is* it well? What do you mean by reducing that crisp 'Prawn' to the flabby dejection of a stranded jelly-fish? What do you mean by dispelling the brooding melancholy of our friend the care-corroded Colonel, only to fan delusive hopes and plunge him remorselessly to a deeper gloom? What do you mean—Ah! lay your hand upon your mouth, do. Yes, what do you mean by flirting your head off—I repeat, flirting your head off with Count Contarini yesterday, and then—here the reprehensibleness comes in—vowing and swearing—well, *affirming,* it's all the same now-a-days— you did not like him one little bit? Ivy! Ivy! Ivy! how is the heart of the coquette become a wilderness, and a grave for the heaps of the slain!"

"Have you quite done?"

"Not yet. If a certain little pin you wear so

persistently is a token that love and luck are inseparably connected, I understand, and will let you off. Otherwise, yes," with a little outward gesture of her hands, "otherwise you are a graceless monster, only satiated with heart's blood like some diabolical idol, and I wash my hands of anything so barbarous."

The blank gaze with which Ivy favours Mrs. Cleveland is very well done, but hers is too vivacious a temperament to assume the gape of incomprehension for long, and struggle as she will, the laughter gleams in her brown eyes like rays of sunlight in forest deeps. The little teeth are involuntarily disclosed, then the red lips close over them jealously, and the small nose is tilted airily as she answers—

"If it were not that I am of so supremely sweet a nature, I should in silent scorn refuse to notice such puerile accusations. As it is, my generosity bids me enlighten you. Poor 'Prawn!' he *is* stranded, and his condition might be described as *melting*, but the shafts that wrought such havoc never flew from *my* hand—oh yes, stare away; and he has unburdened his soul to me and sought my sympathy, since *Nora* will have nothing to say to him."

"*Nora !*"

"Do you mean to say you have not seen it for *days ?* He proposed yesterday morning, and 'cat cousin' was so furious with Nora for refusing him, she prevented her coming with us to Monte Carlo in the afternoon. Answer to charge number one!" holding the thumb of one hand between the fingers of the other meditatively.

"Not so fast, if you please. Staggered I may be,

for I quite thought Nora was engrossed with her Germans, as she struggles incessantly with that knitting, and has been spluttering through Schiller with their assistance; but how will you account for the 'Prawn's' fearful confusion at my appearing last night on the balcony, when he was clinging to your hand, and looking for all the world like a whipped clown? No evasions. Ah! you have the grace to blush. What was it? Did he say, 'If she be not fair to me,' &c., and 'When far from the lips that we love.' You know, dear. Oh, he's coming out in *quite* a new light, really not at all bad for the bashful one! I shall have to put Vyner on to him; he's getting quite dangerous!" and Mrs. Cleveland laughs gaily.

Ivy tears the flap of her envelope slowly. "As to Count Contarini, why I hardly spoke to him. Ask Mr. Cleveland; he was there all the time."

"Vyner says he never took his eyes off you, and he said you were 'splendid fun.'"

"*Did he?* I'm really glad to know what Count Contarini considers 'splendid fun;' it will assist me in rendering myself suitably amusing to him should we meet again."

"Delicious! Don't bite my head off. *I* didn't say it. No, you shall not go. Why, you have not answered half the charges. How about our prowling prophet of moral philosophy, what are you doing with him? I heard him ask you last night to sing 'Love laid his sleepless head,' which certainly has a happy hopefulness about it, and off you went and warbled 'Robin Adair' with heart-broken intensity. Who, I wonder, was standing in mythical Robin's shoes?"

Ivy, pressing a little Indian bangle between her fingers, snaps it in half. Stooping for the pieces, she picks them up, and as she rises looks at Gwendoline. " Tell Mrs. Cleveland about Fane," she says. " I'm going to get some work; one can't be idle all day," and with a bright little nod she leaves the room.

Get some work! Perhaps it was that she could not find it; perhaps none was to her liking; but it was very queer the way in which she sought it; at least so thought the fat little golden cupid who strained his chubby arms round the broken time-piece on her mantelshelf. See how she rushes in and bolts her door, and paces frantically up and down her room, then grasps the bedstead fiercely, disarranging those neatly-draped mosquito curtains as she struggles with an intensity of passion that appears to the small archer perfectly incomprehensible.

" Ivy !"—how the words hiss between her clenched teeth—" Ivy, do you live to say it? Stand up and say it is not true! Say it *shall* not be! Say, I will tear my heart in all its living passion from my being. I will trample it down. I will conquer it; it *shall not* conquer me. I can force it under the iron keeping of my own will. I will bury the existence of this love—*love*, ah !" with a little strangled cry, and covering her burning cheeks with the poor little trembling hands, " I have said it, and it is true, O God ! it is *true !* Cry ? What is there to cry for ? Do you hear ! I tell you," springing erect with head thrown back, " I tell you I am glad; no, I am *proud* that I know what love is. It has come, the glory that brightens our lives but once. I hold it fast, my one leaf from the tree of happiness; so soon it may wither; but now, just now it is *mine.* Ah! I laughed at those who cared. I said, Why make life suffering when it might all be sun-shine? I thought myself so wise. I took so much out of life and gave—yes, and gave so little. And now, Love, you little vengeful god, do you hear?"

Yes, he did. With his highly polished cheeks and nose shining ludicrously, he smiled back at her in fat complacency, clasping the silent clock in token of his everlasting covenant with Time.

"Ivy, are you not ashamed? No, not a bit," with a pathetic little smile and shake of the brown head. "You *ought* to be, you know; you love some-body who does not love you one little bit. You love so much that the whole world is more grand, and beautiful, and good because he is in it. Ah! mother, you did not like me to say, I hoped I should never have a neutral tinted life. I wanted sunlight, if it came blotted across by blackest shadows. It is not wrong—it cannot be wrong to love and no one knows it. Gwennie thought my 'Robin Adair' was Billy, and *he* thinks he is Count Contarini! I will never speak, mother. I would rather know this and have to live it down than exist without feeling. Oh, it is not dreadful to love, is it, when no one knows the truth?" and kneeling with her face buried in her hands, Ivy struggled long to subdue the sudden outbreak that had overmastered her. She knelt until she had conquered and was quiet. Then fear-ing detection if she delayed longer, she strove to remove all traces of suspicious excitement, and bath-ing her face and arranging her tumbled hair, looked ruefully at her reflection in the glass as she ejaculated regretfully—

"Ivy, you *are* an owl!   Why could you not put off all this until you could howl at your ease in the silence of the night?   Remember, you little ninny," with a nod at the glass, "there's no disgrace in —in this, as long as you never let a soul find it out. Openly play at love when it *is* only play, but if it be the 'real thing,' keep its secrecy as sacred as your soul."   Then catching up her crewel-work, she sallies forth to face the others, secure in the conviction that she can maintain her *rôle* of universal friendliness, merely laying herself open to a renewal of the old charge, " Ivy is such a coquette."

Luncheon is over, and Ivy feels happily secure in her gossamer armour of frivolous irresponsibility, aware that its fragile transparency is its chief efficiency, since of course nought but trifling would seek for shelter 'neath so frail a thing.   A "sirocco" blowing steamily from the far south makes the day as hot as June, and the girls in their cashmere gowns are enjoying a turn in the garden, jacketless and hatless.

" I love heliotrope," Gwendoline remarks as on tip-toe she picks some sprays from a straggling mass that covers one of the terrace walls.   " Have a piece, Ivy? You can fasten it at your throat with your horse-shoe.   I wish "—persuasively—" you would tell me really who gave it to you.   I am sure Teddy did not, and feel positive it was Billy.   Was it ?"

" It is so delightful to feel *positive* about anything now-a-days, that I certainly shall not try to rob you of your conviction.   Only, *is* it like me to wear a thing so persistently out of regard for any *one* man ?" Ivy answers. " Had it been a token of the united affec-tion of Fanc's gang of college friends, or a pledge of good-will from Teddy's entire regiment, it would have been credible. But oh! Gwen, you little goose, did you really think I was a sentimental ostrich to wear my heart on my sleeve, on rather at my throat, and think because no initials betray the giver, all is secure?"

Gwendoline is easily mystified. "Then you only bought it yourself!" she cries disappointedly.

"Yes, I only bought it myself," Ivy answers softly. "I gave so little for it, too. It was just worth *that*," holding out a little sprig of heliotrope.

" Ivy, I believe "—— But whatever avowal was forthcoming, it was abandoned as Gwendoline, peeping cautiously upwards, cries, " Count Contarini! coming down this way, and a carriage at the corner !"

"Stop here, Gwen," Ivy whispers. "Turn him back towards the tennis-courts. Say we are going out—say anything, only give me time to escape;" and running along close under the terrace-wall, she flies off.

The whole garden covers only a few acres, and is easily investigated, but Ivy hopes by an impromptu short cut to gain the carriage-drive, and across it to reach the back of the hotel in safety. Being on the side of a hill, most of the garden is terraced, and on the broad gravel walks are benches invitingly placed under palms and pepper-trees. Here the habitués of the hotel sit sheltered by the high walls, whose abundant covering of roses and creeping plants makes them look like soft banks of flowers. Carefully avoiding the flights of steps which lead from higher terraces to lower, Ivy flies along the one she is on until she reaches its extreme limit, and finds, unless she will risk a drop of some five feet or so, she must return to the central means of descent, and risk encountering Count Contarini. This she will not do. Annoyed at the coolness of the man, and his offhand remark about her being "splendid fun," she will have him clearly comprehend that, however fascinating he may appear to others, he is anything but irresistible to her, and, far from putting herself in his way, will avoid him on every possible occasion. She eyes the lower terrace ruefully. From where she is she cannot escape into the carriage-road, for here the wall rounds the corner and is built into the bank above, too high to climb. There is nothing for it but to drop into the lower terrace, and thence by a tiny bypath to scramble up into the drive, so close here above her.

Holding her skirt together in one hand, she pushes her way to the edge of the wall, here fortunately covered with her thornless namesake, and clutching its clinging roots with one hand, slides over the edge with horrible rustlings.

"E-e-e-e—oh! I'm *caught!*" as with a ripping hiss the kilted skirt strains and drags, slipping into close folds under her arms, suspending her in its twisted loop within a few inches of the ground.

To pull herself up again and unhitch the offending garment is impossible; it must drag itself loose as it tears with her weight. Horrible thoughts cross her mind of Count Contarini discovering her in such a predicament. The opportunity it would afford him of displaying his exaggerated gallantry, and the supreme joke it would be ever after; and wriggling distressfully, kicking out the dangling feet with aimless jerks, she decides she would rather *die* than let him help her.

Feeling the pressure of the tightened material

insupportably heavy across her chest, and unable
to force lower the loop that suspends her to the
level of her waist, Ivy recklessly flings both arms
up above her head, and grasps desperately at
the straining dress behind her. One moment she
writhes, a hapless Andromeda, fast bound, or rather
suspended, against the wall of living green; the next,
the thick roll of skirt jerkily unfolds, drags, and then,
with a sudden slip, slides completely over her head
and all, like an umbrella storm-blown inside out.

As she feels herself hanging in the ridiculous
position of a human cracker, with feet dangling in
one bell-shaped half, and head hidden in the other,
Ivy, though mortified beyond expression, cannot suppress an irresistible giggle at her grotesque situation. "If it were only not strained so tight, I could
get my arms down, unhook the band, and slip comfortably out of the skirt," she reflects. "The other
end of me must look like an 'Effie Deans' in that
striped petticoat. Oh, how awful I must look!
I should die of shame if any one came. You detestable thing!" with a wrench that produces no result
but a slow cracking far above her head. "Split, do!
It's as bad as being hanged and suffocated at the
same time;" and wriggling savagely, she creates such
a stir among the ivy, that the lizards fly terror-
struck in all directions.

"If—er—I could assist you in—er—any way, I
should be—er—most happy."

Instant stillness on the part of the pendant
Andromeda. Perseus is evidently wrapped in profound thought. He next remarks—

"I will get up on to the—er—higher terwace and
—er—pull you up."

"You can't!" comes in strangled tones from the enveloped one. "There's nothing to hold on to up there, and no one could pull me up; I'm too heavy. If," with hesitating despair, "you could pull me *down*, I'd be eternally grateful."

Perseus advances, and catching Andromeda's strained garments, endeavours to free them. "I shall—er—tear your dwess awfully," he says.

"Oh, drag away, *only* get me free," she gasps.

A moment of suspense. "I weally *can't*," he remarks ruefully. "There — is — er — some — er — wibbon arwangement besides the dwess, and it is all hooked together on a thick fork, and—er—unless I lift you up and can *un*hook it, I—well, I positively don't know *what* is to be done."

"*Do* lift me, then!" in tones decidedly tearful.

Perseus, seizing Andromeda, raises her slightly, and propping her against her leafy background, wrestles with her fast-bound skirt. A few seconds, then by a supreme effort the mass of "ticbacks" and gown is freed, and with a sudden drop Andromeda sinks into Perseus' arms.

As he loosens his hold of the enveloped one, and the drapery falls into its rightful place, concealing the pretty petticoat and dainty ankles, Perseus sees a face he will not easily forget. A small face with rather a square jaw; a mouth whose delicate sensitiveness make the finely-cut lips traitors to a resolute will; a pair of dark eyes, liquid and clear as a trout-stream, with its red-brown lining of leaves, the heavy fringe of curling lashes, soft dusky borders to those "windows of the soul," as if to screen from the too curious the workings of the mind within; a straight rather short nose, which takes to itself the most ridiculous little crumple when the owner thereof laughs, and which, in company with the dimples that lurk round the deeply-cut corners of the mouth, make each flash of merriment the most humorous expression of overflowing mirth.

Just now the cheeks are stained a vivid carnation, the lips curl and tremble as they part over the white short teeth, the eyelids droop their long lashes heavily as the girl ruffles her hair with her hands, and hangs her head under the pretence of eyeing her gown. "Thank you," she says uneasily; "I am very grateful to you; I can't tell you how much; for without you I might have been hanging there *hours!*" with a nervous laugh. "I can't think how it was I—I—*stuck.* I've been down much worse places before. I don't know *what* I should have done if any one had come—any one else, I mean. No, I mean—oh, I mean, as some one *had* to come, I'm glad it was you," blushing furiously and feeling the futility of trying to explain why, if such a thing *had* to be, it was better to depend upon the tender mercies of an absolute stranger, since he could not make jibes at one's expense, and *might* be induced to keep the whole thing a profound secret.

"I am only too—er—delighted to have been of any—er — assistance; but—er—seems wathur — er peculiar method of — er — descending from one terwace to another. Do—er—you always pwefer that—er—mode of pwogwessing?"

Gratitude makes Ivy much beholden to the stranger, so she struggles bravely to suppress the amusement his slow drawl and peculiar utterance cause her. "I was trying to run away," she says in a confiding tone; "*please* don't tell; and oh, please never let any one know how you found me; it must have looked so *awful*," turning aside as she colours hotly.

"Not at all!" he replies; "it weally looked wemarkably pwetty; wather like Andwomeda wapped in waterpwoofs to pwotect her fwom the woughness of the weather, or the appwoaching dwagon!"

The hearty peal of laughter that breaks from Ivy's lips is so infectious, that the languid stranger is drawn into giving vent to an exhausted "Ha! ha!" that only serves to redouble the girl's mirth.

"By Jove! *there* she is!" and in another moment a tall, slight boy bounds lightly on to the gravel path from the terrace above, and Ivy, with a spontaneous cry of welcome, rushes into his arms.

"Dear boy! when did you come? Oh, what a boon it would have been could you have arrived a few moments earlier!"

"What for? I say, Ivy, what *have* you been doing? You are in a most fearful state, and your gown all torn out behind. Oh," with a whistle and eyeing the wall critically, "is that it? Well, De Trafford, anyhow you're a cool hand. You vow you can't stand family greetings and all that, and don't want to be in the way; and here I find you chattering to my sister when every creature is hunting for her high and low to bring her to her affectionate brother's arms. You seem to have introduced yourselves," he continues, looking from one to the other amusedly, "so it's quite unnecessary for me to go through the ceremony again; but here come the whole crowd, so let's go through with the introductions now." And to the advancing group Fane presents his friend, who undergoes the somewhat trying ordeal with a sort of sleepy indifference, that irritates though it amuses the girls.

Count Contarini here steps forward, and shaking hands with Ivy, remarks in an undertone, "I cannot think how it is that I have missed you. I looked for you everywhere. Indeed, we all thought you must have dived like a mermaid under those waves. It is fortunate your brother's friend did find you; but where were you?" he continues with puzzled pertinacity.

"Oh, only down there," with a comprehensive wave of the hand that includes the entire garden and shore.

"Come and show me the rocks. Do! will you?"

"What! Now, without a hat, across the public road? Oh, no, I really cannot. Besides, it is so grilling; let us all stay here." And as they settle down in their group of chairs under a welcome patch of shade, Count Contarini mutters to himself, "Then she *was* in the garden after all!"

All look so thoroughly happy, and make so pretty and animated a group, that Mrs. Lestrange might be fairly justified for concluding that all the chattering throng were in perfect harmony with their beautiful surroundings. Fane, holding forth on his recent yachting experiences, is keeping his listeners in continuous laughter. Sybil, bending over her work, is outwardly attending, though Lord Egerton, who sits at her elbow, finds it quite possible to converse in an undertone all the time. Mrs. Cleveland, deplorably idle, in listless laziness is talking to Mr. De Trafford, and under her half-closed eyelids has taken his measure—metaphorically speaking—to the veriest fraction. His drawling responses, uttered in the spent tone of extreme languor, are so irresistibly funny, that it is only by sustained efforts that she can refrain from mimicking him to his face. Her husband and General Lestrange are smoking contentedly, and, soothed by the influence of their cigars, can afford to smile at a type of mannerism that, under less pleasant circumstances, would excite them to scathing sarcasm. Ivy is very happy. Count Contarini plays with her crewel-work, and is endeavouring to embroider curious designs upon a corner thereof, to his supreme satisfaction, as it enables him to keep very near to her, and share, if not entirely command, her attention.

How easily we are put off the right track! How blindly we follow the false scent laid so cunningly for our mystification! A word, a gesture, a stare of incredulity, and down go our assured surmises like children's sand castles at the touch of the in-rushing tide.

Mrs. Lestrange had experienced several disquieting hours, musing over the perplexing vagaries of her wayward niece, and had wisely resolved upon a course of quiet observation that should arouse no suspicion. It was true the altogether desirable Billy seemed to be entirely forgotten; but that might be only a form of the girl's pride, that had ever held real affections as treasures to be locked away in the comment-proof safe of silence. Indeed, it might almost be taken as a sure indication of her growing interest in him that she never mentioned his name, and seemed completely mystified by any chance allusions to his well-known attachment. Yet again Mrs. Lestrange had been rendered curiously alert by noting an unusual earnestness and tender gentleness that had revealed itself in Ivy of late, and of which, woman-like, she realised the importance, since the girl strove to conceal it under a greater display of excitable frivolity It could not be that for so lugubrious an individual as Colonel Talbot Ivy could entertain anything more than a sort of awe-stricken regard. Flattered by the grave deference of his manner, and interested in one whose humility and merit were only equalled by his ill-fortune, of course it was but her woman's ready sympathy that made her so gracious and *tractable* when in his society. Yes, of course it must be that; and Mrs. Lestrange smiled as she looked up at the group in front of her. Count Contarini, bending very low over the end of the mantle border he is assisting Ivy in ornamenting, is speaking in the lowest of tones. The remark, whatever it is, sends a flush slowly creeping over Ivy's face. Her lips narrow into a sneer, and with a quick impatient gesture she jerks at her work, sending the plaited skeins of silk flying to the ground. As Count Contarini and Colonel Talbot stoop for the little coloured tags, Ivy catches her aunt's eye, and, without any apparent provocation, becomes absolutely *beetroot* in hue. It does not diminish in intensity as Count Contarini in the most open manner kisses the silks before placing them in her outstretched hand. The little saucy grimace she makes thereat, and the flash of contempt in her eyes as she smiles at Colonel Talbot, are warnings perfectly incomprehensible to sweet " Aunt Amy." Confidant at last of having guessed the truth, Mrs. Lestrange knits away in preoccupied contemplation, wondering what will be the wisest course for her to pursue. It is so extraordinary that in so short a time Ivy should have fallen in love with Count Contarini. True she had *seen* him for some time, but he had only been introduced to her yesterday. Of course he was very handsome and his outspoken simplicity was amusingly novel after the reticence of Englishmen. Yes, perhaps she had better put Ivy upon her guard in case this man's attentions meant nothing at all. Unlike most Italians, he adopted an English freedom of intercourse, and had completely shaken off the national dread of compromising himself, and endeavoured to appear thoroughly cosmopolitan. He was so well known as that most detestable of all things, a flirt, that no one would dream of attaching any importance to his sudden devotion. Was Ivy—poor little heedless Ivy—to be wounded with weapons many said she knew so well how to use ?

Poor deluded lady ! you have revealed the weak place in your system of attack, and the wary besieged one is safe sheltered behind the most palpable of stalking-horses. Slight harassing feints will keep you ever engaged in the wrong direction, while the real work slowly progresses, to culminate in a grand *coup* or a colossal collapse.

Esprit de corps has always made Ivy screen from all but her cousins—to whom it is only too well known —Fane's ridiculous " swagger ; " yet already she has been put to the blush by the cool way in which he holds forth about " *our* yacht, *our* trip," &c., taking to himself all the privileges and honours of host, inviting every one to go over the " G.O.M."—a peculiar appellation for a yacht ; but Mr. De Trafford wisely remarks, " It is weally wemarkably comforting to weflect that no danger is likely to attend us in any wisks we wun, since the G.O.M. always floats!"

Ivy notices with secret gratulation that Fane is deep in an animated conversation with Nora. Long may it continue! She had endured Count Contarini with equanimity because his airy chatter has not succeeded in driving Colonel Talbot from her side, but she feels in the nervous condition of a nurse whose naughtiest charge is unavoidably selected by Fate as the exponent of her system, and expects momentarily to see it disgraced and discredited Love renders us absolutely blind or painfully critical, according to the preponderating influence of heart, or head perhaps.

"It pretty well cleared me out; but I'm going to get square after a turn or two at the tables," Ivy overhears Fane remarking to Nora.

"*Is* he? Not if I can help it," reflectively.

"You will come over?" Fane goes on. "Not allowed? Who won't allow it? Never fear! I'll square your aunt and uncle all right."

"*They* don't mind; it's Cousin Julia who objects," Nora replies dolefully, "and there she comes now to hustle me off," in resentfully dismal tones.

Fane has barely time to whisper, "Introduce me, do!" when Miss Templeton is upon them. Her coming generally produces upon a merry gathering the hushed panic that a hawk creates when swooping suddenly across a chicken-yard. A sort of tremble vibrates through the rest as they see Fane in smiling confidence rise to meet her. Nora introduces him.

"Your niece—*cousin*, of course," recovering himself with a laugh, while the hearts of the listeners sink at the inauspicious commencement, "has been telling me you don't care about Monte Carlo; but you really must come in with us all to-morrow. I've set my heart upon it. We are making up a party, and it won't be complete without you." This with unblushing effrontery.

Ivy almost shuts her eyes in anticipation of the retort. There is a pause; then Miss Templeton's acid tones fall distinctly on her listening ear. "Certainly I will join your party. My objection to the place is purely imaginary on Nora's part. I have not been there lately, because one can scarcely go alone, and I never force my society upon any one," with a glare at Nora, "particularly when I feel it would be an intrusion."

"How proud you are! Do you not know it could *never* be that—only a charming acquisition?" Fane answers softly, looking into the hard face with sweet intentness. "How he can!" Ivy ejaculates mentally. But it certainly succeeds. Whether, poor soul! she imagines her presence will be a pleasure to this tall handsome boy, or whether she is only anxious to participate in a gaiety that always seems just beyond her reach, she conceals her ill-humour under a mask of graciousness, and sitting down in the chair Fane places for her, prepares to launch into the current of conversation.

Fane is equal to the emergency. Promptly realising that Nora is lost to him if her cousin shares his attention, he whispers to Miss Templeton, "Will you let me introduce De Trafford? He'll be *so savage* if I don't!" and at her smile he introduces his friend without any warning, thereby causing him to drop his eyeglass as he turns to make his bow, and preventing the utterance of a suggestion on his part for quite five minutes, while he screws his glass firmly into his eye, and mentally execrates the boy's smartness.

Carrying out a suggestion of Mrs. Cleveland's, her husband has ordered afternoon-tea to be served on the terrace. Here they sit and drink that much-appreciated beverage, which under jealous superintendence is done full justice to in a land where, under ordinary circumstances, it is barely drinkable.

" Such a peculiar thing! The ivy at the end of the terrace is all torn down; I noticed it just now," Miss Templeton remarks, innocently this time. " It must be that horrid little boy Benjamin Dryer, that Nora is so foolish about. He is a most destructive child, and cut out the whole of her tennis-bat to use the frame for a butterfly-net—detestable little creature ! "

" I don't think it can be Benjy," Nora cries quickly. " They have all gone to St. Agnese, and been away all day."

" Of course you will defend him. I know he did it ! I shall inform Monsieur de Sérins and get him punished for his naughtiness."

Ivy is very engrossed with her tea, but cannot repress a silent shake. Mrs. Cleveland, looking up at her, ejaculates quickly, " Good gracious, Ivy, what is the matter ? Beat her on the back, somebody, do ! She's going to choke ! "

Ivy shakes her head weakly for all answer in crimsoning silence. Then Mr. de Trafford hands her a plate of bread and butter, remarking slowly, " Choking is—er—wemarkably uncomfortable sensation. Wather like—er—hanging, is it not, Miss Peyton ? but—er—have some bwead and butter ? "

How dare this half-baked, wholly flabby individual attempt to chaff her ?   She draws herself up with a mischievous smile as she retorts, " No more for me, thanks ; but after such *unusual excrtion*, I feel sure you must require something. Try this cake ? "

" I'd wather not, wcally," then with a drowsy smile like a sleepy baby's, " Some sort of—er—exertion is wather a welaxation after a long pewiod of west."

Mrs. Cleveland is all alert, and her " What sort of exertion, I wonder, do you find a relaxation, Mr. De Trafford ? " has to Ivy's ears a ring of triumph, like the joyous yelping of the hounds when first they cross the scent.   Mr. de Trafford raises his eyebrows and drops his eyeglass. As he replaces it carefully, his face broadens into a habitual contortion.   His mouth is compressed into a long narrow line, which Ivy notices is extraordinarily like a crease in a soft cheese made by the string, for his complexion is distinctly *Stilton,* and the features of so little account, that they do not in the least mar the resemblance.

" I—er—pwefer gardening to most things," he says blandly.

" Gardening !   Oh, I like that !   You don't know a rose from a cabbage," laughs Fane as he comes up with a cup for more tea.

" I wather thought there was—er—some welationship between them, I confess, but—er—I am most interwested in *fuschias.*   There is—er—something so femininely gwaceful about the formation of their —er—flowers."

" *Fuschias !* " ejaculates Mrs. Cleveland blankly. " Why fuschias ? "

" I wather think it must—er—be because their dwooping blossoms wemind me of—er—little pwetty farwies in—er—bwilliantly coloured petticoats," he replies slowly.

Fane eyes his friend for a few seconds, and then laughing as he sees the conscious red in his sister's cheeks, remarks decisively, turning away with Nora's tea, "For the 'fuschia' give up the study. You can see they don't bear handling without all tumbling to bits, although they may be pretty, old chap, and in *these* latitudes climb anywhere!"

Will Ivy's cheeks *ever* get cool? She turns her back on the tea-table and plunges almost eagerly into conversation with Count Contarini, who happens to be near her, and yet is for some time quite unaware of the drift of his remarks. "You have been so kind to me, that I am sure you will grant it," he says.

"I! grant what? What do you mean?" with returning consciousness that he has been reiterating something for the last ten minutes.

"The flower that you are wearing, you will give it to me? It is not possible for you to know how much I shall value it, but," with earnest insistance, "if you grant me that, you give me what I most desire."

"Really!" Ivy answers lightly. "Then you know we never *do* get what we most desire; it is always withheld for a beneficent purpose, they say. So I'm afraid you cannot have this," fingering the sprig of rapidly blackening heliotrope lovingly.

Count Contarini's face darkens curiously. "You *will* give it!" he says passionately.

Ivy glances at him in cool surprise. "I think you hardly quite understood," she replies coldly. "I said no—you cannot have this."

"And you mean it?"

"Certainly I mean it."

"Good-bye! I shall not see you for a very long time. I am going to Nice this evening. I cannot tell when I shall return," he says, looking into Ivy's tranquil eyes furiously.

She almost laughs aloud. Truly foreigners are vastly amusing! "Good-bye," she says, putting out her hand with a smile. "I hope you will enjoy yourself. Nice is just the place for you. Mentone's quiet picturesqueness must weary you unutterably after a time."

Holding her hand in his, he gazes in her face with an intense hopelessness Ivy thinks very well done, as he mutters in a low voice, "Forgive me —I will not go. I will *stay!* You do not understand—it is not *possible* that you understand. I ask too much. Ah!" with a great heaving sigh, "we can feel more in one day than you English in one year! Niente—niente di cuore, Signorina. But one day—ah yes," with a beaming smile like a forgiven child's—"one day you will give me a flower, will you not, Signorina?" pleadingly.

"Oh, no doubt! When I *too* think it 'splendid fun!'" with cutting emphasis.

Count Contarini's face is a study. For a minute he does not understand, then, as the recollection of his remark flashes across his mind, a satisfaction that his words have power to excite her to any emotion at all, fills him with unctuous delight. Rapidly concealing his content under a well-feigned remorse, he speaks in humble deferential tones— "Signorina—Mees Ivy—allow me to tell you— what have I said that you should be so angry with me? Ever since I saw you I want to know you, and for how long I wait for an introduction! until yesterday afternoon Mr. Cleveland introduce me to you. Perhaps you say I have no right to speak. *I* am not English! I do not think for ten years and speak when it is too late! I know at once, it is in me to know at once, and when I say to Mr. Cleveland last night you are 'splendid fun,' I mean it! I mean you are not only quite beautiful."

"I wish you would not talk so loud. I would rather walk up and down until you finish what you have to say," and Ivy jumps up and paces rather sullenly along the terrace, with Count Contarini emphatically gesticulating at her side, often stopping in his walk to enforce some remark with extraordinary asseveration while he confronts her.

"Rum chap that!" Fane remarks; "looks out of place somehow without an orchestra and footlights. What is he?—Contarini? contadine? Any one is a Count! If Ivy is 'sweet' on him I shan't allow it, they are generally as poor as rats," he continues pompously; "and anyhow, though Billy isn't much, his 'ready' is right enough."

"Who is Billy?" It is Nora who asks the question, but there are others who are waiting for the answer.

"Oh! don't you know? Only a fellow at home. He's got a nice place not far from ours." (*Ours!* the old Rectory with its ten acres, and dear garden, more useful than beautiful!)

"Well! does she like him?" Nora asks again.

"Can't say, I'm sure; he is awfully in love with her, but Ivy is like most girls, you know, likes to have a lot of fellows hanging round, and won't decide upon one for fear of losing the rest."

"How can you say such horrible things?" Nora cries indignantly. "No wise girl jumps into a serious thing like marriage in a hurry, she must take time to make up her mind."

"Yes, when she has one to make up—Ivy has only instincts," Fane retorts. Here Nora begs to differ, and they argue the point with a persistency gratifying to none but themselves.

Count Contarini has meanwhile explained, most lucidly for him, that the term he made us of, and which to Ivy was objectionable, was in his imaginings most respectfully complimentary. "If I come back here, do you think your uncle will ask me up to your salon?" he asks after a while.

"I am sure I don't know. One or two come in for music after they leave the smoking-room, excepting Colonel Talbot; as he never smokes, he comes up whenever he likes."

"He! oh, he cannot smoke, of course. If you have no lungs you cannot smoke. Perhaps that helps to make him so *triste.* Mr. Cleveland tells me the best chance he had to see some active service was in Egypt, and there he became very ill at once and was sent to England, and now he is ill ever since; but about the smoking-room—I will join the gentlemen there, and perhaps your uncle will ask me to your salon, and if you will not give me a flower, you will let me bring you one?" He waits with a smile for her answer.

Her indifference piques him. "A flower? oh yes, if you like," she says. But her eyes are fixed in an abstracted gaze upon the far horizon, and her manner is decidedly *distraite.*

"You need not be troubled to think I shall come.

I shall *not* come!" he bursts out with sudden vehemence.

Ivy sighs. Really this man is rather exhausting, with his tender susceptibilities, or overweening conceit. "I was not thinking of you at all," she answers wearily.

"Of who then?" quickly. Receiving no answer, he pulls his moustache, eyeing her reflectively, and noting rather a pathetic droop about the corners of her mouth, he nods slightly several times, weighing the inspiration that has come to him, then smiles, rather a pleased smile, whether at his own perspicacity or at his companion it would be hard to say. "I like to see you are not always gay," he says magnanimously. "Why are you English so afraid to show you have any feeling? I know very well what you were thinking of," he continues in satisfied tones rather trying to his hearer—"I did feel sorry myself, too, when I heard it, but what will you?" with an expressive shrug and outward gesture of his hands; "for the pleasure of so many, one or two must suffer; it was no fault to any one, only his own. It is over now, and, Gran Dio! his was a merry life as long as it lasted!"

"What do you mean?" Ivy faces him with startled vehemence. "Speak!" she cries in a sharp voice.

Wonder has held him silent, and a natural impulse to follow out his own line of thought before answering her. "What is it that she thinks of, if not this subject of which he speaks?" But the brown eyes are angry, and the girl gives a short stamp of impatience. "What are you speaking of?" she questions again.

"I thought you had heard," he replies in his

usual precise way, biting off each word distinctly, tongue and teeth wrangling over the S's and T's "Did you not hear that French boy you saw at Monte Carlo yesterday afternoon, shot himself last night in the woods at Cape St. Martin? He was found this morning; he was alive, but he could not speak, and he died very soon, about two hours after they found him. He was "——

"Oh, never mind," Ivy answers, in a curiously still voice, "I must go and get a wrap"—she shivers —"it is rather cold."

"You will let me get it?"

"No, thank you, I would rather go myself." The tone is not to be gainsaid, and much mystified, Count Contarini draws himself up and bows stiffly as she moves away.

It is not cold, not at all. High still in the cloudless heavens rides the sun, blazing down brightly upon grey olive slopes and orange gardens, white houses and red rocks, making dazzling the foam ribbon that bounds the blue mantle of the sea, and crowning with stainless glory the pure snow-covered mountain peaks in the background far away.

Behind a shed at the extreme limit of the garden, hidden from view, but by no means sure of solitude, sits Ivy. A large parasol and book are all her defences to defy the curious; however, fate is beneficent, and she is undisturbed. Sitting on the ground clasping her knees with both hands, the open parasol balanced over her shoulder, she rather comically resembled a huge crimson toad-stool, placed by adverse circumstances at a somewhat inebriated angle. Coming up from behind, you might smile perhaps at the red excrescence clearly defined against the wide blue sweep of the sea, but the wisdom that looks at both sides would find here as elsewhere, it is well to suspend judgment until we are acquainted with the whole.

There are no tears in the wide open eyes, only a dull hopelessness, that has stilled also the trembling lips with its petrifying touch. The thoughts are strangely apathetic that pass so slowly through her brain, like gently moving shadows on the sea. They do not race by, treading upon each other's heels in a bewildering string impossible to arrest, or even connect; only rise and pass, and fade into the haze of forgetfulness, like birds slow-winging their homeward flight across an evening sky.

The boy is dead—*dead.* Out there with the wide-eyed ancmones under the cold grey olives, whose weird distorted shapes hung like accusing memories between him and the sky. Out there—where the wood had echoed with her laughter, while the sunbeams trod so gaily stately measures with the shadows—out there in all the wealth of beauty and rich flush of life, the boy had died. Not in a moment, but slowly, oh so slowly, the cold waters had come creeping to his feet. He was so young— so young! perhaps the death angel had in pity tarried ere carrying him across the tide. Did the olives whisper still the murmuring echo of his last farewell? Through that long sleepless night had the ripples broken laughingly as they kissed the rugged shore? Did sweet nature, lulled by the breath of the night wind, disregard the dying boy, or had the waves sobbed in soft sympathy to soothe his passion of remorse? Had the stars smiled down through a veil of tears as they gleamed in the bypaths of heaven, and pointed the way across the vast regions of the temporal to the "things which are not seen, which are eternal," and where there is "no more curse"?

And the fluttering butterfly that alighted on her knee, and the soft breath that played with the tumbled hair on her forehead, brought no answer to Ivy. The black scythe of death spanned the wide heaven of hope, and hid awhile its glad rays of glory.

The butterfly has flown away, and Ivy, with a long straining shiver has bowed her face upon her knee. Her hands are clasped tightly together, and the words fall quite steadily from her lips, only with an intensity that makes of them a prayer. "Death!— you must hear me, you are always near, they say— death, why can you not take—*me*? What did you want with that poor boy? and what do you want— —oh, my God, I cannot bear it! not die—not *die!*" with a convulsive sob—"Oh, let him live—just for a little time, only a little time!" She is so insensible to all but the anguish that masters her that footsteps behind her are unheard. Her parasol is pushed gently to one side, and a hand is laid on her bowed head, while a voice whose low tones are to her dearer than all others speaks very tenderly. "My dear child, what is the matter? Something is troubling you. Can you not tell me what it is? Perhaps I can help you—come," speaking firmly, and with a kindly pressure of the long thin hand.

Oh, if she could only weep at his feet and *speak!* Oh, *why* does he not understand? Why can he not see? The touch of that hand steadies her wonderfully, and after a fierce last grip of her hands, she unclasps them and prepares to rise. So absolutely unnerved is she, that when by the aid of Colonel Talbot's hand she is standing by his side, she feels strangely tired and faint.

"Sit here," he says, "Giani is away with his boat, catching 'ricci,' he tells me, on the rocks down there, so he will not be returning to turn us off his much beloved bench."

"What does he want it for?" Ivy manages to say.

"It is his carpenter's bench. Do you mean to say you have not noticed him working here often, mending hotel furniture or repairing boxes for travellers? Oh! he is a very useful fellow," Colonel Talbot goes on, carefully abstaining from looking at his companion—"he mends locks, carves a little, is rather a good fisherman, and drives a fiacre, when he has no other job on hand. He is very proud of his bench, and his hut, himself, and everything about him, and justly remarks *his* view is the best in the garden. It is very beautiful, is it not? That wide expanse of sea is always a wholesome tonic for me. Rolling downs, a clear sky, or a far stretch of ocean gives one a sense of freedom, and resignation, and rest: you know the sort of feeling, when nothing intervenes to throw you back upon yourself—when no restricted outlook cramps the soaring of your desires—when your little finite longings find themselves free to rise and pass unhindered into the Infinite Eternal."

An uncontrollable tightening of his little neighbour's clasped hands causes him unusual distress. Her eyes are dry and bright, but the traces of pain about the compressed lips grieves him. "My child," he says very quietly, "can you not tell me what troubles you? I am an old fellow, and might be able to help you; most misunderstandings can be adjusted satisfactorily with a little arrangement," he adds kindly.

A look of indignation curls the corners of her mouth as Ivy answers, "Did you imagine I had quarrelled with any one and was distressed because I had not made it up!"

"Well," thoughtfully, "I thought it might be something of that kind; some people take offence very easily, and two impulsive natures may inflict a great deal of pain mutually, often quite unintentionally."

"Quite so," Ivy answers drily.

Something in her tone arrests his wandering imaginings. Clearly her distress can have nothing to do with Count Contarini. "I trust you have no bad news from home," Colonel Talbot remarks sympathetically, and yet not wishing to force in the least the girl's confidence.

Blind buzzard though he is, he is so *dear*, that though her heart is beating thickly, Ivy could almost smile at his mystification. Steadying her voice carefully, she answers, "It is nothing—I mean, it is only perhaps, because—because it seems so *awful* that — that I cannot help thinking of that poor French boy," with something very like a sob at the finish.

"Ah!" There is a great deal of relief expressed in that long drawn interjection. The natural relief of a man who finds some logical reason for a woman's tears. "Yes, *indeed* I understand. When we are young death is to us so terrible, and in this case one realises so clearly ' the sting of death is sin.' But do you not think the value we put upon life is almost pagan ? Surely what appears of so little account in the eyes of God need not be of such paramount importance to us! Does not the waste of life here convince us that this stage of our development is but a preliminary process in the 'perfecting' of our humanity ? Why fear for the welfare of another ? Is he not in his Father's hands ? Will you dispute His discipline ? Do you doubt His love ? "

As he speaks Ivy's mental horizon seems to clear. The rebelliousness that pronounces existence purposeless and the preponderance of suffering an unnecessary element in our experience, dies down into a dulled acquiescence. It is like the restful silence of a lofty cathedral after the chaotic clamour of the streets. On no account would Ivy analyse her sensations. The terrible death of the young Frenchman is of course cause quite sufficient to account for her unhappiness. Death was so strangely out of place here in all the full flush of life and gaiety of her existence, that the shock was all the greater from its glaring incongruity.

Once long ago in the joyous spring-tide, when the carpet of the wild flowers was unrolled in all the woods, and the air vibrated overhead with the music of the birds, Ivy, singing in the sunlight, and laden with golden daffodils, saw suddenly at her feet a dying thrush. As the wings ceased to flutter, and the bright eyes closed, and the little songster lay still, the child had cried out in passionate protest, " Go away, death, go away ; not *to-day*—no, you *cannot* come here to-day ! " But the little minstrel's day was done ; the juicy bracken fronds covered him tenderly, and the sunbeams kissed his ruffled coat with warm and loving lips, only he would never sing any more, and yet the thicket was throbbing with the carolling of his kind. The merry daffodils danced on, and the sunlight played bo-peep with the shadows, but the gladness had died out of the heart of the child, and the wood was not any more like heaven. And so to-day too, in the hot noontide of happiness, had death chilled her with his sudden touch of sorrow. Yes, oh yes, it was of course *that !*—only why, when the outer chaos of her mind had calmed, did the keen grip of anguish cling so coldly round her heart ?

"Thank you"—Ivy crumples her handkerchief into little kiltings as she answers in a dull constrained tone—"thank you so much, you have done me a great deal of good. One ought not to feel bad as well as miserable, but I had grown both just before you came. I am all right now. I suppose it is time to go in," rising as she speaks.

Colonel Talbot rises too. Looking down at her earnestly, "Is there no other way in which I could help you ? Have you not some other trouble ?" he says gravely.

The little face is raised and the eyes look straight into his. They darken slowly with an intense hopelessness, as the fluttering lips smile bravely and reply, "What a question ! Trouble and I, of course, are strangers ; but indeed I feel your kindness more than I can say, in trying so carefully to keep us still apart." She lifts her book and parasol, and turns to go.

Far away behind the terraced gardens and quiet olive slopes, the mountains gaze down upon them in grand serenity. A feeling of regret perhaps prompts

Colonel Talbot to exclaim, "How untroubled and at rest it looks up there!"

Ivy's glance travels on, and lingers lovingly upon the far snow-tipped summits. "I wish I could fly there!" she says with a little sigh.

Her companion hardly seems to hear her, though in a moment he speaks musingly. "Few indeed mount up with wings as eagles," he says. "We cannot fly, but all of us may climb." Perhaps it is the consciousness of life's toil that makes Ivy so tired as she walks along thoughtfully and enters the hotel.

CHAPTER VIII.

"No man knoweth either love or hatred by all that is before them. All things come alike to all."—*Ecclesiastcs.*

SOME people impress their personality upon their surroundings in such a manner that all things become invested with their individual charm. Mrs. Cleveland's salon reflected her artistic proclivities in comfortable disorder. There was no strained regularity about the folds of the Abruzzi blankets that formed the window-curtains. The hard, un-inviting chairs belonging to the inevitable set of crimson Utrecht furniture have been banished, and the uncompromising rotundity of the sofa judiciously concealed under more Abruzzi drapings, and a luxurious pile of cushions. Small tables, lounging chairs, two draped easels with unmounted sketches upon them, photographs in all varieties of frames, a fire snugly blazing in its setting of sea-green plush, the shelves above studded with rare specimens of Venetian glass—an open piano, books and litter of papers, with a wealth of flowers everywhere, in brass pots or unpretending pottery ware, completed the catalogue, and created by their harmonious combinations a most satisfactory whole, save to the soul of the rigorously neat. Lounging before the fire in a low chair was Mrs. Cleveland. The glow from the red logs lit up her figure in rosy distinctness, burnishing into golden ripples her glossy auburn hair, outlining her beautiful form proudly, as it pencilled the embroidered peignoir with brilliant tracery beyond the imitation of even Parisian art.

Silence proclaimed it the dinner hour. No steps hurried along the corridors, or whirr of electric bells broke the stillness of the deserted étage. Mrs. Cleveland, being in no mood for conversation, has remained in her room, availing herself of the 'nerves' or 'neuralgia' she has established for occasions like the present, when, to put it plainly, she was a prey to undeniable sulks. Waving away everything presented to her by the faithful Brigida, she ordered tea, and relapsed into silence. Having given the necessary orders, Brigida noiselessly retraced her steps to her mistress's side, and running her wiry fingers through Dora's hair, stood silently behind her chair, ruffling the auburn tresses lovingly. Dora must indeed be irritated when that failed to soothe. Turning her head impatiently she shook off the old woman's hand. "C'è una pina?" she cried peevishly.

Without a word Brigida kneels before the fire, having supplied herself with the *pine* (the fir cones always used with wood fires), and arranging the logs carefully she lifts glowing embers with her bare fingers, then dexterously kindling her fir cones, she produces a brilliant blaze.

As the flood of light illumines the old woman, playing on the gaudy kerchief folded across her shoulders and down upon her spotless apron, making curiously distinct the myriad wrinkles in her weather-beaten face, out of which the keen black eyes glow strangely, Dora feels the qualms of an accusing conscience. Stretching out her hand to her kneeling attendant, "Mi sentivo di mal amore" (I was cross), she says simply. Quickly the old grey-headed creature clasps the outstretched hand. Raising it in both her own she kisses it, invoking a blessing from Our Lady the while, then rises to go in quest of the much-desired tea.

To strangers it appeared curious that this wizened old Italian should be elected as Mrs. Cleveland's handmaid, but those who knew the story of her devotion to the mistress she had tended from childhood wondered no more, and perhaps reflected regretfully that faithful loving service is not common nowadays, and cannot be purchased with money.

The tea probably inspired Dora with a more cheerful view of things in general, for when her husband returned from the smoking-room she was contentedly listening with eyes closed to the vivacious chatter of the antiquated domestic, who ruffled and combed with tireless fingers the long rich masses of hair most tenderly.

"Well, Dora, you *do* look comfortable ! This room is nice, after the salle-à-manger. 'Pon my word, we shall have to break the windows, or set up an air-pump," Mr. Cleveland exclaims, throwing himself into a chair opposite his wife. "I can't think how people stand it ! The whole crowd are in the hermetically-sealed salon now, while the new

German plays. I looked in to see who was there—none of our set, except Nora Bingham, playing dominoes for a wager with her two German satellites, and Fane swearing in the hall, vowing all sorts of rude things; 'that only an Irishwoman could stand it, &c.,' as the salon was 'worse than a monkey-house.' That boy will be a nice boy, some day, when the nonsense is knocked out of him," he continues, stretching out a hand and feeling aimlessly over a small table for matches.

Brigida places them in his hand, and, with a final touch to the lamps, departs to her mistress's room at Mr. Cleveland's well-known signal, "Thank you, old girl, now you can clear."

"Will it be bad for your head, Dora?" he asks, with his pipe in his mouth, hesitating ere applying the lighted match to the tobacco.

"No, I like it. Brigida, shut my door!"

There is silence between them for some moments, while Mr. Cleveland draws at his pipe absently, blowing the smoke in thin curling whisps through his pursed-up mouth. "Talbot was not there again to-night," he says suddenly. "Sorry it annoys you, Dora, but I *was* right this morning. I met Martin as we were going down to dinner, and he told me Contarini was right enough in what he said. Martin doesn't know how it got about—servants, I suppose—but Talbot has had another attack of hæmorrhage."

Mrs. Cleveland does not answer.

"He'll pull through this time," continues her husband, "but—Dora, don't you think you could advise him to go away; he might be the better for a change, you know."

Perhaps it is a good thing he is engrossed with his pipe, and does not see his wife's face. "Vyner," she begins after a moment's pause, "go on telling me stories. Was every one else there? How did they all look? Was the concert good this afternoon, and has Fane been as lucky at the tables as usual?"

"Strikes me," Mr. Cleveland rejoins readily, "it would be the best thing for him if his luck were to change; he's getting a deal too fond of the excitement. Ivy doesn't like it, but she can do nothing; and it's my belief the Boronowksy encourages him in it. It is strange the way in which she has taken up that boy?"

"The *strangest* thing about it is that Fane imagines it is entirely due to his many attractions," Dora remarks cuttingly.

"Well, isn't that so?"

"Of course! nothing more natural! A woman who creates a perfect furore wherever she goes, and is idolised by society everywhere, would undoubtedly prefer a youthful unknown to a host of fascinating celebrities!"

"Women like a change."

"If I did not know you only mean to be irritating I should begin to tremble for your sanity! Don't be tiresome, Vyner, as if you did not see that nasty mean jealousy is at the bottom of it all."

"You surprise me; I was not aware Nora had such a rival."

"Nora! Who is talking of Nora? I wish you would be serious, for really this is giving me a dreadful amount of mental agitation, and I don't see why you should not help me with all my worries."

" My dear Dora "—impressively—"*don't* worry ! "

" How supremely selfish, and how like a man ! Fortunately for society at large, when *women* see catastrophes impending they do their best to avert them."

" And make confusion worse confounded. Now look here, Dora"—taking his pipe from his mouth with pleasing and profound attention—" I'm not going to run my head against a stone wall to please any one. If the Boronowsky choses to make short work of Fane because Contarini has thrown her over for Ivy, that's their own look out. Hints to Contarini are sparks to a powder-magazine. You don't suppose he can't see her game and laughs in his sleeve all the time ! Fane's conceit effectually blinds *him* as to the true bearings of the Boronowsky's course, and nothing but the eventual *denouement* will convince him that he has only been a convenient tool whereby she hopes to distress Ivy. What you expect to gain by irritating the Boronowsky and urging her to prompt retaliation I fail to comprehend. Leave them alone. If Contarini is in love with Ivy and means more than mere fooling around, it yet does not follow that she will have him. If she does not, the Boronowsky's jealousy will die a natural death and Fane be all the better for the lesson."

" What makes you think Ivy won't accept Contarini ? "

" I don't say she won't accept him ; I said it does not follow that she will have him even if he does propose."

" But what makes you think that perhaps she may not accept him ? "

" I think it is probable because woman's unselfishness (as you call it) is a factor that produces most unforeseen results. In the ordinary course of things it would have been only natural for her to like him, but when unselfish women introduce conflicting elements embodied in an interesting rival with one foot in his grave; a girl's—pity sympathy, call it what you will—plays the mischief with her common sense, and then—well, then, the unselfish woman may have a good deal to answer for."

Dora plays nervously with her handkerchief, and then desperately resolves upon an attack. " I quite understand what you wish to imply, Vyner, but allow me to remark that it was but natural that any woman with good taste should prefer Colonel Talbot to Count Contarini, and think him an infinitely more desirable husband for Ivy. Of course, *had I known* he was in such a deplorable state of health, nothing would have induced me to introduced him to the girls, or countenance in any way an acquaintanceship that might be attended with distressing results; but naturally, if one is not *told* of things—one may blunder in one's ignorance, only— the responsibility is removed from the shoulders of the unconscious agent, to the broad back "—pointedly —" of the silent onlooker, who, aware of the danger, sat still, *like a man,* and did nothing."

Mr. Cleveland has a pipe. He is naturally a good-tempered man, with a keen sense of the ludicrous. Silently the smoke-wreaths curl upward as he leans back in his chair, with half closed eyes. A slow smile of amusement creeps round his thin lips, as he removes his pipe, and remarks, " You've been right all through, Dora, stick to that, only, next to woman's social generalship, I'll place their extraordinarily retentive memories. I can't compete, but, being a man, I am at liberty to sit still and do nothing."

Dora struggles to subdue the smile that comes too quickly, and, looking pathetically at her husband, trusts he will accept her unexpressed penitence. He will not look at her, but pokes at his smouldering pipe in engrossed pre-occupation. She stretches out her hand. He is too far off and does not see the movement apparently. Making her handkerchief into a ball, she flings it at his head, crying out, "Vyner, you are detestable; you have not a grain of pity for me! What was the good of your telling me the man was awfully ill, when there was nothing but your assertion to make one think so. No, *nothing!*" at her husband's gaze of exasperating incredulity. "Any one else under the same circumstances would have displayed in a thousand ways their severance from all the trammels of society; but when one sees a man give the same scrupulous attention to his toilet, grow no beard and shave regularly, wear stiff collars instead of soft wraps, I consider one is justified in supposing he retains his hold tenaciously of this life; and really, now I come to think of it, I am not at all surprised I was misled, only I think it rather strange in a man of Colonel Talbot's character, for it bespeaks a clinging to life that puzzles one in so unworldly a mind. Don't you think so, Vyner?"

"I don't profess to understand the logic of women, but I can't say I see anything worldly in the fact of a man, however good he is, wishing to dress like a gentleman as long as he lives: only. it might be wiser in future to get medical certificates for all whose matrimonial prospects you propose to influence," Mr. Cleveland replies drily.

No remark follows this speech, and looking up at his wife after a prolonged pause, he sees that her eyes are full of tears. " Come, Dora, never mind," he says kindly. " I only want to warn you about playing with edged tools. I daresay you have not done Ivy any harm ; perhaps she may be in love with Contarini, who knows ? and even if not—if she does care for Talbot, summon fatalism to comfort you, and say, if it be so, it was destined to be so. It is a very comfortable creed, and shelves one's responsibilities effectually."

" You are very unkind, Vyner, and have made my head ache dreadfully. I am *much* too tired to sit up talking any longer "—moving towards her room— " and please open all the windows, there is nothing I *detest* like the smell of tobacco smoke ! I thought you would be nice and amiable if I allowed you to have a pipe here, and your arguments have only increased my headache, and your smoking has made me sick !" and disappearing into her room she shut the door.

Left to himself, Mr. Cleveland kicks the logs together with cool decision, smiles in a way that would have irritated Dora, as he muses upon the peculiarities of the gentler sex, and then with careful consideration prepares to carry out her behests. As the cool evening air sweeps through the room, making the lamps flicker, and sending papers fluttering to the floor, it brings on its wings the sound of Sybil's ringing voice, throbbing in the piteous melody of Denza's " Se." " I will get ' Ideale ' out of her," Mr. Cleveland says briskly. " How her high notes peal out like clear bells; that's the sort of voice I like." And a few minutes later finds him in the Lestranges' crowded salon. I say crowded, because somehow it always did appear so. A stranger might experience a momentary sensation of being decidedly *de trop*, and ruefully reflect that his room would be preferable to his company; but the cordial circle possessed most expansive qualities, and a warm welcome was never wanting. Mrs. Lestrange and the General were engaged in conversation with some old Mentone residents, who had left their charming villa to accept the only hospitality the Lestranges could offer, " table-d'hôte dinner, and music in our little salon afterwards." Barricaded behind small tables they sat and discussed politics or personalities, Mentone's virtues *versus* Monte Carlo's vices, and the many dissipations of Nice. Sybil was engrossed in conversation with a rather dirty-looking German professor. His hair was of that luxuriant tropical growth rarely seen in our nipping English climate, his coat was somewhat greasy, and his collar an old acquaintance. He stands with his rusty elbow almost rubbing against Sybil's rounded arm shining whitely through the beaded black gown that, being high to the throat, does duty for hotel dinner toilet. In rapt attention she turns over her music for his inspection, receiving his criticisms and short comments as utterances from an oracle. Gwendoline, with eager eyes and parted lips, leans against the piano, her slight figure stooping as she bends forward to catch the full significance of the unwashed one's spluttering opinions. Nora has evidently done with the Germans downstairs, and sitting in a window seat with Fane is having a low and somewhat snappish conversation across a draught-board. Lord Egerton, looking decidedly bored, rises from his place near the pre-occupied Gwendoline, and moving to where Ivy and Count Contarini are winding skeins of silk in a very desultory manner, watches them silently with a glance decidedly vacant.

Ivy looks up at him and speaks simply. "So nice for you musical people having such a treat. I can hardly say I thoroughly appreciate Herr Krachen-Schlag; he is a trifle beyond me, but Sybil and Gwendoline are enchanted with him; indeed, Sybil is completely conquered, and says now social barriers are rightly swept away at the approach of genius, and that the superiority of intellect should be the only qualification requisite for society's passport. You must feel gratified at having brought them so much pleasure," she concludes kindly.

Lord Egerton does not speak, but lays his hand over his mouth, and then slowly smooths his short beard as he answers, "Your cousin has decided opinions and very much common sense."

"She has! She *is* so sensible. When once she has learnt to overcome the ridiculous old-fashioned prejudices that make good birth and breeding essentials for friendship, she will unhesitatingly stop at nothing. I assure you"—Ivy says with slow emphasis—"she will put her hand into his grubby paw without a qualm, only considering his nobility of soul: now, I couldn't, not without gloves."

Lord Egerton does not smile, indeed he is looking somewhat sullen. Dropping her hands in her lap, Ivy leans back contentedly. What her mischievous smile preludes remains unknown, as Fane, followed by Nora, now joins them, the former growling irritably. "Can't sit over there. Can think of nothing but that Pongo's pomposity and his beastly hair. Do they all grow it like that?" Fane concludes, with an expression of lofty disgust.

"Don't think of his hair, think of his talents," Ivy replies severely.

"Think of his talons! Not if I know it! Nebuchadnezzar was a *joke* to him: they ought to keep them caged, or give them a change of raiment when they let them out," he continues irritably.

Here the excitement at the piano reaches a climax. "But you will sing, 'Ideale'?" Mr. Cleveland implores.

"'Ideale'! Tosti! puiff!" and snapping his fingers with a shrug of contempt, Herr Krachen-Schlag selects the song he wishes Sybil to sing, and attacking the piano with a tremendous prelude he breaks into Elizabeth's prayer out of Tannhauser. Not a word is spoken while Sybil sings, and the beauty of the music appeals to all, and silences the annoyance created by the dogmatic decision of the musical authority. Only Mr. Cleveland ventures to remark at the conclusion, "Now, Miss Sybil, I don't want to be stirred up any more, may I have my soothing 'Ideale'?" Sybil smiles, and petitions the ruffled genius to accompany her, and with a shrugging protest he complies.

Music may often be an annoyance, unless in defiance of all decency conversation clatters on unchecked. However, to-night even to the veriest chatterer it is a relief. Mr. de Trafford thankfully pauses in his laborious exertions to make conversation with the daughter of the "residents," an altogether dabby girl, like a washed-out water-colour with nothing distinctive about her but an abnormal length of back and flat feet.

> "Torna, caro ideale, torna un istante
>   A sorridermi ancora.
>   E a me risplendera, nel tuo sembiante,
>   Una novella aurora."

How often Ivy had heard the words, and always with an intense appreciation that almost taught her suffering by sympathy; now it is different, however, and unfurling her fan she keeps her eyes upon its swaying feathers, drawing in her lip to still its trembling. The power of music is so absolute, because it expresses for us feelings we dare not put into words. The gladness we strive to hide will break out into a pæan of triumph through the medium of another's melody, and the ice-bound torrent of our longing or regret sweep down all barriers and rush tempestuously onward in the passionate outpouring of some composer's rhythmic woes. The last "torna" breathes through the hushed room, and even on the unprepossessing face of Herr Krachen-Schlag is gracious approval depicted. They crowd round the piano, and compliments, and the hubbub of conversation, recommences. Count Contarini, twisting a piece of silk in his fingers, leans towards Ivy and speaks gently. "You like that 'Ideale'? What Ideale do you think of? Do you think for yourself or for some one else?"

"How do you mean 'to think for some one else?'"

"I mean, is it your Ideale to return to you, or are you thinking for some one else's Ideale to return to them?"

"Oh! I see. Well, of course I don't think about it at all! It is quite stupid enough to have ideals, without expecting them to return," and Ivy smiles rather bitterly.

"We have all an ideal!" Count Contarini replies sagely "Wait, I will tell, I have an ideal, sometimes I see her, and I say, now I am happy because I have found her, and then it is a disappointment, for she is not ideal at all—quite—quite *tiresome*," he cries joyfully, having expressed himself as he thinks so clearly and well. "Oh yes, you have an ideal," he continues, looking at Ivy with a smile, "of course he is a very handsome young man."

This is suggestive of something so eminently "shoppy," that Ivy smiles. Edging his chair a little nearer her, Count Contarini answers her smile with another very significant one, and twirling his moustache, drops his eyes modestly as he answers, "Is that not so? For you, he must be very handsome—very handsome," with a clicking intonation that puts one in mind of a mechanical toy.

"No, I always *hate* handsome men," Ivy says sharply.

This is so overpowering that for a moment the astounded Italian gazes at her without a word, then as the blood rushes to his head, and his eyes blaze, he looks so horridly excited that Ivy dreads some reckless outburst. Lowering her fan she peeps over its edge, and laughing a low little laugh looks at him coolly.

"How could you expect me to say anything else—to *you*," with a deprecating gesture, and moving her left hand a little towards him. "Come, you can't be really angry, you know; shake hands and be friends."

He takes her hand and holds it in both his own. "Dio mio!" he gasps, "you are a cat"—a disgusted start on Ivy's part—"to like to play with the mouse as you do." Here he raises her hand slightly, and bending down kisses it gravely. "We are friends," he says as he relinquishes it, and sits up stiffly.

"That's a comfort!" Fane remarks to Nora, with an uncontrollable laugh, as they sit silently near. "But are you still thinking of your Germans, you aren't attending to the game a bit. There—I huff those three," dabbing his draughts over the luckless captives as he speaks. "Come, crown me; you have not a chance, the photo is mine."

"Wait till you have won."

"Go on—you have only one move; what are you waiting for?"

"I am thinking 'the best laid schemes of mice and men gang aft a-gley,' as you doubtless know," with one finger laid upon her lips. "Ah—oh! take care," as with a dexterous movement the board is overturned, and the draughts sent rolling in all directions.

"Of all the mean tricks that's the most vulgar," Fane ejaculates wrathfully. "*Worse* than vulgar, downright low! I don't care. I'll have the photo. It is in 'A Roman Singer,' I saw it before dinner," and leaping to his feet he makes for the window seat.

Nora is before him, however. Holding the book tightly she faces him angrily. "You won't have anything of the sort. The idea of *taking* a photo! I thought you were above that sort of thing; or are you, I wonder, the original Terry told me of, who kept a book full of pretty girls' photos, his 'Chronicle of Captives,' he called it, and of which he had bought or stolen every one!"

"Well, you've no conceit about you," Fane says sarcastically, "that's one good thing; and I should have remembered that truth and honesty are scarcely to be looked for—in a Paddy."

"As much to be looked for as politeness in an Englishman," Nora retorts furiously.

Fane smiles. "Are you imagining it might be rare?" he says.

"I don't imagine anything. I know it is as ridiculous to expect manners from an Englishman as merriment from a mummy."

"Your simile is most inaccurate. Mummies are a frequent source of merriment. I saw one once causing an infinity of fun. I didn't see why. Poor old chap was all tied up in rags and dripping with brown varnish sort of stuff: I couldn't see much to laugh at, but the other fellow held me there, and we heard a fat old woman explaining to her daughter; 'Lor! now, ain't it wonderful! two thousand years old and more, and he's quite fresh yet, *perspiring still!*'"

Nora laughs readily, then frowns, as Fane makes a futile grab for the book. "Leave it alone. What makes you think it is here at all?"

"What makes me? 'A Roman Singer' would be a degree flatter than I take him for, if he no longer held your photo."

"Take him," Nora says, presenting the book, "take him and see for yourself that, like the rest of his sex, he is flat and empty and disappointing."

Fane flutters the leaves vigorously. "It *was* here, I'd swear."

"Not before me, please."

"You've taken it out. You've got it, you"—as **a**
horrid thought darts into his mind—"you couldn't
have given it to that *sickening* German!"

"He is much better now, thank you, in fact nearly
well. He told me he thought happiness had cured
him."

Fane makes a peculiar noise expressive of extreme disgust. "There is no accounting for taste,"
he sneers.

"There is not! Ostriches *prefer* nails, and I,
equally remarkable, esteem brains more satisfying
than beauty," Nora remarks.

"I thank you for the compliment."

"Oh, don't trouble, beauty is common enough, you
can be included," with a gracious smile. "A puppy
—a dear little puppy—a small calf, a young ass,
besides the whole insect creation from drones and
moths down to the common or garden earthworm,
are all beautiful. Some, of course, may require
strong magnifying glasses to convince the uninitiated, but the beauty is always there, only unfor-
tunately no brains—no brains," regretfully.

"Your ignorance is only equalled by your insults.
Like other very *young* girls you imagine you are
being 'smart' when you are merely extremely rude,"
Fane says hotly.

"How dare you!" Nora cries, her eyes filling with
indignant tears. "Never—*never* will I speak to you
again. For Ivy's sake I have tolerated you hitherto, but really this is too much. Germans forsooth!
Is it to be wondered at that I so infinitely prefer
their society, when, at least, they behave as *gentlemen.*"

"My dear Nora, what are you two quarrelling

about? You really look quite tragic. *Not* the old feud of 'The Roman Singer'? Why cannot you let us all adore him, Fane, if we like," and Ivy lays a soothing hand upon Nora's arm. "Come, Nora, they are going."

It is true. The evening is over, and the "good-nights" are being said. Lord Egerton has no opportunity for a last short conversation with Sybil, for Herr Krachen-Schlag is proudly talking to the group at the door, and after eulogising the taste and capabilities of "zis von yung leddy," he takes her hand, and shaking it up and down proudly, declares her his approved disciple in these remarkable words: "I haf much bleasure to blay ven you vish, an' I am hap-py zat I haf found zis yung leddy—ze iss my von leetle chile!" Then bowing to every one in the room with a most exhausting-looking motion from his waist, he makes his exit with a last dip of his mop, and muttered "adieu!"

Fane barely allows the other guests to depart before he executes a wild dance of savage exultation round the unruffled Sybil. "I congratulate you! This conquest is *a triumph*. What a pity parading victims in gala processions is not in vogue now! Think of the effect you could produce by leading this last captive carefully chained and combed out for the occasion! Really, Sib dear, properly advertised it would be *the* event of the Carnival week. See, you lead him like this; at the end of the Corso, bestow a rose, so"—bowing and holding one out— "then he kneels at your feet, kissing your hand"— attempting to kiss it. "Don't struggle, Sib, we'll take your maidenly modesty for granted. Oh, come; don't pretend there is anything novel in having your hand kissed—I'll bet you've had it done often enough. Don't blush, too, we are all looking, and it is a painful sign of self-consciousness."

"Get up, Fane; what an intolerable boy you are! Ivy! Nora! you might help. Get up, Fane, you are kneeling on my gown—there, now you've torn it! Oh! Fane, *do* go," pushing him away, while the others laugh and refuse to interfere. "Father! oh, do make him let go my hand—he is such an intense plague," despairingly.

Fane rises, and carefully holding both Sybil's hands, turns to his uncle gravely. "I resign all claims, uncle; here is her hand, bestow it upon whom you will. Take both, uncle, do—she is dangerous; and though the links that bind me to her are many and enduring, I would"—edging off carefully—"rather not be handcuffed," and waving a kiss from the tips of his fingers, he retreats promptly from the room.

Darkness and sleep brought silence, and sorrow fled, and care stood still. The tears that lay wet on Ivy's eyelashes had sprung from a lightened heart. Gwendoline's chance remark, "Colonel Talbot may be so much better now, Ivy; people often are after a hæmorrhage," had filled the earth with richest gladness, driving into nothingness the bitterness of doubt.

CHAPTER IX.

"Be not anxious about the morrow. Do to-day's duty, fight to-day's temptation, and do not weaken and distract yourself by looking forward to things you cannot see, and would not understand if you saw them."—CHARLES KINGSLEY.

IT is the last week of the Carnival. As Ivy hurries through her morning toilet, she is revolving plans for beguiling Fanc from the dangerous lure of the Boronowsky by the magic of Nora's wiles. Their ridiculous quarrels must be patched up, and Nora induced to soothe, not irritate him further. And Contarini, too, was aggressive, and demanded a certain amount of consideration; his attentions were tiresome, and she would rather like to make him hopelessly in love with her in return for his pronounced flirtation with her : it would serve him right, but she would not do it—she might regret it afterwards; she would continue to treat him in the friendly tolerant manner she had always adopted as suitable for an excitable individual very indifferently understood. What a comfort he did not even interest her! her heart beat just as placidly whether his mood were anxiously tender or one of raging indignation; he amused or bored her, that was all, she was sublimely invulnerable—of course she was. Self-analysis is impossible when one is hurried. It takes time for fair examination, so just set your teeth hard and go ahead with a rush, only obey the guiding impulse and go—straight.

"Ivy, let me in!"

It is Nora. Ivy admits her, and returns to the occupation of brushing out her hair; it gives her time for a careful survey of her visitor's petulant expression. "What is the matter now, Nora?" she says cheerily.

"I shall not go out for the *confetti*-throwing to-day."

Doing one's hair is as absorbing an occupation as shaving perhaps. Ivy is pre-occupied apparently, as she slowly questions, "Why?"

"I don't want to go—I shall not go; it won't be the slightest fun for me, as there is no one going I care a straw about. Neither of the Germans are going. It's all very well for all of you, who have men to look after you; I have no one. I might have enjoyed pelting Fane (I certainly should not have spoken to him), but he is off to Nice, so there won't be even him," speaking pettishly.

"He cannot be going to Nice, Nora, for he said last night he should be here."

"He told me this morning he was going."

"This morning? Why, it's very unusual for Fane to be early, and it is only a quarter to nine now! Did he say he was going at once?" anxiously.

"He said he should be off before eleven, as he wants to see about his page's dress, and had business on the way, in Monte Carlo."

"Nora—now don't jump at me—I want to ask you something. If Fane had not been so rude —yes, *horridly* rude—to you last night, you would have let him escort you in the Corso to-day— wouldn't you?"

"If neither of the Germans had been going, nor Mr. de Trafford, nor Mr. Dalmatic Cumin—well, then, yes, if he had been *sufferable*, I suppose he would have escorted me."

"And you are not going now; but Mr. de Trafford is going, and I think Mr. Dalmatic Cumin too.

Why should you not come? It cannot be on the Germans' account, because you told me you *knew* they were not going. If, then, you remain at home now, when we all go out and enjoy ourselves, I think—well, I think it might look as if you cared whether Fane was rude to you or not, and "——

"Care!—I ?—really, Ivy, how ridiculous you are! As if the ill manners of a boy of that age are of the slightest consequence to me," and the blue eyes flashed angrily, as Nora looked up at her friend.

"That is just what I thought, Nora; how could it matter to you? Only if you do not go, any boy in Fane's place would say it was because he was not there. You should go, of course. Talk to Mr. de Trafford, or any one; pretend you are enjoying yourself even if you are bored to death, and vow afterwards it was splendid fun. You must see it is the wisest thing to do, and anything else would count a point to the opposite side."

A radiant smile breaks out and hovers in Nora's blue eyes and on her saucy lips. She looks up gaily. "Right you are, Ivy; ' Vantage out' the score may be now, but I'll back myself to make it ' deuce all!'" and with a merry laugh she leans back, clasping her hands comfortably behind her head.

Ivy looks down at the girl and sighs slowly with satisfaction. This graceful, petulant child (Nora was barely seventeen, with a manner that savoured more of the nursery than schoolroom) was indeed a most effective weapon if wielded with discretion. Fane (as susceptible as most young fellows of his age) was decidedly attracted by this tall, slim young beauty, who dispensed her smiles to old and young, ill and well-favoured, with equal liberality, and an impartiality anything but flattering. Her dainty head, with its raven black tresses drawn back from the low forehead simply into a burnished crown, shone with all the dusky brilliance of a starling's coat, and the blue eyes danced beneath the thick fringed lashes, and borrowed ever-varying shades from sapphire to a stormy black. With her head thrown back proudly, and her slight figure drawn up to its fullest height, Nora had that very morning rejected Fane's overtures of peace, and excited anew his admiration, though he avenged himself by designating her to Ivy shortly after as " that coxy, long-legged young spitfire."

Yes, Ivy had succeeded in entrapping Fane into a five minutes' *tête-à-tête*, and was exerting every influence to prevent him leaving the place that day.

" I'm sorry for you, dear boy," Ivy remarks considerately, " for I can quite understand how annoying it must be to be entirely ' cut out ' by those Germans, for of course Nora is remaining at home on their account."

An angry " bosh ! " is all the answer vouchsafed.

" Bosh !—not at all ! What can be more clear ? They do not go, therefore Nora will not go. Surely that is plain enough ? "

Fane throws his cigarette with a jerk into the bushes, and retorts in no amiable tone—" If I were not *bound* to go to Nice to-day I would just stay here and prove to you effectually that *the Germans* "—in a tone of withering contempt—" have nothing to do with it ! "

" How ? "

" Simply because if *I* go, she will go."

" A bold assertion, but nothing unless proved true."

" Do you doubt me ?   I tell you I *know!* "

" I think you possibly magnify your importance."

" Do you ?"—hotly—" then I'm *hanged* if I don't stay and prove to you I'm right ! Only mind, no hints to Nora, and not a word but what I choose to tell her myself."

" I promise not to interfere," Ivy replies coolly, while stifling the sigh of relief this promised security affords her.

Fane works the toe of his boot abstractedly into the gravel—" You make things beastly awkward for a fellow, Ivy," he breaks out crossly. " Now I think of it, I hardly see how I can get out of going to Nice to-day, and I promised to be in Monte Carlo by twelve."

" Ah ! You begin to doubt your powers. I can quite understand your not wishing to court disaster," Ivy answers with slow disdain as she turns away.

Not a very pretty expression is flung after her by Fane, but the obnoxiousness is atoned for by the concluding "—— Take it all, I'll stay ! "

It is so bright a morning Ivy cannot be tempted from the garden, and eluding a few conversationally inclined pedestrians, she wanders along sunning herself in the satisfaction that her laudable efforts are likely to be crowned with success.

It is no light thing to steer her own little craft through all the shoals and quicksands that impede her course, how much more difficult then to tow a rudderless, unwilling brother overloaded with conceit through shallows of vanity against the slow current of indolence ! But Ivy is singularly light-hearted, and the gladness of the moment beguiles her into singing softly as she flits along the terrace—

> " What made th' assembly shine ?
> 　　　　　Robin Adair—
> What made the ball so fine ?
> 　　　　　Robin Adair."

She is nodding her good-day to a tangle of purple pimpernells, and almost trips over Colonel Talbot before she is aware that he is indeed there. For a moment she catches her breath and colours nervously, then seeing him about to rise, her wits return to her, and she waves him back imperiously.

"Don't move!—if you do I'll go this minute! Nonsense, I won't have you get up; here is plenty of room for me, and I will talk to you and you can listen, and sit still in the sun and obey orders"— and calmly sitting down beside him she leans back and nods at him reassuringly.

"May I not even say you are welcome as the sunlight and bring gladness in your looks," Colonel Talbot says in a very low voice.

"No, not even that! though I like to hear it; but *I* mean to talk, so please you will kindly listen, and not interrupt. In the first place, tell me truthfully, shall I tire you too much if I stay here chattering?" She speaks gaily and looks up with a smile, but is struggling with the sense of oppression his altered looks and listless attitude causes her.

"One hot summer's day I saw a tug towing in an old wreck, to be broken up. Upon its useless spars and worn-out timbers the sunlight played; and round its sombre, slow-gliding hull the martins were wheeling in happy gaiety—

> ' Sleepe after toyle, port after stormy seas,
> Ease after warre, death after life, doth greatlie please.' "

He seems to have forgotten the listener by his side,

and his concluding words are more to himself than to her, but she is answered; and in the silence that follows his quotation is nerving herself for a revival of his wandering attention. How slowly, how almost painfully he labours and pants for breath as he speaks, and how white and thin that hand is that grasps his stick. A curious tightness about her throat warns Ivy to be on her guard, and to refrain from further investigations until her self-control is assured.

The sudden smile with which Colonel Talbot turns to her tests it sorely, but she is prepared.

"Are you so afraid—of my interruption, that you will not begin your recital?" he says lightly. "Do not be afraid." The concluding words are spoken in such calm brightness, that they convey the sensation of reliance he intends to impart.

"I hardly know where to begin. There is not much to tell. We never went to Castellar after all, and —and we have not been half so—so jolly while you have been ill." Ivy feels this is pitiable.

"Thank you; that is one of the especial kindnesses we invalids enjoy, the ready sympathy of friends, and Cumin was always bringing me fresh proofs of it, in all the inquiries about me that he reported."

"Mr. Cumin!—Mr. Dalmatic Cumin!—did *he* go and see you?"

"Often, and stayed with me as long as that careful old Lee would let him. Ay, what matter if a man mould himself upon a system, and encase his mind in the cramped hard shell of dogma, so long as his heart beats true to human sympathies? Yes, child, he is quite a wholesome creature in an old resuscitated shell, that opens readily enough to the touch of another's needs."

Ivy is regretfully conscious of having missed much consolation at his hands. How much he might have told her! of how much needless anxiety might he have relieved her!

"He is coming to the Corso to-day, isn't he?" she asks.

"I believe so; he tells me he promised to join your party. He tells me—many things," smiling significantly.

"Indeed! What does he say?" a little defiantly.

"He tells me of a certain little lady who emulates the great warrior, and might cry with him, 'Veni, Vidi, Vici,' but who seems almost unconscious of her triumphs."

"Triumphs!" Her eyes blaze. "Do you call it a *triumph* to command for a time the attentions of —of—a creature like Count Contarini?" Colonel Talbot looks very surprised. "At least I suppose he meant that," Ivy adds, blushing hotly.

"And if he did mean it, if he did imply that so well-known a trifler was in earnest at last—that this man, so changeable and unsettled of purpose, had now thrown all his heart and will and energy into the pursuit of one happiness, the attainment of one desire, what then?"

"Then he wilfully implied what he knew to be untrue, or he—he is a blind owl!" Ivy rejoins angrily.

Colonel Talbot smiles, then remarks rather gravely—"You will pardon me speaking to you upon so personal a matter, but some friendships entitle one to certain confidences, and"—with a questioning glance—"I think ours will bear the strain."

The frown departs in Ivy's smile.

"Do you wish me to believe you consider Count

Contarini simply to be trifling with you?" His tone is itself a reproach. Certainly crudely put into words it sounds unpalatable.

"I—I do not believe he could be in earnest about anything; it is all a sham, and a manner he can put on just as he pleases."

"Do you really believe that?"

"Most certainly I do! Why?"

"Pardon me, but you demand an answer. Since you believe that, I am amazed at your speaking to him, or permitting him to speak to you."

The sting to her pride and self-esteem is so keen that for a brief mad moment Ivy feels she must right herself at all cost in the eyes of one whose opinion she values above all others, even if it be effected at the risk of disclosing the secret she has hitherto guarded so scrupulously. "What must he think of me? Oh, how contemptible I must appear!" she reflects wretchedly.

"I cannot explain anything," she begins hesitatingly. "I know it must look *horrid* to any one who—who does not understand. I cannot say anything except that I am *sure* Count Contarini is only —only pleasant and attentive, but does not care really a bit about me."

Colonel Talbot is evidently bewildered. "It is very extraordinary," he begins; "so extraordinary that unless you have a very strong reason for such a belief, I think you may reject it as—as only some hallucination of your own brain."

"You say that as if the belief in his devotion would cause me satisfaction."

"Well, are you not anxious to know whether— whether the man be true or false?" in an amazed tone.

"Not a whit! I think to such a man there are no such things as truth and falsehood, and his likes and dislikes constitute his *very* personal religion. But what, after all, has he done to cause so much remark! Sent me a few bouquets" (until uncle stopped it), "carried my parasol in the mornings and my fan in the evenings, sat by my chair and turned over my music—of course all evidences of an absolute devotion!"

"I am at a loss to understand why you grant so much intercourse to one whom you evidently dislike."

"Please do not say I dislike him."

"Ah!—do you wish it to be thought that you like him?"

"Yes."

A silence of some minutes, then Colonel Talbot resumes—"Your motive for acting in this manner may be a most laudable one, but have you considered that to Contarini it may prove rather misleading?"

"I never take Count Contarini into my calculations at all, any scruples I might have had about him having been effectually banished long ago."

"May I ask if the opinion you hold of Contarini has been formed by your own judgment or that of others?"

"I really do not think the subject worthy of so much discussion," Ivy replies testily; "but—yes—I have the weight of other judgments in support of my own."

Colonel Talbot remains silent for some time, his eyes looking out to the far line of blue distinctly dividing earth from heaven, as he deliberates gravely upon Ivy's peculiar confession, and tries to divine her motive. It is evident she encourages

Contarini as a sort of safeguard, but—from what? No one else is being thrust upon her, indeed her natural independence forbids the idea of her being inveigled into a marriage contrary to her inclinations. How gladly he would help her! He is conscious of a strong sympathy with this impatient child, who acts upon impulse, and scorns advice: looking down upon her now, her firmly closed mouth reveals a determination that effectually precludes all hopes of any amicable discussion of the difficulty. He has learnt to know her so well too, and she talks to him more freely and spontaneously than to others: perhaps during his illness events have occurred to alter the relations of all this group he is so interested in — complications unnoticed by Mr. Cumin may have arisen, and the purposes have become crossed. Well, all the more need for careful observation, and patience may soon disentangle the trouble.

And so with a tact that is the result of kindly nature and not diplomatic art, he gradually draws away Ivy's thoughts from the disagreeable topic, and leads them to remote subjects that rouse attention and revive her animation.

About an hour later the terrace is invaded. The entire English community seems congregated in the approaching group. Colonel Talbot becomes for some moments the centre of interest, and receives the solicitous gratulations of his friends—then chairs are arranged, groups formed, and conversation broken into separate channels. Mr. Cleveland, Contarini, Fane, and Mr. de Trafford are prevailed upon to put away, at least for a time, the hideous masks which they had donned in honour of its being Carnival time.

Nora, with her hand on Gwendoline's arm, is jibing merrily the unusually indolent Mr. de Trafford, —his serenity is undisturbed, and his wide unexpressive smile is duly recurrent. The regularity with which it is reproduced is remarkable.

Fane is irritated at Nora for the determined way in which she avoids him, his efforts at reconciliation have been steadily ignored, and in no amiable mood he is reflecting that after one more try he will resign the attempt as useless. Ivy watching him is aware of the critical condition of affairs, and yet dare not raise a finger to further the much desired peace. Her wandering attention and short replies are unnoticed by Count Contarini, but bear a significance not overlooked by the observant invalid; Fane, then, is a disturbing element; but what connection can he have with the *rôle* Ivy is playing regarding Contarini? Time will show, he reflects.

Here Nora's voice rings out above the others. "There, Mr. de Trafford, that is a bargain! I'll throw all the bonbons and flowers, and do all the tiring work ; and you shall only carry my basket, and keep it replenished—an easy part, for which you are admirably adapted."

"I shall be delighted."

"Very good ; then, as you are my especial cavalier, we must arrange about badges. Don't you see, when we are all disguised in our dominos, no one knows any one, and with our masks it will be perfectly impossible. So, come, let us concoct a device. I know! I will make bows for you and me, so that, however we get mixed up, we shall know each other."

"A verwy satisfactorwy arwangement."

" But the men don't wear any disguise, Nora," Sybil remarks amusedly. "You are not likely to experience the slightest difficulty in identifying Mr. de Trafford. We three tall ones will, of course, look much alike, but our voices will sufficiently distinguish us."

"No," Nora rejoins pettishly; "I will make our rosettes—it's much more fun; and then, you see, Mr. de Trafford is *bound* to speak to no one but the one decorated like himself. Do you hear, Mr. de Trafford, I command you !"

And, smiling weakly at the haughty young beauty, he replies, "Your commands are my gweatest pleasure."

Here Fane, abruptly quitting Mrs. Cleveland's side, advances towards Nora and Mr. de Trafford. As he approaches, Nora turns her head aside, and catches at the leaves of a bush growing near her. With one glance at her Fane turns to Mr. de Trafford. "I have altered my mind," he says, "and so, old fellow, if you could oblige me."

"Of course—of course," the other rejoins hastily. "certainly, my dear fellow," and they turn and walk away together.

The rose that Ivy is holding snaps off by the head. She does not stoop for it—she hardly seems conscious of its sudden decapitation. As, however, Count Contarini picks it up and places it in his pocket, she smiles faintly.

"Poor rose, please give it to me. I did not throw it away."

"No, you dropped it at my feet."

"I assure you"—stiffly—"I never intended to give you that rose."

"No? then you give it without intention."

"Only the flower without any stalk—it must soon die," spitefully.

"The sweetest rose without any thorn," he whispers tenderly.

"You cannot have roses without thorns," Ivy retorts quickly. "*That !* you cannot call *that* a rose ! A wired specimen strangling in a florist's window is its only counterpart. See, I picked it for the sake of its beautifully veined leaves and this tiny bud, without them, and the accompanying thorns, it is worth nothing."

"You will give me the rest, then."

"No; yours is scarcely a nature to appreciate thorns. I think," toying with the spray, "I had better keep it myself."

"*I* am not afraid of thorns. Will you give it to me ?" Colonel Talbot speaks quietly, and smiles as he holds out his hand for the flower. Whether actuated by a kindly impulse to assist Ivy out of the dilemma, or to test still further her intention in the matter, the result is the same. She blushes one of her uncontrollable blushes, and then with unusual gravity and precision places the flower in his hand. Uttering something unintelligible in Italian, Contarini opens his large blue eyes, and fixing them upon the Colonel regards him with an astounded amazement that puts one in mind of a small child beholding for the first time the marvels of a conjurer.

"Come ! come ! let us fortify ourselves with lunch, and then to our buffoonery," and following Mrs. Cleveland they rise and leave the terrace.

Not long after, the Corso is thronged with a motley crowd grotesquely attired, some in dominos, and others in their ordinary dress, only disguised by hideous masks. All are engaging in a running fire of *confetti*-throwing; which fortunately here is limited to mild volleys of bonbons, some wrapped in coloured papers with long kite-like tails attached to them; and very little of the vigorous pelting with the small *confetti* (a concoction of sugar and lime), which breaks into a fine dust blinding to the eyes, and annoyingly adhesive to any wearing apparel, no matter the texture. Flowers, too, are being hurled down into the carriages from the crowded balconies above, and the windows are full of laughing faces gazing down upon the throng below.

The party with whom we have to do are advancing in a knot up the crowded Corso. Nora is nearly right. Clad in long-hooded dominos they all look wonderfully alike, and the masks, edged with thick lace to cover the lower part of the face, permit only a peep of the eyes, that renders recognition almost impossible.

Mrs. Cleveland has consented to drive once through the street, and they are waiting for her now with the intent of making a sharp onslaught upon her as she passes. There is a greater freedom about the crowd to-day, and were it not that the girls are most watchfully guarded by their father and Mr. Cleveland, they would not have been permitted to go down the street on foot. As it is, they are enjoying it immensely; the very fact of wearing dominos is an excitement to them, and pelting and being pelted is capital fun.

Nora is indefatigable, and flings with an accuracy that does her credit. Mr. de Trafford has no small difficulty in keeping her supplied with missiles, and guarding her store from the haunting little gamins who hover round and grab whatever they can lay their hands on.

Sybil, with Lord Egerton stalking rather aggressively by her side, is engaging far more calmly in the fray. Wherever a child's eager little face meets her eyes, she throws her bonbons readily. She returns a fire whenever it appears particularly noteworthy, as a necessary civility, but hitherto has not retained a single bouquet she has caught—just flung them away again soon after, and Lord Egerton is willing to allow that if people blessed with intelligence can really be amused by this sort of foolery—well, there is certainly no harm in it. Gwendoline, under her father's wing and with Mr. Dalmatic Cumin on her other side, is happily enjoying everything and saying little. She is very hot under her mask and closely drawn hood, and sitting clothed comfortably in a carriage had been more enjoyable yesterday when she could see all their acquaintances and recognise them at once, flinging flowers to them as they passed. Still, to-day was very amusing, and when some laughing young Italians threw a bouquet to her, her foolish blushes were so safely hidden under her uncomfortable but concealing mask !

Ivy has been in so varying a humour that Mr. Cleveland fears at one time the exasperated Contarini may call him out as the cause of her preoccupation and fitful attention. There is almost a feeling of contempt in her mind for this gay Italian, who abandons himself to the amusements of the afternoon with a hearty intensity that appears to her perfectly childish. All her instincts are in revolt against the exaggerated merriment, which under different circumstances **would** not have struck her as extravagant. She is angry with herself for not being in harmony with her surroundings, disgusted at being considered stupid or a spoil sport, envious of Nora's overflowing gaiety, and determined to put away, at least for a time, the oppressive anxiety that weighs upon her. So for a while she is as eager as even Contarini could desire, and her merry laugh and bright remarks send his already excited spirits up to an almost idiotic pitch.

In the string of carriages they recognise, not long after, Mrs. Cleveland; driving with their flat-footed young acquaintance and her estimable mother. Already this carriage has encountered a hot fire, the stolid gravity of the English servants on the box calling forth many jocular remarks, as the crowd aim cleverly for their tall hats, and succeed in bonneting the footman, who adjusts his without betraying a sign of annoyance—only stares ahead, with the laudable intention of not moving a muscle, or letting "them jabbering fools of foreigners see whether hi cares."

A very rain of flowers falls into the carriage as it passes our party, and Mr. Cleveland succeeds in sending a well-weighted bonbon straight through his wife's protecting parasol.

"Ivy," whispers Nora, "I am sick of my compact and weary to death of Mr. de Trafford. Take this bow, and relieve me of his society. I wish, after all, Fane had been here; it is horridly slow without him!"

As they turn to retrace their steps, Ivy executes a clever manœuvre that leaves Nora ahead with Contarini, and herself by the side of the placid Mr. de Trafford. Mr. Cleveland is talking to some friend, and is a few paces behind them.

"Are you waiting for Cleveland?" Mr. de Trafford asks.

"No, let us walk on."

"One gets wather sick of this after a—er—time, don't you think?"

"Yes."

"You are—er—wather tired?"

"No."

He may screw his eyeglass in securely and scan his companion closely, but indeed to-day she is impenetrably masked. After a silence of some minutes he ventures upon another question.

"Awfully hot, isn't it, under those—er—things."

"Rather."

"She must be ill," he concludes hopelessly. By Jove, a pretty fix if she faints in this crowd and smothered up like that! "Hadn't you—er—better —take my arm?" he suggests uncertainly.

Ivy's laugh sets his anxious doubts at rest. "I am only horridly cross," she confesses.

Perhaps for this very reason he is more scrupulously attentive and briskly conversational than ever before. Ivy is grateful to him, and has a sense of security while with him never enjoyed when with the inflammable Contarini. The folk we affirm will "never set the Thames on fire" are often a relief, for the very stagnation we experience in their society.

At last the Corso is left behind, and threading their way through some narrower streets they regain the hotel garden, and rapidly divest themselves of their cumbrous dominos and masks. Here tea is brought to them, and gradually even Ivy's spirits revive. Contarini, on the contrary, is becoming momentarily more savage, and Ivy, with a certain satisfaction which is but natural, increases in affability while conversing with Mr. de Trafford. He, poor man, is a little bewildered, but very much charmed, and his smile becomes almost a fixture, and his eyeglass drops certainly five times in a minute.

Contarini eyes Ivy furtively several times. He appears to be weighing something in his teaspoon as he balances it upon his finger—probably a corresponding process is going on in his peculiarly active brain: at last he speaks. Turning to Mr. Cleveland, he begins in a curiously distinct tone—

"Ah, you saw De la Valliere to-day. I saw you speak to him. Did he tell you about the match? He was very much elated. He says Mr. Peyton was nervous or he should not have beaten him, but as it was, he won by ten consecutive hits, and so has secured his thousand francs." There is something peculiarly disagreeable about the manner in which this is said.

"Fane is a good shot, but De la Valliere is more certain," Mr. Cleveland replies in an easy manner.

As for Ivy she says nothing. If Contarini hopes it will produce upon her some sudden expression of consternation he is much mistaken. Only to the observant eye of Mr. de Trafford is her anxiety discoverable in the unsteadiness of her lips as she answers some hastily suggested question.

There is something about the manner of this uninteresting man just now that does not escape the notice of Mrs. Cleveland. A sort of decided assertive air, that struggles somewhat comically with his usual studied indolence.

Ivy rises from the group, and with a rather unnatural laugh declares she is seized with a sudden desire to go down to the rocks and inspect their beauties at low tide.

"Two inches of tide, Ivy, and no very intrinsic merit about them, I assure you," remarks her uncle. But she laughs and goes, and to the no small disgust of Contarini, Mr. de Trafford goes too.

Ivy's preoccupation is rather embarrassing, but Mr. de Trafford is quietly persistent. *Why* he should be enlightening her upon his family history, personal experiences, and future aims she never even troubles herself to reflect, and it is with a shock of consternation that she feels his soft flabby hand clasp hers! This action has caused him to drop his eyeglass; he hastily restores it, and turns to watch the effect of his manœuvre, but by this time Ivy has mastered any expression the surprise caused her, and all the result is a blank gaze seawards.

"I twust you understand why I have—er—been twubbling you with all these pwivate particulars. I am terwibly affwaid of being pwemature, but your manner to-day has wevived my hopes, that—er—er— I might one day pwevail upon you to be my wife."

Ivy is so absolutely dumbfounded that for a moment her very sight seems to fail her, and the rocks at her feet to be racing past in a strange medley with the softly eddying sea.

A renewed pressure of her hand by his, which suggests the contact of a dead fish, recalls her quickly to herself. Withdrawing her hand with some difficulty she speaks with slow decision.

"I am so *very* sorry, Mr. de Trafford, more sorry than I can express, that anything in my manner should ever have led you to believe I—I could ever be anything more to you than a friend. I never had the slightest idea you ever thought of such a thing! I think," she continues easily, being perfectly collected now, "this must be some sudden idea that this grotesque day is answerable for. I thank you, indeed, for the honour you do me," looking kindly at the turnip-hued visage near her, " but you are the last man in the world to marry. Think," she continues quickly, "you love roving about, yachting, you love shooting and fishing, smoking, and never being disturbed ; now, a wife would drive you distracted. When you wanted to go yachting she would want you to remain on shore, and if you took her with you, you would be ill all the time. She would stop your smoking, share your fishing, and give your shooting to her friends."

Mr. de Trafford watches Ivy with rather an odd look in his light eyes and a smile about his mouth that one might almost have called *pathetic*, had it not stretched itself out such a long way round.

" You are wight," he says at last. " I'm not the sort of fellow to marwy, and never should have thought of it had I not been almost ' badjered ' to do so."

" Indeed—may I ask who ' badjered ' you ? "

" Well—er—to tell you the twuth it was—my gwandmother," he replies confidingly.

It is well for Ivy that it is dusk, it is well that Mr. de Trafford's perceptions are not of the keenest, or her almost convulsive silence might have conveyed to him some idea that her speechlessness was not solely due to remorse.

" Fane will be verwy sorwy, I'm affwaid," he continues ; " not that he ever gave me much hope, but said of course I might twy."

The mention of Fane recalls all Ivy's uneasiness, and strangely enough it is apparent to her companion. After one or two uneasy shuffles, and a few contortions, he speaks, staring out to sea. "Don't worwy about Fane—I think he is not in any gweat difficulties, and he has squared De la Vallicre long ago."

"Thank you," Ivy says almost bitterly; "your generosity may relieve his present embarrassments, but I am afraid there is no way in which I can *ever* recompense you for the loan." The moment the words are uttered she regrets them, for with all his defections the man she speaks to is a gentleman.

A faint colour creeps into his sallow face, and then Mr. de Trafford answers quietly, "I am sorwy you should think I assisted your bwother in order to buy your gwatitude, Miss Peyton."

Bitterly ashamed of herself, Ivy holds out her hand, as she cries quickly, "I beg your pardon; indeed, I hardly knew what I was saying. Oh, I am so sorry! and only hope you will forget what I said. I know it was only your natural kind-heartedness that prompted you to help Fane, only—only—if you knew how—how reckless he is, and how impossible it is for my father to help him any more, you would understand how anxious it makes me when I know he is spending money so lavishly."

Mr. de Trafford holds Ivy's hand in his for a moment, and then with a slight pressure resigns it heroically, as he says, "It is unnecessary for you ever to excuse yourself to me,—you never could do anything to annoy me. I will look after Fane as if he were my own bwother, and as I shall leave Mentone the day after to-morrwo, we shall both "

—with rather a dreary though far-reaching smile—
" be beyond the weach of temptation."

And then clambering back quietly they leave the silent shore and rejoin the others, who chaff them good-naturedly upon their protracted inspection of the " tidal peculiarities," &c., whereat Ivy waxes unusually inventive, and Mr. de Trafford more than usually silent, while Contarini glares angrily, and muses over many things, and perhaps more particularly about the fate of a rose stalk, and the possible attractions of its present owner.

CHAPTER X.

' Yet to be loved makes not to love again."
—Tennyson.

Don't you know, Ivy, that the most necessary thing for a woman is an equable temperament. *We* may not drink away our morbidness nor smoke away our sulks, so, my dear child, cultivate it—cultivate it. I am aghast at your mercurial tendencies ; come here and account for them."

Ivy laughs as she seats herself by Mrs. Cleveland's side, and blushes at her aunt's comprehensive smile, but she does not say a word ; and reflects with satisfaction that the episode of the rose-stalk would not have attracted her questioner's notice, and Mr. de Trafford's suspicious guardianship of Fane need also never become a public fact. Of course she is happy ! Her anxiety is lightened, and the very fact of Colonel Talbot being among them again creates a gladness she does not clearly define.

"Where did those Neapolitan violets come from—spoils of war?"

"No, I kept none to-day; these Mr. de Trafford gave me."

"In token of perpetual peace, I suppose?"

"Yes. Peace and friendship."

"Well, I like him," Mrs. Cleveland remarks reflectively; "he is so restful, like a sleepy cow in a sunny meadow, and soothes one's sensibilities unconsciously. I am afraid I am intolerably idle. I would so much rather be lulled to acquiescence than incited to action."

"You always wrong yourself, Dora," Mrs. Lestrange remarks, smiling. "You are not idle. Your interests are many and your influence far-reaching. Yours is a life of great mental activity, dear."

Dora fans herself slowly, after one look for all answer into Mrs. Lestrange's gentle face; and then her eyes contract with some humorous reflection as she rejoins thoughtfully, "True, I bask upon a sea of pleasure like a jellyfish in the sun, and my far-reaching tentacles bring me into contact with the many all around me, whether for their benefit or my own we won't say; perhaps you have never been stung by one! No, I am afraid I am not sympathetic, the joys or sorrows of others never affect me *deeply*. I am absorbed in the affairs of another for a time, and watch a crisis that develops or reveals the latent force in their character without experiencing any uncomfortable sensations myself. Society amuses me, humanity interests me, as a study, only that—as a study."

Perhaps it is the consciousness that she will not be believed that enables Mrs. Cleveland to disclaim so dispassionately all human sympathies. It is certain no one does believe her; and the minds of her listeners are only speculating upon the motive that prompted a statement so palpably false. Ivy has always felt that in this beautiful pale woman, with her almost exaggeratedly gracious manner, there existed a fund of unselfish kindliness that would never be exhausted by the petty frictions, or large demands of friendship. It is not necessary for us to prove our beliefs—their existence is enough for us. Logically to defend or demonstrate them may be beyond our powers, but the keenness of our perceptions is an instinct more akin to wisdom than the minutely reasoned doubts of knowledge.

There is a world of trust in her brown eyes as Ivy smiles at her friend, and presents a pretty little *bonbonnière* for her inspection.

"Leave it here by my side and go and sing to me, child. I will allow you one 'Gianduga,' and shall expect additional mellowness in consequence. There, go before the contingent from the smoking-room breaks in upon our harmony. We are a picture of supreme content at present—even Nora looks sleek and comfortable, there being none on whom she is anxious to try her claws."

Nora laughs, and then leans back more snugly against the window curtain, and continues her dreamy inspection of the elongated bag she designates a sock! It is her first; always at the same stage of development, rarely with more than two needles in it at the same moment—a tangled, lacerated production that promises to be a veritable Penelope's task; but in such hands it does not matter, for looking at the worker one forgets the work, and agrees with Fane's adaptation—

> "There's a divinity that shapes our ends,
> Rough hew them how she may!"

Ivy looks round to see if any one can be caught in the desultory do-nothing condition, when playing accompaniments is welcomed as a resource. No—no one. Sybil and Gwendoline are engrossed with their books, and indeed are already in the world where their heroines and heroes move, quite apart from the real around them. With a resigned sigh she sinks out of sight behind the barrier of a cottage piano, and presently her deep voice rises from behind its ornamental-draped back and *chevaux de frise* of pottery and flowers.

She sings on, and her overflowing gladness, or the "Gianduga" perhaps, invests the timbre of her voice with a thrill of joyousness that she cannot suppress. The intensity of relief, her undefined but growing hope, her natural trust in the durability of happiness, contribute to dim all forebodings and disarm distrust. An undercurrent of merriment almost runs through the rich tones like the low laughter of a brook in the chorus of the birds. It is delightful to listen to, unless one be of the superstitious turn of mind that augurs a sudden rise in the barometer is inevitably succeeded by a sudden fall. The nursery augury is familiar to most of us, "Don't laugh before breakfast, or you'll cry before night," and whether invented in the furtherance of order, or to suppress irrational hilarity, of its truth we are well assured. Our greatest joy stands blurred and indistinct before us, dimmed with our doubting tears, and to how many of us comes the sudden anguish that makes us cry—

"The sun has gone down while it is yet day"?

A preparatory bang of the music-book slipping on to the key-board announces Ivy's intention of moving.

"One more, Ivy; Colonel Talbot wants 'When sparrows build.'" Unhesitatingly she complies.

What is there here! Such a blending of passion and remorse, the sorrow of experience, and a life's epitome of pain. Clearly this bright-faced, happy hearted girl can have no conception of the emotions she reproduces by mere artistic effects and natural sympathy. Only in the concluding words—

"We shall part no more in the wind and the rain,
Where our last farewell was said;
But perhaps I shall see thee and know thee again
When the sea gives up her dead,"

came a tremolo that proved nature had triumphed over art with her usual success.

Mrs. Cleveland steals a look at Colonel Talbot, but the lamp-shade serves to keep him in shadow, and his hand is also across his eyes as he leans one arm on a table, resting his head upon it as a prop. Where are his thoughts—with the present or the past? Is he engrossed by a sorrow of to-day, or has he mournfully resuscitated a dead memory to revive a dormant pain? "These self-contained people are capable of anything," she reflects; "one cannot fathom their emotions. Any indication of feeling now cannot be relied upon, as it may be the outcome of some decayed passion called fitfully to life by chance association."

As Ivy leaves the piano, Colonel Talbot rises to

meet her. There is no trace of passion or pain in the grave face, only a smile that seems a sad victory of sorrow over self—a sort of look that brands the wearer with almost a leper's isolation, while lifting him immeasurably above the petty pleasure-seekers of society. Ivy feels again the wide distance between them, the unapproachableness that divides them as effectually as an existing palpable six foot wall, or a wide unforded river. How ridiculous to think any singing of hers could affect him. St. Augustin lost in holy meditation might just as well be moved by the melodies of the Moore and Burgess minstrels. It is humiliating—very; but perhaps she is learning to like humiliation, since she finds the happiness his society affords her outweighs effectually all annoyance.

"You have given me very much pleasure," Colonel Talbot says, as he leans forward in his chair that is as usual close to Ivy's. "That is a wonderful gift, and you have it in no small degree—representing, through the medium of your voice, all varieties of emotion and passion as though they were your own. I am glad I can believe in the sensitive adaptability of a sympathetic nature, and need not include you with those who 'learn in suffering what they teach in song.'"

"No, I certainly hope not; I have no wish to suffer!"

He looks rather curiously at the defiant expression on the round little face that to-night has been beaming like a midsummer full moon. "Have any of us the wish? but it is inevitable; we acknowledge it the seal nature prints on every life. Confess that it is so—a divine yet inexorable law, and your very acquiescence lessens the bitterness that a useless resistance engenders, and provides you with the necessary fortitude to endure."

"I won't *endure!* I hate submissive people who bow down at the first breath of adversity, and carry a load of trouble just because they won't kick it off! Life is meant to be happy, and we can make it so; it depends entirely upon ourselves."

"Quite so! when our happiness is not concentrated *in* ourselves. But how can I, through the tried glasses of experience, see the subject in the same light as you, gazing at it through the rosy mist of youth's illusions? Only what, in the first place, do you call happiness?"

"The state of being happy," promptly.

"Yes"—smiling—"but there are many opinions as to the means for attaining that end. What thing or things are necessary to you to produce that condition? Is it to you a clearly defined physical enjoyment, or an impalpable satisfaction of the mind?"

"Oh," Ivy rejoins rather peevishly, "I am not going to analyse abstract happiness. To me it is a great solid fact, as food to the starving, sight to the blind, the glorious relief of waking to reality after the torture of a hideous nightmare. I believe absolutely in happiness. Every one can be happy in one way or another, because of the beautiful harmonious law that has endowed us all with such different tastes. If people would only be properly good-natured, nothing need clash, and the whole world would work easily, oiled by conciliation."

It was unusual for Ivy to resent any statement of Colonel Talbot's, but to-night the gravity of his nature, and the sombreness of his views, jarred upon her. "He could be happy, too, and do his share of the oiling, if he only cared to ; but with your head in the clouds how can you see all the little flowers you trample at your feet!" she reflects a little bitterly. Experience, like knowledge, cannot be inherited, bequeathed, bought nor stolen, and to whom has it ever been an acceptable gift ?

Colonel Talbot has not answered Ivy's outburst. He is leaning back rather wearily, and even in the redly-tinted light he looks pale and terribly worn. A rush of compunction makes her whisper pathetically, " Don't you think, if one isn't selfish and horrid, one *can* be happy though ? I know such a lot of happy people, and they are all *good*. I'm afraid " — rather unsteadily — " I never could feel good if I were unhappy. If we bring sorrow upon ourselves by our wrongdoing, I understand it, otherwise it seems to me—I can't help it if you think it wrong, but a great, useless, unnecessary sorrow *does* seem to me—unjust."

The reproof Ivy expects is not forthcoming, and in the grave face there is only such intense pity that her opposition seems to droop before its dispassionate influence.

" My child," he says very gravely, " the only one who could have questioned the use or uselessness of sorrow bore in silence the crown of its supremest suffering. Was it ' unnecessary ' that the God of Love should be also the Man of Sorrows? and is it ' unjust ' that we His children should but sip of the cup He drained to its bitterest dregs ? God forbid that I should cloud the sunshine of other lives by useless, ill-omened prophecies—only by-and-by we shall understand that sorrow and happiness are twin sisters, the tender-hearted children of Love. Do not think," he continues after a pause, "I take a pleasure in painting your future darkly. You seem born like a humming bird for the sunlight, and how willingly I would shield you from the shadows if I could! Give me your thorns and keep the roses— it makes me imagine I am of some use still. Remember, it is the greatest kindness you can do me to let me serve you. The morning's shadows have vanished now, or I think I might have been impertinent enough to ask their cause. Here come all the others; Fane, too, so Miss Nora's knitting will suffer. I shall say good-night now and leave you—*in the sunlight!*" with a bright glance and shaking her hand warmly.

Furling and unfurling her fan, conscious that the room is alive with people settling down to their accustomed corners, and " sorting " themselves by mutual agreement to the enjoyment of each other's society, Ivy is yet absorbed in her conversation with Colonel Talbot, which is now, alas, but a memory. Why has this man with his austere views, against which her youthful impulses rise in rebellion, a power to interest and influence her so strongly? Why does she feel that a life passed in penitential observances, clad in sackcloth, with a monotonous Gregorian for all its melody, would be a far greater happiness, if blessed by his companionship, than one of idle pleasure with any one else?

Why do her cheeks flush hotly even yet at the foolish hopes those few kindly words suggest, "I would shield you from the shadows if I could; give me your thorns. Remember, it is the greatest kindness you can do me to let me serve you." Oh, is he blind; how can he talk of leaving her in the sunlight, when his absence is her only shadow! What *can* he imagine! Surely she has enlightened him as to her feelings regarding Contarini. Who does he think she cares for—not Mr. de Trafford surely, or perhaps he does not think about her at all. It is very bitter, but this is the first time in her experience she has failed to secure the homage of any one whose devotion she has desired. There *must* be some reason for it, she argues not unnaturally. "He thinks I care for some one else—he thinks I am a flirt—he thinks I am too foolish and fickle! Oh!" with a long suppressed sigh, "I'll be as sober as Sybil; I'll give up useless dissembling, and let him read me like a book. Womanly reserve is all very well, but if it is the rock on which my happiness will split, away with it." She smiles as she forms the resolve, feeling invigorated at the prospect of such plain sailing after the troublesome "tacking" of her recent course.

Now, she need no longer tolerate Contarini when he becomes uninterestingly persistent. Now, Aunt Amy, Mrs. Cleveland, and all of them may think what they like, for she will no longer play the rôle of coquette, for the assumed callousness is in danger of being believed in. Now, yes—that is, to-morrow—she will inform her mother (no longer vaguely), under pledge of secrecy; that she loves some one so utterly that the only honourable course to pursue, is to let poor Billy know that she can never care for him—only she will commit herself to no particulars, and they must imagine what they like. Yes, she must be careful though, for after all it is impossible to prance before society as a love-sick maiden, and in plain language that is what she has been meditating! The consciousness that even for a moment she could have entertained such an idea, makes the shamed tears burn under her eyelids, and the resolve never to betray her secret, most especially to Colonel Talbot, becomes more firmly fixed than ever! A mental postscript that cancels effectually all the previous decisions, leaving her exactly situated where she was before—an exercise of feminine argument not unusual.

Her reverie has not been broken in upon, because it is Mr. de Trafford who has taken Colonel Talbot's vacated chair. Now, however, he leans forward, and presenting a little roll of paper to Ivy, says with perhaps a more pronounced drawl than usual—"I have—er—bwought you the photogwaphs, and—er —I would not—er—take much notice of Fane if I were you; it will—er—pass off, but just now he is wather upset. You see, as soon as—er—he weturned, I told him of the alterwation of plans, and he—he doesn't like it."

Ivy can barely help smiling at the simplicity of his statement. She is so grateful to this poor little man, and very remorseful at the consequences of her few hours' conversation with him, for she cannot believe his declaration was anything but the sudden resolve of a moment's infatuation.

"I must ever be grateful to you," she answers softly, "for your friendship; how much so I am afraid you will not understand, although the demands I make upon it might prove to you effectually that I realise its depth and strength. I cannot bear the thought that I am depriving you of so much pleasure. Just this last week of amusement is worth all the rest! I know there are loads of things you want to wait for,—the Veglione at the theatre on Monday, the ball here on Tuesday. Why, I heard you arranging about your dances with Nora! No, indeed, I cannot have you give up everything for an idea. A week more or less will not matter, and as you are looking after Fane so kindly, I am relieved of half my anxieties, so please don't go on that account; and—and I'm going to ask him, quite gently I assure you, to be careful—so you *will* stay?"

Mr. de Trafford's colourless hair moves backwards and forwards, under the influence of the contortions requisite on getting his eyeglass into his eye. For a man who performs this action about three thousand times a day it is singularly troublesome. He leans both elbows on his knees, and gazes at the carpet, or his own boots, for some moments speechlessly. His words come at last—slowly, like his ideas.

"It would not be any—er—pleasure to me to wemain here now, and I weally don't—er—think I could. You must not—er—wegret anything, because —er—I—don't—only I would pwefer to go away I—I—daresay I shall not find it so—so "——

The sentence is not concluded, and the poor little man's hands are clutched rather convulsively. But to Ivy there is nothing ludicrous about him now. She never liked him so well—his total collapse appeals to her ready sympathy, and she feels very like—sobbing!

Mrs. Cleveland stifles a yawn cleverly to hide her irrepressible amusement at Contarini's rage. He too has been a keen observer of Mr. de Trafford's agitation, and as Ivy rallies her self-control and turning to him prepares to say something soothing, Contarini leaps to his feet hurriedly, and walking up to Ivy stands directly before her while he says abruptly—

"I very much wish to speak to you!"

"Really!" with slow disdain. "How remark-able!"

The lazy movement of her fan maddens him. "I *feel* I'm going to be rude," she reflects; "I *won't* be glared at!"

"Is it not possible for me to speak to you *at once?*" he cries rather savagely.

Mr. de Trafford rises from his chair, and with an astonished glance at the irate Italian, bows to Ivy, and walks off to the furthest end of the room. Flinging himself into the vacated chair, Contarini draws it closer to Ivy, and looking very fierce as he pulls his moustache, he breaks out in no dulcet tone—

"What have I done? This afternoon in the Corso you were unkind to me; then you think, 'Oh, he is proud, I must not vex him too much.' So you smile at me and are kind. Then you become altogether separated from me, and talk alone to Mr. de Trafford. Oh! do not think I am jealous! Ha, ha, *jealous!* With all his money he is not worthy for my jealous—no, it is not that, but it is *you.* What do you wish to make me think? You will not play any more with me, as if I were a child! I am not jealous—that you know very well; but there are some things I—I do not like. You think in the morning to make me jealous by giving the rose-leaves to Colonel Talbot." Here a look of peculiar intensity causes the steel blue eyes to contract, and Ivy again ex-periences a sensation of repulsion that she has felt once or twice before. He is waiting for some ex-pression—some sign to guide him over the delicate ground on which he is treading; but Ivy is wonderfully self-possessed. Her cheeks have paled a little, and her eyes are darker—that is all. She rages inwardly, but feels that in such an excited condition it were unwise to give vent to her indignation. "Oh, she will be cool, so cool!" So in a voice whose contemptuous indifference chills like the whispering heralds of snow, she answers—

"Surely you must be labouring under some strange delusion. Allow me to enlighten you. In the first place, it may be well for you to thoroughly grasp the idea, that whatever I do, or say, or think, can *never*, under any circumstances whatever, refer in *any* way to you. 'What do I wish *you* to think?' I assure you it is perfectly immaterial to me *what* your thoughts are. *I* am kind to please you, and unkind to vex you, and make peace, because *I* fear your annoyance. You are dreaming! *I* try to rouse your jealousy! What for? As an amusement? *Hardly;* I find you quite amusing enough without that! Let me give you one little scrap of advice. Look at existence from a different point of view. Do not imagine yourself the sun, round which all minor satellites are wheeling, but know yourself as one wee speck, in only one system, in infinite creations."

She stops, feeling a sort of proud delight in the knowledge that the words she has spoken are clear enough to enlighten the dullest comprehension; and Contarini is by no means dull, his rapid perceptions are for ever leaping ahead, though landing often in most inaccurate and far-fetched conclusions. He has not moved, only he is breathing as if in danger of suffocation, and the veins on his temples have risen and are standing out like cords, while his face has grown horridly pale, almost *green.*

Ivy fidgets with her fan. His unusual repression is infinitely more alarming than his sudden flashes of childish rage. What *is* he going to do!

Apparently he has mastered himself completely, for in steady tones he speaks at last in a low voice—"I am not so foolish that I do not understand, Signorina. *Basta!* I have had my lesson. Will you allow me to fan you?—the room is hot." And taking her fan he proceeds to wield it dexterously, with a deference and gravity very unusual and quite amazing in one so supremely self-satisfied.

If you have ever struck out at a dog and caught him on his nose instead of his back, you will have some idea of how Ivy felt at this moment. Contarini's submissive meekness is so unlooked for, and his respectful deference so unexpected, that she is seized with remorse, feeling she may have been too severe. Well, anyhow it is a relief to know he is vulnerable at all, and since he has learnt his lesson so promptly, he may be permitted to sit fanning her quietly while Sybil sings.

At the other end of the room sit Nora and Fane. It would be hard to say which looks the more sulky. Fane, conscious of his approaching departure, is too savage to do more than vent his ill-humour upon Nora, who, ignorant of the cause, justly resents being its recipient. The evening wears on slowly; to Ivy it seems never-ending. True, Contarini has been having a most reasonable and eloquent discourse—for him, and her attention has been excited and disgusted by his reflections upon life and its use, or rather uselessness.

Success, that is, social success, seems to be the only goal—a short happiness to the favoured few who reach it; to the rest—only a monotonous oblivion! He only disgusts her by the triviality of his views, and fails to interest her enough to arouse her indignation; his littleness seeming all the more apparent when compared with the calm wisdom of her large-minded invalid hero.

The welcome signal comes at last, and the "good-nights" are being said. What evil influence prompts Nora to remark audibly—"You may shake hands, Fane; but please don't consider your contrition gives you *carte blanche* to be as grumpy as you like. I tell you it will take *wecks* of politeness to make up for your past evil manner, *indeed* they live in *brass!*"

He holds her hand, and then says rather bitterly, "All that time required to efface them, Nora? then I can't do it. I've only one day more in which to make amends, so I had better leave your last impressions undisturbed—it doesn't much matter."

"*One day!* What do you mean? You aren't going away?"

"Yes, we are. De Trafford and I go on Saturday."

A chorus of astounded exclamations, checked in several instances by a flash of possible conjecture that freezes opposition under the safe seal of silence.

In all the perplexed group, whose astonishment is perfectly apparent, though accepting with varying expressions the reason given by Mr. de Trafford—"An unexpected call home"—none look as disturbed as Ivy and Contarini. Ivy is just aware that Contarini is fixing upon her eyes that seem almost to scorch her by the intensity of their gaze, and that, deprived of all sensation except "frizzling," she is feebly grasping a chair, while the room wheels hazily round.

"Good-night," he says, and Ivy gives him her hand mechanically. The firmness of his grasp, the steady coolness of the eyes, give a sensation of aggression she resents but almost quails under. What is it? only a morbid ridiculous impression. Bah! it is nothing; she can breathe now he has gone.

Among the murmur of departing voices on the landing she catches quite distinctly a question and reply.

"If you are not going to the billiard-room will you come to have a cigar with me?"

"With you! Oh, yes, with pleasure if you like."

The voices belong to Contarini and to Fane.

CHAPTER XI.

"Our passions dictate to us in all our extremes: moderation is the effect of wisdom."—MASON, *On Self-Knowledge.*

"THREE times over your left shoulder with your right hand—Ivy, do do it; I've no wish to quarrel with you, and as it lies between us, it means that, or else if you leave it alone it *may* be only ill luck for you."

"Superstitious 'gooselet' you are, Gwen!"

"Well, do do it!"

"Certainly not!"

"Then I shall." Gwen succeeds in conveying a few grains of the overturned salt over her shoulder on to the carpet behind her, and appears much relieved as Ivy, with an answering smile, engages in the same futile rite.

"I hope I'm safe now," she remarks, as she watches the third pinch falling to the floor. "I would not ruffle the Fates now for anything—times are too critical!"

"Do you know I am rather longing for Lent," Sybil remarks gravely. "The unceasing excitement palls upon one. I would give anything not to be hustled off to the Cliffords to-night; but, Gwen, you need not go. Don't you think, mother, Ivy and I, are enough to follow in your wake?"

"Need *I* go, Aunt Amy?"

"Not unless you like, dear; but it is the last party for Fane and Mr. de Trafford, and I heard Contarini say he was going too."

"Ah! of course that makes a difference," Ivy answers lightly.

A little later and Ivy's scratching pen is suddenly arrested by its handle being grabbed, while a hand is thrust over her eyes. An untidy splutter across her letter and a rapid twist result and leave her gazing mutely at Fane. Not having seen him since the previous evening, when his irritated resentment made him anything but agreeable, Ivy is simply bewildered at the extraordinary change in him : he stands looking down at her with a smile, the picture of blissful content, and as he kisses her, calls her "A rum little beggar," in tones deeply affectionate.

"Good morning, my dear boy. What wonderful news have you heard to make you look so radiant? Nora's smiles will hardly account for it."

"Hardly! I say, put your hat on and come out for a minute, I want to talk to you. We may be interrupted here."

"All right," scrambling her things together and

mentally scanning the horizon for signs, but in vain. "Stamp those—I'm ready."

She returns with her hat on, and walks off with Fane, feeling that whatever be the cause of his gaiety it somehow means fresh anxiety for her. Her morbidness is the result of a restless night, of course, of an excited imagination, ridiculous, hysterical : she thinks of her mother and tries to feel temperate and calm.

"Now, Fane, tell me, I'm dying to know. Sit here and have a cigarette ; do, it helps you to talk— and to keep his temper," mentally.

"Well, I must say, Ivy, I am inclined to think you are not half bad after all. I can't understand fellows being such fools as to be infatuated about you, but as it is so I am glad you are 'fetching,' though you're so very insignificant to look at ! Well (laughing at her nod of amused assent), we will leave your personal appearance alone, and I'll only stick to what I have to tell you. That fellow, Contarini, isn't half a bad sort of fellow ; fact is "— musingly—"I have not been quite fair to him. One is rather hard on foreigners—insular prejudice, I suppose; but it's hard lines on them. Always thought he was rather theatrical, and his ties such beastly form ; but hanged if I don't think he's the right sort after all. A little 'loud,' but you can easily tone that down by bringing him over to us ; and—oh—well last night he asked me casually to go and have a smoke with him, and was awfully nice and friendly. Finding out quite accidentally that—that I was rather upset at De Trafford's leaving in such a hurry, he went on to say he would be only too delighted if I would stay with him."

"Stay with *him !* why, how preposterous, you hardly know him at all!   Of course you refused ?"

"It was not a mere invitation to stay on for the ball, as you seem to imagine. He said—oh, he said a lot of things; said he had taken a great fancy to me, &c.—liked having another fellow with him (he is sociable, you know that), and really begged me to remain and see the Carnival out, and then go on with him to Nice—altogether put in about a month more here."

" Well ? " stiffly.

" Well! By Jove, you do rile me sometimes, Ivy. Naturally what could I say except that I was awfully obliged to him, and would like it above all things."

" You didn't! you couldn't. How in—— I mean, surely even—— Fane, you must realise that—that there are reasons that compel you to return with Mr. de Trafford. Surely after—after what I know he has done for you, you will see that *the least* you can do is to go with him, and be grateful."

" Pray don't excite yourself. If Mr. Philip has been the means of assisting me *for a time* in any pecuniary difficulties, it's no more than any other fellow would have done in his place. Don't you bother yourself about my affairs. De Trafford is a friend of mine, and these little transactions are nothing between men; girls, of course, don't understand—with them it is perfectly different," patronisingly.

" Fane, I know nothing but that you owe Mr. de Trafford money—how much I cannot tell—but I only ask you if you are doing a gentlemanly and an honourable thing in leaving him in this cool way to suit your own wishes—in putting yourself in the way, to say the least, of spending *more,* when you already owe him what it will take you ages to repay ? I know you will do as you choose, only, dear boy, just for once—oh, only this *once*—think of mother ! " Ivy rises as she speaks, and holds his arm, while looking into the handsome, passionate face.

" Don't talk such confounded twaddle," shaking off her hand impatiently; " I'm not leaving De Trafford coolly a bit. I'm going to join him later. I suppose I can leave him for a few days if I like ? "

" You said a month."

" I didn't ! I said I could stay a month if I chose; perhaps I *shan't* choose. Don't look so glum about nothing; when I give you grounds for calling me dishonourable you can make as many faces as you like. But I'd have you know whatever debts of honour I incur I invariably pay them, and—hotly"—" *at once !* "

" Do you mean to tell me "—sarcastically—" you owe Mr. de Trafford nothing ? "

" I owe him *nothing !* "

" Fane ! "—passionately—" you can't have allowed him "——

" To give me money ? Not quite; calm yourself, let it suffice that I have paid him."

" How ? Fane—Fane,"—wildly—" I *will* know. Oh ! "—clutching at his coat—" tell me, Fane, you don't mean it—you don't mean "——

" Upon my word, I think you are raving mad. First I'm *dishonourable* because I *don't* pay, and then, Heaven only knows what because I *do.* Hang it all, what d'you mean ? "

" Fane," in a curiously still voice, " where did you get the money to pay Mr. de Trafford ? "

" What's that to you ? Mind your own business."

" No, Fane, you must tell me," still gently.

" Oh, hang you, I won't ! "

" Fane, only—only *one* thing; was it—was it Contarini ? "

" Well,"—coarsely—" don't be afraid it will choke him off—if it was ? "

For one moment Ivy stands passively silent, her eyes darkening with a sort of horror, then the white lips curl and the blood comes surging back madly.

" You *idiot*, you miserable weak *idiot !* are you so blinded by your pitiable conceit that you do not see you are only a tool? Oh, my God, forgive me. Fane ! " brokenly, while the tears rush to her eyes, " Fane, only hear me. Oh, I see it now; I always distrusted that man, and last night I—I *feared* him. To punish me he means to make a tool of you. He has no pity, no kindliness; he hates me, I cannot tell you why, and this—this is his revenge."

Across the boy's angry face steals a smile almost of pity.

" Poor little Ivy ! " he says kindly, " you are clearly bang off your head, so I'll forgive you all this frantic outburst. Contarini is to chum with me, to encourage me in evil ways until I blow my brains out at Monte Carlo? Oh yes; and all—all out of *revenge*, because he hates *you !* Oh, Moses ! if you aren't capable of working up a sensational drama, I don't know who is." He laughs heartily. " You are —yes, you *are*, without any exception, the greatest little fool I ever saw ! Why, you idiotic little donkey, he *adores you*, worships the very ground your silly little feet tread upon, and only hangs on to me, I verily believe, because I'm your brother, and he wants to spin yarns about you unceasingly. Now are you satisfied ? or still do you imagine he's got a slide all 'fixed up' for me on the downward path into which I'm to be promptly hustled, or that he keeps a stiletto up his sleeve to stick me in the back with?"

She does not answer. With both hands clasped behind her head she is leaning against a tree, her eyes looking out blankly as the crowded perplexed thoughts surge through her bewildered brain. She does *not* believe Contarini cares for her. His passionate outbursts of admiration and furious jealousy are mere intermittent phases of feeling, not proceeding from the heart, but the result of confirmed habit.

"Ta-ta, my sensational small sister; leave these mundane matters for men's cool common sense to master, and confine yourself to strictly *feminine* interests, such as decorative arts and the entrancing pursuit of angling," and with a cool nod, Fane turns away and saunters off, leaving Ivy in the horrible condition of having been snubbed, and feeling conscious of deserving it.

There are moments in life when, dizzy with the rushing of events, we pant for a breathing space and feel a desperate longing for privacy—happy are we when we can get it. To some, action follows action with no time for thought, we fly through gigantic emotions and grotesque situations at a rate that defies reflection until the inevitable happens—the collapse of the overtaxed powers, or the final respite of a crash.

Ivy, with a laudable desire to drink in consolation in solitude, is fleeing to the olive woods behind the hotel, when she encounters Mr. de Trafford.

She cannot pass him without some greeting, and holds out her hand with a smile.

Mr. de Trafford shakes it limply, and with a faint

smile in answer murmurs, "I won't detain you," and moves determinedly away.

Not until he has disappeared does Ivy move. A little astonished smile gives place to an angry gleam of amazement as she opens her eyes wide and ejaculates, "Of all the cool things I ever heard, absolutely shunting ME!" with an indignant shrug.

"Good morning! You are going to the olive woods; will you permit me to accompany you?" and Contarini, aggressively radiant, stands before her, with a light in his eyes and air of general jollity about him that is to Ivy, in her dissatisfaction, trying.

"I wanted"—"to be alone," she means to say, but fears it will sound hardly polite, especially if all Fane has been telling her is true. She does not at all wish to believe in this man's devotion, and steals a look at him curiously to take soundings for herself. The surreptitious investigation meets with its just reward. A pleased proud smile answers her shifting glance, and she crimsons at his satisfied detection.

"You wanted—*what?*" he says, smiling. "Ah!" rubbing his hands together briskly, "when we want very much we can get, only it is to persevere, *always* to persevere; there is nothing we cannot have by this persevere; she is the axe to cut our way up to the highest peak; do you not think so?"

This is rather awkward. If, as Ivy suspects, she is the present "peak" his aims are fixed upon, it will hardly do to assent that perseverance is the only thing necessary to assure his triumphant ascent.

"What can have raised his hopes so since last night!" she reflects; "he seemed precipitated into the lowest depths then! Perhaps Fane has been saying something wildly idiotic. I'll pull myself together, go warily, and see how the land lies," therefore wisely she remains mute.

He laughs lightly. "It is not necessary that you understand. With you I want—I like—*presto*, you have it! With us? With me it is my good axe persevere that will get for me all my best wishes." He speaks happily, decidedly, as if there could be no contradiction, and from Ivy none comes.

"I was speaking to Mr. de Trafford," he continues, "just before you came. He is—ha! ha! *what* is he? —the 'type Inglese,' that has no more feeling than a stone, and sleeps always because it knows not how to be happy when awake! You forgive me that I speak so of your friend; but you, you are not very fond of him, are you?"

"Fond of him!" stiffly—"that is hardly the correct term. I like him extremely," emphatically; "he is most wonderfully kind-hearted, most generous, and a perfect gentleman."

Contarini looks down at her questioningly. "It is *you* that are generous to those who serve you; you will grant much kindness, and against them hear no bad; you are right."

"I think I do not care to go further. Aunt Amy is not sketching, so will be in the garden; I think I'll go back," Ivy remarks, as, reaching a little plateau with a ridge of broken wall, that was a favourite spot for petticoated artists, she finds that she and Contarini have the olive woods to themselves. Solitude had been very desirable, but a protracted *tête-à-tête* with Contarini anything but a joy.

"Wait!" Contarini stands before her, smiling. "Will you speak with me a little? You are angry, and I am very sad. I—I think you have not very good thoughts for me. I think you say, ' Mr. de Trafford, oh, he is very good, he is *English*, he is very kind, he is very quiet; I am glad my brother shall be with him, he will be careful with him. Oh yes, I like him '—and then, then you hear something else. You hear there is another who will be kind to your brother, you hear he will like to keep your brother to stay with him. Ah! what is the matter? you are not angry with me?"

A shake of the brown head, but no words.

"But you do not speak, you will not let me see your face, and I think you have tears! For why? You are afraid? You do not trust me? And I would do everything in all the world for *you ! Now* I will speak; it is no use that I am silent, it is not for you to understand me when that I am silent; but I will tell you, I will tell you, and then you will know how much I love you. Ivy, Ivy, I love you so much that I could stab every other man who speaks to you. My darling!" seizing her hand and holding it tightly, "when you smile at me I am in heaven, and when you are cross to me I am in hell."

"Hush! indeed you must not say such things; I am afraid I don't understand you after all," Ivy interrupts piteously.

"That is true; you do not understand, but I will *teach* you. I will show you every day, every hour, every minute how much I love you! For you I am anything you wish. I become English, I will give up these high heels, buy some racehorses, and go to church—ah! you smile, do you not believe me yet? No, you cannot take your hand away; you will tell me you love me—a little?" stooping until he can look straight into her eyes.

"I—I—oh, I don't know *what* to say! I think," beseechingly, "you are imagining a lot of things until—until you believe it is all *real*, and, and it isn't real, really! Oh, please wait! You are not really in love with me; it is only just for a minute you think you are! You were not in love with Contessina Alberta, or Lillian Williams, or Geraldine Parker, and yet you thought you were, or they did, and it's much the same thing."

"It is not at all the same thing. You see I am not angry,"—drawing his fingers together, he raises both hands to his lips, thence blowing a beneficent kiss to all corners of the earth as he continues. "Let them be! For me they do not exist; like the smoke of yesterday's cigarette, they are gone! You are not so foolish that you will listen to silly stories like *that!* Some cross old lady has told you, and calls it *kindness*, because I have not married her child! I see now why you were so proud to me; but you know *now* how much I love you, and you will let me speak to the General."

"No! no! oh, indeed, no—I—I hardly know how to explain. I'm afraid it will sound rather rude, but I don't know how to say it, only I never, *never* thought you cared one bit about me, or "——

"That is not true!" fiercely. "Never cared! you thought *I* never cared," scornfully. "What is possible to do to show you my care that I have *not* done? All the society know, and only *you* do not know! Oh, it is not true, it is not true; but now, *now*," grabbing her hands and crushing them rather mercilessly, "you know — you *know* I love you. I love you more than it is *possible* for you to understand, because you are English, because you are so

careful that you never think of love until papa says,
' You may love him, my dear, he is a good man.' *We*
are not like that ! we love, and we love altogether,
without any so wise carefulness. Did Fane think I
do not love you ? no, he could understand at once.
When he spoke to you, for he told me he would
speak this morning, you did not believe him ? you are
quite surprised to hear that I love you ? it is quite for
you a revelation ? but that is funny, is it not, because
all the others they know very well I love you ! "

His eyes blaze and glow like a cat's in the dusk,
he is wrenching her fingers horridly, and jamming
her rings until it is absolute agony, but it is almost
a relief, almost a satisfaction, that she must steady
herself to endure physical pain.

"I am so sorry," she begins simply, "that I did
not know you did like me."

A long loud laugh from Contarini utterly unnerves
her ; he throws his head back, and as he gives vent to
this unseemly mirth, eyes her with insolent disdain.

Furiously she drags her hands from his as she flings
herself free. "Don't you believe me?" she cries hotly.

"No, I *do not !*" he says recklessly. "For what
reason will I believe you ? For *no* reason ! ' You *did
not know,*'"—sarcastically—"oh, you did not know ?
It is nothing that I care only to be with *you*, to
speak with *you*, to sing with *you*, to walk with *you*,
to dance with *you*, to watch *you*, to think of *you*, to
dream of *you*, that is nothing ! all *nothing !* You
have ears, they hear all the words that I say to you—
you have eyes, they see the too much love that it is
not possible to speak, you have somewhere a heart,
an English heart, that is a *stone !* Yet the stone
can feel the fire, and grow colder with the rain ; and

your heart will be a stone, but I will be the fire, my love is a fire, a fire to make hot your heart of stone."

This is downright alarming; he is beginning to rampage about like an infuriated lion, the olive wood is deserted, and he may have knives!

Buttoning her glove with a calmness that belies her agitation, Ivy ventures upon a gentle interruption.

"I do not want to quarrel with you—I want to tell you how dreadfully sorry I am I was so stupid—of course I ought to have known you really did care for me—but"—firmly—"I did *not!*"

Springing at her, Contarini grasps her wrists in both his hands, his face is livid. "You will look in my eyes," he cries passionately, "and you will tell me *the truth.* You will tell me that you know very well that I love you. Say it!" he cries, as he gives her an unmistakable shake in his ungovernable passion.

"I know—yes, of course, I know you love me," Ivy answers with white lips.

"Ah! And you will tell no more stories—and you will promise that you will marry me when your papa and mamma will write me their consent."

His face is very near hers, and his blue eyes are positively blazing.

Firmly, but wretchedly, hers look into his, for oh, she is so sorry and ashamed. "I cannot marry you, because I do not love you," she says.

Frizzling over a slow fire must have been agonising torture, requiring the fortitude of holy martyrs to endure. Ivy is no heroic martyr, and the scorching contempt in Contarini's eyes is to her intense pride unbearable pain.

"I have said I am *sorry,*" she cries indignantly.

"You ought to—to understand I did not do it on purpose," with a gasp.

Holding her hands as in a vice, Contarini speaks His words hiss through his lips like drops of water falling on red-hot iron. "*You do not love me.* You will smile at me, you will talk to me, dance with me, walk with me—you will be oh, *so kind* to me, but you *do not love me.* I shall be all things for you, your servant, your friend, your slave, your *lover.* I shall give you my time, my pleasure, my best happiness, my altogether love, for what? For an *amusement* to you! For your *pleasure, pour passer le temps!* No! no! *no! Dio mio! I* permit? *Mai mai!*"

Compelling her by a convulsive jerk to lift her frightened eyes to his, he continues—

"It is not permitted that for your *pleasure* you shall do such a thing. You do not love—me, you will say, *perché?* You will love another. Where will you find him, this other? It is Mr. de Trafford? No! It is the American gentleman, Mr. Cleveland's friend, you have met at the ball? No! It is the English gentleman, that lives near your house in England? *No! Who,* then? They will all marry you, it is not possible that you marry all. Who then will you marry? You do not speak—you will *tell!*" fiercely.

"I do not want to—to marry any one you have mentioned," softly.

"I cannot hear, speak loud; there is no one you want to marry!" jeeringly. "Very funny, but I do not believe you!"

Above the loud drumming of her heart beating quickly, Ivy just feels that she is saying—

"There is *no one* in the whole world who would marry me that I want to marry."

A long-drawn sigh from this terrible Italian, and then he leans back and surveys her coolly. "*Diavolo!* it is enough! you have not in you *anything* of a heart, yet I will marry you."

She is too frightened and unhappy to venture the mildest protest.

"You will listen," he recommences, in dogmatic calmness. "You are altogether to be very much blamed. You are as cold as ice. You are English— it is a pity! but it is not to be helped. You have no heart at all, only a *stone*. I know that it is only a stone, but I am Italian—I love this stone, I will have it. You say you are proud, you English! you nation of *shopkeepers*. Very well, where shall I see it, this great pride? You will steal from me all that I have, my good happiness, my great, not understood love—for why? You cannot love, you are not permitted to understand, but," and the voice grew bitterly sarcastic, the eyes intolerably contemptuous, "you are pleased to take *my money* also! It is nothing to you that the foolish Italian gives his money to the young Englishman because he loves so *altogether* his sister. For you there is no love, no gratitude, because you have no heart, no generous pity, because you have no *pride*."

Bowing her face in her hands, Ivy shivers, for the passionate words sting her as sharply as a lash.

"Is it for my *pleasure* I give your brother twelve thousand francs? Because I *love* him, that I ask him to stay with me? Is it not because I try *every* way to make you love me, because I see for Mr. de Trafford you have pity, you have almost love, because he is good to your brother. I say, ' *I* will be good to her brother, she will love *me*.' You take my good, you take my money, you laugh. Ha! ha! foolish Italian, you give money to my brother; it is nothing to me, for your love, for your money, I owe you nothing—nothing ! "

Oh, he is brutal, ungenerous, unmanly. Oh, does he know of her absolute indifference for him, and yet desire to *buy* her love. Does he imagine it can be bought ? Does he goad her by his intolerable insults to a deed of reparation that is more horrible than death ? Is this the end ? Has she striven and struggled and steadily steered for the far, faint light o'er the troubled sea to be wrecked on the bar at last ? Oh, hope had given her golden wings, but honour held her fast. Oh, fair sweet joy that smiles on the horizon of the possible, die out in the blackness of despair, for you could only come now shrouded in dishonour ! The olives laugh mockingly, as they close their grey arms round her, waiting like weird sentinels to hear her doom. There is no open sea and free wide sky, only the solitary hillside for a prison, with that angry, wronged Italian for the gaoler!

Why does not something happen ? The ground could open and swallow her up, lightning could strike her dead, *at least* she might faint, but no, she does not feel a bit like fainting. This is the same world that she had waked in that morning; the same sunlight is shining down upon the same groups in the hotel garden, out there it is all the same; uncle smoking, auntie reading, the girls sketching or working, children playing, people laughing and talking; out there on the sunny sheltered terrace there is—oh! out there he, *he* is in the sunlight, and here, here *for ever* she is in the shadow. How still it is! Somewhere there is such a beautiful world; the sun always shines there, and all the people are happy; men are noble and brave, and women are sweet and fair. Love and goodness appoint for all their work, and the monotony of toil is brightened by hope's rosy beams of happiness. That was such a beautiful world, and she had gathered her flowers there only that morning! and now, now one deed of thoughtlessness had sealed her doom, and the Angel of Justice guarded its gateway with the drawn sword of retribution in his hand.

Who is that man there, that man with hard pitiless eyes and tremulous white lips, that man of whom love can only make a savage, and hatred a devil. Who is he? Oh, wretched desperate alternative, sole refuge for all pride and honour, this man, against whom every pulse throbs in passionate rebellion and every instinct recoils impulsively, must be her lord, her master, her *husband!*

A little yellow butterfly flutters past her, flitting onward through the shady olive wood, into the glad white sunlight beyond. "Good-bye," Ivy whispers. It is her farewell to the gladness of all her girlhood.

"Count Contarini,"—is that Ivy's voice, that bitter, even tone?—"I deserve your censure, I have behaved abominably to you; being English, you will understand easily that I have no heart to give you; but you appeal to my *honour*, it is not in vain. I thank you deeply for your *great generosity*, and—and there is my hand."

The bitter irony of the tone matters little, for is

not her cold little hand in his own ?   Contarini kneels before her, and baring his head, kisses the trembling fingers wildly, passionately. " My darling," he cries, and there are tears in his eyes, " my darling, you give me your hand, and I will win your heart. Have you put it so high as heaven, I will tear it down ! have you locked it up tight in a box of iron, my hands will force it open to set it free for myself ! "

" Footlights and a little subdued music would make it quite perfect," Ivy is conscious of thinking, and then wondering rather blankly if Contarini is right after all.   Perhaps she has no heart, until recently she had often thought it might be so, or why does this man's masterful emotion move her not at all ?   Her pulses throb not a fraction faster for all the fierce feeling that reveals the strength of his devotion, every sign of his affection only creates a bitterer repulsion.

" Shall we go back now ? " she says drearily, knowing that wherever she goes henceforth it will be all the same, living a miserable lie by dint of hourly hypocrisy.

" Go back ! " blankly, " why, I have only this one minute just opened the gate of Paradise.   Come, sit here, I have millions of things to speak with you, *carina carissima mia !* "

So they sit on a ridge of bank, where wild white violets are growing and a wealth of monkshood and anemones are crowded at their feet; and Contarini holds Ivy's hands, pulling off all her rings and fitting on his own; talking proudly and a little pompously of all *they* are to do; and Ivy listens, but hears little, for her senses seem strangely numbed, and all emotion wonderfully controlled by this apathy of despair.

"Ah! the gong! *Madonna mia!* with you the day is a dream! Yes, we must go. My one, my darling," trying to slip an arm round her waist and draw her nearer, "is it not possible that I kiss something other but your hand?"

Is this apathy, this rushing wave of absolute repulsion? Ivy springs up crimson. "No, no, indeed you must not! indeed, indeed, I—I cannot possibly permit anything of the kind," pantingly.

"But," smiling broadly, "it is permitted. I know in English engagement very well, it is permitted. You are not Italian! *then* of course I understand very well it is the same for always. With you it is different. It is *better!* I can talk with you, walk with you, write to you, alone—*quite alone!* Ah, you know very well it is nothing to be wondered at if I kiss you; I have been in England—I know very well."

"You are right," Ivy answers steadily. "An engagement between English people sanctions all those things which are unheard of with Italians; but surely it is clear to you that—that this is quite a different thing! *You* are Italian; it is impossible that the privileges that are distinctly national should be granted to a *foreigner*. You must feel that I am right; you know what is expected of an Italian *fiancé*, and I—I trust to your gentlemanly feeling to act up to that established standard."

The sudden blaze of fury dies into an expression of discontented resentment.

"*Diavolo! A stone!*" he mutters. "*Basta!* We will go."

Gwendoline's familiar grey shawl and well-worn parasol, lying innocently on a chair, recall Ivy from

her stupefaction to the details of to-day. Turning
to her companion, she speaks hurriedly—

"Please pull off that ring of mine until—until
after you have spoken to uncle; and remember your
—your promise to keep this—this engagement secret
until—until I hear from home."

"No!"—furiously—"I shall *speak!* It is engagement, you do not deny? In *Italian* engagement,"
sarcastically, "it is permitted! To-day I shall tell."

"Oh!" with sudden pallor, and laying her hand
on his sleeve beseechingly, "please wait. I will tell
auntie and the girls, and"—rather breathlessly—"Mrs.
Cleveland—but please, oh, *please* wait." After a moment's pause, in which Contarini watches her keenly,
she continues more steadily, "You can tell uncle
and Fane; but it cannot matter to you, and only—
only for a day or two, till we hear from home you
see—don't, don't give it out—don't tell every one."

Her agitation is so apparent that she feels the
uselessness of trying to hide it—her lips flutter,
rendering speech almost impossible.

Pulling his moustache coolly, Contarini looks down
at the hand that lies upon his sleeve. He makes no
movement to touch it, and glancing from its little
clinging fingers to the pleading brown eyes, smiles
disagreeably.

"You think two days will be enough? I do not
know! What a pity"—insolently—"you have for
the poor man! Oh yes, you cannot tell him; it would
make him sad. You are very kind, and I am not
jealous, that is true; but "—fiercely—"for my wife
it will be different. *Take care!"*

Throwing his hat down hurriedly he strides away,
and Ivy, with every nerve strung to passion pitch,

walks into the salon, past the long rows of bobbing heads, to her place at the far end. The disagreeableness of being late produces no nervousness. She is conscious of nodding her greetings, of answering her cousin's questions perfectly calmly, of struggling with something on her plate, and of laughing at Sybil's astonished " What are you doing, Ivy, cutting up your bread with your fork ! "

No man, and not many women, would have been able to detect anything amiss with Ivy. She talked incessantly, if rather inconsequently, laughed and joked about the coming gaieties, made so good a pretence at eating that it answered for the real thing, and when, with a little grimace at her cousins, she linked her arm in her aunt's, saying she had something very particular to tell her, Mrs. Lestrange thought she never had seen her brighter or happier.

"The postponement of your parting seems to have raised Ivy to the seventh heaven," Nora remarks to Fane, as she watches Ivy disappear up the broad staircase with her aunt. " What an affectionate family you are ! Of course "—meditatively—" it is that ; it cannot be anything else."

" Why, of course ! " Fane answers, with rather a significant smile. " Don't you think there are other circumstances that might produce the same effect ? "

" I don't know of any."

" No ? Talk of the peculiarly keen insight of women ! it's all bosh. A reputation with no foundation, like a guinea-pig's tail. A thing as plain as a pikestaff of course they won't see till it raps them over the nose, but the crazy creations of their own fancy are the only facts, the only real, the sacred flame of pure truth, that their finer perceptions alone can discover—extraordinary mare's nests, idiotic delusions, the result of morbid imaginations or a trumpery digestion."

"Dear, dear!—this is very interesting; do go on with your explanations. It is early in the afternoon; there may be time."

"Pshaw! I mean it!"

"Just so, that makes it interesting. Vague statements cannot be twisted into bones for wrangling over. Come to the tennis-courts, and fight it out between the sets."

"But the heat? and just after lunch!"

"Just pleasantly mild to-day, and unless your digestion is 'trumpery' you won't mind." And being young and enthusiastic, they go.

Life can hardly be unendurable when we desire to sit still and analyse it. It is when we plunge ahead frantically, straining every power to the uttermost in the fierce desire for action to banish thought, that we merit the greater pity.

Mrs. Lestrange was amused, and perhaps a little puzzled, by Ivy's manner of announcing her engagement. She flattered herself upon her prophetic instinct, which had clearly revealed to her the inevitable; but she felt an uncomfortable conviction that the actual hardly realised her expectations. After all the girl's strange unaccountable fits of irrepressible joy, and moods of dreamy abstraction, there was something peculiarly wanting in her manner now. Her rattling chatter seemed to lack the rich ring of gladness that surely should bespeak such fulness of content. The vivacious gaiety seemed hardly suitable for a young lady who should "thank heaven fasting for a good man's love." It was too shallow, too frivolous, too artificial. No, poor child, she would not judge her by the severe standard suitable for such characters as Sybil and Gwendoline. Ivy was a distinct creation, one of the butterfly tribe not endowed with deeper feelings. Her character was flighty and her temperament fickle. What absurdity to expect the depth and power in the laughing stream that one finds alone in the sea.

So she had listened and laughed, and forbore to lecture, though Ivy drew comic pictures of her happy future. It was very satisfactory that all their investigations about this man revealed nothing to his disadvantage. True, he was Italian, and there the objection ceased. His religion was of that elastic nature that could be stretched to any limit deemed expedient, or totally ignored if found objectionable. His liberal views embraced not only Churches but sects with bland impartiality. He would carry his candle at a requiem mass, attend the English Church, or avow himself an absolute materialist, with equal fervour. Therefore without doubt he could be satisfactorily moulded into a good churchman.

Mrs. Lestrange was a gentle woman with a dominant husband: she lacked many qualities, but possessed to a remarkable degree that charity which "hopeth all things," and "believeth all things."

"Dear, dear child, I am so glad. Of course you will write to your dear mother at once, and so shall I, and tell her your future husband is the handsomest, most popular, most kind-hearted, and—I truly believe at heart, darling, the *best* man in all Italy. It is delightful to hear how well he is thought of, and I think little Ivy will be able to retain the love she has so surely won ; only I am sorry for poor Billy, and only hope he will not feel it as keenly as I fear. Do not be vexed, darling, I do not mean to grieve you. These things cannot often be helped ; unconsciously often suffering is given or received ; but I must not dim your gladness to-day. Run away now and write the happy letter. Is—what do you call him, dear ? —*Enrico* going to add a postscript ? There, don't blush ; everything will end in ' issima.' " And after kissing her tenderly, Ivy goes.

That letter is written, written by a brain of fire and a hand of iron ; it tells everything and reveals nothing. It confesses to the love that comes but once, and the faith that shall last for ever. It speaks of the fervour of Italians, and the attractive qualities of one in particular, until the whole works up into a satisfactory recital of supreme joy. The most astute reader would be puzzled to make it any- thing but a pean of love's purest homage to Contarini, and yet Ivy is scrupulously honourable in writing only the truth.

Written, stamped, posted, and then Ivy rushes with eager haste to the tennis-courts to play wildly, exhaustingly, until almost dinner-time.

Sybil, watching her that long evening as she is whirled through endless dances—so many times with Contarini—smiles at the reckless gaiety, the almost ridiculous high spirits, and wonders, as she notes Mr. de Trafford's flabby dejection, and thinks regret- fully of Billy, why Eros can't be more wholesomely radical, and dispense his favours liberally to the needy many, instead of limiting them to the fully- satisfied few.

An unavoidable engagement had detained Lord Egerton in Nice.

CHAPTER XII.

"Oh, it is excellent
To have a giant's strength, but it is tyrannous
To use it like a giant."—*Measure for Measure.*

"YOUR breakfast and the letters, miss; and if you please, Miss Sybil, you are not to get up if you are tired, mistress desired me to say. It is half-past nine now, and I was to ask if your headache was better, Miss Gwendoline."

",Um—m—oh—ah—" and a few prodigious yawns; then, "Oh, Hammond! and I was having the most *perfect* dreams. Now you've spoilt it all!"

The persistently lazy never know the unctuous satisfaction of an occasional late morning.

Gwendoline's headache was better, and Sybil, at the sight of her letters, seemed no longer loth to leave the land of dreams. That a short note in a very distinct, decided hand should with Midas touch transform all the grey morning into gold, is no doubt too improbable to be true; yet a faint tint of the purest sentiment has been discovered in the coldest colouring of to-day.

So Gwendoline studies Sybil's programme with affectionate interest, demanding a faithful description of any unknown partners; and receives a concise and disinterested account of the evening, which, seen in the clearer light of to-day, does not appear so unsatisfactory after all.

"Ivy was in the wildest spirits—*would* dance everything, though it was suffocating during the greater part of the evening. Contarini was simply *silly* with delight—never taking his eyes off her, and never hearing a word one said to him! I must say I think a man need not make himself a laughing-stock because he happens to be in love; but then, of course, Italians are different, so—so transparently childish."

"But then, Sib, he is so bright and amusing, one rather likes his unusual—candour, don't you think? And then he is so *nice*, and they say his old father perfectly worships him, so he must be good."

"You good, kind child, what do *you* know about him! For my part, I prefer reserve; and, too, the worship that is wafted from a remote distance always seems to me to vanish into nothing on the way."

"That's unkind, Sib, isn't it?"

"*Truth* is often unkind, Gwen, that's why it isn't polite or right even to say it unless one is bound to. Only when we are alone it is different!"

"I see."

"You lazy people! Why I have been up *hours!* How's the head, Gwen? Tired, Sib?" and Ivy, looking keen and brisk, enters the room.

After a few minutes' chattering she departs, taking off with her three volumes of a novel which she declares only takes her an hour to race through!

"It's quite immoral the way in which you just tear the heart out of books, and you cannot *possibly* have finished 'In the Golden Days.' You only began it yesterday after dinner!"

"Well, I *have*, and after that—oh, nothing. Well, ta-ta, get up, lazy ones!" and she goes.

"Don't you think Ivy is rather funny, Sib. How can she have read all that?"

"Very simple, in her sleep. There—read that," throwing Gwendoline a letter, and glad to clear the calm little face of the slightest shadow. Undoubtedly Ivy *was* queer.

Slowly, slowly, the *G.O.M.* is fading from her sight, and Ivy stands shading her eyes with her hand and watching the graceful motion of the little yacht she had learnt to like so well. Poor Mr. de Trafford! Well, he had not gained much by his intimacy with her family, she thought somewhat bitterly. To both brother and sister he must feel he owed a grudge, and the thought was disagreeable; it was repellent to her generosity, and irritating to her innate love of popularity. The more she became conscious of Fane's intense selfishness that made him ignore the many kindnesses of his friend, and accept benefits at the hand of a comparative stranger; the more she felt possessed by a fierce desire for self-denial to immolate herself without a tremor upon the altar of her family honour. Where *he* disgraced, *she* would ennoble; where he failed in the sacred trust of his father's name, she would conquer by an absolute though unknown sacrifice.

Tranquil souls who pursue the even tenor of their way without being agitated by any extraordinary oscillations to one side or another, should deal gently with their more impulsive brethren who bounce from the regulation orbit of reason to some illogical extreme. Fetish worship is never out of fashion. Human sacrifices are offered to the god of love—even yet.

"Good-morning! If you do not wish to appropriate the entire bench, I will sit here too. How pleasant it is, and I am glad to find you—in the sunlight."

Ivy's answering smile is a little stiff; she is not so troubled about her self-control now—the intensity of despair has made her strong. What if she loves this man with an unreasoning devotion, what matter? Has not even the palest ray of hope died out for ever from the desert where her life-long journey must hereafter be? Contarini is away; he has gone into Monte Carlo, anywhere, to get her trinkets, she feels sure—more galling links of an intolerable chain. Oh yes, she will wear anything he likes when he comes back, but, thank God, just now she is free of him! She pushes away her books eagerly, and sitting down by Colonel Talbot plunges into a conversation that is more reckless and rattling than she has ever held with him before.

Understanding perfectly that all the defiant frivolity is but a mask for some new bitterness, Colonel Talbot endeavours to narrow the range of subjects gradually, and trace home the poisoned gladness to its root, but in vain.

A blind groping for guidance in the future made Ivy arm herself with Contarini's arguments to question in mockery the use of life, the good of good, the ultimate benefit of self-sacrifice. And then Colonel Talbot talked with laboured breath but earnest purpose that could not fail to elevate the lowest aspirations. "Success," he questions at last, "fame, honour, riches, and immeasurably greater power, are the best you say life has to give us? To stand unchallenged upon the summit of one's ambition, that is success. Is it worth the struggle, is desire ever crowned with satisfaction, ambition with fruition?"

"Certainly it is. The will of one man governs empires, the money of another secures honours. They are happy, but it is happiness for the favoured few—there lies the sting."

"Not so, believe me. For the self-seeking there is no *happiness*, it is the crown of hard-earned self-restraint. That which success can rarely teach, but failure finds almost easy, is not for the few but the many—the cross of submission and the crown of content."

"A cross of iron and a crown of thorns!"

Colonel Talbot looks down regretfully. "No," he says; "the iron nails have been drawn from this cross, and the crown once kingly is a halo of glory."

Ivy is silent.

"Life is not worth the responsibility of being alive," she remarks after a while with extreme bitterness.

"Life is work; our indolence exhausts us, not our exertions. Training serves but to make us strong."

"Strong for fiercer strife, I suppose!"

"Yes, or "—quietly—" for the harder inaction."

Ivy is desperate and miserable. Advice that seems possible, or a sanction for the inevitable, she must extort from this uncompromising prophet. "You speak as a man," she begins defiantly, "to whom life is a distinct duty, a defined purpose, that is because men must adopt a course of action, a career or profession, and must keep to it. With us where are our duties? making a few flannel petticoats, and teaching in the Sunday-school—being of use at home and pleasant in society. If we had work—hard, enforced work—life might appear more reasonable. As it is, who will show us our ife's work?"

"Your life itself. Directly through your circumstances, whatever they may be, lies the path of duty. Keep to that, it will broaden and lead to nobler work at last somewhere."

"Circumstances are bewildering. This path of duty, how does one find it?" Ivy questions quickly.

"Its portals are generally self-sacrifice," Colonel Talbot replies thoughtfully.

The knowledge of the influence every human creature possesses *consciously* over others of his kind is at times an appalling thought. How should we stand aghast, then, at the consequences our *unconscious* influence unwittingly evolves.

Colonel Talbot was desirous of directing his heedless young companion to the safe and undeviating highroad of duty, and would have been justly amazed had he known he only gave some hysterical impulse towards the most miserable blunder of her life.

So it is, and often where we seek to soothe we only wound. When we remember the heel of even the invulnerable Achilles, surely we should have a care lest those "shafts at random sent, find mark the archer never meant."

Not fifty yards away, in the same garden, are Nora and Fane. A certain sympathy certainly draws them together, but when within a range of possible contact, an adverse force of cool indifference springs up, upsetting the attractive influence, and producing most irritating results.

That such is the case now may be inferred from the fact that Nora is sitting with her back to Fane, who inhales his cigarette with well-feigned indifference.

Silence is unbearable, so after prolonged pause she speaks—"You know *perfectly well* I have no wish to quarrel with you, but if we can only keep friends by a meek surrender of all my wishes to yours, a mental 'grovelling' to your superior intellect, then don't flatter yourself I think you worth the sacrifice. You are all very well, but after all you are only *a boy*," pointedly.

"And *you*," Fane replies with slow impertinence, "are only a petulant baby!"

Nora starts up passionately. Languidly he is barring her way down the path. Grinding her little white teeth, she bursts out furiously, "*Oh*, I should like to—*scream in your face!*"

"Do!—infantine rage generally relieves itself in that way, doesn't it?"

"I hate you! I will never speak to you again. Will you move, please, I wish to pass."

"Certainly not; after grossly insulting me in every possible way I consider you owe me an apology."

"An apology! Yes, *you* shall apologise; *you* shall beg my pardon. Do you think because I tell you the truth—do you think because I put into words what others only think, and dare to tell you you are selfish, and conceited, and unkind, and are making Ivy miserable—yes, *miserable*, that, for *that* I will apologise. You are much mistaken! Because I love Ivy I have *condescended* to notice you, I tell you what I know to be true, because of my great friendship for her that *even* included you. I tell you she is *miserable;* that she is skylarking about merely to hide something that is making her perfectly *wretched*, that even last night after the ball she never slept. I saw her light under the door between our rooms *twice* when I woke, I heard her opening the *persianni* at daylight, and I with all my toothache was in paradise compared with her. I *will* speak. *You* have made her miserable, and you just smile, and smoke, and try to look calmly superior, knowing that you have done something horrible, and that she is *suffering tortures ;* and you won't say what it is, because you are mean and selfish, and altogether detestable."

It must be a *man,* and he must be very much in love indeed, to tolerate an outburst of this kind from even the most adorable fury. Fane, however much he disliked the assertion, was very much of a boy. His manhood being tender, was tenacious of its position and dignity, and rose with prompt assertiveness at the slightest attack. He had borne much at Nora's hands, from a sort of conviction that although her imputations were unjust, and Ivy's woes were not of *his* making; yet—that somehow he had something to do with them. That she loved Contarini he never doubted, and indeed flattered himself as being the means of clearing up the misunderstanding that had existed between them. A hazy solution occurred to him—that she resented his treatment of Mr. de Trafford—it was just like the fastidious scrupulousness of a girl; but anyhow, whether he had anything to do with it or not, he'd be shot if he would allow any one to speak to him as Nora did.

" You will retract every single word you said, and you will say ' I beg your pardon, Fane, for being so rude to you. I was *quite wrong,* and I hope you will forgive me.' " He has thrown away his cigarette now, and stands in front of Nora, looking very determined, and very—strong !

How the queenly little head is flung back, and the lithe figure drawn up like a proud young palm ! With a mocking laugh she curtseys low, " Does your immaculate conceit demand anything *more ?* "

"Yes, by George," with a quick gesture, "I'll—I'll"——

Steps and voices the other side of the myrtle hedge arrested all speech and motion with the instantaneous effect of the most approved brake on the most well-ordered train.

"Because you do not love me—you think I do not care! It is too much—it is *too much!* Come to the olive wood, I will speak there."

"What you have to say you can say here."

"But *I* say—come to the olive woods."

"And *I* say—I shall stay here."

Dear, dear, Contarini and Ivy within three feet of them, in a condition of feeling much resembling their own, and unaware of their vicinity! With all the starch of indignation evaporating from their figures, Nora and Fane gaze blankly at each other, and then Fane makes pantomimic signs to indicate the desirability of flight. Nora shakes her head, and with sundry waggings thereof, which suggest latent feelings of triumph, lays her finger on her lips, and with a downward patting of her hand in the direction of the other two, clearly expresses her intention of staying where she is.

Supercilious contempt, and the faintest movement of turning on the part of Fane, produces a slow crunch of the gravel.

A silent grasp from Nora holds him fast, and with imploring eyes she beseeches silence. Her eyes perhaps, or her eager grasp—one or the other or both, arrests him. Close together, her hands on his arm, scarcely daring to breathe, they stand like two figures in a tableau.

The myrtle hedge is thick and high. It might be

possible to get a peep at the other side; yet so keen is Nora upon *hearing*, that at present she has no inclination to exercise any other organ.

Ominous impatient stampings, then Contarini's voice—"Very well! you prefer to stay here; we can stay. If you like that any one shall hear what I say to you, you will remain. If you think it is better that I speak to you alone, you will come. But, if you go there, or if you will stay here, it is one thing—I shall speak!"

"As you will," icily. "You have nothing to say to me that the whole world might not hear."

(Satisfied signals on the other side of the hedge.)

An insolent laugh—then Contarini, leaning nearer to Ivy as he sits on the bench, stares at her with the coolest scrutiny and speaks slowly—"You are right—you are *always* right. If you do not object that people might hear, why should I? Only I did not know—not *quite* know you. It is one thing to know that you have no love, that also you have no pride. Ah! pardon—perhaps you will say, you have shown to me that you *have* pride. I am not so sure now that it was so! I think perhaps you have another motive, but"—lightly—"just now we do not speak of that, just now I learn one thing—that is, you have no shame!"

"Indeed!"—dangerously calmly—"why?"

"Why? why?" excitedly. "*Why?* Because when you are engage to one man it is *a disgrace* that you make love to another! Because, when you promise to me that you will be *my wife*, I find you altogether content with the love of—of"——

"Take care!"

"Take care! I to take care! That is very good!

I *take care!* Yes, *Gran Dio!* I *will* take care! If you think that is no shame, while I go up and down everywhere, everywhere, to buy for you beautiful things, that *you* will sit alone to *encourage* that old man to make love to you, I"——

"*Stop! What* you believe, or what you do *not* believe, I do not care in the least! But" (with a curious tremble in the voice) "never *dare* to speak to me so again—I *forbid* you!"

Nora's hands here tighten on Fane's sleeve. He gently removes them and holds them in one of his, while he places an arm round her waist. Every faculty is concentrated upon the drama being played on the other side of the hedge, and she is perfectly oblivious of the manœuvre. Fane, too, is much interested, but is dominated, as usual, by the self-interest that rarely fails him. It would be more pleasing if Nora seemed conscious of the action, still, no matter, there is something very satisfactory about it, and he can be so triumphant—afterwards.

Nora, by dint of much prying, has discovered a peep-hole that affords her a glimpse of the iron bench and its occupants. Upon this aperture her eyes are glued; her head craned forward eagerly, while Fane clasps her hand unnoticed and undisturbed.

Oh! how ghastly Ivy looks. She is standing, one hand grasping the arm of the old rusty seat, looking down, ay, in more senses than one, looking down so wretchedly, so desperately on Contarini. Once or twice she pulls at the collar of her dress as if it were choking her. Her eyes are half-closed, but the quiver that plays with sudden tremors over her features, reveals as clearly the intensity of her emotion as does a flash of lightning the black wrack of a storm. Contarini has been watching her in silence for a few minutes, then he speaks—

"That is enough! You do it very well, and you look so fine and proud all the time, but it is enough! You must be *so good* because you are English—very well, but you will please to behave now like an Italian girl, and permit" (disdainfully) "that the man you *will marry* shall be the only man to make love to you. I" (with concentrated insolence and hate) "can *forbid too.* I forbid, *forbid* that even once more you speak with Colonel Talbot."

At the mention of his name some inexplicable change transfigured Ivy's face for a moment. A brief gleam, "as if a door in heaven should be opened, and then closed suddenly." Contarini saw it and it maddened him.

"You hear!" he cried, seizing her arm; "you hear —and you will *obey.*"

"I shall *never* obey you."

"To *love* me, to *honour* me, to *obey* me—you will have to say them *all.* What you *say,*" with a shrug, "is nothing. *That* I know very well. If you love, if you honour, that is for *you* to know—if you *obey,* that is for *me !* and I "—slowly—"am a *man !*"

With a little piteous gesture Ivy flings out her hands, as she cries brokenly, "Oh! because of that— because you *are* a man, hear me; because you *are* strong, pity me. Oh! I cannot, I *cannot* marry you! I was mad to ever dream of such a thing. I do not love you; *how* can I marry you? I never *can* love you! Set me free. I appeal to you by the very love you say you have for me. Oh, see! I *pray* to you—I *kneel* to you. Oh, be generous, forgive the wrong I did you, and "—with an uncontrollable sob—" let me go."

"To marry that old man! *Never!*"

"To marry no one—*no one!* Oh! you know it—you know it! Why do you taunt me? Is it not enough that you can see, that all can see now—now—that "—brokenly—" he is—*dying*."

Kneeling before him, her face hidden in her hands, she is shaken with a very passion of suppressed sobbing.

"Get up," he cries roughly. "Suppose that any one should come! There!" seizing her wrists and raising her, "now sit here, and stop the crying. Can I help that he is dying? Can I make that the old and the sick shall be young and strong? You are too foolish—but you are a child. I am a man—I forgive you, because that you are a foolish child. It is not possible that I forgive *him!* That he will steal your love from me, when too it is no use for him, oh! it is too much—it is *too much!*"

Oh, but the lassie can speak out bravely. The long sobs shake her still, but the words ring proudly through the pale lips—

"You speak falsely, and you know it. He could not steal my love from you, it was never yours—it was his always from the very first. I told you I had no love for you, none—and you knew it. Do not lie to me. You have nothing—nothing to bind me to you but my word, my poor little word. Listen to me; I will never rest until I can pay you this debt of honour. I do not know how, but God will help me. Give me time; you shall not lose a centime—only spare me, and let me go. You can trust to my honour, and forgive my brother. In time—in time, I will pay you all, *all.* Oh!" with intense earnestness, "let your twelve thousand francs buy my eternal gratitude, and not, oh *not* "—wildly—"a wife to *hate you.*"

Fane's arm falls from Nora's waist; and looking up quickly she sees the boy shrink and cower, while his blanched face looks haggard and his eyes wild. He recoils from her quick gesture of warning, but she catches his arm, rigid as an iron bar, and whispers, "Not *now*—not a word—wait."

Contarini is silent. It will be a struggle perhaps, but even *he* will grant such a prayer and free the poor child now!

Drawing her left hand from its fellow's frenzied grasp, he pulls off slowly the rings on the third finger. As the unbarring of the prison door to some despairing captive sends the pulses wildly throbbing, so at this action Ivy's bitter anguish is brightened by a rush of hope.

"These rings, I have given them to you, now I will take them back. You did not very much like them, that I could see, for always, always you wore your glove. Ah!" smoothing the little hand tenderly, "it would be such a pity to give this little hand without you give also the heart—that is great pity. And, *carina, carissma mia,* only *one* know very well where is your heart. You are very clever, very clever, oh yes—but Enrico is clever too. Always, *always* he could see that to the old blind stupid man who knows nothing but the 'Miserere' this foolish child had taken all her heart. You are English, quite English, you tell me no lie; you say always 'I do not love you,' but Enrico," smiling curiously, "is *not* English; Enrico is Italian, and to-day he will take away all these rings you do not like, and on this poor little finger—poor little finger, he will"—with a sudden vindictive intensity—"put on this *big* one, this new *strong* one, to hold fast for ever—HIS WIFE."

Ivy rises, staggering; her disengaged hand is pressed against her heart, and her breath is coming in long-drawn gasps. She seems to totter and sway as she speaks stranglingly—

"You—do—not—mean—it. You—will—will—let—me—go."

Drawing her nearer, nearer, Contarini clasps the slight form in his arms. As she falls against the big strong man, he stoops and kisses the white face passionately. Only a moment, and then—then she slips heavily, droops forward, and with a muttered curse Contarini lays the senseless girl at his feet.

Why Nora did not scream she never knew. The loud banging of the luncheon-gong broke upon her ears like a call to battle. With her teeth clenched, and the delicate little nostrils dilated like a young thoroughbred's, she dashed down the path, and darted through the opening to the other side. Contarini was there, looking down helplessly (perhaps remorsefully), as he knelt at Ivy's side.

"See this foolish child," he cries, as Nora rushes up, "she suffers so much fear for me that I did not return, she has faint when I come."

"*Joy*, of course!" (grimly). "Here, move, let me come; go—you can't do anything—go and bring a glass of water;" and a little blankly, he goes.

"Fane! come quick, come and move her before he comes back," calls Nora. As they raise her, Ivy opens her eyes. Soon, oh so soon, all consciousness returns to her. Her face is rather set and white, but her words are quite calm; only her voice sounds cracked and broken like an old woman's. "How stupid! I was rather—tired, I think. You need not look at me—I am all right—only—I don't want any luncheon—say I am lying down."

They do not answer. They stand back, and see her walk slowly away. Contarini is coming with the glass of water. She passes him without a sign, and disappears behind the indiarubber plants that flank the broad stone steps to the hall.

Contarini returns to the hotel. Nora and Fane are alone.

Fane has never spoken, his sole struggle has been to maintain his self-control. The indignation, the anguish and the bitterness of shame, are too much for him; and as Nora lays her hand on his arm he shakes it off as if it were some noxious insect, crying, "Don't touch me!—you know now what I am, not only 'mean and selfish and altogether detestable,' but a liar, who has sold his sister to screen himself; a scoundrel with no honour, a brute who would sacrifice everything to suit his disgusting selfishness."

He hurls the words at her with a sort of proud recklessness. The defiant misery in his face makes the tears rush to Nora's eyes. He laughs—"It must be a satisfaction to you to have all your suspicions about me so clearly verified!"

"Don't, Fane, *don't*," with a sob. "I know, oh *of course*, I know you didn't know—didn't understand. I knew there was something wrong—I never thought it was *this*."

"By ——, I would die gladly for the satisfaction

of strangling him with my own hands. What can I do? *Nothing!* If I could return his accursed money with one hand I could shoot him with the other, otherwise "—bitterly—" I'm afraid it would be bad form to square the account with a trifle of lead. To think "—with a wild attempt at pleasantry—" Ivy should deem it necessary to sell herself to a blackguard and a cad rather than try an appeal to my—honour! flattering, isn't it!" Oh, how horrible to hear him laugh!

"By George! Nora—happy thought—cheer up, I'll go into Monte Carlo with this," fingering something in his pocket, "and have a run of the devil's own luck—he's sure to patronise me to-day! I'll win back every centime, pay that brute, and blow his brains out afterwards!"

"Much more likely to blow out his own," thinks Nora wretchedly. "Now *think*, Nora, you scatter-brain, men never can solve these difficulties it always devolves on us." "Sit down here, Fane," speaking decidedly, "and don't talk nonsense. You won't do anything of the kind. You are not going to risk another *farthing* of Contarini's money. You and I are going to think out how this money can be paid back, and you can settle about blowing out his brains afterwards. Now *think*, you have no money nor have I—there *is* a difficulty, of course; because I don't know who we can borrow it from. Why on earth didn't Ivy go to your aunt!"

"So likely, when she is here as their guest as it is! I can, though I have none, *understand* such a thing as family pride."

"Well, I can't! I think it's perfect nonsense. Under the same circumstances do you think *I*

would have acted so ? No, thank you ! I would
have *extorted* the loan from *any one*, the merest
stranger. I'd rather be a little humble for five
minutes than wretched all my life ! Couldn't we
go to the Clevelands ? " dubiously.

" Certainly not," fiercely.

" I couldn't squeeze one soldi **out of** uncle or
aunt, or I'd try with the greatest pleasure. There is
—oh, there is—I suppose "—shamefacedly—" we
could hardly ask—him ? "

" Hardly ! " dryly.

" Do you suppose he knows ? " insinuatingly.

" Yes, I suppose so ; oh "—miserably—" *stop*, Nora,
it's no use, there isn't any one."

" If there were any one else awfully rich in love
with her, that's the way," Nora continues musingly.
" Some old generous thing, who would only be overjoyed at the chance of doing her a service ; I can't
think of one just now—can you, Fane ? Oh," with a
sudden start, " *where* is Mr. de Trafford ? "

" I—oh—I don't know."

" What's the matter—you are thinking of something. What is it, Fane ? "

" I'm thinking of a fellow who would give every
penny he has in the world for one smile from
Ivy."

" You *darling !* Who ? "

He realises that the tender epithet is for his
intelligence, not for himself, and smiles a little
drearily, as he answers—" A fellow at home. Dare,
Billy Dare. He loves Ivy more than anything on
earth. He has loved her for years."

" How can we get him ? "

" We can't."

"Can't! Must, you mean. *Must*, and at once," briskly

Fane shakes his head as he answers firmly, "*Never!* Do you think I have sunk too low even to grasp the *meaning* of honour! What are you proposing to do? Free Ivy from the power of one man with the money of another?"

"You owl! one is a perfect brute, the other a dear darling. Do you mean to say you would leave her in that—*savage's* hands, rather than ask a dear, honourable, brave thing to do her a service that would be the best happiness of his life!"

"You don't understand. I could not ask him. Ivy shall be set free; I must do it myself. I shall think of a way; but what you ask—no, I could not do it."

"You mean to tell me you are *not* going to tell him?"

"I cannot, Nora."

"Very good!"—setting her teeth together firmly —"then *I shall!*"

"Don't talk nonsense. In the first place, you don't know his address."

"Oh! yes, I do. Quite enough. Let me see, 'Billy Dare'—Billy? that's William. 'William Dare, Esq., near *Mudsbury!* ——shire, England.' There! I have got exactly twenty francs. I daresay I can say all I want for that, and "—with a firm little nod—"I am going to the telegraph office, *now!*"

Expostulation was useless. Nora but waited to equip herself with hat and gloves, *and* her twenty-franc note; and then fleeing timorously past the open door of the salle-à-manger, she hurried through the hotel gardens into the hot white road, and took her way to the town.

Fane, with aimless restlessness, accompanies her. He is so intensely miserable that Nora is glad his dejection should not be remarked by prying eyes. She allows him to interfere with her in *nothing.* Worms out of him the correct address, as she *will* send it anyhow; but strictly guards her telegram from his anxious scrutiny. She is some time about its construction, but when finished, she eyes it with satisfaction, for the message that is sent pulsating along those wonderful wires to that quiet country village will surely bring back this much-desired Billy! Yes, Nora, I think it will, for the brief message runs thus—

" *William Dare, Esq.,*
         Horston, ——shire, England.

" Only you can save Ivy. Come; bring a lot of money, and a big stick.

         "Nora Bingham."

CHAPTER XIII.

"A fellow of plain, uncoined constancy."
—*King Henry V.*

A grey fog is clinging coldly about the brown fields, and lies in hazy folds round the wooded ridges; where a few disconsolate pipes from the unhappy songsters conveys to the world in general their respectful protest at such a protracted winter. From the far hollows the pealing of the church bells rises in broken echoes, as the cold breeze plays like a juggler with the sound; pocketing a whole chime with one airy sweep, and then dropping out an entire measure in regular intervals with the precision of a barrel-organ.

The message of the bells comes with varying voices to hearing ears to-day. Down in the clustered hamlet the call of duty blends harmoniously with the instincts of devotion; and the groups of villagers are wending their way to the little ivy-covered church, with no very exalted sensations perhaps, but contentedly satisfied with the routine of the day of rest, and quite willing to be worked up to a higher level of emotion by their beloved and honoured vicar.

On the upland farms the case is different, and a few personal "cons" are mingled with all the more weighty "pros," varying in number and intensity according to the distance to be traversed by the scattered pedestrians.

A little higher—a little further, and its echoes come to an attentive group as the reiteration of an inexplicable doom.

The woods round Horston are showing a billowy mass above the slow-creeping mist. Their brown heads have thrust their bare tracery of twigs up proudly, conscious of the glory that shall crown them again ere long. Round the house itself the decree of man has created a vast gap. It almost appears as if the leafy monarchs disdained a nearer contact with anything so supremely hideous, and had bid their sycophants, children of a lower race, go forward and create a befitting barrier of shrubberies.

Standing obtrusively in a red sweep of gravel, Horston rears its unlovely head. A wide expanse of white-eyed windows, regular, unvarying; no delicate tracery or rich mouldings, no picturesquely pointed gothic eyebrows to relieve those blank, unsightly eyes. Like a great blind giant rearing its gaunt ugliness in sullen discontent, it scorns all signs of animation, and even the few open windows in the furthest limit of the left wing, does not convey the impression of a partial humanising wink!

A glass door—an innovation of recent date—opens directly on to the gravel sweep. About its threshold are gathered a disconsolate group. A huge tawny mastiff stands eyeing ruefully the turning through which his master has taken his short cut to the valley below. At his side two black and tan collies; an old setter, three terriers, an indolent-looking Clumber spaniel, a black retriever, and an old bull dog, are gathered. The woebegone expression is universal, and varies only in degree. Discipline decrees that when their adored master hies him to the valley at that mysterious chiming summons, he speedeth forth—*alone.* An absolute obedience they render; but as the first echoing vibrations of the church bells strikes upon their attentive ears, the iron enters into their souls; and it requires a strong sense of duty to prevent unsabbatical yelpings as they note his preparations for departure, and finally watch him disappear.

Through the soaking wood-path Billy tramps. There is about him to-day none of the effervescence of glad content that habitually broke into disconnected whistlings, or snatches of not untuneful song. A strange silence had grown upon him of late, and the blue eyes did not look quite so hopefully out from under those fair prominent brows. Leaning upon a small gate, opening into a cart-road, Billy waits; his head a little on one side, his ungloved left hand raised to his face, where the first finger and thumb caress his short moustache. It is a familiar attitude; it denotes little but that Billy is thinking. This in itself is remarkable no longer, for his brain has been for some weeks set a-working, grinding up old material from a debris of chaff to extract in perfect faithfulness its rich store of pure grain. Poor Billy! What matter if the past holds the fairest flowering hope, when a great cankerworm born of to-day's doubts is eating out its very heart's core? Mrs. Peyton's carefully worded suggestions have conveyed for some time past, that in Ivy's affections he has a formidable rival. Who, or what he is, he knows not. Only that while he waits, another may win. And that the lingering uncertainty of helpless inaction is almost more insufferable than certain despair.

Setting his teeth firmly, he looks up rather drearily, and with a little decided jerk seems to pull himself together. Some sixty yards of cart road is traversed in rapid but erratic fashion, skirting puddles and selecting the firmest-looking ridges; and then but one more gate stands between him and the everyday highroad of local life. A broad, muddy, but tolerably decent road; lovely in summer, with its banks and hedges a wealth of unpretending beauty, just now rather a trying link from Horston village, some five miles away, to this scattered, beloved Mudsbury.

Passing through the groups around him, Billy makes his way towards the little Norman church. Of course he is punctual. Has he not timed it to a second, so that behind the flock of school children he should always encounter Mrs. Peyton, and of yore,

Ivy. Giving a hand to leaping Cyril (a child with kangaroo propensities who never walks), he paces soberly by Mrs. Peyton's side, hungering in silence for any crumb of information she will vouchsafe him. She has nothing much to tell him. Ivy's letter that tells so much and yet means infinitely more, the letter that announces her engagement, and would blot out from Billy's horizon every ray of light, is lying harmlessly in the postal deeps, and cannot arrive until the following day. Full of an infinite kindness and blessed tact, Mrs. Peyton always softens disappointment, extracting its bitterness, and leaving only its wide inevitableness that makes it seem almost reasonable.

As Billy, with new-born resignation, is about to follow her into the porch, his elbow is touched by a fiery-hued yokel.

"Please, zur, ears a 'telligrum.' Jim, what oughter brought it, 's took bad. Mr. 'Arding sez to me; don't e take it up to th' 'ouse, take it 'long with e and bide by t' church, and mind un give it un, fore un goes in.'"

With puzzled curiosity Billy took the brown red envelope, and stepping aside broke it open, speculating vaguely upon its probable contents.

> " *William Dare, Esq.,*
>   *Horston, ——shire, England.*

"Only you can save Ivy. Come; bring a lot of money, and a big stick.

>   "Nora Bingham."

He read it through. The words were meaningless —to him they expressed nothing. Lying outside

the orbit of his imaginings, it required mental leap-
ings into the unexpected that bewildered his essentially masculine reason. A woman grasps the wildly
improbable without any difficulty; a man must first
concoct his inductive ladder logically, and it takes
time. The third time he read it the words assumed
some comprehensible shape. "Can save Ivy"—
"save her," from what? "Only *you* can save Ivy."
For a moment the strong rush of bewildered relief
is so great that Billy puts out his hand blankly,
feeling for something tangible to tell him this is no
dream. The stone buttress meets his grasp. Yes,
he is alive—very much alive; and, with a sharp in-
drawing of his breath, he feels all the quickening
excitement of strength called suddenly into action.
Ivy is in trouble—no matter, thank heaven rather,
for he can save her! Oh, the unspeakable relief of
having something to do! "'Bring a lot of money'—
Fane, I'll take odds!—'and a big stick.'" Here a
somewhat humorous lifting of the eyebrows reveals
Billy's perplexity; then, with a sudden frown that
completely alters his face, his hand is clenched with
a quick fierce grip, and his lips tighten ominously.
Who is it from? "Nora Bingham!" "Nora Bingham! oh, of course, she is the pretty girl who
turned out to be a cousin—the hot-tempered young
beauty who is at present Fane's divinity."

Standing there, while the bells boom out over his
head, Billy ponders deeply. That he does not at
once flee away to plunge into action is due to a
thoughtfulness that is indeed rare. Mrs. Peyton
will wonder why he never entered the church. She
might hear something about a telegram—nothing
like a small parish for retailing trifles. She might

suspect something. No, the train does not leave until 2.15—plenty of time for church, explanations, and everything. With a confident little shake, the outcome of new-born gladness, Billy bared his head and entered the church.

I will not say his faculties were concentrated and absorbed in "the imperfect offices of prayer and praise," but I will say that with dim instinctive childlike trust he offered up his gratitude to God.

Billy was no saint. I would he had been. I use the word in its true sense, not as a cloke for any form of hypocrisy. But Billy was possessed of many unsaintly qualities. His easy-going sociability made him tolerate, if not participate in, many amusements that were decidedly "unregenerate." His temper when roused was very much of the "old Adam" order; and his language worthy of the House of Commons. But with all his faults Billy was dear, and stood a good chance of scrambling, in a blundering fashion perhaps, up "this great world's altar-stairs that slope through darkness up to God." With a sort of dual consciousness he kept himself in touch with the service going on around him, though at the same time his innermost interests were involved in endless speculations. He never had entertained extravagant ambitions, he did not ask of fortune exceptional favours, he had a simple rule of right which he thought he followed pretty well; and that was to act as became a gentleman and leave other fellows alone. Love had made him humble. His vigorous manhood and calm reason worshipped the pure perception of right that is a divine gift to all good women; and made him, from an excess of chivalrous deference, singularly shy and silent in their society.

He loved with all the intensity of a strong and constant nature, and though the deadlock in his wooing had depressed him greatly, he had clung to the conviction that success must crown him at last. The bitter doubt that had sprung into being so lately had seemed unbearable because it tortured him *now*, but in his heart of hearts he had never resigned the idea that some day this greatest happiness should indeed be his—and now, was it not about to be granted him? This "other fellow!" Why, he was a myth! for how could *he* be the only one to "save Ivy" if she had another who was dearer still! Not a bit of it. Fane had got into some row, the "other fellow" was some d——d scoundrel; he only *hoped* it might be that Russian puppy with the long hair that was always near Ivy in all the groups she sent home (photographic soarings on the part of Mr. Cleveland). And he—he, strong, steady Billy Dare—was forging ahead most surely, and would leave the rest nowhere, coming in easy, a glad and triumphant winner!

An involuntary movement causes the pew to creak audibly. Under cover of this slight disturbance old Granny Hedger lets slip her cough, and it gets well away with her before all the other old folk can rally to the hue-and-cry. The coughing contingent have it entirely their own way for some minutes, and Billy is perforce recalled to the real around him. Then across the ebbing current of chokes comes Mr. Peyton's voice, drawing towards the end of his sermon. He has been pressing home the few practical facts he wishes his hearers to take to heart. He has been preaching exactly ten minutes, and is already at the close. "Take home these words with you, my friends, 'He saved others, Himself He cannot save.' In irony are they spoken? Are they not the sublimest truth, however unwittingly uttered? No, He cannot save Himself. Why? He *saved others*. As the keynote of Christianity is self-denial, so let us learn this lesson He will teach us, and blot out—it may be only with our heart's blood—those four branded letters of *Self*, and trace—it may be only with tears—the imperishable letters of *Love*. A hard lesson, my friends, but the first we are taught with the alphabet of God. We *shall* learn it somewhere; here, with slow, dulled senses, or hereafter, in the clearness of perfect comprehension. In child-like humility, or shamed contrition: with loving gladness, or in broken anguish; ' *Till we* ALL come in the unity of the faith, and of the knowledge of the Son of God unto a perfect man, unto the measure of the stature of the fulness of Christ.' "

The stir of the congregation rising at the concluding words sounds to Billy like the inrushing of life's commonplace commotion. His dreaming had exalted him to the summit of gladness. Confident of success, he seemed to bask in the enjoyment of all he desired; and then—then from a cloudless sky came a bolt unbidden. The words had nothing to do with him; undue sensibility made him attach unnecessary importance to very natural precepts from a pulpit. " 'He saved others'—'He saved others.' So I will, I will save Ivy. Am I not going to do my best to save others now? Ay, but—' *Himself* He cannot save!' "

Mr. Dawson is well into the concluding voluntary; the choir boys are with bounding pulses but decorous steps filing to the vestry door; and with a strong wrench of passionate protest Billy frees himself from his spectral mentor, and rises with a jarred sense of difficulties ahead, to join the diminishing crowd, and plunge once more into active reality.

A few words to Mrs. Peyton, some muttered reason to the vicar about " being away for a time with a fellow I know;" a promise to Cyril to " bring *all* the dogs when next he comes to see them," and then striding rapidly through the gossiping knots of villagers he finds his way to Horston.

The 2.15 is puffing in the deserted station, when the wandering wits of the one remaining porter on duty are nearly lost to him for ever by the sight of a dogcart swaying behind " Zazel," spinning into the small enclosure. That it is Mr. Dare, and that that raking chestnut *is* " Zazel " he knows most truly; but the excitement is so unusual and the apparition is so unexpected that it requires an imperative yell from its occupant before he plunges forward to haul out the portmanteau.

A few minutes later and Billy is *en route* for town.

As Mr. 'Enery 'Oldup drives the now steaming " Zazel " homewards; he gives vent to the following soliloquy—" It's *the pace* as does it ! 'e ain't agoing to catch this evening's boat for nothink, I'll lay long odds ! Blest too if I don't think that 'orsewhip 'e's such death on taking means mischief ! "

In which sentiment his master would entirely concur.

CHAPTER XIV

"You talk of suffering being pure waste; I tell you it is all pure gain. You talk of self as the motive to exertion; I tell you it is the abnegation of self which has wrought out all that is noble, all that is good, all that is useful, nearly all that is ornamental in the world."—WHYTE-MELVILLE.

CERTAINLY, calamity is the best cement for friendship. The consciousness of their mutual woe, and the knowledge that they alone were aware of Ivy's miserable secret, drew Nora and Fane together in a most incomprehensible manner. Sybil said little, but reflected that the unusual truce would only be followed by more open and revengeful war. It was a pity Ivy was not there to see the fun; but, poor child, her headache had been so severe all Saturday afternoon and evening, that she had been prone in her darkened room, a prey to most unusual pain, asking but silence. So unfortunate, for Contarini grew quite cross at her protracted absence, and on Sunday afternoon did "caged lion" round and round the garden-beds, glaring at every one, and suggesting irritably all sorts of impossible cures. Sybil's faculties were engrossed by other interests at this time, or she might have noticed the straws that engaged the attention of Mrs. Cleveland. More than once Nora had felt those dreamy eyes regarding her with studied indifference; more than once did they rest upon Fane—such a queer impassive Fane, as he replied to some question of Contarini's, and once—oh, Nora you "daftie," could you not feel those wonderful eyes upon you when you turned scarlet to the tips of your ears as Colonel Talbot inquired most impressively about Ivy?

Certainly, nothing could well have been more depressingly dull than that long Sunday, but its dragged-out hours were over at last, and with a hungering relief Nora awaked to the fact that another day had dawned.

How she had looked forward to this Monday—the day of the Veglione; and she had never seen a masked ball; and to-morrow, to-morrow was the big ball here—here in this very hotel, and every one was coming; all the nice people, that is, for Mr. Cleveland and General Lestrange had the chief management of the list of guests. Yes, *how* she had thought about it, and now? now she seemed hardly to care whether it ever took place at all! Only one craving absorbed her—"Would Billy come?"

Her first opportunity of addressing Fane in private is after breakfast while they saunter out into the garden. They neither of them care to dwell on their morning's interview with Ivy. "She is quite well, she says, and means to get up, but—but she thinks she won't leave her room, she is so afraid of—of making her head bad again," and with perfect sincerity they support her opinion.

No defiant merriment lingers about Nora as she nods at Fane impressively. "He has got it, Fane; when do you think he will come?"

"Can't say—depends when he started."

"I suppose so! Any one can say that! But supposing he started as soon as he could, *couldn't* he be here to-day?"

"He *might*—steady wind and a 'through' balloon would do it."

"There is a time for all things," she begins severely, when Fane interrupts

"That's exactly what I'm saying — there *is* a time for all things. The question is entirely one of time—it is a question of *our* time, *the* question of the time."

"Have you *no* heart?" with angry contempt.

"None," briefly.

"I think," she continues persistently, "he *could* come to-day."

"In the balloon?"

"Pshaw! I mean properly."

"Certainly, so do I. I promise you he shan't come improperly. I won't allow it."

"I should have thought," with sudden anger, "that considering all things *you* would have been the last to make senseless jokes about the subject."

A glance at Fane fills her with remorse. The muscles of his jaw move as he clenches his teeth firmly. He does not speak; only at her impulsive "Oh, I didn't mean it—I *am* so sorry," he smiles at her readily, but there is certainly something funny about his eyes.

"It is no good thinking of it, Nora," he begins seriously enough. "He could not do it; charting a steamer and running a 'special' wouldn't land him before to-morrow morning. He could not come until the afternoon train to-morrow, *possibly;* even if he got the telegram at once, and—he might have been away."

This contingency never having occurred to Nora, causes her a fresh access of dejection.

"Cheer up," Fane says, "I *feel* he will come all right. The only thing that plays old gooseberry with me is, who's to tell him?"

"About Contarini?"

"No, of course not. *Contarini*—why, what the —— I beg your pardon, but what am I going to tell him about, if *not* about Contarini? I mean, who's going to tell about—about "——

"About Colonel Talbot? Leave it to me. I will—that is, if it's necessary."

"Of course it's necessary."

"Very well, only don't *you* say anything about it; you'd only make a hopeless hash of the whole thing. Leave it to me; you do *your* part—free Ivy, and get Billy to break every bone in his body."

"What! Billy can't do it unless he gets himself mangled."

"You know what I mean; you get Billy to 'pound' Contarini, and—and it's a *fait accompli.*"

"*Who's* a fat accomplice? Billy? He isn't a *bit* fat; broad if you like, but *fat*—heavens! no, he won't thank you for *that.*"

They laugh, but feel it is under protest. A moment later and Contarini stands before them.

"Does she come down?" he questions eagerly.

"Oh, yes," Nora answers sweetly, "she is coming down muffled up in shawls, and Colonel Talbot has lent her his invalid chair; so kind of him, but then he always *is* so kind."

"But—but," begins the Italian passionately, "it is not possible, it is—I do not desire that Mees Ivy will have his chair."

"I beg your pardon," lifting her eyebrows perplexedly, "do you speak of Miss Peyton? *she* is not coming down, she is *much too ill.* I spoke of Miss Templeton. Her neuralgia is well enough to enable her to be out in the sun, and Colonel Talbot has lent her his chair. I presumed, of course, you meant her when you waved your hand in its direction. I'm so glad she is better, aren't you ? a morning like this makes one feel amiable towards everybody."

Over the Italian's face comes an expression that can scarcely be termed pleasant, and he turns away abruptly.

"Oh, Fane," cries Nora impulsively, " are you not *thankful* we can save Ivy from such a *fiend* as Contarini ?"

"And I," Fane cries equally loudly, " fool that I was ! actually believed that she *loved him !*"

" And does she not ? "

They turn, startled, and close to them is standing Colonel Talbot.

Nora gives but one glance at the grave face looking down with intent scrutiny upon them, and then with nervous confusion mumbles some lame excuse and basely flees. As for Fane, the irritated turkey is not more red than he, and as he stands pressing in the corner of his upper lip with unsteady fingers, he is racking his brains for some excuse that will sound probable.

"Miss Templeton is coming here in a moment, my dear boy, therefore I should prefer talking to you on the lower terrace; I shall be there in five minutes, and shall not keep you long."

The quiet words are almost a command, and Fane, rebellious but obedient, saunters off to comply.

A fresh cigarette has a soothing effect upon him, but its glowing tip throws no light upon his difficulties, nor illumines the depths of his perplexity. Thus when at last he feels Colonel Talbot's touch upon his arm, his sole resource is the idiot gape of incomprehension.

"Sit here; now just a word or two with you. Judging by Contarini's conduct these last two days one may imagine there is some understanding between him and your sister—is there?"

"Well, of course! didn't you know they were engaged?" in a genuinely surprised tone.

"I had not heard it," quietly. "What was the reason for this engagement?"

"The reason? I—really I—I suppose she had the same reason as other girls have for being engaged to fellows generally,—liked it, I suppose."

"Why stigmatise yourself 'a fool' for imagining 'she loved him' then?"

"Well, perhaps she doesn't love him as much as some girls love the fellows they are engaged to, but perhaps she likes being engaged all the same," persistently.

"Indeed! the satisfaction of being *engaged*, no matter to whom, outweighs the—the disagreeableness—to use no stronger term—of engaging herself to one whom she does not love, and one whom you agree in considering 'a fiend!' My dear boy," turning to the young fellow with a keen smile, "the assumption is so palpably false, that it is not worthy of consideration. If you are unaware of any circumstance that led to this unfortunate engagement, you cannot of course assist your sister in this difficulty. I happen to know from her own statement that she *dislikes* this man Contarini. Knowing this, it is the duty of all who are interested in her to discover why she has engaged herself to him, and if possible, free her at once from so odious a compact." He speaks sternly.

"I suppose you think I was aware that she hated

him from the first. I assure you I knew nothing of the kind!" Fane retorts.

"Until when ?"

Fane's blue eyes are fixed gazing into space, then with a short nervous laugh they are turned on his companion's grave ones as he ejaculates, " Caught out, by Jove !"

"Yes, caught out! and therefore, Fane, don't make any more stand for a bad cause, but bring your young knowledge to help my old experience, that together they may aid your sister."

"I can't do more than I am doing! I think," digging up the gravel with his boot; "we're in such a first-class fix I may as well 'show up' and let you into the whole thing," and this with much bungling and brief self-contempt he proceeds to do.

Colonel Talbot listens attentively. Had Fane been less wrapped up in his own recital, and the perplexities it presents to his own imagination, he might have noticed the concern it caused his companion. To Colonel Talbot it appeared scarcely credible that a girl with such an idea of duty as Ivy undoubtedly had, should be so lamentably misled by a perverted notion of honour that she should sacrifice principle for pride. Surely it was acting in opposition to her most cherished precepts and natural instincts. What miserable folly had her impulsiveness led her into. And it was rather hard upon Contarini ; that he should endeavour to attach the girl's affections by any means, carry the position by sharp assault, or undermine it—well, he was an ardent lover, and to an Italian it would appear lawful strategy and not in the least unscrupulous.

"That your sister should have engaged herself

to one whom she does not even like is to me the most amazing thing. For Contarini I am not surprised. I do not defend or attempt to extenuate the fact that he lent you the money solely to advance his cause with your sister. The action was natural, and it will be a most painful duty for us to enlighten him as to the true state of things; and explain that a mistaken sense of duty made your sister consent to the engagement, and that, poor fellow, it is quite impossible for him ever to win her love."

"What!" the words come in reckless haste from Fane in his exasperated disgust. "Let him know he can never win her love, when the miserable brute swears that he knew *all the time* who it was that she really *did* love!"

"He knew all the time who it was—and *who* was it? Mr. Dare?" Colonel Talbot speaks slowly, a look of bewildered indignation lighting his dark grey eyes. He has turned towards Fane, and grasping his arm is looking into his tell-tale face with masterful firmness.

Above the conflicting emotions depicted on the lad's ingenuous face, remorse seems to reign supreme. The faculty for lying forsakes him; the dusky flush rises in wave after wave to his very hair, and he sits twisting his fingers nervously, just conscious of Nora's wrath above the confusion of his own deadly shame. What had he done? What *hadn't* he done? Let out every single cat out of every known bag! What an arrant ass even the smartest fellow could be sometimes!

That touch on his arm becomes firmer.

"Well, Fane, *who* was it? Who is it, rather? Is it Mr. Dare?"

“No ”—stranglingly—“ not Dare.”

“ Who then ? ”

No answer.

“ My dear boy, I do not ask out of idle curiosity ; but surely, rather than imperil your sister’s happiness, you will confide this—knowledge to me.”

“ I can’t—indeed I can’t ! ”

“ How is it possible for me to help you, if you will not ‘ let me into the whole thing,’ as you proposed ? ”

“ Oh, yes, everything but *this !* You couldn’t help this. You’d be the very last—I mean you’d be the very first to—to tell me *not* to tell, if—if you only knew, if ”—with desperate clearness—“ you only *guessed.*”

The hand is withdrawn sharply from his arm. Half dazed, Fane raises his eyes to the face of the man beside him. It is ghastly ! Contracted as if with mortal pain, and blanched into the dead white of chalk. For some minutes the fearful pallor seems but to deepen, as the short gasping breaths break from the closed lips. Then the blood creeps slowly back, and dies with fleeting brilliancy the wan, grave face.

“ Impossible—incredible—impossible ! You must be mistaken ! ”

“ No,” rejoins the lad brokenly, for a curious tightness is making itself felt about his throat, and he *dare* not look again. “ I—I heard her tell—tell Contarini so—herself.”

“ God help her ! Poor little girl ! poor little girl ! ”

A harrowing silence of some minutes, in which Fane hears only the strong pulsations of his own heart’s beating, then—

"And Contarini knew—this?"

"I heard him say he knew it from the first."

"From the first!" a wondering pause. "From—*the—first!* Oh! eyes that are dim with death, how should you see the dawn!—Oh! life, why ere you leave me—bring me—love!"

They are almost bitter, these few words of sudden protestation. A silence, in which Fane is only conscious of the fierceness of his companion's struggle.

The life that laughs all round them seems to mock the majesty of death. How strong this man is! how intensely calm. Those hands are clasped tightly—very tightly—and the eyes are looking far away, over the changeful sea. A whisper, that, blending with the humming of the insects, and the plashing wavelets on the shore, steals abroad into the tremulous air.

> "Sweet love, that seems not made to fade away,
> Sweet death, that seems to make us loveless clay—
> I know not which is sweeter—
> No, not I."

Then, "Thank you, my dear boy, thank you for the sweetest knowledge that ever came—too late. Give me your arm, will you, Fane; I"—rising slowly—"I am blinded with—with the sunlight, I suppose, and can hardly see my way." And then slowly, very slowly, they walk back and enter the hotel.

.

"Oh, there you are, Fane! Come here; you have not seen the new *Graphic*."

Nora is sitting in the Lestranges' salon, where all but Ivy are gathered waiting for lunch. Fane joins her slowly, "Oh yes, I have," he replies.

"Dullard!" in a whisper. "Well"—aloud—"come and try this Pears' soap advertisement. It isn't fair; *I* can't see it; I ought to have a thousand pounds."

He makes no response, but leans on the window-sill looking out absently. Nora, placing the paper upon the ledge between them, gazes at it critically.

"There, don't you see! that spot (go on, what did you say to him ?), that spot—spot you see (how did you get out of it? Speak, do, they are not listening a bit), that spot—well, *that* spot makes Cadbury's cocoa in *five minutes*. Can you do it? I can't. What on earth," savagely, "are you stopping for ?"

"I told him."

"WHAT! (turns green!" hastily; "never!—*red*, you mean.")

"I mean, Nora, I told him."

"Are you mad ? What, everything!"

"I told as little as I could. I told him about the money part of it, and my share in the matter. I naturally only spoke of the fact of our finding out how she hated him. I—I never said anything about—about what we heard about *him*."

"Indeed!" sarcastically. "You told him about Billy ?" questioningly.

"I had to."

"You told him *everything?*" in low, but indignant tones.

"I told him little, but—he guessed everything," Fane replies.

"Then"—making a little contemptuous grimace—"commend me to your honour for a transparent oaf. It's all very well to cook Contarini's goose, but you need not roast the poor dear Colonel in the same oven. Do you truthfully mean to say he knows about—that she cared for him?"—in whispered, anxious tones.

"He does. And if a fellow of that age could have any feelings, I'd almost bet he cared for her."

"As you're clearly distraught, I have done. Don't speak to me—you plainly are not responsible for either words or actions."

Then the welcome gong calls all to the mid-day meal, and the little salon is left to desolate tranquillity.

"Hammond, is anything the matter?" Mrs. Lestrange looks up inquiringly from her writing as she speaks, for the entrance of the maid, and her sudden halt inside the door, suggested a quest of some sort.

"I beg pardon, mum; I did not know you were here. I was only looking for Miss Ivy; I was to give this note at once, the waiter said."

"Is Miss Ivy not in her room?"

"No, mum; and what with her hat and jacket being gone out of her drawer, I thought she might have gone out."

"Very possibly. You can leave the note here. A little walk will do Miss Ivy good. You can say the note shall be given as soon as she returns."

"Yes, mum."

Mrs. Lestrange looks at the envelope and then lays it aside with a sigh. There is something very peculiar about all this—Ivy barricading herself in her room in this extraordinary manner; Contarini prowling about in a state of sullen fury and sending a hot fusillade of notes all day long that excited only the curtest verbal replies to be delivered second-hand in answer. What did it all mean? Ah, how satisfactory. Mrs. Cleveland!

She enters smiling.

"How wicked of you, how absolutely wicked, to be indoors on such a day. Vyner has gone with the General to take the girls to the band. The gardens are crowded, all the world there. I did my share of gossiping and came back to drag you and Ivy out. A little drive will do her good."

"She is out, Hammond tells me; did you not see her in the garden?"

"No one but Contarini, chewing his moustache and looking murderous—a bad moment for her to fall into his hands! Don't look so alarmed, he will walk it off. At the rate he is now pounding round and round the central flower-beds, he will be reduced to steaming exhaustion and the gravel walks to plough in another five minutes."

"But, Dora dear, do enlighten me. What does it all mean?" Mrs. Lestrange looks up anxiously as she speaks. "These letters! this one here is, I think, about the fifth to-day, and Ivy absolutely refuses to write one line in answer. Her uncle is beginning to notice Contarini's extraordinary manner, and augurs all sorts of evils; arguing that all the favourable opinions we have heard of him are so much worthless evidence, as they proceed entirely from his friends. You know Richard's distrust of anything foreign—he made me miserable just now by remarking that he hoped it meant 'a split' between them. Very probably Contarini was only a 'plausible hound' (Richard is so terribly outspoken), and Ivy would be 'very well out of it.' What do you think yourself, dear; you surely thought the engagement a most happy circumstance at first?"

"Well"—with her head a little on one side—"this is the fourth day of it, and for three of them Ivy has remained *perdu*, not an unwilling prisoner apparently, but rather seeking refuge in despair; while her inamorato, ramping without, woos her—not with soft breathed *seranatas*, but with a very tornado of assault. Can't say it *looks* well! Now don't, Amy, don't worry, dear. I mean to get right through with this, and find the truth out somehow. You come out for a drive with me; leave Ivy, she has evidently given her explosive lover the slip, and therefore we shall find him steaming round the same ring on our return, unless by that time he has dropped down foaming."

"Hammond will have told him Ivy is out. Suppose," tremblingly, "he should find her?"

"Oh, he won't," comfortably; "you come with me. I'll go and settle him!" nodding sagely.

The sight of Contarini stalking tragically beneath the palms causes Dora secret amusement but outward surprise.

"Not at the band?" she cries gaily. "Why, how is this?"

"Where is she?" he questions for all answer, looking angrily at her as he stands near the carriage. "Where is she? I wait, I wait. I walk, I walk. I watch, I watch. I write, I write. Not *once* do I see; not one little letter do I have. She is not ill; she is gone out. Where is she gone? You will tell me?"

"Gone out, has she?" in slow sleepy tones; "ah, that's right. I advised her to take a little turn. I also advised her to be sure and not speak to a soul, to keep *perfeetly quiet*, to get a few gasps of air, and sit still. It will relieve her headache, and enable her to go to-night."

Contarini's keen eyes are fastened on Mrs. Cleveland's face, but she appears quite unconscious of his scrutiny.

"Then you think she will go to-night? '

"If she could have perfect rest and quiet now, yes. I think she could go to-night."

"She is alone? you say she is alone?"

"Oh, yes, quite alone, resting somewhere in the garden, I believe (does she), and only anxious to avoid you; yes," nodding gravely, "to avoid you, because, like most lovers, you are utterly unreasonable, and expect speech or letters when she is quite incapable of either."

"I will not speak, I will just see her."

"As you please, she will be sure to creep back presently. Ah! here you are, Amy—that's right. *A riverderci*, Count Contarini," and smiling still they are driven away.

"Why did you tell him Ivy would be back soon and keep him guarding the entrance, Dora?"

"For the very good reason that I wish him safely located here, while Ivy roams elsewhere."

"Do you know where, Dora?"

"No; but I suspect she has taken refuge in Italy," with a wave of her left hand to a rocky summit that seems here towering above them.

All familiar with Mentone will remember a terraced garden just beyond the Pont St. Louis. Passing the group of soldiers at the douane, one traverses the ascending road, and climbing the steep hillside to the left, finds a walled garden with paths that lead ever higher and higher, from one terrace, heavy with the scent of orange groves and flowers, to others yet more beautiful, with all the glowing varieties that seem crowded together from every clime. In luxuriant abandon roses raise their radiant clusters to the caressing air. Hyacinths and narcissus, with anemones, snowdrops, and lilies of the valley, lie around on every side; and the banks of myrtle and heliotrope send up rich heavy odours to mingle harmoniously with the prevailing scent of the orange blossom.

But nowhere in this modern Eden is Ivy. Girls carrying baskets of weeds or mould upon their heads are passing lightly and gracefully from terrace to terrace. Gardeners are at work, planting, potting, and gathering in golden stores of ripe oranges and lemons. This is a busy hour, and only those who are fortunate enough to possess a private pass may visit this spot to-day.

The signorina is known to all the dark-skinned merry workers. Often indeed have they seen the three signorine laughing, as they tried desperately to reduce to sketching blocks the wide sweep of the circling hills, or to catch the fleeting lights of loveliness on sea and shore. Often have they heard their master talking to these merry lassies, and listened to the melodies as they sang song after song in yon quaint Moorish tower. Ah, they knew them well enough! and when, swiftly gliding through them came the "little one;" passing quickly on from terrace to terrace, up the stony steps breathlessly, they took little heed. Perhaps she had only come like many another foolish one, to watch the wonderful shadows on the ever changing sea; and dream in the ignorance of presumption she could reproduce in opaque blotches the glories of that vivid colouring.

And so, unheeded, Ivy climbed on—on until the walled and terraced garden lay below her; on until the cultivated merged by a sweet neglectful borderland into the surrounding waste. Here, beyond the ken of intrusive humanity, above the world of little bustling to-day, she was alone.

Oh to be alone! away from the hotel with its thousand eyes and busy tongues. To be out in the glorious light, on the free hill-side, alone. She flung herself down wearily, and laid her head against a rock. Above her a great bush of " woolly-headed niger " stretched its downy little tufts to the cloudless sky, yellow butterflies flitted aimlessly about; and the undercurrent of all sound was the hot harmonious humming of myriad drowsy bees.

For some time she lay content to drink in the dulled relief that crept over all her senses, while her mind was deadened with a most blissful torpor; then all too quickly woke again the pitiless questionings that neither stern resolve nor time could silence. Was it not wrong to marry Contarini? Was it not right to shield Fane? granted that to marry Contarini was wrong, how was it to be helped now? To whom could she go to free her. To free her! Yes, but at the same time ask for twelve thousand francs for Fane! To free *herself?* Had that been all, oh, that was easy enough; be termed fickle, false, what you will, but by telling a soul she hated this man she had promised to marry she would be freed at once she knew. How about Fane then? How about that high standard of honour for which she was to sacrifice everything. So easy to dream of ideal standards and pursuing the path of absolute self-sacrifice, when duty is leading on through flowery ways one loves to tread. Wait until leaving all love and happiness behind, she bids you follow her into the blackness of despair; until she strips from you your sunny crown of flowers, and shuts for ever from your soul the light of hope and gladness. Wait until then—until with awful relentlessness she bids you tread in the tear-stained footprints behind her, across the weary wastes of monotony, to the iron summit of right. Will you follow? Will you throw away all that makes life enjoyable for a sentiment that may be but some morbid hallucination after all? Oh branded in burning letters that scorch her dizzy brain flashes the question once again—

"This path of duty, how does one find it?"

"Its portals are generally—self-sacrifice."

A great horror comes over Ivy, a great terror of her utter hopelessness. The world is so exquisitely fair, the present so full of possibilities, that hope had been hard to kill. During her long seclusion she had devised a thousand escapes, and always evaded an ultimate decision on the plea that so many things might happen; nothing was defined but anything possible. The money might drop from the sky and she might be saved, nothing was too wild for her to anticipate, and now? now she had learnt that in putting the question honestly she had heard her doom. "Self-sacrifice!" Yes, truly, if self-sacrifice is duty, then her duty is plain enough, for is she not sacrificing everything — everything for duty ?

And how about being a liar and hypocrite, Ivy ? How about the wrong done to all who love you, and would die rather than see you make such havoc of your happiness ? How about the false oaths you must utter before man and before God ?

If such thoughts do rise, they are stifled by her blind infatuation for a self-denial that shall effectually prove she will follow Colonel Talbot's precept at all costs !

These lopsided ideas of duty only overturn much happiness that otherwise had been well-balanced. Thank Heaven, misguided one, thy destiny is in other gentler hands than thine !

Wearily rising, Ivy looks out over the sea drearily. Her eyes are full of a hopeless calmness, her white lips resolutely closed. Everything about her bespeaks extreme physical exhaustion, and in the changeless darkness of her eyes lies only defiant despair. By the time she reaches the hotel she is so utterly weary that Contarini meeting her, struck by the wretchedness of her looks, forbears to reproach her, only asking with puzzled curiosity, "You are tired ; you have been away very long ; were you alone, carina ? Quite alone ? "

"Quite alone," she answers wearily, and then— "I am sorry you waited."

He holds her hand tenderly, until she looks at him. "I will forgive," he says benignly, and she makes no reply.

———

CHAPTER XV

"Use every man after his desert, and who should 'scape whipping ?"—*Hamlet.*

THE theatre was crowded. The masked multitude had danced through the first hours of the evening's fun. The grotesque dresses, the hideous distorted monkeys and frogs, the Turks and Templars, Red Indians and *diavoli* of every colour, were as amazing to Nora and Ivy as the astonishing "masquerine," their partners. All effectually disguised, they had been allowed to leave their box, and each escorted by some gentleman of their party, had gone down to inspect the throng more closely; and indeed Nora and Fane had joined in many a valse. Contarini had been in most jealous attendance upon Ivy, but she was strangely silent and too tired to dance, she said. He brought her back to Mrs. Cleveland, and shortly after obeyed that lady's behest to "fetch Vyner." Scarcely had he left the box before Mrs. Cleveland, taking Ivy by the arm, walked her off to another box some few doors away.

"We are going to call on some people, do as I do," she said hurriedly.

Their knock was replied to by the door being flung wide.

Two contadine girls, a veiled lady in white, with a tinsel crown, who might have been "Elsa," from Lohengrin, a dejected Boadicea, or a rather unhappy "Night;" a roguish-looking nun, one devil, two priests, and a rather inebriated white rabbit, rose to receive them. Chattering in a high-forced falsetto, Mrs. Cleveland entered into smart badinage with the group; while Ivy, thoroughly perplexed and mystified by the Italian dialogue, stood silently regarding the flapping ears of the rabbit, with a sickly suspicion that he was splitting up behind, and that she was on the verge of hysterics. How they got out of that box without betraying themselves was a wonder to both, but Ivy noticed with no small surprise that when they left Mrs. Cleveland took the gay young nun with her.

"Now, Maggie," she whispered, when they turned into the passage, "do me a favour. I knew you through all your decorous disguise. Change dominos with my little friend here, will you? Vyner shall tell your husband. I want to take this child home, and as you are both of a height, the size will suit. Where is your box?"

It was soon accomplished, and Ivy, beneath the nun's austere drapery, gazed from behind her mask as charming little Mrs. Smarte-Payce pranked in her discarded red domino and mask.

No one could have suspected that the slightest transformation had been effected. About the same size and height, both with dark eyes, and speaking in feigned voices, the disguise was perfect. Mrs. Smarte-Payce was overjoyed.

"Don't let your husband tell Charlie," she cried merrily. "This" (holding out the red domino delightedly) "opens vistas undreamed of! I disport unsuspected, undetected; now for something really refreshing, now"—with solemnity—"for Charlie!"

"You must have an escort."

"Certainly, the rabbit will do; he is so delightfully silly, he understands nothing! Unconscious that he is fatally cracking behind, he is recklessly energetic, and flops his limp old ears with a pertinacity that hastens his untimely end."

Mrs. Cleveland exchanges a few remarks with the transformed Ivy, and then leaving her in care of the ill-fated Rabbit, conveys her silent little nun through the jostling crowd to the hall. Explaining matters to Mr. Cleveland, she leaves him with sundry injunctions which he takes with an audible chuckle; and then hurrying into a carriage she and the little nun are driven rapidly away.

It is very annoying to Dora, but she has not been able to extract much information about the present crisis, and no one seems willing to throw any light upon the affair. Nora and Fane know something, but seem sworn to secrecy. Contarini and Ivy are so guarded that watching them is time thrown away; and Sybil and Gwendoline are only vaguely unhappy, in ignorance perhaps greater than her own. A little shock produced unexpectedly may startle the truth out of some one. Ivy shall be victimised no more. She looks utterly broken down, but Contarini! oh, to be even with Contarini!

Above them the dark vault of heaven is studded with gleaming stars. Beyond the flaring lights along the shore, beyond the noisy laughter and gay clamour of the streets, beyond the twanging of guitars and mandolinatas and the echoes of shouting song, lies in grand serenity the silent sea.

Ivy, who has removed her mask, is gazing out over its dark expanse in earnest abstraction. Dora lays her hand upon the listless little figure, and giving her a shake asks rather suddenly, "What she is thinking of?"

It seems some seconds before the longing dies out of those dark eyes and they come back regretfully to the brilliant gaiety around them. She smiles as she puts up her hand and smooths back her tumbled hair. "I don't think I was thinking of anything," she answers slowly; "only the difference here and out there struck me, and I thought perhaps if we understood, nothing really matters much."

A reply from which Dora elucidates little, only confirming her in the opinion that Ivy would be best in bed.

Not long after she gives the tired child into Hammond's care, and with no small satisfaction is driven back to the theatre.

Here Mr. Cleveland is waiting for her, and Faust is once more seen escorting the veiled Egyptian lady to the boxes.

"Dora!" he whispers, "I suppose you don't mind how many become corpses through this trick of yours? Contarini means to have Smarte-Payce's blood before the dawn."

"Don't laugh, Vyner, put me somewhere where I can see the fun?"

"Only the General and Gwendoline are in the box. Keep your 'yashmak' as it is, and you may enjoy a comfortable chuckle undetected."

The Knight Templar and Breton peasant girl rise as they enter; then, recognising their visitors, Gwendoline pulls Mrs. Cleveland forward to the front eagerly.

"Mrs. Cleveland, do look; can you tell me who that tall jockey is?—there, over there, in a bird's-eye jacket, talking to that enormous Carmen?"

Mrs. Cleveland lets her eyes rest on Captain

Smarte-Payce for a moment before she questions—
"Why, Gwen, has he eclipsed your Spanish student?
Fickle, fickle Gwen!"

"Oh, no, it's not that!" Gwen cries nervously;
"only—only Ivy has been dancing with him so
much, and—and I don't think Contarini likes it.
He was standing near me, and when I said,
'There's that jockey again,' he looked furious,
and muttered something that sounded like 'damit,'
only I didn't know he knew German."

"Most men know as much as that, dear," Mrs.
Cleveland answers quietly. "Of course he meant
he did not like any one to be with her."

"Yes, I suppose so; but it isn't correct—'mit'
is what he should have said."

Mrs. Cleveland looks at Gwen curiously. Blushing, timorous, gentle Gwen—wrapped in cotton
wool, and never at ease away from the parents'
wing—you are indeed charming!

Not long after, Mrs. Cleveland is considerably
startled by seeing Mrs. Smarte-Payce enter the
box, followed by Contarini.

Gwen, with an appealing grab at the Knight
Templar, rises and they vanish from the scene;
while Mrs. Smarte-Payce, coming forward, leans
her arms contentedly on the front of the box,
and laughs gently as she remarks in a high, forced
tone—

"For the strongest essence of pure fun, give
me a masked ball!"

Contarini, sitting down, draws a chair near the
two masquerine. He looks very well in sixteenth
century doublet and hose, and is an exact copy
of one of his Venetian ancestors; but what can

velvet and satin do against the disfiguring effect of a mask? Nothing. Perhaps it is as well he wears one though, it conceals so much; even his voice betrays his wrath, and his hand plays uneasily with his jewelled dagger.

"You are pleased to have fun now, bella masquerina," he says, looking fixedly at the red domino. "You are not tired, then? To dance with *me* I suppose is what would tire you?"

"I do not know, signor. I have not tried."

"You *will* not try."

"Because I have told you before, the jockey is enough, and when *not* dancing with him, I must rest. Are you not content for me to talk to you?"

"And dance only with the jockey, no."

She laughs.

"You are prejudiced, signor, he dances divinely. I feel like gliding into Paradise when his arm is round my waist." One of the brown eyes deliberately closes behind the red mask.

"They say, masquerina, the two who find Paradise must be always fools."

"But such *happy* ones, signor, until the devil came."

"Signorina!"

"Well, signor?"

"You insult me."

"A matter of history surely, signor; but," airily, "his dancing is not the only adorable thing about that jockey. His voice! such a sweet voice, so low and—and thrilling. His eyes too! I," with a curious tremble in her voice, "I shall never forget them."

Sounds as of strangulation from Contarini.

Here the fictitious Ivy lays a caressing hand on the veiled Egyptian.

" Cara Incognita, if *only* I knew who he is; do you? Oh, those *hateful* masks! I can only see his moustache, it is such a beauty, so silky and—so soft."

" How do you know that—that it is soft? " comes in strangled tones from Contarini.

" I know it is," loftily; " *how*, I do not think it is necessary to say."

" But *I* do! It is all very well that you choose to talk as if, as if—you were unknown to me. You are no incognita masquerina. Why pretend all this nonsense—it is too much! Why will you not speak in your own voice? You think" (with low intentness) " you will frighten me to do as you wish? You hide yourself for all these days, and think I will leave you to do what you wish? No. You were a little sad to day when I see you, because you think ' it is no good, he will always be too big for me, too strong for me,' and for a little while you try to make peace with me. Then you think, ah, then you think, I will try other plans. Oh, you are clever, very clever! You think to-night to make me too jealous with this—jockey. Bah! jealous! Do you think I do not know very well it is only you that pretend? that you have no feeling at all, no feeling for any one in all the world, only for an old man that goes already out of it!"

Behind the red mask steals a smile of satisfaction; the ruse is not wholly in vain—not wholly.

What a brute this man is. Poor dear little Ivy Peyton, what could have induced her to be engaged (so Mrs. Cleveland said) to such a creature? Well, perhaps, she may not be able to discover *that*, but at least she can give this handsome villain rather a nasty ten minutes. She sees that Mrs. Cleveland is enjoying the roasting process that is going on; although she can hear little if anything of the dialogue.

Here a sudden movement of Contarini's makes Mrs. Smarte-Payce lift her head. Gazing at her from an opposite box is the tall jockey, her husband. In an instant she flutters her handkerchief with little pantomimic signals. The jockey steps to the back of the box, bows and retires.

"He's coming!" she cries gleefully.

"He is *not!*" Contarini rises, and bolting the door at the back of the box, stands with his back against it.

"But I say he *is* coming." The little red figure rises too, and stands back from the full glare in the front.

"He may come," Contarini cries insolently in his own natural voice, "but I say he shall not come *here*."

"He comes because I invited him. Pray do you mean to tell me that *you* are to dictate to me as to who I may and who I may not speak to!"

"At present, signorina," speaking with slow rage, "*I* am here. Supposing only that you keep to the *rôle* of a masquerina—no more; yet I am your partner now, it is my right to talk to you, you cannot have another."

"I can't have another if you keep the door shut, that's quite clear! Our dance was over long ago. The rest has done me a world of good. I'm quite ready for another valse, and—unbolt it quickly, there he comes."

Obstinate stillness on the part of Contarini.

The jockey without — " Are you there, bella masquerina ? "

Domino within—" Woe is me that I am."

" Why does it cause you woe, and may I not enter ? "

" That is the cause of my woe that you cannot enter, and I cannot come forth ! "

" But why ? "

" A dragon, a veritable dragon, guards the door."

" He must be overcome."

" But how ? my charms have failed, it is now time for thy sword "—and tearfully, " thou hast none ! "

" Beautiful masquerina, listen to me. I will indeed help you; but first, oh first tell me, have you seen my—er—a little nun anywhere ? She belongs to our party—in fact she is under my care, and I cannot find her anywhere. I'm in an awful stew, because her mother will be in such a state about her, you know."

A pinch, that nearly extracts a yell from Mrs. Cleveland, then the domino answers feelingly—

" A nun—a little nun ! rather a frolicsome little baggage she seemed to me—have I seen her ? Of course I have. She has lovely little feet and ankles that she seems rather fond of displaying, and tiny hands in black *gant de suede* gloves, hasn't she ? "

" Y-es," doubtfully.

" Ah, well, you need not worry about *her*, she is having no end of ' a time.' About two hours ago I saw her with that fascinating dominican; she had evidently a good deal to confess, for they went off and have not been seen since."

A crash behind the door, ominously like a kick!

"Do you know where they went?" irritably.

"Do you suppose I should tell if I did? Oh, don't think of the nun, think of *me;* you promised to help me," tearfully. "Have you forgotten? oh, have you forgotten, love, so soon?"—a sob.

"I say, it's all right, course I haven't forgotten. Who is this silly oaf against the door, or have you bolted it yourself? Cheer up, I know the people to whom this box belongs; I'll go and fetch them, they will soon cart out this 'dragon.' Who is he, the over-fed rabbit, or the sulky dog you wouldn't dance with?"

"The—d-dog," with a burst of tears.

For one moment Mrs. Cleveland trembles; for Contarini, with a quick execration, wrenches the little domino's hands from her face, as he hisses between his teeth—

"You defy me! you insult me! You think I am tame cat English, I shall not care. I shall show you I am not a game for you. This jockey, he is your lover, he is not your lover—I do not care, I shall *kill him!*"

With a quick movement Contarini flings open the door of the box, and the jockey, who has been crushed closely against it, perforce tumbles almost on to his head, as he lurches unexpectedly among them.

Contarini takes a step forward, but before he can make any sign of hostility, the red domino is between him and the jockey. Stretching her arm backwards she draws the jockey's hand over her shoulder, and clinging to it with both her own, faces Contarini bravely.

" You shall not touch him," she cries, with a little gasp. " Have I not told you to dance with him is sweeter than a dream; have not I told you that his eyes, his voice, will haunt me to my dying day? What if I *never* know who he is—what if—if he never sees me again, has not to-night been beautiful as Paradise? You who would mar my happiness, what are you but——"

" It is not necessary you will tell me again, thank you, I understand; then it is true? You tell me plainly, quite plainly, you *love* this," with a gesture of scorn, "jockey"?

The jockey's face (all that could be seen of it) is carnation; he pulls his moustache as he tries to back a little from the red domino, on whom he is looking down with feelings more akin to terror than anything else.

" Don't you love me even a little bit?" asks the domino in a heart-broken whisper.

" I—er, that is—good heavens! what *am* I to say! I—I'm awfully sorry, you know; 'pon my word, never knew—this sort of thing—thought— Oh, I say, hang it all! didn't you know that little nun was *my wife?*" desperately.

The red domino collapses into his arms. Contarini stands silent for quite half a minute, and then bursts into demoniacal laughter. At this moment Nora, Fane, and Mr. Cleveland enter the box.

Fane, with wide open mouth, stands transfixed against the wall, while Nora flops helplessly by Mrs. Cleveland as she gasps—

" So you know. Goodness! this jockey isn't Billy, is he?"

Mr. Cleveland is about to speak, when his wife

grasps his hand firmly. "Not a word," she says; "'tis the last act in a short farce—wait."

Contarini's mirth still explodes in hateful little squeaks as he chuckles out—

"Ah, ha! this is too fine! So you love this jockey, this very English jockey. Ha! ha! but he has no love for you—no love for you; the little he has is all for his wife. Ha! ha! for his *wife!*"

The red domino is hanging like a limpet to the bewildered jockey, but one hand is skilfully loosening her mask; perhaps she thinks it is time the jest should cease.

"You may laugh," she begins defiantly. "I do not mind! Who are you that I should care whether you are angry or no? I cannot deny I love this jockey—I do not want to! That he is so English and loves his wife, only more honours—*me!*" and pulling off her mask, she looks up into her husband's face with a smile.

"Maggie!"

"Ah! can't I make love nicely, Charlie? Really nicely? I hope you appreciate the honour I did you in selecting *you!* I had my choice, and the world before me, and I chose—you."

Blank mystification has kept the others mute. Fane's mouth shuts with a snap, Nora draws a long breath of relief, and Contarini bows sarcastically.

Before another word can be uttered, Mr. Cleveland, cool and self-possessed, steps into the breach.

"Count Contarini's chivalrous gallantry does not easily take offence, we all know, therefore I am sure a little explanation will suffice to clear up any misunderstanding. My wife tells me, Count Contarini, that Miss Peyton being very tired, she took her home some hours ago. This lady, who wished to play a practical joke upon her husband, begged to be allowed to exchange dominos, and disguised as Miss Peyton has been able apparently to mystify him to her heart's content. If at the same time she has quite unintentionally caused you any—annoyance, I am sure she most heartily regrets it."

The note of warning in his voice is sufficient to steady Mrs. Smarte-Payce's gaiety at once.

Coming forward with outstretched hand to Contarini, she says very penitently—"Indeed I am truly sorry if I annoyed you, Count Contarini. I was so engrossed with Charlie I'm afraid it made me rather callous about everything else. Do shake hands with me; you are not jealous of my jockey *now?*" smiling.

Contarini barely touches her fingers, as he answers stiffly, "Madame amuses herself no doubt excellently. The joke is very fine, but you will pardon me if I say I do not see—the fun," and bowing with elaborate ceremony he abruptly quits the box.

"Well, ladies, if your programme for the evening was to conclude with a duel, I am sorry to have upset your arrangements. Let me know beforehand another time and I'll promise not to interfere," Mr. Cleveland remarks slowly.

"You don't mean that really, Vyner, not really?" Mrs. Cleveland questions in rather a frightened voice.

"Of course he doesn't—nonsense! for a trifle like that! Gracious me, who would the firebrand fight with? Charlie had nothing to do with it—I take the credit of the whole thing. Pray, would the creature call out me?" and Mrs. Smarte-Payce draws herself up to her maximum five feet two inches, and shakes her little ruffled head defiantly.

"My dear lady, if you are pleased to play these pranks upon foreigners you are at perfect liberty to do so; only you will excuse me again repeating that for any such action they consider themselves quite entitled to the satisfaction of calling out your husband."

"Monsters!—Oh, Charlie dear!" with an agitated grab at him.

"Pompous puppy! should like to kick him," growls Captain Smarte-Payce angrily.

"Then I fear my interference has been unwelcome," Mr. Cleveland remarks drily.

General Lestrange, with Sybil, Gwendoline, and Lord Egerton, now make their appearance. A very Babel of conversation ensues, in which partial explanations are rife and enlighten nobody. Then all leave the grotesque scene and are driven homewards; the men rather morose, the women outwardly jubilant but inwardly remorseful; conscious that their own heedlessness was to blame for a farce that very nearly became a tragedy, and determined never to acknowledge the concerted part they had played in the affair.

Before Nora retires to rest Mrs. Cleveland has extorted from her all the information she desires.

"Now then, what did you think I knew? Who is this Billy you thought Captain Smarte-Payce could be? No prevarications, tell me the whole and entire truth."

After much haggling and one concession, that for at least *one* more day Mrs. Lestrange should be told nothing; Nora unburdens herself to her sympathetic friend, who promises to wait another twenty-four hours for the much-desired Billy, and in the meanwhile assist with all counsel and advice. It is late before sleep comes to any of them; over all seems to hang some indefinite dread, the anticipation of excitement, the sure instinctive foreboding that tells of the coming storm.

CHAPTER XVI.

"Let your own discretion be your tutor : suit the action to the word, the word to the action." —*Hamlet.*

MR. CLEVELAND is a clever man and a cool one, but as he listens to the string of facts his wife retails, with lucid brevity, he feels distinctly "cornered" and a trifle put out.

"You have the most extraordinary faculty for gravitating into rows brewing in the neighbourhood, of *any* woman I ever knew, Dora. Your joke last night was in danger of proving rather serious for Smarte-Payce. Surely you have learnt by this time that Italians can't be trifled with, and that anything in the way of practical joking is perfectly incomprehensible to them, and always resolves itself into an insult to their *amour propre*. I don't expect a woman to possess common sense, but I am surprised that experience can't teach her caution. About this engagement of Ivy's too," he goes on solemnly, "what on earth have you to do with it? Granted you did know there was something in the wind—why in the world steer into other people's squalls out of pure curiosity? What have you gained by learning the 'rights' of the case? Saddled yourself with additional responsibility and tied your hands at the same time! You cannot help Ivy in the smallest degree or report Contarini to the General, you say, because of this senseless promise to say nothing for another twenty-four hours! What for? To satisfy Nora! Really, Dora, doesn't it strike you both the General and Mrs. Lestrange will think that rather a trumpery excuse for letting this state of things go on? You know how the fiery old fellow would positively enjoy chucking the money out of the hotel and kicking Contarini after it. He will be perfectly furious when he knows the true state of the case, and that you were cognisant of it. Who is this fellow Dare? Why should everything wait for him? By what right is he elected Ivy's champion and the defrayer of Fane's debts? Is he engaged to her?—a sort of indefinite reserve! That a child like Nora might commit such a *bêtise* as sending for the fellow is perhaps scarcely to be wondered at; but truly, Dora, I should have thought *you* would have been the first to see how very questionable it looks."

"Well, Vyner, I *don't*. That Ivy would rather *die* than ask for the money from her uncle I suppose you can understand—that by a fluke Nora has discovered the only one Fane could or would take the loan from I consider a stroke of exceptional good fortune. I am sorry you don't see it in the same light."

"Fane! The only one *Fane* would take the money from? A very delicate way of putting the fact that Dare is the only fellow who would give the money to Ivy. I won't argue, my dear; you have let yourself in for an unpleasant business, and refuse the only plain way of getting out of it. You know what I would do, go to the General *at once*. Who has more right, pray, to know about Ivy than her own uncle and aunt? If it were merely a case of paying off that—scoundrel, you know I would do the thing right off myself; but as an outsider I have no right, and the only one in my opinion qualified to interfere is undoubtedly the good old generous General, and no one would relish it more. To kick that fellow Contarini would positively rejuvenate the dear old boy and knock his gout clean out of him."

"Only for another day, Vyner; I *must* wait for another day—I promised."

"Very good, Dora, as you choose, only a good deal may happen in a day," and Mr. Cleveland, taking out a pipe from his pocket, rises and walks off to the door.

"Vyner." Dora has moved up to him and stands holding on to a button of his coat, twisting it round and round as she looks up into his face. "You—you aren't angry with me, Vyner?" sorrowfully.

"What is the use of being angry, my dear child? I shall just go and have an hour's fencing, one may as well be in good practice for the inevitable *dénoucment*," and with rather a grim smile he goes.

Surely never in the life of mortal man did the hours creep by so slowly. That Ivy passed the day in Mrs. Cleveland's salon was scarcely a relief to Nora; for Contarini was loose, walking up and down on the earth, and the very air seemed fraught with danger. The jest of the preceding night had excited him to a very frenzy of rage. That *he* should be made sport of to amuse a parcel of idiotic women, that he should betray his private affairs to a mere stranger— it was scandalous, it was worse than scandalous, it was unpardonable.

He had accepted Mrs. Smarte-Payce's excuses, because most undoubtedly it was true she had wished to impose upon her husband, and certainly had most successfully done so. But had she and Mrs. Cleveland any ulterior design? And above all, had Ivy had anything to do with this—had she sanctioned or been cognisant of so abominable a trick? He would know.

"She was tired." "She was lying down." "She could not see him then, but would by-and-by." Any excuse served, but, "see her he shall not," said Mrs. Cleveland, and keeping the child a listless but willing prisoner, she left her in blissful ignorance of her lover's importunities, employing Nora and Fane, her excited allies, as trusty messengers and scouts.

Ivy is apparently reading; her eyes are upon the pages of her book, but she has not grasped the meaning of a line. She has forgotten Contarini, forgotten the hopeless wretchedness of her position, forgotten the inevitable meeting at the dreaded ball to-night, forgotten the part she had resolved so resolutely to play. Forgotten the past, and the horror of the future, in an overmastering craving of to-day. Oh! if she could see Colonel Talbot once more, only *once* more—only for a few moments, only to do away with the wrong impression he must have of her ever since their last conversation. To tell him she did not mean a single word she had said. To tell him the ideas she had vaunted as her own about life and worldly success, &c., were *hateful* to her. To tell him that his standard of duty should be the guiding principle of her life, that—that she was not—not *really* frivolous, that she so often said what indeed she never thought. And then—then, when he understood (for he always understood), then it would not be so hard to—to never see him again. A sort of desperation seemed to come over her. Oh, it was unendurable, it was cruel, it could not be right. Was he to leave her, thinking what he must think of her, believing she was just a heartless, heedless, frivolous flirt, without a thought beyond merry-making and society? She could not bear it—oh, she could not bear it!

Why had she never spoken the truth, been open and honest like Sybil and Gwendoline? Oh surely it would have been better to let him guess *every-thing*, than believe — what, of course, he must believe.

Your tired brain will never tell you why, Ivy. The why and the wherefore of even little things are necessary cogs in some whirling wheel, moved by gigantic tireless engines quite hidden from our sight.

Dream on, Ivy. Death does not seem so dreadful now it is so near. "Only before he must follow you great grand King, let us meet and part as friends."

"Are you dreaming, Ivy? Asleep! Run away with Nora and get ready for dinner; it is half-an-hour earlier, because they want the room for the supper. Of course none of you will dress until afterwards."

"No, of course not. Mrs. Cleveland, where has everybody been—in the garden?"

"No, in the Corso. Such a rabble, seeing the last of King Carnival. We shall see the fireworks when they burn him to-night. Run along, girls, all your bouquets have come; and—oh Ivy, dear, you will find a note or two from Contarini—I would not have you disturbed, so you can answer all at once when you meet him." And dismissing the two girls, Mrs. Cleveland walks off to her room, sighing thankfully with satisfaction that so much of this detestable day had been safely lived through.

Nora is to Ivy as her very shadow. She remains a fixture by her side even when Contarini accompanies them upstairs again to the Lestranges' salon, He looks down grimly upon Ivy. "You are too ill to answer my letters—is it not a pity you will see no doctor."

Oh! the comfort of Nora's touch upon her arm. Ivy answers almost independently, "No, thank you, the only medicine I required was rest. I feel much better now, only I won't promise to stand much dancing."

"I do not ask it. I wish to talk to you. Why, how is this—surely it is not possible that you are going to dress now?"

"Indeed yes," Nora answers laughing, "we have a thousand things to arrange, and our hair takes—*hours;* it is six now, and no girl ever took less than three hours to dress for a ball—especially as for this foreign dancing our clothes have to be double-stitched on!"

Contarini bows as the girls walk away, but his sensations are by no means pleasant. Surely every one is less cordial to him than of yore. Mr. Cleveland, Fane, and even the General seem to have drifted from the state of *bon camaraderie* into a stiff neutrality. Why? Can that young ass Fane have suspected anything, and imparted his impressions to the others? No, impossible; he cannot *suspect*, or his outspoken rashness would have found its vent in some unguarded speech—and of one thing he is certain; that Ivy would never tell. That is a bad traffic trading upon pride; there are those who will barter love, happiness, hope, all things for honour. Wise economists call them fools. Contarini was not certainly one of these, he would always get his money's worth; he flattered himself that he was astute, and he was generally considered successful. He wandered about irritably, abused the floral decorations, the hurrying waiters, and general confusion consequent upon the preparations for the ball—hindered porters, hustled about the bureau; and finally swore long and loudly on finding the billiard table converted into a buffet. That Fane seemed nearly as restless as himself he never noticed, nor that as time went on each sudden flit round deserted rooms, corridors, and garden marked him with added melancholy. No, he noticed nothing, thought of nothing, but his own particular annoyances.

"Nora!" Fane calls, "come to the door. Are you nearly ready? It is eight now, so I am going to dress; every one comes at half-past—and, Nora," softly, "he has not come!"

"Perhaps he never received the telegram—do you think?"

"Perhaps he's *dead!*" Fane whispers in return, and then walks away, while Nora returns dejectedly to manipulate her silky hair into little extra twists and turns in honour of the evening.

An hour later, and over the "Hotel Bellevue" has passed a singular change. Among wonderful decorations of coloured paper and cotton wool, wrought into garlands by energetic waiters, gleam groups of candles, and flares the more commonplace gas. Corridors, passages, stairs, and all the rooms *au premier* are filled with shrubs and flowers; while lounging smokers and knitting old ladies have vanished into the limbo of things that were.

Strains of gay music float out on the sweet tranquil air. Prettily dressed girls chatter merrily as they perambulate up and down with their partners, or linger in out-of-the-way corners to prolong some pleasant *tête-à-tête*. Gorgeous dowagers are ensconced in all the places of honour, where eyes find plenty of material for tongues, though sight is a bad second to thought.

Mrs. Smarte-Payce is looking extremely pretty in a simple costume of grey tulle, against which a few diamond stars flash out like torches in a fog. The consciousness of being well dressed always makes a woman happy, and serves more than anything else to put her perfectly at her ease.

She is happy but cannot endure the sensation of being eclipsed, and to-night she most certainly is. All the dear girls in white gowns are sweet visions of fluffy innocence—fresh, but insipid, they scarcely count. Mrs. Cleveland, in pale green, graceful and languid, crowned with the rich coronal of her own glossy auburn hair, is the artistic triumph of the evening—quite a full happy Burne Jones note, if one may imagine health effecting this combination with harmony. But Mrs. Cleveland does not trouble her—their paths lie too widely apart. One commands triumphs, the other seeks successes; one prefers the game driven to her—the other, more sporting perhaps, stalks it.

But who—oh, who is this? Slight and rather small, holding herself like a queen, dressed in a rich white silk stiff with its design of woven gold, and trailing in courtly magnificence along the floor— opals and diamonds encircling the slender throat, and studded cunningly in the dusky pyramid of hair; with a skin like death, lips a blood-red cupid's bow, and eyes more darkly brilliant than all her glowing jewels. Who is she?

Watching the unknown as she dances with Contarini, Mrs. Smarte-Payce is only the more impressed by her extraordinary beauty. It is so aggressively vivid that when once seen can never be forgotten. She forgets her partner, a somewhat dull one 'tis true, and watches these two as they whirl round—the handsomest and most striking couple in the room.

"I should put a stop to that if I were engaged to Count Contarini, and yet she takes it calmly enough, doesn't she?" Mrs. Smart-Payce says suddenly, indicating Ivy to her partner as she speaks.

"What! that little girl over there in white— colourless little thing; pretty smile though. Seems quite happy with those two young fellows. Has been quarrelling with the good-looking one because he wanted to stand with his arm round her waist. Stickler for custom, or afraid of 'mama.'"

"It's her brother," Mrs. Smarte-Payce replies ere being launched cumberously into the whirling, compact crowd.

And Ivy is happy, very nearly happy. True to her resolve to submit to Contarini, because hateful though he is, he represents her absolute duty; she has done her best to soothe his ruffled feelings, and danced solely with him up to the present time. That Princess Tina Boronowsky should unexpectedly make her appearance caused her a certain amount of anxiety, until she saw that the beautiful Russian's fascinations has no effect upon Fane. What was the matter with the boy? he had grown so silent and distrait lately, his intercourse with Nora seemed but to increase his mysterious melancholy, his shallow vanity could not be even fanned into life by the lovely Princess's smiles; and above all, he had developed an extraordinary interest in his sister! It was very dear of him, Ivy thought, to rescue her from the toils of an energetic partner, and give up dancing to talk to and keep guard over her. Poor, dear boy! She had been unjust to him, for in spite of all his apparent selfishness, here he was looking after her with a gentle consideration worthy of Teddy! So they laugh together, beguiling the energetic youth to quietness, while they criticise the throng, and make endless feeble jokes about Nora and her Italian partners. She can only dart helpless looks of anguish at them, as she is spun past at about a hundred miles an hour, and with very high action. Soon, however,

Contarini returns for Ivy, and walking off to a lounge in the corridor sits down rather glumly by her side, and begins abruptly in no amiable tone:—

"You are looking very pale to-night; it does not please me to see you pale; you want a colour in your dress, in your hair—you are too white."

"Has my hair turned white *already?*" Ivy answers. "I hardly expected it so soon."

"You mistake me, or you are please to be very rude. Why"—angrily—"did you not wear the diamonds I gave you to-night?"

"I have not taken them off. Do you wish me to go without my glove? Of course I can do so if you desire it."

"Your glove! You know very well what I mean. You know I wish very much that you will wear the diamond stars that I give you, and you do not wear them. Why? You are engage to me, you can wear the things that I give you. What pleasure is it for me to give you beautiful presents, all the lovely things I buy for you, if you do not wear them?"

"They are too handsome; they are much more like—like a married woman's things. I—I could not wear them now. They are—I have never been accustomed to such things," Ivy concludes aimlessly.

Contarini eyes her quietly. "That chain you wear round your neck—you think that very beautiful! It is very light chain, and you think my one is too heavy, do you not? But you must put on the things I give to you, *carina*, because I like to see you beautiful."

"I am sorry I do not please you," Ivy answers, "I cannot help being pale—I am tired."

"You are always tired! If you are pale, do you not know you must put on some gay colour? Where are the flowers I sent you? Why do you not put plenty of the pink roses in your dress? What is the use I get you so many flowers, and you choose only this?" He touches disdainfully a spray of white lilac as he speaks.

With Griselda-like meekness Ivy unfastens the flower from her dress, and tosses it aside. As she replaces the pin that has secured it into her dress, Contarini makes a sudden movement as if to seize it; Ivy draws back haughtily.

"That pin!" Contarini begins, "again you have it—always you have it—it is too much! You will give it to me! What is this pin, that you will always wear it? Who gave it to you? *My* things you will not wear—my beautiful, pretty things—but this little, *poor* thing, this common little pin, it is for ever, ever, ever in your dress. I ask over and over, and you never tell. 'A friend,' you say; that is very good; but I do not choose that you shall wear the present of any of your *friends!* Give me the pin at once!"

Ivy slowly rises from beside him. "I think you are dreaming, Count Contarini; I wear what I choose, and shall be dictated to by no one. I have worn this pin always—long, oh"—with maddening tenderness—"long before I ever saw you! I *have* always worn it, and"—firmly—"I *shall* always wear it!"

"You can be very proud, oh! very proud, *now*," Contarini answers, with a swift look at her, as he rises too; "you think you will do what you like. I tell you *no*. Do you think I do not know quite well who has given you that pin? You are wise to make me angry here, in this place where all these people are; you see Mrs. Cleveland coming, so you think I cannot take it now—that is true; and also I can be generous, *carina*, because *now* you are altogether mine, and "—bending towards her, he whispers—"your lover is —*dead!*"

Ivy's hands go out to grasp his arm as her eyes turn in startled horror on him. She gives him a little shake before the words come from her pale lips—"What do you mean?—say it—at once!" she cries.

"Dr. Martin has just told me your lover—the miserable old man Colonel Talbot—is dead," he says brutally.

A moment Ivy stands, her eyes wide and staring, then with a little strangled cry she makes a few tottering steps forward. A group of people are coming towards her. Uncertainly she stretches her hands to them as to fleeting visions in a dream. Some one—some one, strong and tall and gentle— catches her ere she falls, lost to the overwhelming horror in the blankness of unconsciousness.

    .   .   .   .

We must return for a little while to Nora and Fane. Their natural brightness of disposition made the gaiety around them enjoyable, though across the gladness of the hour came moments of doubting despair. Why, oh why, had Billy never come? What would happen when Mrs. Cleveland reported

the whole affair to the General and Mrs. Lestrange?
Nora was dejected, Fane desperate.

"There is something so humiliating in the thought
that we must go to uncle after all," Fane remarks
blankly, as he stands by Nora on the steps of the
hotel.

"The collapse of my brilliant idea distresses *me*,"
Nora replies, as she twists a crochet chair back
round her shoulders, in deference to the coolness of
the evening air. So still is the night, that to those
blessed with entire lungs the garden is a very
possible joy. A few couples are sauntering slowly
round the flower-beds, their eyes roving heaven-
wards in rapt contemplation of the myriad stars,
their thoughts possibly very much on earth. How
still, how calm, how exquisite is the beauty of the
tranquil world without—how glaring, how noisy,
how restless the turmoil of the scene within!

"I shall tell uncle myself, Nora," Fane remarks
presently; "it is simply sickening to think of spong-
ing on him, but there's nothing else for it."

"Oh!" Nora cries, with a little break in her
voice, "everything would have been all right if only
my telegram could have brought Billy."

"I came as soon as I could. An accident beyond
Nice "——

"Dare! Good heavens!" Fane springs up and
grasps the arm of a man who has just stepped from
the dimness of the garden into the flood of light
from the Hall.

"He is a great big man," is Nora's first thought.
"He is in evening dress; that shows he was not in
much of a hurry," is her second, and then—then a
sudden shyness at the remembrance of what she had

done makes her shrink back a little as she blushes a most royal red.

"This is Miss Bingham, Dare," Fane begins nervously, and Billy comes forward at once.

"You sent for me. I cannot tell you how grateful I am. I came at once. Train came to grief beyond Nice, engine broke down, had to wait; came by next one, found no one at the station, so came on to this hotel. Found you were all in the middle of a ball, got a room by strategy and a tub by bribes, dressed, and here I am, and for Heaven's sake tell me what you want with me."

"Ivy," begins Nora nervously.

"What about her?" Billy cries quickly.

"I'll tell him, Nora, I'll tell him. Wait in the Hall, sit round the corner, leave me to tell him out here," and Fane, giving Billy a push into the friendly darkness, walks off.

"Look sharp, Fane—you have come to grief. I've got the coin, but what in Heaven's name about Ivy?"

"She is engaged to the fellow who paid my debts. He is Contarini, an Italian. I thought she really cared for him, but we found out—Nora and I—she *hates* him. Only, somehow, he had bound her down to marry him because he lent me the money," Fane begins, in spasmodic jerks.

"Well—go on."

"That—there's nothing more, that's all," Fane answers, wondering at Billy's coolness.

"Do you mean to say you allowed this . . (not being a parliamentary reporter I consider myself entitled to leave gaps) this . . Italian fellow to keep Ivy to such a . compact for a miserable

handful of coin! What in the   . own name is
the General thinking of. Here, stand back—where
is this   cad, this low, sneaking hound? Oh
wait, wait—we must be properly equipped."

"Dare, for Heaven's sake," Fane begins imploringly, "do keep quiet; these Italian fellows are
the very   .   in a row. There'll be a beastly fracas
if you can't keep cool," eyeing the great big fellow
with secret joy.

Billy is fumbling in his pockets. "Come on,"
he cries suddenly, "must have left it in my room
—thought I crammed my cheque-book in here.
What is the figure? Come on, I'm in some out-
house they call a ' dependance,' suppose because it
is only for poor dependant beggars who can't get
anything else." He is striding along, talking as
he goes, and in another few moments he is striding
back. He looks rather stern, but his whole bearing is exultant. In his pocket he carries a leaf
from his cheque-book, and in his hand a business-
like cutting whip.

Nora springs up as they enter the hall. Billy
looks round him vaguely. "Go ahead, Fane," he
says, and Nora, with quick apprehension, glides
after them, her eyes seeking desperately for Mr.
Cleveland or the General.

Mr. and Mrs. Cleveland are half way up a
corridor; they step forward to meet the coming
trio, but Billy never halts a moment. These people
to him are nothing, for just beyond, not half-a-
dozen yards away, he has already caught sight of
Ivy.

Across the doubting misery of these days of
parting, out of the darkness of her past, see how

she is stretching imploring hands to him in a dumb appeal for help. A great wave of tenderness sweeps away every other feeling but the intensity of his love, and with a proud gratitude Billy puts his arms round the little figure and holds her fast, indignation and vengeance alike forgotten.

Nora and Mrs. Cleveland are at his side. " Give her to us, we will take care of her—here, before any one comes, bring her here," and flinging open the door of a chaotic cloak-room they sign to him to follow. He does so, and lays her gently down upon a well-piled sofa. As he steps back to give them his place, he sees that one or two men are standing in the doorway.

" You will let me come," one of them is saying; while the other, a dark smart-looking man, is keeping him back. " It is nothing, she has faint. I tell her she shall not dance, she *wish* to dance with me, but I will forbid now; she is too tired. Let me come, please."

" Get back, man, get back ! Leave her to the ladies, my dear Contarini, you can do no good—let us clear."

Billy turns sharply round. He looks the fair man straight in the face, and then steps up to him —" A word with you, if you please." Something in his aspect causes Mr. Cleveland to pull Contarini into the corridor.

" Where you like, gentlemen, only not *here*—this will do," walking along until they reach a small salon at the extremity of the corridor, at present silent and deserted. Fane is following with the determination to see the row which his knowledge of Billy tells him is imminent.

Standing near a small table Billy turns to Contarini—" You bound Miss Peyton to engage herself to you, because you paid twelve thousand francs for her brother—that's right, isn't it, Fane ? " He nods. " Good ! here is a cheque for the amount; that will cover the debt Fane owes you; the General will satisfy you that it is right enough. Take it, you   scoundrel, you contemptible cowardly cad," coming nearer Contarini, and now speaking in a voice unsteady with passion.

Contarini raises his eyebrows and absolutely laughs, as he bows in answer—" This gentleman —is he a friend of yours, Mr. Cleveland ?   I am sorry for him; he is of course mad.   You, sir" (looking at Billy), " are very kind, but I do not want your money.   Fane is my very good friend.   What do you want, poor man ? do you want to try and take away my *fiancée*, my little Ivy, that shall be my wife !   Ha ! ha ! it is good joke ! it is "——

" Look here ! " Billy says quietly, if a little pantingly, " you drop that. You know as well as I do, that you've done as dastardly an act as any fiend unhung. You can't *buy* a wife now-a-days; not an English one, anyhow.   There is your money; take it or leave it, as you like—that's your own affair; but *this*" (suddenly letting out straight at Contarini) " is *mine*, and hang me if you don't get it *hot !* "

Contarini parries one or two blows, but then Billy is upon him. Seizing him by the collar of his coat he shakes him as if he were a rat.   " My cutting-whip," he gasps. Fane hands it to him silently, and then—then for all the insults Ivy has undergone she is amply avenged.

Beyond the swish of the whip and sundry tramplings over the floor, there is not much noise, but General Lestrange, aided by a horror-struck whisper from Nora, feels that anyway he must be upon the scene. Fane opens the door cautiously to his imperious kick, and with a thrill of unrighteous satisfaction he surveys the groups before him—Contarini leaning against the wall, livid and in rags—Billy, erect and crimson, his whip still grasped firmly in his hand—Mr. Cleveland and Fane very cool apparently, though a trifle anxious.

When it is made clear to the General what it all means, his wrath knows no bounds. In a perfect storm of invective he upbraids his nephew; heaping upon him such contemptuous terms of reproach that the boy is completely cowed, knowing in his shamed humiliation that he has no word to say. Mr. Cleveland does not escape, his recent knowledge of the facts of the case justifying the General's keen indignation at being kept in total ignorance by every one. His abuse of Contarini comes out in such rich streams of scathing eloquence that even those who know him best are surprised, and realise the occasion does him credit.

"Dare, my good fellow, I am as grateful to you as a man can be expected to be to another who has defrauded him of his just and enviable rights. I am not a young man, perhaps, but—me, sir, I've strength enough to thrash half-a-dozen such as—that," indicating Contarini contemptuously.

Contarini has been watching them speechlessly. Nothing could exceed the villainous malevolence of his look. He comes forward now, and laying hold of the back of a chair, grasps it firmly as he speaks—

"Gentlemen, you are all very please with this affair—very well. This Mr. Dare, he is great bull Englishman, and because he is very strong ox, you think he is above all things gentleman. We shall see. Oh, he is very brave—he will give his money, he will fight like drunk sailor man for Mees Ivy— my Mees Ivy, his Mees Ivy. Ha! ha! I think "— sarcastically—"I will be kind to this great stupid Englishman. You Englishman, listen to me! Do you think your Mees Ivy love you? I tell you—no! Do you think I think she love me? No—no, *che!* I am no fool. You see her just now, you think she go to meet you, she is glad, you think she faint for joy that you have come, I tell you, no—no—no! Shall I tell you why she faint? shall I tell you why she go from me? shall I tell you why she is sad? Yes, I will tell—I will tell." Contarini leans forward and fixing his eyes on Billy speaks a little faster—"I am Italian—if I love it is for my pleasure, if it makes not to love again I shall not care. *I* am Italian—*you* are English. With you I think it is different. You big dog Englishman, you do not care to have wife who cannot love you! I know very well—you think Mees Ivy love you! No—no, not you, not you! She faint because I tell her that her lover—*her lover*, the poor old man with his cough and his prayers, the old *triste* Colonel Talbot— is dead."

Billy has been listening attentively, but the Italian's speech is almost unintelligible to him. His bitter venom makes itself felt—little else. Looking round on the others—"What does the fellow mean?" he asks.

"What I mean?" Contarini cries quickly, "what

I mean? You know what I mean. I mean you think Mees Ivy love you, and that is lie. She does not think of *you*. She loves always—always—always, only one—and this one I tell you is Colonel Talbot! You understand—not you, not me—*always always* Colonel Talbot!"

Over Billy's face passes an irrepressible quiver. In a minute he speaks. "Is this true?" he asks, looking at the others.

"A   lie!" shouts the General—"another of his   . lies!"

"No, uncle," Fane says with stiff lips, "it is the truth."

What matter the rolling execrations of the General—they are unheeded; for in the boy's blue eyes Billy reads the answer that seems more cruel than the grave. He stands very still, and all the hubbub round him might be the crashing of the waves upon the shore, then he draws himself up to his full height, with a strong might that made even the men feel uncomfortably choky. He turns to the Italian, and looking him straight in the eyes, says with splendid self-control—

"You are right, sir ; you say perhaps Englishmen and Italians are not alike. I don't think they are. I utterly refuse to discuss Miss Peyton with you, only would have you know that she is at perfect liberty to—to love whom she will. She is in *no* way bound to me—I am nothing to her." How still he is and how strong.

Mr. Cleveland is silently admiring the man's "grit." As Contarini looks up and remarks, "You are prepared, signor, to meet me to-morrow morning," Billy merely nods carelessly.

"If you will allow me. Mr. Dare, I should be proud to act as your second and arrange matters for you," Mr. Cleveland says at once.

"Thank you, much obliged. I don't know much about this sort of thing. You understand the necessary etiquette. You can let me know if you want me. Do as you will, only let it be as soon as possible. Come, Fane, come along, I want to go and get a drink," and Billy shakes Mr. Cleveland warmly by the hand and walks off.

It is very mean, horridly mean, Nora thinks, the way in which men keep all their excitement to themselves. Here has she prowled, waiting for a crumb of intelligence, and then Billy and Fane march out calmly and go off with irritating tameness to "get a drink." "And I thought they would come reeling out covered with blood and mad for swords," she ejaculates with disgust.

Bloodthirsty young damsel, you have a measure of satisfaction in store for you. The ball is pronounced a splendid success, and is kept up with spirit. Ivy is safely hustled upstairs without hearing of Billy's arrival, or attracting any one's attention. She is informed that Contarini had been misinformed, for Colonel Talbot was just the same, " of course very ill and Dr. Martin with him, but certainly, oh certainly he is 'about the same,'" Mrs. Cleveland assures her, having heard the ruthless falsehood that had so upset the miserable little girl. Nora, having fallen a prey to an obdurate partner, perforce must dance, and misses the vision of a tattered Contarini that flees past Mrs. Cleveland out to the blessed darkness of the garden. She is talking blandly to a deaf old gentleman; the conversation requires much facial expression and a little shouting, but it is not as trying as one might imagine, for it is quite possible at the same time to keep one ear cocked for the sound of her husband's voice.

Mr. Cleveland is speaking. "Of course it is a mistake," he says, "but the General is to blame. He let out that Italians always think a fellow a tailor if he can't handle a sword. So nothing will do *but* swords! They say Dare is an A1 shot, so is Contarini. However, Dare won't hear of anything but swords, and knows as much of fencing as I of surgery. It is a species of bounce, but I like the fellow all the better for it." Then taking Captain Smarte-Payce's arm the two men walk off together.

"Nora," Mrs. Cleveland whispers, as they stand speeding with smiles departing guests, "I kept my promise to you in spite of Vyner's protestations. All this mystery has been a miserable mistake, and now has led to—murder!"

"What!" with a clutch.

"The same thing, Nora dear—a duel!"

CHAPTER XVII.

" I think if thou couldst see
    With thy dim mortal sight,
How meanings dark to thee
    Are shadows hiding light,
Truth's efforts crossed and vexed,
Life's purpose all perplex'd,
    If thou couldst see them right,
I think that they would seem all clear, and wise, and bright.

" And yet thou canst not know,
    And yet thou canst not see
Wisdom and sight are slow
    In poor humanity.
If thou couldst *trust*, poor soul,
In Him who rules the whole,
    Thou couldst find peace and rest.
Wisdom and sight are well : but trust is best."
                              —ADELAIDE PROCTOR.

THE Carnival is over. Venetian masts, scaffoldings,
and portions of triumphant arches give to deserted
streets the dissipated air of a ballroom by daylight,
when glittering candles, faded flowers, and frag-
ment-strewn floor fill one with a curious shrinking
at unblushing incongruity.

Banners, bunting, and coloured rugs may still
hang in scattered disorder from balconies and
windows. The Corso may yet be strewn with
withered flowers; and rifts of coloured paper lie in
every angle and gutter, but they impart no air of
gaiety—rather desolation. No late revellers are
singing snatches of song; no early shopmen are
busy erecting stands, and disposing wares on their
several stalls. Restaurants and cafés are alike
closed. After the mad fever of excitement and
continuous revel of these last few days, the whole
place seems sunk in sleep.

An absolute stillness holds the hushed earth in

mute suspense, not a leaf quivers, not a creature rustles in the rank grass, no single pipe of early bird breaks the intense silence. The mountains, wrapped in their eternal calm, rear snowy crests, serene, stainless, up to the tranquil sky, where pale stars are fading in the hazy veil of deepening light that ushers in the dawn.

In a walled garden behind a villa, where enthusiasts have devoted the central space to the demands of lawn-tennis, there are others too who are waiting, like the hushed world round them, for the coming of the day. Wrapped in greatcoats, several men are pacing the gravel courts, conversing in low tones; the constant glances at the sky overhead and the comparing of watches proclaims the fact that light is scarcely " up to time."

A little apart, Billy is standing with his arm through Fane's. The boy's face is wretched, and it is all that he can do to keep the tears out of his eyes; welling up in his heart is so great an admiration, so strong an affection for this great big fellow at his side, that he is taking refuge in silence, feeling wretchedly conscious that all his penitent regrets would only choke him in their utterance. Billy is so strangely unimpressed, rather absent perhaps, but when recalled to the present, courteously attentive, listening with a good-natured smile and such complete nonchalance, that one would imagine the matter in hand was of very trifling importance indeed. He listens while the seconds discuss the supreme question of the light, arrange all preliminaries, and carefully examine the ground, but he offers no suggestions, and indeed seems to care very little about the matter, except once remarking that "Surely time was up, and they could see well enough now."

Fane is an impressionable youth, with quick kindly feelings under his calm conceit and satisfied selfishness. He had never liked Billy Dare before; the cool indifference or silent contempt he had always shown towards him had irritated him intensely, though for "Teddy's rough diamond" he professed to care not a straw. Now, however, the case was different. Without any self-assertiveness, without any bluster or brag, Billy seemed to have stepped from the quietude of his natural obscurity into a position of enviable notoriety. Certainly fate in the attractive person of Nora had forced this *rôle* upon him; but from the moment when he learnt the truth from Fane's own lips in the garden last night, he had acted with a prompt determination and cool self-reliance that excited the boy's admiration. That Contarini had dealt him a blow, more deadly than any he had received when he proclaimed Ivy's affection for Colonel Talbot, Fane also knew; and the silent endurance and gentle quietness of the man seemed no longer the evidence of stupidity, but of strength. There are so many things that he would like to say—so many matters all unexplained, and that must appear to Billy incomprehensible; but there is no time; and oddly enough, from the mesh of misunderstanding in which he must be involved, Billy does not appear in the least anxious to emerge. Poor Billy! he knows one thing, and to him it seems everything. He knows that his dream is over, his hope vain. The gladness of his brief greeting had raised him to the summit of delight, only to he thrust into the outer darkness of despair when from his maddened rival he learned the truth. What did explanations matter to him now? Of what use were regrets or repinings? Failure and loss had come to him in the place of success and gain; it seemed hard somehow, but he was scarcely in a condition to analyse the situation, only dominated by the stubborn courage that strove in silence to conceal the fact of having received a " facer."

To Fane the hour is an experience so unique, so vivid, that it lives in his memory as a distinct revelation. The very nasturtiums growing in the plaster vase on the pedestal against which he is leaning become woven into his sensations, and for ever after bring back to him in the scent of their gaudy blossoms the whole details of the scene.

He wonders how his uncle can smoke so calmly as he stands here in silence by his side. De la Valliere, the doctor, and Mr. Cleveland appear to take the whole thing very coolly too; and were it not that there is that in Contarini's expression which forbids the thought, the affair might seem only some absurd farce. This is the first duel he has ever witnessed, and as he watches the two men fencing in this still hour of early morning, he is regretfully aware that the tragic glamour he had expected has faded for ever in the face of this crude reality. Even to his inexperienced eyes it is patent that Billy is no match for his opponent. Contarini seems but to dally with the Englishman, to place him at a disadvantage over and over again, merely to set forth his superior skill; and his contempt for his adversary is plainly expressed in his smile, that has in it something of insolence.   Contarini is perfectly cool; Billy, conscious of his inferiority, is gradually losing his self-control. Fane is bewildered, and an odd sensation makes him feel as if the whole garden were throbbing with his own excitement. A few quick passes, a sudden step forward on the part of Mr. Cleveland, a sharp thrust from Contarini, and then Billy stumbles heavily backwards to the ground.

Even while Fane springs to him, and a cry breaks from his lips, ten thousand carts seem to be unloading bricks against the garden-walls. The plaster vase reels from its pedestal, and is crashed into fragments as it falls. A low roar rolls in grating reverberations under the ground at their feet, and then the whole place heaves and shudders, while the stone walls tremble and totter, falling in yawning gaps across the well-kept paths.

Too astounded for speech, Fane just feels his uncle's grasp on his arm as the General ejaculates, "Good God! an earthquake!" The General's pipe is still alight, and as he turns deliberately towards the villa, he draws at it involuntarily. It is the act of a moment, but even as they turn, the house rolls, and with a quiver rights itself by a swaying lurch, sending the entire roof slipping off it to the ground. Chimneys, tiles, plastering, showers of broken glass and starting window-frames flash across Fane's horrified vision, and then, with a sharp cry of consternation, Contarini, shouting something unintelligible in Italian, dashes past them through the little door by which they had entered, and under the still shaking house out to the open street.

De la Valliere, with every expression of terror,

is standing in the centre of the open space, with wild eyes watching the flying missiles that are hurling round him. Better remain where he is than rush into the more dangerous street, he deems; so, panic-stricken, he stays.

The doctor kneels at Billy's side, and is binding up the wound that has dyed his white shirt crimson. Mr. Cleveland is beside him, and no word passes between him and the General as they assist the doctor, and watch the big, half-conscious fellow, looking so tall and powerful as he lies here at their feet.

"Go and see, Fane, if the carriage is where we left it, or if that scoundrel has fled."

Through the empty and now dilapidated villa Fane runs. Emerging into the roadway leading to the town, he becomes at once aware of the general panic. From every corner people are rushing madly; yells, execrations, and shrieks ring out from all quarters, and half-clad creatures are darting in aimless terror in every direction. Catching sight of a *fiacre* at a distance, Fane pursues it, and ousting the driver by main force, whips up the miserable old horse into an unaccustomed gallop until he halts at the open door. Shouting to his uncle, he keeps guard over his prize until slowly they come out to him.

Billy is quite himself now, and, as they help him into the carriage, he smiles at the boy with rather a pitiful attempt at cheerfulness. "Go ahead," he says, "I'm all right;" and Fane, giving his attention entirely to the still panting horse, carefully refrains from another look at his friend.

Animated by a thousand fears for those left

behind, and desirous of getting Billy safely out of sight, Fane hurries the old animal along at a good round pace, and hustling through panic-stricken fugitives, gallops down the long white road that leads to the hotel. General Lestrange and Mr. Cleveland are crushed into the small carriage, and keep a sort of protective guardianship over Billy—not with the tender officiousness of women, but in the rough, undemonstrative manner of men. Each moment adds to their uneasiness, for on all sides wreckage and ruin meet their view. Garden-walls lie in heaps, giving peeps of dilapidated houses beyond; entire windows protrude their broken frames, as if just pinched out by the strong grip of the surrounding masonry. Groups of curiously-enveloped human beings are gathered in every open space, or fleeing in terror from streets and alleys to the sea-shore.

Climbing the short ascent that leads with a sharp turn to the front of the hotel, Fane stops.

Beyond the gravel sweep directly before the door, scattered along the winding walks, and forming grotesque groups in every open place, all the hotel inmates are gathered. Sofas, chairs, and benches have been carried out into the roofless haven of the garden, and on improvised beds invalids are lying almost buried under their coverings of rugs. Several ladies in conventional night attire are evidently playing at the popular game of "follow my leader," for with childlike fidelity the slippered leader, trotting along with a little jewel-case in one hand and grasping the corner of a blanket that sweeps royally behind her in the other; is unhesitatingly imitated by a few others identically the same as regards garment and garniture. Passing this trotting string of distressed dames, General Lestrange pressed onward to where, sheltered by a cluster of rhododendrons, he sees two blue dressing-gowns that seem familiar. As he nears this chair encampment, Gwendoline suddenly perceives him. She flies towards him with outstretched hands, her long fair hair hanging in half untwisted plaits far below her waist. She is very pale, and the tears rush to her eyes as she throws herself into her father's arms. "Oh, father, it was so dreadful, and we could not open the door."

"Never mind, my pet; all are safe now, I see. Don't cry, my pretty one. What a wan little Ophelia it is!" smoothing back the thick heavy tresses tenderly; then, with his arm round her, he moved on to where Mrs. Lestrange sat wrapped comfortably in a long fur cloak. "Well, Amy," he says; but as he clasps her hand and bends over her to arrange the·rugs more comfortably, the look that passes between them has all the eloquence that so rarely finds expression in words. His whispered conversation is unheard by Sybil and Mrs. Cleveland, who are engaged in manufacturing an elaborate couch out of two iron benches and some heavy chairs. With a collection of pillows, shawls, &c., they succeed in converting the uncomfortable materials into a veritable nest, where they ensconce themselves with much careful deliberation. "Come, Gwennie, pull your cloak round you and climb in. Hammond has ordered coffee brought here, father, and when you have all completed your toilet, I suppose you will join us at breakfast—eh, father?" Sybil questions, smiling.

Mrs. Cleveland looks at the General. " Yes, you have been some time about your toilets to-day. National coolness, was it? Vyner and Fane have been deliberating upon a choice of garments, or the colour of their ties, I suppose ?" She speaks lightly, but looks appealingly at him, and is crushing the heavy folds of a rug with nervous fingers while waiting for his answer.

"They are all right," he answered, looking at her, "but—but they are looking after a young fellow who was hurt somehow. Nasty blow, knocked him senseless, and they won't allow him in the hotel, as they say it is not safe. He is on a bed somewhere out here, and Martin with him."

He spoke easily in a comfortable tone; but disentangling herself and throwing off the cosy coverings, Mrs. Cleveland rose at once, and calling out "Don't drink my coffee," walked rapidly away.

Taking the path indicated by the General, she passed groups of people with a hasty survey, encamped in family parties all along the garden-walks. Many ridiculous sights and absurd situations brought an involuntary smile to her lips, but a gravity that was not born of the universal dread was upon her, and in increasing anxiety she pressed onward, longing to catch a glimpse of her husband. All round the central flower-beds, under the motionless palms, along the orange-walk, and down several myrtle-bordered paths she passed hurriedly. Again and again some knot of people have been mistaken for those she is in search of; and at last, feeling convinced that, notwithstanding obstruction, the "young fellow who has been hurt" must have been conveyed under cover, she turned abruptly, and passing Gianni's shed, and through the aloe hedge that divided the hotel from the dependance, wheeled round on to a lower plateau reached by a short flight of stone steps. Here the scene is far quieter, doors and windows stand open, and a few articles of wearing apparel are littered about, but there is no one to be seen. A little farther, and with a dumb expression of consternation she shrinks back behind the shelter of a large seringa. The plateau on which the dependance is built sweeps back on the right, and is built up in a solid bank and strengthened by a high wall running up the ridge, until lost to view in the olive woods above. The bank, wall, and about half of the ground before the low building have entirely disappeared, half the plateau having slipped into the narrow road below, completely blocking it. A slope of earth with the roots of shrubs standing out against the shore-line, and tree tops and flat-roofed houses sweeps away here at her feet; and past the low verandah of the dependance on her left, against a background of camelias she espies—Nora and Ivy!

Hurrying forward, she lays her hand on Nora's arm. The girl turns a startled white face to hers. "We came upon him accidentally up there," she says, indicating the hotel terrace above. "He knew her; he wants to speak to her; they brought him here, and now—now he cannot speak—he is dying."

Mrs. Cleveland puts both hands up to her forehead; pressing her fingers against her temples, she stands a moment with bowed head, overcome by a passionate regret, and then with one hand loosening the strain of the heavy cloak at her throat, she moves hesitatingly forward.

With her back to the treacherous land-slip, the gardens, and houses below, with her little dishevelled head and grey-robed figure distinctly outlined against the broad sweep of the glassy sea, with hands clasped in agonised passion, wide-fixed tearless eyes and pale parted lips, stands Ivy.

Propped up against a pile of cushions on a couch before her is a man wrapped up closely in a huge astracan-lined coat. Above its heavy collar a face blanched with the hue of coming death is turned to her, as if in mute entreaty. A great throb of gratitude makes Mrs. Cleveland close her eyes in sudden relief as she recognises in the man before her, not the " poor young fellow," whose blue eyes, dim with tenderness, have haunted her ever since she had seen him bending over Ivy last night, no, not the young strong Billy Dare, but only—yes, only poor Colonel Talbot. She involuntarily steps nearer. Old Lee, standing at the foot of the sofa, has his eyes fixed upon his master's face, and watching in breathless silence every fleeting change of expression, has no thought for anything else in the world. Mechanically Dora brushes her hand across her eyes. What a scene! What an hour! The first fright and horror of her waking; the weird half-crazy figures flitting about everywhere; the comical creatures that danced across her recollection like grotesque characters on magic-lantern slides; the horrible anxiety about this miserable duel; the uncertainty and suspense—it was like the ever-increasing chaos of a fearful dream; and then the sudden silence and this terrible stillness. She looked round nervously. Not a leaf trembled overhead. Jasmine tendrils stretched wreathen sprays unflutteringly from out the terrace walls into the cloudless blue. A graceful date-palm might have been carved in marble as it stood in motionless majesty between her and the sea. It was unreal, a weight of oppression deadened her faculties, some spell was being cast over the land. Oh, horrible! they were being magnetised into the silent sleep of death. She felt half-paralysed, and then a soft sigh broke from her thankfully.

Over the line of terraced walls, over the low broken ridge on her right, behind the date-palm and that small motionless figure swept a sudden flood of palpitating light. A wave of golden sunbeams showered through the silence, an echo of life and glory; brighter and brighter grew the land, and the dimness even here has departed. With the divine touch that beautifies all, the sunbeams are flashing on broken window-panes and rent earth, decking them with lavish tenderness in a glory not their own.

Over the date-palm already is woven a network of delicate shadows, and round the ruffled tresses of Ivy's bare head glows a halo of dazzling light. Behind her the limpid ocean is barred with lines of colour, as the world blushes into more radiant beauty at the warm kiss of the day.

And over that deathly face, too, has passed a change. Leaning a little forward, the dark eyes, full of wonderful light, the man gazes in earnest sweet serenity at the little piteous figure before him. The full glory of the rising sun illumines his face, and flashes a sheen of living colour over features blanched by the touch of death.

This little grey figure stands full in the blaze of golden light, an aureole of sunbeams twined lovingly in the tangle of her hair. As he sees her standing thus, outlined against the flood of dazzling sunshine, he stretches out his hand to her and speaks with evident labour, but quite clearly.

" Good-bye   dear child   God bless you. I —I understand all—*now*. Me you will forgive, and you ?—God keep you always—in the sunlight," he smiles a bright calm smile as he utters his farewell, but with a little sharp cry Ivy bows down her head upon his hand that she holds in both her own, and an uncontrollable sob breaks from her lips. Stooping forward, Colonel Talbot kisses the little bowed head slowly, then—then a nerveless hand falls from Ivy's grasp, and Mrs. Cleveland holds her closely—oh, so closely !—clasped tenderly in her arms.

Drawing Ivy away in her protecting grasp, she turns to leave the spot. Straining the little figure to her in breathless terror, she stands motionless. Here, not two feet from her, in front of Nora, is standing—Billy !

He is a little pale, and as his eyes meet Mrs. Cleveland's he smiles rather defiantly. His left arm is in a sling, and his heavy ulster hangs over it loosely. His expression is not easy to read, and Mrs. Cleveland, dreading another shock for Ivy, would have passed him with a mute appeal for silence, but at this moment the girl slowly lifts her bowed head from Dora's arm and sees him.

A terrified cry breaks from her lips, and with wide frightened eyes she gazes at him for several minutes in speechless bewilderment. With a pathetic gesture she presses one hand over her heart, while Mrs. Cleveland holds her other firmly in her soft grasp. No word comes from Billy, his eyes are fixed in longing bitterness upon the pale small face he loves too well. At last uncertainly, in choked unsteady tones, words come from Ivy's trembling lips.

"You—are hurt, Billy, and what are you doing here?"

He does not move any nearer, only at the sound of her voice a softer expression sweeps over his face.

"It is nothing," he says shortly. "A beam struck my shoulder and dislocated it, so I have to wear a sling."

"But—where were you? Were you—here? When did you come?" breathlessly.

"I came last night on business for a fellow I know at home. It was entirely a money transaction, in which this fellow had got mixed up with some foreigners." He hesitates a little here.

"Well?" quickly.

"Well," firmly, "I came too late; the gang of scoundrels had already been discovered and forced to fly, and the head of the whole concern, a fellow called Contarini, escaped this morning in the general confusion, and will never dare to show himself in Europe again." As he finishes, he looks from Ivy to Mrs. Cleveland, and smiles a little haughtily, as if to say, "I defy you to contradict that!"

Dora, however, attempts nothing of the kind, only with a swift appealing glance at him she says, "I think Ivy is hardly able to bear any more conversation just now. I want her to come with me," and drawing the girl towards her, she

T

would have moved on. Ivy, however, remains trans-fixed and gazes into Billy's eyes with a world of doubting bewilderment in her own.

Swiftly stepping nearer him, she lays one hand convulsively upon his arm ; over her pale face passes a sudden light, then incredulous hopeless-ness kills the fleeting eagerness, as she whispers in low tones that struggle to be calm, " Of course you could not mean that ; you didn't mean *Count* Contarini just now—not that he had gone—not that he will never come back any more ? You could not—could not mean *that ?* " piteously.

A fixed, hard look came over Billy's face as he felt Ivy's clinging touch upon his arm. Looking down upon her, he replied, apparently quite un-moved, " There is no mistake. Count Contarini has gone, never to return."

A moment those little fingers tighten their hold upon his sleeve, the brown eyes look searchingly, imploringly into his, then Ivy threw back her head and stood erect, with one band slipped into the fur collar of her peignoir. Standing so, she struggled with a rush of emotion that almost over-whelmed her ; across the fleeting lights and shadows of her ever-changing face came a flood of gratitude that filled her eyes with tears. " It is true—it is true," she murmured, "and I am free !" Almost proudly she uttered the last words, and then some rapid thought flashed a great agony into her wide-open eyes ; and raising one hand to her temples, she gave a bitter little cry, as with a swift unex-pected movement she darted past Billy and round the ruined dependance, running with desperate fierceness up and across the hotel garden, on and upwards into the dense olive woods, deserted and silent on the slopes above.

A strong passion seemed to possess Ivy as she scrambled up banks and broken walls from one half-ruined terrace, knee deep in grass and flowers, to yet another higher and ever higher. Her little stockingless feet were cut by the sharp stones that pierced her thin slippers; and long trailing sprays of briers and thorny undergrowth tore her bare ankles remorselessly; yet wrenching free the soft grey peignoir from every spiky hindrance, she climbed on until the limit of the wood was reached, and under the clear sky she stood at last on the rounded shoulder of the ridge, that, joining here another tongue of land, formed one of the irregular spurs of the mountain chain behind. On her right ran the narrow gully with its deep walled road, blocked far down below her by the landslip near the dependance. Farther away on this side, the lovely range of Cannes hills were bathed in shimmering hues of morning's early light. The wooded tongue of land known as Cape St. Martin run in bosky softness out into the glassy blueness of the soft sleeping sea; and the jutting promontory of Monaco, and all the sweeping lines of mountain gorge and curving shore, were traced in lucid harmonies by the clear fine touches of that great master (an early one perforce), and that is—morning.

The wealth of loveliness unrolled before her brought no answering gladness into Ivy's eyes. Almost blankly they travel over the fair scene on her right, and then are turned to where the "red rocks" are glowing pink, and Bordighera lies a violet bar under the rising sun upon her left.

Springing from the ground, where she had thrown herself down after her weary climb, she stands erect with her hands flung up above her head. White and rigid is her face, her attitude might suggest supplication, but there is only protesting defiance in the passionate words she seems to hurl upwards into the vastness of that blue vault above.

"For nothing! for nothing! to suffer so for—nothing," she cried out, bitterly. "Ah!" clasping both hands behind her head, "I was too happy, I suppose. They say each soul must be broken by sorrow before it can learn to love. It is not true! I tell you it is not true!"

"Oh," spreading out her hands with wide entreaty to the far-smiling ocean, "speak, you quiet sea. In calm as well as in tempest, does not life teach us love?"

The blue waters gleamed an unruffled plain below. No answer came from the stillness of their deeps, nor a whisper from the curling lips that caressed the pebbly shore. Above the coldly smiling sea, under the blankness of that boundless blue, whose vast infinity dwarfed this little earth to nothingness, suffered and struggled one little human soul. *One* soul! suffered only *one* soul! Ah! God, whence comes the universal moan making the lives of millions unvarying misery? Omnipotent queen, deathless sorrow, crown with your thorny wreath this little bowed head, stamp on brow and lips the erasable seal of suffering, take from yet another heart its treasures of hope and joyous gladness, and teach it that only through crystal tears can it gaze on blinding truth. "O God," Ivy cried wildly, "what have I done that you should punish me like this?"

She shrunk back, and, with her hands clasped over her eyes, seemed to be waiting in trembling awe the answer to her passionate words. "Ah!" it fell from her lips drearily, as with hopeless wretchedness she flung herself down, burying her face in her hands and lying motionless, half hidden among the tangle of weeds and grass.

The placid sea, the unresponsive earth, the vast void above her, were alike silent. And the Eternal God also. He who spoke in every whisper of life's countless voices, to-day, to-day, He had cast her into the outer darkness of absolute silence, the darkness that may be felt—the black valley of despair.

A little bird, perched on a neighbouring bush, glanced down with his bright round eyes at the still grey figure lying low in the grass. With the extreme caution of an unprotected foreign bird, distrusting everything in human shape, he hesitated long ere giving vent to his "cheep cheep" of sympathy. With a little nervous flutter he got through it, however, and then, frightened at his own temerity, flew away. His tiny trumpet-blast woke in the numbed chambers of Ivy's consciousness a throng of hurrying thoughts. Thought thrilled dormant passion; and she lay racked by the memories of recent events and new experiences, mingled in such inextricable confusion, that pride and hate, love and bitterness, longing and remorse, tortured her in their fierce struggle—a warfare so overpowering and remorseless, that only a sullen resolution to passively resist crept with chill defiance over the poor little heart. She had always been happy—*always*. She had a right to expect happiness, to demand it. Others were happy, why not she? Why had love only come to her at the very portals of death? Why had she been made to suffer for the faults of others? Why had she been racked by the long struggle between desire and duty, self-seeking or self-sacrifice, if it were quite an unnecessary and superfluous exercise of suffering? What was the use of it all? Had any good been attained by it? None! Fane would under any circumstances have been freed from Contarini, and all her bitter humiliating surrender was so much high purpose thrown away! Ideal action looked only childishly ridiculous in the clear light of common sense; she had played the part of a silly coquette, mistaking it for the highest *rôle* of bartering everything for duty. And what was it really? in what light must she appear to others? Surely as a girl who, unable to appreciate anything truly worthy of love or reverence, had been dazzled, like dozens of others, by a handsome face and insinuating manners, and had only been delivered from the spells of this soulless puppet by a happy combination of circumstances. Oh, it was bitter; it was not to be borne! Oh, where is the comfort of self-esteem when you are conscious that to the eyes of all others you are playing the part of a pitiable fool? Ivy clenched her teeth firmly, and covered her burning cheeks with her cold little hands. She lay motionless and stiff, battling with a bitter struggle of scorn and shame. Oh, she had wanted to act so, so *nobly!* Yes, she had wanted to act in such a way that she might feel worthier of Colonel Talbot. Yes, of course she had never thought, never dreamed she would be anything to him but one of the crowd of poor insignificant commonplace people above whom he towered so immeasurably; only she had visions of a time when this great prophet of denial should look from his high range of iron right, and see far, oh! far below him, toiling in the path himself had trod, a poor little tired pilgrim, climbing with slow labour but dauntless trust, the stony stairs of duty. Then, oh! *then* he would have looked down upon her and said, "You were governed by no fleeting fancies. I read you now aright. I have learned your motives, child, and now I know."

Across her dizzy dreamings flashed the words of his farewell, "I understand all *now*." The seething whirl of storm-tossed fancies, that only dazzled as they branded their hideous passions into her tired brain, hushed their ghoul-like dancing, and died out as glowing torches are extinguished one by one. A great hush held her consciousness captive, then gradually, like stars in a twilight sky, pale and passionless passed before her memories of the dead.

A long while she lay with her face buried in her hands, listening in a tempest of tears to these voices of the past; then wearily half rising, she leant back against a lichen-covered rock, and looked up into the tranquil sky with a slow, sad smile. He *knew!* He understood! Nothing mattered very much now. The bitter tears she had shed and the sorrows she had endured were but as trifles compared with the great knowledge that had come to her. To realise that misconceptions and misrepresentations had no more power to pain; that in the clearness of that light where "we shall know even as we are known," subterfuge and shadow can never come. Was not this enough ?

We agree with Novalis, that "to know a truth well, one must have fought it out." But at twenty such struggles sorely tax one's strength, and comfortable commonplace facts seem more satisfying than unrealised ideas; only sometimes we are suffered to see things as they *are* and *not* as they *seem*; and then life's bitterest gall and death's relentless cruelty become but as motes in the golden sunbeams that sweep through the vastness of time, and ultimate good and everlasting right work out by grand eternal laws framed by a changeless love. And when we have learnt these things, and truth has taught us trust, the dimness dies in the day's clear light that dawns on the night of sorrow.

CHAPTER XVIII.

" The blue of heaven is larger than the cloud."
—MRS. BROWNING.

" Let thistles grow instead of wheat, and cockle instead of barley. The words of Job are ended."

" Helpful care, a mother's perfect sway."
CHARLES KINGSLEY.

CHILL in the deepening dusk felt the breeze that swept with tender remorseful touch through the deserted woods. The light on this short December day was fading already in the western sky, and above the low-banked sullen clouds only faint tints of dying glory lingered to bless the sorrowing land.

Lights began to gleam from cottage windows; and rolling uplands and distant ridges grew more mistily indistinct beyond the rough stone wall and near foreground of winding road, where, leaning on the little gate that opened from a square of cottage garden into the highroad, was Ivy.

There was a greater gravity about the small face, and the listless attitude bespoke a weariness and dejection that had been undreamed of in the sunny days long ago—ages ago now it seemed; and yet, counted in measures of regular time, it would not make two years, though from the gladness of youth the present was divided by a chasm deep as the grave.

How lonely, how miserable, how deserted the whole world looked! The last faint flush faded from the western sky, as slowly ebbing life pales in the shades of death. Drear and grey grew the darkening land, and the little squares of lighted windows served but to make the surrounding scene more dim. The colourless quietude of daily life seemed never more oppressive than at this hour, while Ivy stood idly dreaming, letting her personality drift, so to speak, unprotesting, unresisting, into the passionless torpor of the dying day. Oh, yes, it was over now, and there was no use in repining; she had had her measure of happiness, heaped up and overflowing, all through the golden years of her glad youth; and now—now that life lay before her, no longer in a sunny haze of possibilities, but stretching far into the dull level of monotony, she must endure the coming shadows; and further, be for ever thankful that for so long a while her steps had been stayed in the light. Poor little Ivy! she had been making a brave fight for resignation during the long months that dragged their glorious days through exceptionally lovely seasons. The return home after the foreign tour had been like gaining a placid harbour, when broken and spent by storms, and the consciousness of returning to her mother's keeping restored the old restful sensation of resigning responsibility, and living again, untroubled by scruples or harassing moral perplexities, a life of unquestioning calm. In the undeviating routine of home-duties, Ivy found the necessary counteracting influence for combating morbid depression, and in the healthy optimism of her father the moral tonic she needed. But with all the best endeavours and most strenuous resolves, the present could not fail to appear terribly dull and triste, and the plain highroad of common duty very wearying indeed. Well indeed for Ivy that her mother understood her so well, as through long months she helped her to regain quietude and content by perfect sympathy and comprehensive love.

As at this moment Mrs. Peyton closed the cottage door behind her and passed out into the darkness, her heart was full of loving tenderness for the listless little figure that seemed so lonely leaning against the gate. She longed to be able to take every burden, and ache, and sorrow away from the heart of her child. It seemed so terrible to see her children suffer, and be powerless to prevent it. She would so gladly drink their allotted bitterness, and give them her own content. But she never thought of repining, no bitter regrets passed her lips at the troubles through which her dear little daughter had been made—it almost seemed unnecessarily—to pass. There were lessons that perhaps could never be taught while hedged about with all the careful barriers of home; and these lessons that life must *sometimes* teach, had not Ivy been learning them lately, when, beyond the range of her parents' protection, she had, nevertheless, been perfectly secure in the all-powerful guardianship of God? Ah! truly the tender discipline of home would never mould loving, joyous children into heroes and heroines. No; time and circumstance are the tools life uses in her forge of slow experience to bend, and to beat, and through trouble to temper the tried metal to nobler use, and thus the work that breaking hearts and trembling hands could never do, is done so effectually for them by the relentless anvil of universal suffering.

As Mrs. Peyton fastened the latch of the cottage door behind her, Ivy rose from her leaning posture, and turning to her mother, smiled in the darkness. The very presence of a great soul seems to bring a wonderful sense of security and strength, and the sweep of her mother's gown, brushing the stone-flagged path, passed a spirit wand over the discontent of Ivy's dreaming, banishing all cobwebs of distrust by the mere motion of her coming.

"You must be quite cold, darling, waiting. Have you been here long?"

"Oh, no!" (it does not seem long now). "I took Mary Budd the pudding; saw Grannie, but couldn't talk, mother, for the old thing kept up a continuous cough the whole time, and Joe roared louder than ever, and every two seconds kept asking me if I didn't think *at last* the old 'oman was breaking up? And really, mother, trying to evade an answer one imagines would be heartless only irritates. Would you believe it? Grannie almost *burst* with indignation when I said, 'Oh, I hope Grannie will be better as soon as the days get warmer.' She snapped out, in a perfect paroxysm of chokes and coughs, 'Lord! what more do 'e want. Bain't I shook a 'most in two, days and nights, with ne'er a bite inside me but what I drinks, till I be gone to a shadder, and ha'n't n' more strength than a cat, and that a be nothing! *Better* indeed! If *I* ha'n't a right to die, I dunno who 'as.' And she was quite disgusted at me, mother, for suggesting a possible recovery," and Ivy smiled as she looked up.

"Poor old Grannie!" Mrs. Peyton answered softly. "One must recognise her right to candour, for in life's real struggle, where poverty and hardship are hourly experiences, reserve appears a luxury limited to the rich. But do not think bluntness necessarily denotes absence of feeling; it is at times its mask, and you will find, even in its most repellant form, it is but a consequence of the stern teaching of their daily life. Let us be thankful for the delicate veil that enfolds ours."

"Our illusions, mother darling! Surely the sooner we lose them and see the real as it is, the better." Ivy speaks with a touch of bitterness, and her head goes up with the little defiant jerk her mother knows so well.

Mrs. Peyton holds Ivy's hand beneath her warm cloak and walks on silently. "When the flowers of

our illusions fall, we must wait awhile, my child, for
the fruit of fact to form. The real is no barren
tree," she says at last.

"The flowers were so beautiful, and the facts so
hard and sour," Ivy answers, half smiling.

"Facts need mellowing; do not judge before the
time, or your judgments must be crude and soured.
Perspective is very puzzling when we see certain
things in their absolute, not relative capacity."

"I know," Ivy sighs; "the fairest view is distorted
by bad, discoloured glass; one's mind is the dull
medium through which our impressions come. No
wonder they are so often vague and colourless.
I envy the people who plant their opinions as the
Romans did avenues, regular, unvarying, never to
be cut down or uprooted. Dogmas are hateful, but
they must be a strong solace to those who hold
them. A kaleidoscopic mind like mine, that changes
at every new jar, is particularly embarrassing."

"Never mind the jarring," Mrs. Peyton answers,
smiling; "there is only uniformity in life for the
colour-blind; progress is a series of surprises."

"I want shaking up, I expect," Ivy replies. "I
feel monotonous. I think a vivid surprise would be
agreeable."

"Shall I ask your Aunt Amy to let Gwendoline
come and stay here for a time? I do not know if
she could be spared before they go abroad. We
might write to-day."

"Please don't! Gwennie is very dear, but she is
not 'a surprise,' mother. I know her so well, and
she is never original. She is so like a pat of butter,
the faithful copy of the last person who has smoothed
her down and stamped in their individuality. As

she has been at Tyneford, it will be a blurred outline of Lord Egerton's liberalism, and I always want that clearly defined. Oh, mother, turn up here, will you? There's—there is—good dog—Shotty dear, keep off!"

"Come here, Shot; get back. Good evening. I hope Shot did not jump up on you, Miss Peyton." Mr. Dare is shaking hands with her mother while he speaks to Ivy.

"It would not kill me if he had," she answers: "but do not distress yourself unnecessarily; he treats me with marked politeness."

She bends down to stroke the spaniel's head as she speaks, and does not apparently notice Billy's outstretched hand. He turns abruptly and walks by Mrs. Peyton's side, and strives to appear unconscious of Ivy's presence, while the conversation becomes a dialogue in which she has no part.

For countless reasons, Ivy yearns for Teddy's coming. Fane is a source of comfort now, and Sandhurst has made a marked improvement in widening his perceptions and clipping his pretensions; but he can never take Teddy's place, and in one matter it is Teddy alone who can assist her. Billy's surliness must cease. Because the old order has changed, the new need not be a stiff neutrality. Why will he not understand that the basis that will not support love is firm enough for friendship? He is so unreasonable; he will be genial to all the rest of the family, but treat her with distant politeness. It is ridiculous. To be hated would be preferable to being ignored; it proclaims assured strength and a measure of scorn. Teddy must inject common-sense into his friend.

Why bear ill-will towards the inevitable, and seek to inflame comfortably healed wounds? It is morbid and unmanly, and unworthy of that great strong man tramping on the mother's other side. Of course she has nothing to say to him; her kindly interest only irritates, though silence scarcely soothes. Indeed, Teddy must restore peace and harmony and the old placid friendship. So mused Ivy, and wrapped in the consideration of so desirable a consummation, she unbent sufficiently to shake hands at parting with a grain of cordiality.

Billy strode savagely away. She could afford to be considerate when he had just announced that he must be away for three weeks. A sign of satisfied relief perhaps. Well, if it were not for pheasants and fox-hunting, a man might almost be driven mad by a pair of brown eyes, that contradicted their owner's clearest statements.

Mrs. Peyton rarely reverted to the past now; she knew all that its experiences had taught Ivy. She realised the magnitude of the mental crisis through which she had passed, and would never imply that its effects would be less than lasting. No alleviation is caused by doubting the depth of another's sorrow, or suggesting its bitterness is transient. Ivy's imagination had been completely enchained by the high-souled mysticism of Colonel Talbot, but she did not believe her affections were completely embalmed with his memory. Time would do much, and Teddy, with his practical sunny temper, might do more. He knew very little about Ivy's affairs and nothing of Billy's participation in " Fane's fracas," as the elder brother termed it. And Ivy too had at Billy's urgent request been kept in ignorance of his action in the affair. The repayment of his loan had been accomplished without exciting Teddy's attention, and as far as possible Billy had escaped what he appeared particularly to dread—a store of gratitude. It might be he still hoped for some other reward !

CHAPTER XIX.

" Hope is a lover's staff :
Walk hence with that and manage it against despairing thoughts."
—*Two Gentlemen of Verona.*

"WE will carry all the baskets home, Cyril, and then take the dogs for a turn, if you like." Ivy collected together a miscellaneous heap of odds and ends as she spoke, and piled them into the baskets waiting for them. It is New Year's Eve, and Ivy and small Cyril have been rejuvenating the decorations in the Church for the morrow's festival. Saturday afternoon always has a sort of tidy respectability about its preparations for the coming Sabbath. To-day, not only is there an air of satisfied content breathing in the orderly rest that has crept over the village, but a peaceful expectation seems to hover about animate and inanimate nature alike. The empty Church, decked with its evergreens and flowers, breathes of preparedness even to the soul of small Cyril, who, with satisfied industry, is sweeping the open space round the font, and vainly endeavouring to fill his dust-tray.

"I think there isn't anything more now, Ivy; it's quite ready, don't you think, 'cept the baskets?"

and Cyril stands shouldering his dusting-brush, and glowing with his late efforts.

Ivy gazes up the aisle, and lets her eyes rove round the flower-decked chancel, now dim in the fading light.

"Yes, it is all ready," she says; and then while the little boy bustles about, carrying the paraphernalia of brushes away to the vestry, and arranges the baskets to carry home, she lets her thoughts roam, hurrying with the racing hours.

From out the darkness of a great shadow this year had brought her into the calmness of a passionless twilight. She was quite content that it should be so. She only trusted it would last for always, and that the coming years would not draw down upon her a growing dimness. What! she already resented her life's darkness! Never! She knew it could never be anything but dark—no, hardly dark with such a home, and so many things she still so loved, and Teddy coming! No; she smiled, and realised that between deep gaps of regret lay spaces of very enduring satisfaction. She would not think of herself or for herself at all any more. Whenever she felt her thoughts gravitating towards selfish retrospection, she would revert to the cure she had adopted often before, and dash into some other interest at once—playing with Cyril, or still more effectually banishing useless regrets by absorbing all ideas in any book she could find. Oftentimes the most trifling rubbish and improbable adventure served best, and tore her from the introspection that must be conquered at all hazards.

"You can carry one, Ivy; me two, as I am a boy,"

Cyril says, lifting the largest basket, and clasping it affectionately, then with tottering determination stooping for a second.

"You can carry both, Cyril, but I wish you would only take one, and run on and let out the dogs—I'll follow with these;" and Cyril willingly accedes to a suggestion, not a command, and flying off, leaves Ivy to follow more slowly. As she is about to turn in at the Vicarage gate she encounters Billy. Of course, he can stay there chatting all the afternoon, since she has been safely out of the way She feels rather irritated as she nods her good-night. Billy, however, stops, and seeing her heavily weighted, asks permission to relieve her of her burden as far as the house.

"Pray don't trouble; I can manage very well. Do not let me detain you," Ivy says, in a cool tone.

"This short distance will scarcely detain me, and I should insist on helping any lady," Billy replies equally coolly, laying his hand on the baskets, and calmly taking them from her. They walk in silence up the drive, save for Billy's dogs, whose yelping and effusive greeting to Ivy is a welcome relief. As, however, a dear spaniel and leggy setter leap aggressively upon her in the exuberance of their joy, Billy shouts at them angrily—"Down, you brutes. Get out, Blucher! Keep off, Shot! Get away with you!"

The dogs slink off with lowered tails and up-turned pleading eyes, and Ivy bites her lip, and unreasoningly winces at what seems another sign of hostility, since even his dogs must not be her friends.

As the baskets are placed in the Hall, Cyril races round to the front of the house with Rollick, Dormat, and Dick."

"Tea has gone in, Ivy," he shouts, "so we are only to take them across the field and back. Oh! you're not going!" as Billy begins looking round for his dogs, and steps a little apart. "Oh, *don't* go; I want to race all the dogs together. Oh, I'm the huntsman, and they are my pack of hounds, and I'm going to practice keeping them all together"—cracking his dog-whip, and looking up eagerly into Billy's face. "Only *one* run?" he says pleadingly; and as Billy smiles at his eagerness, he gives a war whoop of delight, and tears off with his rampaging pack gyrating frantically round him. Ivy follows slowly, and as she tramps over the short grass, wonders why it is that conversation seems so impossible with Billy now. He walks by her side, but his eyes are upon the leaping dogs and the yelling child, and he hardly seems to know that she is even there. Well, she will not talk either. So they walk over the brown, dull grass speechlessly, and halt by the further wall waiting for Cyril.

After several frantic dashes which excite his unruly crew, and send them far afield, necessitating an instant halt, and futile efforts at restraining them, the little boy relinquishes the vain attempt, and returns to the silent two crimson and panting. "I'd like to be a huntsman all the same," he says, "but you couldn't keep them from running all over the place if they've not been broken in properly, could you?"—to Billy.

"No, I'm sure I couldn't. Hullo! what are they after—a rabbit?"—as with quick short yelps of excitement the dogs race for a flying object tearing down a distant field—all sweeping along in scattered flight, tailing away to the fat and now excited Dick, who is puffing painfully in the laudable endeavour to show he still retains some love of sport, and by no means regards his day as over yet.

The dogs are left to themselves; and after a rush of Cyril's to see the chase, he returns and rejoins the other two walking demurely back to the house. He is so thoroughly at home with Billy that he skips along chatting ceaselessly, until passing a big beech-tree, a few whirling dead leaves attract his attention.

"Catch them!" he cries, making erratic leaps in his endeavours to secure the fluttering dried fragments; "catch them! This is the last day you can catch 'happy months,' remember."

"What do you mean?" Billy asks, smiling.

"Don't you know?" with an amazed face. "You must catch them when they're flying off the tree, and if you catch twelve before the New Year, you'll have twelve happy months. I've caught all mine. It's very difficult, and Ivy wouldn't try; but it's a most important thing if you *want* to be happy," Cyril concludes sagely.

A gust of wind blows down a shower of curled-up morsels that once had been soft sweet leaves. As one flutters close to Ivy she stretches out her hand involuntarily, endeavouring to grasp it, but it whisks off at a tangent, and with a smile she shakes her head at the little boy as she says, "No use."

"You don't *try*," Cyril shouts, as he grabs wildly in every direction. "You've got to try *hard* if you want to be happy, 'cause nothing comes for wishing, you know."

Ivy does not answer at once, then remarks, "And nothing comes but what is meant to come."

Had she been looking at Billy she might have perceived his brows contract for a second. Then with a quick movement he turns to her suddenly, "Will you have some?" he says shortly.

Ivy looks up surprised—his tone is so imperative, and the occasion so trivial. She is unprepared for the decision, unimportant though it is, and hesitates ere answering.

"Will you?" he repeats.

"I—well, really, I hardly believe in catching happiness for oneself like that, you know," with a doubtful smile at him.

"So do I," he rejoins quickly; "it is usually futile. Still, will you have them?" And as she stands smiling dubiously, he clutches dexterously at the leaves fluttering past, and after a few moments walks up to her with a handful, counting them into her hand as he says, "There! there are eleven. I thought I had another. Wait, and I will catch it."

"What!" breaks in Cyril quickly, "what *are* you doing? You can't catch happiness for other people, 'cept, oh, Billy, 'cepting you have given up all your own"—in a horrified tone.

Ivy glances at Billy amusedly as she places the leaves compactly together, but the smile dies out as she meets the steady, rather grave look of his eyes; and a little embarrassed, she fumbles with her fragile gift, and wonders if this is another reminder of the wreckage she had wrought. It is rather bad taste in Billy to revive this old grievance.

Why cannot he generously let bygones be bygones, and allow their intercourse to assume a general friendliness?

A little stiffly, therefore, she remarks, "Thanks; please don't trouble about me any more—at least keep one month for yourself."

"Yes, do catch it, oh, do!" Cyril cries eagerly. "There's another gust coming. Look out! here come the leaves."

"No use," Billy says coolly, looking down with a smile at the child. "I don't agree with you, Cyril; I could not catch my own happiness, I am quite sure. Some one else would have to do it for me. Here, old man, I'll give you as far as 'The Swab,' and catch you before you reach the gate;" and yelling with delight, off darts the small boy, with his big pursuer behind him, surrounded by the wildly barking dogs.

As Ivy follows in staid calmness, not with the rush of old, she is conscious of a desire to be very kind to Billy. She wishes he would wait for supper and meet Teddy. He is not like a stranger, and could not mar the harmony of Teddy's first evening, and it will be so lonely for him spending his New Year's Eve all alone at Horston. Yes, he *must* stay. She will conquer the irritation he creates by any reference to old times. Perhaps his allusions are often unintentional, and woman-like, she magnifies the importance of utterances which to him may contain no hidden meaning. Women are so liable to exaggerate chance trifles, and conclude spontaneous actions are the outcome of deliberate thought. Poor Billy, she will treat him with exceptional kindliness always, because somehow the blow she had dealt him in the heedless happy days long ago, seemed tender and sore at the slightest touch, and after all, she only desired to make things pleasanter for him, and lessen the bitterness in his life, as she would try to in all others henceforth and for ever; and thus full of virtuous intention, Ivy hurried rather unusually to overtake her small brother before Billy should leave him. They were engaged in an animated discussion as she reached them.

" He says he's going, and I say he shan't," Cyril cried, as she came up. " Tell him, Ivy, tell him he *must* stay. Remember it's New Year's Eve! He's always been here, hasn't he, Ivy, every New Year's Eve ? "

" Yes," Ivy answers, looking at Billy kindly. " Of course he must stay, Cyril, and we will all go to the midnight service together. Did you not mean to go to it ? "

" Yes, but the walk is nothing—I don't wish to intrude; and besides, here are all the dogs. I really must take them back," Billy answers.

" I wish you could stay," Ivy says, in a tone she has not used for years. She does want to be kind to Billy, and his manner of ignoring her, and then suddenly awaking to the fact that she is there—the odd way in which he had almost forced these fantastic symbols of fortune upon her—created a curious interest in him; and she wished to satisfy herself that though he might be resentfully irritated towards her at times, yet most surely, gradually would she be able to re-establish the old friendship on its earliest comfortable footing. Therefore she has something to effect, and Billy becomes interesting, and a small scope is opened to her for the

exercise of power; and scarcely realising how dear
is this exercise to her essentially woman's heart,
she experiences a reviving desire to exert her
influence over this big rebellious man—of course,
entirely for his own particular welfare. It is a
wish not born of any personal instinct or smouldering pique—a purely charitable sympathy that merely
includes him among the general multitude deserving one's kindliness and pity. Was it not a truly
wise man who said, " Know thyself," realising that
he had placed the unattainable for ever before his
aspiring pupils?

Billy collects his dogs together by imperious
shouts and whistling. As he turns away and lifts
his cap—"I will take them home, and then—I—
will come back," he says; and with a little gratified
smile Ivy enters the house.

CHAPTER XX.

"Home is the sphere of harmony and peace,
   The spot where angels find a resting-place,
When, bearing blessings, they descend to earth."
                        —MRS. HALE'S *Poems.*

How contentment breathes in the very atmosphere
of home! Outside interests sink into insignifi-
cance, exterior worries are forgotten, when, with
a sigh of relief, tongues and actions are liberated
by unconventional ease. Each possess individual
rights; no one metaphorically steps into another's
shoes. Capabilities and opinions may be questioned amid shouts of derision, yet when in opposi-

tion to the outside world, they carry weight, and unhesitatingly the family support any member when it is a question of "us" *versus* "the world!" What a satisfaction to reflect that, though the great multitudes are absolutely ignorant of one's existence, yet each has his own especial little groove, making or marring the big mountain of man's endeavour. Teddy's stories, Fane's inventions, and even Archie's puns were received with appreciation. Billy woke up genially, and his sudden laugh was as ringing as it was rare. To the Vicar the evening was his only relaxation. Parish matters were never mentioned but in the privacy of his sanctum, and therefore village tragedies and petty transactions did not form the subjects of conversation. The daily papers, magazines, or any light reading occupied the hour after dinner; then, while Ivy sang or played; besique, cribbage, or whist—when he could secure a four—beguiled him. Mrs. Peyton sat reading or working, hearing and answering all her children, although they generally spoke all at once. Teddy had twice trumped his father's best cards; but as the conversation was kept up between players and onlookers, and every chink of silence carefully filled in with a song, it was not much to be wondered at.

"Go on singing, Ivy," cries the Vicar, making a mis-deal cheerfully; "you have driven that irritating Commission and County Councillors out of my head. I am sorry, Dare, to offend Crotchet again, but I can't advocate Stickphast merely because he is a good churchwarden. Broadley, from his practical knowledge of county matters and local questions, and his liberal toleration, appears the most fitting fellow for the post, and I consider it my duty to support him."

"Broadly speaking, he's the only one," Fane supplements with a grin, returning Billy's lead with care; "only, father, owing to the limited capabilities of other people's visions, they can't get him focussed into their views all at once. Diminutive representations might render this possible— midget 'proofs' of him will be issued by the opposite side, and haggling over the width of his head, they will never get down to his 'sole,' eh, pater ?"

The Vicar laughs. "True, most big things, ideas or facts, have to be dispensed homeopathically, to be swallowed. *Hearts* are trumps, Ted. Another song, Ivy."

Ivy and Archie have been prowling round, peeping at the different hands, and exchanging exasperating signals of amusement. She is rather tired, and not very inclined for singing, and Billy has noticed her reluctance before.

"Sing something short," he whispers, as she passes his chair.

"Certainly," Ivy acquiesces quietly, while he is making room for her to pass. "I have several with one verse. I am sorry you should be victimised. It will soon be over."

There is a flash in the blue eyes that look down upon her. Then, almost coldly, Billy says, "I was thinking, of course, it would tire you."

"How odd !" Ivy answers, raising her eyebrows lightly, "when I was thinking just the same for you !" She smiles as she plays the prelude to her song, for Billy's rigid jaw is always a sign of suffering, and to possess the power to wound is in itself something!

As she finishes Teddy calls out for something out of " Dorothy " or " Paul Jones." " They are awfully pretty; Nora sings them," he says.

" Nora! Why, have you been seeing much of Nora? She has never mentioned you in her letters."

Teddy plays his card with careful deliberation. Ivy waits in vain for an answer. It comes later as he turns to his father and says abstractedly—" By the way, pater, as Nora's mother was the sister of your sister's husband, aren't we cousins? Lady Templeton says no."

" Certainly not. My sister's niece by her first marriage is no cousin of yours, unless you desire it. Taste decides those relationships. And now, come, we must be off to church. Mind the dogs don't escape, or we shall have Dormat heading the procession again, and fresh wiggings for heterodox innovations."

Midnight service was an institution in Mudsbury. Cyril has gone on with his father; Mrs. Peyton walks between her big soldier sons; Billy stalks at Teddy's side; and Ivy comes blundering along in the darkness, behind the others, wishing for silence, and yet doomed to suffer at Archie's hands. She does not know that his remarks ring out on the night air with penetrating distinctness. Teddy gives his mother's hand an amused grasp as it rests upon his arm. Billy pays no attention to Fane's jibes; his ears catch every syllable uttered behind them.

"Sell," Archie grumbles, "when New Year's Day comes on a Sunday. Shame to roll an exceptional institution in and get nothing for it. It's like blending fish and *entrée* with the everyday joint. Amalgamation doesn't pay. Always think you have been 'done' somehow."

"Solace yourself with the reflection that it is exceptionally 'lucky,' and foretells the seven 'fat kine,' the seven 'full ears' that are to bring in the period of prosperity."

"But then the other blasted—(it *says* blasted)—things ate up all the good ones, and their latter state was worse than the first, so I don't call the outlook cheering *that* way!"

"You have evidently missed the practical lesson in this illustration," Ivy replies loftily. "If you recollect, the dream inspired actions to checkmate fate. It really means in one way, use your opportunities so well that they place you beyond the range of reverses. Think, in seven years you might be Prime Minister; that is if you never fell short of that ideal Pitt!"

"Never knew an ideal pit," Archie responds gloomily; "gigantic, impossible, *American*, I'll be bound. I'd much rather fall short of such a thing, than *into* it!" he adds firmly.

How they laugh as they come stumbling along behind! "What use are *you* going to make of your 'seven good ears'?" Archie asks Ivy suddenly.

"I! Oh! in our case everything is quite different. *We* can't make our destiny—destiny makes us."

"That's the neatest excuse for twirling your thumbs till your Duke comes by that I ever heard," Archie retorts.

"Twirling my thumbs indeed!" Ivy reiterates quickly; "I should be miserable without work. I desire above all things work."

"Then be comforted—you shall have it! My entire wardrobe requires renovating, Teddy's and Fane's are in rather a poor way too, and then, what with parish work, household *dusters*, and sock-knitting, you may flatter yourself you shall be kept fully occupied."

An indignant "Pshaw!"

"Are you not proving yourself as illogical as every one of your sex? You crave for a thing—I offer it you—you scorn it. Shall I tell you why? Because when you say you want work, you are talking pure twaddle. D'you mean to say you look out into the future and ask and expect and desire nothing but work! If you do look forward at all, and of course you do, you don't a bit want only work—you want just what every one else wants—a fair share of prosperity, and a good deal of happiness. Now, don't you? Answer fair—you want prosperity and happiness?"

"Prosperity! I don't know! Prosperity doesn't always mean happiness."

"Don't haggle about the key fitting the lock—anyhow, you desire happiness."

"I really," Ivy begins hesitatingly, "I really never asked myself if I did want it; but," after a pause, "I suppose if you put it in that sort of way—well, I suppose it is only natural to hope one may have it."

"Of course, it's only natural. Pray, don't think I blame you for being natural; it was entirely the other way. The dread horror I entertained was

solely upon the score of having an *unnatural* sister.
Now I look at you and breathe freely, knowing
you are exactly the same as every other little petticoated darling all over the world. You are quite
content with your destiny because you all hope
it is a sort of comprehensive name for—Duke."

Archie has arrived at the hectoring self-assertive
age when manhood's prerogative reaches stupen-
dous proportions, and "the boy" very much
regards himself as "father of the man." Mrs.
Peyton would have diverted Archie's remarks, that
might, however unintentionally uttered, seem to
Ivy somewhat pointed; but all things considered,
it seemed better not to interfere. Archie really
knew nothing about Ivy's buried romance; and
besides, all girls with brothers are more or
less accustomed to the ordeal by fire. They are
nearly at the Church now, but Archie has time
to cry—

"Under the very shadow of the Church speak
the truth, and ' own up ' to the Duke."

" Be quiet; I don't want anything of the sort ! "

" What a ' corker.' You want happiness, and
you know the gods never send it to a woman
except by the hands of a man."

"Don't they ? " Ivy rejoins impetuously, speaking without a moment's thought. "Then, of course,
I've *had* my allotted portion—eleven months—it
came to me to-day."

The consternation of an afterthought dyes her
cheeks crimson, but a hurried glance round relieves her. Billy is not there. No, Ivy, not anywhere where you can see him, but the words have
reached him all the same, ere with prompt con-

sideration he effaced himself into the outer darkness beyond the flood of glowing light that streams from out the porch. Ivy follows her mother calmly, happily, and some distance behind the brothers strides in Billy. Perhaps all the flaring candles and mass of brilliant colouring have thrown some answering reflection into Billy's earnest eyes. Colour and light are tonics old as time. It may be! Yet, when the service is over, and the joyous bells are clashing out their glad greeting to the silent presence of the New Year, the darkness of the night cannot dim the brightness lingering in them still; and Ivy feels he is at her side, and is glad he should be the first to wish her "a very happy New Year." He holds her hand rather impressively, as she smiles and utters the same wish for him; but then, perhaps, the occasion sanctions that—only he did not do so last year. Of course, it is only chance though—the fact of his being near her, that made him speak the dear old greeting to her first. Of course, only the purest chance. She knows far too well to judge men by merely a woman's estimate. Women think so much without acting. Men, on the other hand, act so much without thinking.

Overhead clashed the bells, while from distant hollows varied echoes answered, heralding with happy auguries the new-born son of time. And out into the silence the New Year passed, tenderly greeting the tired world, as he traced athwart the darkened heavens the golden letters of Hope.

———

CHAPTER XXI.

Phebe. "Youth, you have done me much ungentleness." . .
Rosalind. "I care not if I have : it is my study
To seem despiteful and ungentle to you ;
You are there followed by a faithful shepherd :
Look upon him, love him ; he worships you."
                              —*As You Like It.*

THERE is so much to be done on a Monday morning
that it is perhaps only natural that Ivy should be
"in a fuss." Cyril, in contented eagerness, has
trotted about in her wake endeavouring to participate in all her avocations. He is so happy—children
always are when busy. If dejection troubles them,
one may be sure they are unwell, or have nothing to
do. He has raced backwards and forwards to the
pit house and tiny conservatory, changing all the
plants from the drawing-room, and quite surpassed
himself in eloquent pleading for any particular pot
of maidenhair he fancies. The doves and canaries,
accustomed though they are to his erratic attentions, have been simply staggered at the wholesale
thoroughness of his operations. Perchless, waterless,
seedless, they still suffer his relentless scourings,
and cower at the bottom of the cage until the dread
hour of scrapings and shakings shall at last cease.
Ivy, entering the room, with a pile of clean linen
in her arms, is aghast.

"What *are* you doing, Cyril ? Not done the birds
yet ! Why, they all look dead with fright ! Come,
hurry up; I'm going to put away the boys' things,
and then want you to help me brush Nelly."

"All right," Cyril replies, his dear little brown
head rather on one side, as he stands lost in

admiration of his handiwork. "I've scraped every single thing," he ejaculates emphatically—"*everything* except the birds. I didn't touch them, Ivy, not even their feet!"

"For which let's be thankful, as you wouldn't have left them a leg to stand on," she rejoins, as she turns away with a smile.

Why is this an exceptionally busy day—a day on which the slow accumulated jobs of weeks are taken in hand and carried through with desperate energy? As Ivy laboriously sorts through the piles of music, and dresses the drawing-room in clean chairbacks and fresh ribbons, she struggles to ignore the fact that in all her keen expectancy lurks a dimly felt regret; and why? Because to-day is coming to stay with them, for some months at least, bright, beautiful Nora Bingham. Ay, there's the rub; Nora is *beautiful*—report says so—every one says so. Ever since her presentation her social career has been one long triumph. *Why* she wishes to bury herself in the stagnant solitude of Mudsbury, while Sir Noel and Lady Templeton are abroad, is more than Ivy can understand. Julia is married now to a Manchester manufacturer, with a gorgeous palace surrounded by cotton mills, a little unpretending body and an enormous head for business. It is natural, all things considered, that Nora should not care to stay there. Julia had never been very friendly, and had seemed to regard her beautiful cousin with daily increasing disfavour. But why should Nora not have gone abroad, or with Gwendoline? If she were such a friend of Gwennie's, nothing would have been easier than for her to join them on their southern flit. Aunt Amy would

X

have been only too overjoyed to obtain so bright a companion for Gwendoline. What *can* have made Nora suggest, in a rambling effusive letter to Ivy, that to be dragged abroad was the most wretched of all fates, and that if only she might live in the Vicarage coal-cellar, life would be Paradise!

Ah! there was something below all this—Mudsbury's placid attractions would scarcely explain this unaccountable desire; and Ivy, with a little disconcerted sigh, felt very much puzzled, and not half as delighted as of course she ought to be. Life had been so untroubled of late—ever since Teddy came a fortnight ago things had gone smoothly. Billy had been in a most placid frame of mind— he often stayed to supper; and whenever they got back early enough from hunting, would come in to afternoon tea.

The hunting had been excellent. The boys—Fane and Archie—occasionally had a horse lent them by friendly farmers, and at rare intervals had one of Billy's fliers; but that was not often, as he regularly mounted Teddy four days in the week. These two were greater friends than ever, and now—would Nora's coming upset the general placidity?

At afternoon tea time, when the drawing-room seemed a tangle of wicker tables, and the boys' long legs, Nora comes.

"Put the buns in the fire and mind Dick," Ivy cries, as she rushes into the hall.

A moment later, then Nora's voice, "Well, I thought the fly never was coming here. Though I'm not partial to tough meat, I'd rather eat the beast that brought me, than drive behind him again;"

and then the door is flung wide, and the two girls enter the room.

Nora comes forward with just the right amount of eagerness, and perfectly assured. To Mr. and Mrs. Peyton she is prettily deferential; to Fane friendly; to Teddy wholly indifferent; but when Billy comes forward, her blue eyes flash, and with an eager little gesture she stretches out her hand, saying, with much *empressement,* "Oh! how *very* charming to meet you again."

The expression may be a surprise to some; to Ivy it is startling as a thunder-clap—a proclamation of an intimacy undreamed of. She is indignant, puzzled, and consequently lost in illogical speculations, and very silent. Nora's radiant gladness depresses her strangely, and her exquisite beauty troubles her, and fills her with foreboding, and an undefined apprehension.

Fane may worship Nora with ludicrous impertinence—his friendship excuses his effrontery; Teddy may look on with an amused smile; but why is Billy drawn into the conversation, and kept carefully engrossed by Nora's nonsense!

Time has flown; candles have come, and Billy rises to go. Ivy is not in the least desirous that he should remain for supper. His refusal is a relief. Nora looks up as he shakes her hand. "Horrid of you," she says, smiling. "*Au revoir.*"

Ivy has dropped several stitches, and has no hand for Billy's farewell. "Good-bye," she says, without looking up.

"Good night," he answers, standing stiffly still for a moment, ere he and Teddy leave the room together.

" Well, you *are* a happy family," Nora says emphatically; " I want to join the circle. Mrs. Peyton, I am going to call you Aunt Mary— may I ? "

Mrs. Peyton smiles as she answers, " Certainly."

" Now, give me some work," Nora continues. " Here, Cyril, you may sit on my lap. Oh, my goodness! is that a cat ? "—springing up with alarm.

" Cyril need not sit on you, and if you wouldn't mind *not* sitting on the cat, I think we could find chairs enough," Ivy remarks, feeling suddenly savage.

For her rudeness the others make ample amends. Fane ousts the cat without ceremony, and Nora promptly appropriates him, and, to Ivy's infinite chagrin, the tawny favourite submits to her coaxing with a good grace, and lies in her lap contentedly.

" Now, Cyril, will you come ? " Nora says sweetly.

" No, thank you," the little boy replies; " you see I'm rather too big, and I like to sit where I can see you "—with flattering honesty.

Ivy is racked by most unchristian emotions. She is jealous of her brothers' undisguised admiration of Nora, puzzled by Billy's preference, and could almost tweak Paul for purring as those dainty fingers pass over him. She struggles and is silent.

" Nora," Fane says abruptly, " have you seen much of Dare lately ?—I mean, since that time in Mentone, when—— I say, look out! Did he scratch you ? You mustn't jerk him suddenly— Paul is a gentleman who hates surprises."

" Does he ? " Nora replies, looking at Fane;

"well, I prefer those sort of creatures to the placid stamp, on whom the greatest surprise produces no lasting impression." She nods at him almost scornfully.

"I don't understand," Fane begins hopelessly.

"That is painfully apparent," Nora retorts.

"Well, but," Fane continues, "what on earth have surprises and Paul to do with what I was saying? What *was* I saying? oh, asking you "——

"If I loved you as much now as I did at Mentone—well, I *don't*—not a thousandth part as much. Sandhurst has made you strangely stupid."

"You haven't lost the art of making polite speeches," Fane says, rather nettled.

"It is only with you I have to exercise it," Nora replies. "Oh, are we going to dress for supper? Here, Paul, get down; and you "—in an undertone to Fane—"dare nothing retrospective!"

Fane whistles to himself as he ruminates awhile, and confides to Teddy not long after that Nora is evidently "awfully gone on *Dare!*"—at which his elder brother merely requests him to "go and be hanged!"

To Ivy it is a miserable evening. She is aghast at the sensations that from the dry bones of buried sentiments leapt into sudden life. She had watered with tears the grave of her dead illusions, and decked its mound with deep-rooted memories, stamped hard into the sod; and now, from the ideal dust-heap of her crumbled hopes, sprang a rancorous disaffection, poisoning to the core her slowly grown content.

There are men who fail to appreciate their wives until they are taken from them, we are told. It

may be. The buried hunter was ever the best, the
pipe just broken always the favourite one. It is that
curious craving for the unattainable, that pathetic
longing for the lost, that writes "sacred" across
all that is past. An experience shared by some
women.

Ivy had been content to picture her future in
a mixed pattern of no very decided shades, but a
wrought out harmony of all the hues blent round
her to-day. The possibility of one strong tone of
colour being withdrawn—not only that, but appro-
priated by another weaver—well, it certainly made
the continuation of the pattern more dull. Ivy did
not choose to ask herself what she thought about
Nora and Billy. The tacit understanding, the
mutual comprehension that existed between them,
could not fail to mystify her, as of course she was
quite unaware of the share that both had taken
in unwinding the greatest tangle of her life. She
was puzzled, she was unhappy ; and when Nora, in
the gayest of voices, insisted upon her going to sit
by her fire for a brush and comb conclave, she felt
that even her citadel of silence was threatened.

"Do you know, Ivy," was Nora's first remark,
"there's something very *taking* about Mr. Dare."

Ivy shakes a long wisp of hair if possible
more over her face than before, and disentangles it
methodically as she answers in the most indifferent
tone—"We have known him for a very long time ;
yes, he is—nice."

"Oh ! but it is not only *nice;* he is so different
from most men—so unassuming, and self-contained,
and—strong."

Ivy's hair is sadly knotted. Her little pinky finger-

tips are combing through the tresses ceaselessly,
always over the same ground, so to speak. Nora's
lips curl a little mischievously as she continues—
" You don't often meet men like that—there may
be crowds of them, but one does not meet them.
He gives me the impression of a man whose life
has been a hard one—there is a curiously stern
look about him when he is not speaking, but that
is not the case, is it ? He has always had very
much what he wanted all his life, hasn't he ?"
The tone is cordial, only broken by colons and
full stops for sundry tuggings.

" He has always been very well off, I believe,"
Ivy answers under her hair.

" Yes, but that's just it," Nora resumes reflectively;
" he seems to me to be one of the rare men that
money and leisure won't satisfy. With all his
eagerness (and of course about hunting one can
see he is eager), he cools down into a reserve that
seems to almost petrify him. He wants more
interests ; he ought to go into Parliament, or—he
ought to marry."

" Perhaps he would prefer the first alternative,"
comes in somewhat resentful murmurs from behind
a brown veil of hair.

Nora's irrepressible squeak she promptly attributes to having inadvertently burnt her toe. " No,
I think not," she continues musingly. " No, he
is just the sort of man that could be made almost
perfection by a woman. He wants a little soften-
ing, a heap of sympathy, and—if he loved her, she
could turn him round her little finger. Oh, dear !"
with a long sigh, " I wonder if *I* could make any
man *really* happy ! Ivy "—abruptly—" if any man

that—that you were interested in, wanted to marry me, what would you advise him to do? Would you speak a good word for me, or would you recommend him to be quit of the bargain?" Nora laughs a little nervously, but her tones are almost touchingly eager for all that.

The brown head is very still, then all the wavy mane is flung backwards with a quick jerk, and two brown eyes look straight into Nora's, as Ivy lays her hand on her arm firmly—"I would tell him," she says quite quietly, "that if he had won your *love*, he might indeed be happy, as well as—proud. Good night, Nora—it is late, and I am rather tired—sleep well;" and kissing her tenderly and gravely Ivy rose and left the room.

Nora's eyelashes are suspiciously bright, but she laughs as she stretches her hands to the blaze. "It was cruel," she says; "but oh! you certainly deserve something for the way in which you have made him suffer for two years—*two years!* and two *hours* have made me almost in love with the poor thing! I should be, if it were not—how does it go? 'I really could love thee nearly as much, loved I not some one more.' Is that right, I wonder? Well, anyhow it is what I mean, and that is the great thing."

"Sleep well," Ivy had said, and restful and happy indeed were Nora's slumbers. Ivy slept too, at last, when the morrow was some hours old, and her pillow had been turned again and again, until it was well saturated with a bitter storm of long continued tears.

CHAPTER XXII.

"Love took up the harp of Life,
  And smote on all the chords with might—
Smote the chord of Self, that, trembling,
  Passed in music out of sight."
                              —*Locksley Hall.*

THE days have dragged their heavy laden hours through another week of time. Nora has satisfied herself that Ivy is coming to her senses sufficiently, and has implored Billy to try his luck once more. But though he cannot fail to perceive that Ivy seems more conscious of him, he mistrusts her reserve; and once bit, twice shy, waits for some plainer evidence than Nora's belief before making his second venture. Beaming with satisfaction at having broken down all obstacles between the two, and paved the way for their mutual happiness; Nora has been graciousness itself to the much mystified Teddy, and made him at one moment dizzy with hope, and the next cynical with deliberating distrust. It *did* seem to the uninitiated that Nora enjoyed the very suffering that now all the world might see she could inflict, although poor Teddy trusted his sorrow was safely wrapped in stubborn silence and solacing tobacco smoke. Coming round from the stables, where he found a satisfaction in Rat Trap's sympathy, he turned into the drive, singing mournfully, as he emerged unexpectedly upon Nora—

"Shall carry me, with steps, silent, mournful, and slow."

"You shall *not* sing that," Nora cried sharply, standing still before him. "It is miserable, morbid, unwholesome. I hate it. You do it because—because you know I can't bear it. I think it is most disagreeable of you, and most unkind."

Teddy smiles a little bitterly. "I don't want to be disagreeable," he says, knocking his pipe against the heel of his boot to empty it; "but I really can't see why you should object to my singing my own requiem, if it pleases me—morbid perhaps—but it *is* a satisfaction to know I shan't go to my grave unmourned, even if I've had to chant my wailings entirely myself. You see, India may polish me off pretty quick. I don't take kindly to stewing, so it is as well to be prepared."

Nora's head is turned away, but as they reach the front door, Teddy hears a choked "I think you are p—perfectly—b—brutal," and the next minute he is looking into the loveliest eyes in the world, blazing through angry tears.

"If I thought" —— he begins, with a great gasp of amazement.

"Think what you *like*," Nora whispers, with the most adorable smile, as she held the lobby swing door, and looked back at him. "Hush! here's Cyril."

How brilliant dear old Teddy became. Ivy watched and grew glad, wondering; the Vicar peeped over his paper several times; and the mother knitted gravely. Billy sat by Ivy's side, and felt a novel satisfaction in her almost timid gentleness, but kept himself in guarded commonplaces for very fear of frightening her, though his manner, even to misguided Ivy, could not fail to say much. It was a disquieting evening. A certain air of suspicion effectually banished content, and every one appeared anxiously expectant, or on the *qui vive* for some fresh surprise from Nora. None came, however, and the agitating evening closed without any further revelations, though Billy and Teddy were in boisterous spirits, and Fane took to openly chaffing Nora for her fit of shyness.

The morrow broke in a hazy mist—no wind, and Teddy in raptures about the scent "lying." As the meet was a near one, there was little need for Billy to appear at breakfast time. Nevertheless, looking exceptionally smart, and with violets in his buttonhole, he entered smiling. What has happened to Nora —not a word has she for Teddy, but devotes herself to Billy, and seems only anxious to have speech with him; and when the girls stand out on the doorstep in the soft uncertain sunshine, and men and horses come round from the stable yard, he is still ignored. Grooms walk the waiting horses up and down the gravel sweep on the right. Here, in front of the door, Teddy lights a cigarette, and keeps himself clear of the admiring dogs. Cyril has run off to watch Fane overhauling Rat Trap, and Ivy leans against the trellis-covered wall alone. How can any one understand English weather and women! Could anything be more variable and incomprehensible, more irritating and more swift in fresh surprises? What did Nora mean by her manner to Teddy yesterday, and her manner to him to-day? What does this renewed interest in Billy denote? or had it really never relaxed? and was Teddy merely an assumed solace for spare moments, like press atrocities for dull times? How eagerly she has been conversing with Billy all the morning, and how his face lights up as she whispers words so softly while they saunter up and down.

"You'd better chain Rollick and Dormat," Teddy remarks, looking at Ivy, and they both turn in at the door moved by the same impulse. It is only one moment before they see a chain flung down by Cyril — only one moment, but in that brief space of time Nora and Billy have come much nearer to the door. Walking from the school-room corner they do not see the two inside, and their voices are perfectly audible.

"Keep them, Nora, in exchange for the hope you give me," Billy says tenderly.

And then comes Nora's answer. "It is *more* than hope, it is—love."

A lightning flash of—was it scorn?—in Teddy's eyes, and then the red gravel, the oval plot of grass, the horses moving by, and the black dabs of the dog's backs seem to heave a little confusedly, while Ivy stands quite still ere she steps out into the sunshine. Mechanically she links the chains into the dogs' collars. She knows she smiles and waves her hand at the rider's laughing farewell— she has even spoken once or twice, and the words have caused no amazement, so presumably they were sense; but she is conscious of nothing, and can see only two things distinctly—Billy's parting smile at Nora, and the purple bunch of his violets she keeps close clasped in her hand.

"Ivy! aren't you going to take Rollick?"

"No, Cyril. Keep all the dogs with you, and ask Nora to take you to Cross Farm; you may see something of the field, as they are going to draw Bamley."

"Aren't you coming?"

"No I am going to Mill End."

The Vicar often said one of the greatest charms of his parish was its variety. Probably to one who knew it less intimately this would have appeared a statement difficult to substantiate; but when from the woods of oak and beech on the far ridge by Horston, over rolling uplands and flooded valleys, from every larch spinney to each thicket and copse, from hedgerow elms and brook-side pollards to tumbling stream and thymey pine-wood, every foot of ground was familiar, there was indeed an infinite, an hourly, a glorious variety. No matter what the mood may be, nature is always in harmony with it. In idle dreaming she draws cloud pictures to the sound of the drowsy bees humming; in joy she magnifies the gladness by every ray of sunshine, by every tone of colour, and sets the single notes of sweetness to her full orchestra of sound; and in sorrow she soothes by the evidence of changeless law and infinite love.

And so Ivy crept with broken spirit and bitter soul to where unnoticed and unsuspected her passionate sorrow could find a safe and speedy vent. Mill End was a small outlying hamlet on the extreme limit of the parish. Here the cottages were of the poorest description—their occupiers the day labourers employed on the neighbouring farms. Here was always some struggling soul to cheer by the smallest gift and a few words of kindness. Here, too, always overjoyed to see visitors, lived Grannie Budd. Ivy's district duties were somewhat hurriedly performed, and her interest in Grannie's ailments the result of undeniable force of will. It was over at last, and then with a sort of uncontrollable desperation, she hurried by by-path and field track to the crest of the sweeping hillside, crowned by the darker masses of pine-wood. A good time to come here, for no one would be about—no women gathering faggots—for at this hour all would be engaged in getting ready the mid-day meal. No children searching for fir cones, for it lay out of their route to school. Yes, here, with a sense of utterly unfettered feelings, Ivy could be alone. For a time she sat with her hands pressed over her eyes, trying to shut out everything but the thoughts that should be forced into some sort of order. Was that fact of to-day's disclosure the result of her own folly, or the inevitable consequence of vengeful mocking fate? If she had known, if she could *only* have known what she knew, oh, so terribly clearly now— could she have gone forward long ago and taken the happiness that had been held out to her slow un- willing hands? For oh, once, and she could almost have dreamed not so long ago either, he *had* cared. And why, oh, why had she only learnt how utterly she loved him when it was just—too late? Perhaps could it be that she was mistaken, and that all this time he had only been anxious to show her his indifference? Could it be that she was offering her friendship unasked?—that she had given her—her love unsought? The shamed tears crept between the fingers that covered her glowing cheeks, and for some time Ivy cowered and shrunk down in silent agony, feeling through every nerve and fibre the burning breath of this slow scorching suspicion. Oh, it was horrible! Was that Billy's revenge? Because she had sacrificed him for—for something— something that had been beautiful, but a dream, a revelation of abstract goodness, as it almost seemed now, oh, had he, by his quiet gentleness and long continued kindness to all of them, woven himself into the network of her daily life, just to show her how great a wrench his severance would be! No; that was scarcely worthy of Billy. No; he had not mapped out a course of slow retaliation—this thing had come suddenly—it was a new thing. And then memory recalled a thousand vanished tokens and half forgotten signs, and strove to prove by a long connected chain of arguments that he had never altered, excepting to seem more friendly, until Nora came— yes, until Nora came; and then, oh, and even *then*, when she had learnt from Nora's own lips what had brought her here, she had still almost fancied the liking might be all on Nora's side. How blind she had been! Even yesterday she had been half frightened at Billy's curious manner to her—such a mixture of proud reserve and tender deference; and it had never meant anything at all. Oh, how contradictory and how puzzling it was! No, she was sure, whatever Billy had thought, he had not meant to be quite so remorselessly avenged. She could not wrong him by any unworthy suspicion. If it were a case for blaming any one, was it not Nora. Yet how was Nora to know that Billy was everything to Ivy, when it had been the struggle of every hour to ignore him, and misrepresent her feelings for him?

Spring was in the pine-wood—spring, with its lesson of hope written broadcast everywhere; but to Ivy the message could not come, for her soul was dead. Long, long the rolling billows of sweeping sound rocked her in the strong solace of their cadence, and over her impassive desolation breathed an unheeded balm. The brambles, with last year's leaves still green upon them, stretched long sheltering sprays across the leafless hawthorn; in the banks of the ditch nettles were growing ; and every barren twig was blessed with its store of brown sheathed buds. Some little ants were very busy running over a root of the pine-tree, and toiling up the interstices of the bark to a branch above. Backwards and forwards, up and down, passing and repassing, moved the tiny creatures, and Ivy watched them with an interest and pity that seemed called forth for all the labour of life's endeavours. Then the pines breathed over her softly the grand song of the sea, the flood-tide of noble striving, the listless ebb of wrong, the ceaseless contest of forces regulated by unalterable rule; and lulled by the roll of their rhythm Ivy learnt the mystery of suffering, the littleness of self, that happiness rarely crowns us with her laurels of success, but presses into trembling hands her hard-won palm of sacrifice, that love has stamped all the sorrows of man with the seal of the Cross of Christ.

And leaving passion and scorn and hot agony of tears to be blent by thousand thymy strings of the harmonous pine-wood into soft sighs, Ivy crept out of the clinging shell of self, and lifted by invisible angel hands to a higher, clearer level, asked nothing but that " Billy might be made happy —and—Nora too."

There was a glad echo in the pine-wood, and Ivy passed out in peace.

The afternoon sun was still well above the brown elms by Hedge's Farm when Nora, standing near one of the drawing-room windows, shouted with sudden interest—" Oh, Ivy, look; who are these people coming up the hill?"

Ivy stands with her eyes upon the approaching group, then enumerates them confidently—" First of all, Teddy and Mrs. Martingal; then Billy and her husband, Major Martingal; and that battered Jew is Fane. I must order more buns. Oh, Nora, do be careful; she is too killing for words."

Mrs. Martingal is indeed more amusing than she has any idea of. Her only interests are hunting and her husband. A tall masculine woman, a little deaf and very absent, her conversation is a standing joke. Her husband has been discussing different methods of treating mud fever with Billy and the Vicar. Mrs. Martingal has been an absorbed listener, and it is long after the subject has been discarded, and other topics introduced, that she declines the muffin Teddy offers, looking up at him gravely, as she utters the startling statement—" No, thank you, we *never* wash our legs; do we, Jim?"

Nora laughs aloud; Fane and Billy choke silently; Cyril gapes in blushing incomprehension; and Teddy collapses to place the muffins on the table's lower shelf.

Major Martingal has his glass in his eye, and gazing at Nora, has not heard his wife's remark. He is speaking to the Vicar. " Oh, really," he says, " your niece—Irish—plenty of 'go,' I should say," smiling broadly.

Mrs. Martingal, catching something of her husband's speech, assents eagerly—" Irish! oh, yes— he told me — first season — Galway blazer — well-shaped, but—er—kicks!"

Y

This is too much. Mrs. Peyton struggles to preserve her gravity behind the shelter of the tea-pot, but all the boys are rolling weakly, and Ivy's tea is shaking over in convulsed ripples on to Puff's back.

"You were in the earthquake, weren't you," the Major says abruptly, looking at Nora. "Met a fellow—Bicester country—other day; told me knew you all. Smarte-Payce—nice fellow—rides fourteen stone. Said there was pretty girl—devil to pay—general shindy—masked ball—and a duel. Earthquake quite cleared the air. By the way, he said—why, so he did! Why, Dare, he said *you* were out there—mixed up in the whole thing. How's that, Dare?" Nora and Fane are frozen into speechlessness. Billy stirs his tea slowly. "Yes, good fellow, Smarte-Payce is. Gunn trains for him—won a lot with Mermaid at Kempton and Sandown this year. He has put me on to several good things."

The danger is averted. All breathe easily.

"Horrible that earthquake, horrible!" Mrs. Martingal here joins in, late as usual. "Dear me, Jim, some one died; don't you remember; some one you know—the man we bought Cheese Cake from. Well, his sister was out there—nice girl—sprained her off hind in the beginning of the season—we had to sell her—he hunts with 'The Vale' now, you remember."

"Oh, yes, I remember her telling us all about it—fearful scene—many injured—one poor fellow "——

"Put on his tall hat and dived from the third story," Fane continues quickly. "He *was* a little jarred because he took his opera hat by mistake, otherwise he vowed he always chose that method of exit in earthquakes and fires—perfectly simple if the hat acted as a sufficient 'buffer,' otherwise a little rough stopping suddenly, as he hadn't yet invented a brake."

Mrs. Martingal is silent while the others laugh. "The old lever brake is the best I know," she says suddenly. "I don't believe in his new invention—at least don't ask *me* to try it, that's all."

It is hopeless. The boys are speechless, and Ivy crimson. Cyril is utterly bewildered, and quite relieved when the Major, anxious about Cheap Jack and Checkmate, hurries his impassive wife away. Then the inappropriate remarks are improved and coloured according to fancy, until the mother deprecatingly interferes.

Billy is feeding Dick, hoping thereby to extract some remark from Ivy. She takes no notice for some time, then looks up to say diffidently—"It really makes him so ill, I wish you would not, if you don't mind."

"And suppose I do mind," Billy replies.

"Then—I have nothing to say."

Billy looks up quietly. "Seems to me," he says, bending low over Dick, and speaking too softly for any but Ivy to hear him, "it is not that you have nothing to say, but you won't say what you might."

Ivy stoops for her ball of worsted, but Billy has it, and as he puts it into her hand he holds her fingers a moment while he whispers—"Are we not friends *yet*, Ivy?"

The tears rush to her eyes, and she feels half choked, as she answers—"Yes, oh, yes, of course we are;" and then Cyril springing forward cries out gaily—

"Oh, Billy, Nora has just told Ted those violets were given her by her 'only love.' *You* gave them to Nora, didn't you? *Are* you Nora's 'only love,' Billy?"

Ivy does not see Billy's laughing grimace, or hear his answer. Swiftly, silently, stung by passionate jealousy, and strong in sensitive pride, she passed out quickly from the drawing-room, and tearing upstairs two steps at a time, gained the haven of her own room, to find again, after torrents of tears, the lost calm of the morning's victory.

CHAPTER XXIII.

"I'm not denyin' the women are foolish : God Almighty made 'em to match the men."—*Adam Bede.*

THREE days' frost had stopped the hunting. The bitter wind swept once more over a wintry world, and the rich, soft furrows were iron bound, and dusted with powdered snow. That sense of duty that forces English girls to abandon firesides and face hurricanes, had driven Nora and Ivy to seek their daily constitutional along the Mudsbury Road. Teddy and Archie, with the three dogs, had gone to Horston; Fane to Houndsley-cum-Sentum for the afternoon letters; and the only companions for this exhausting walk were Cyril and Nelly. Now Nelly, under the most favourable circumstances, was a somewhat unsatisfactory creature. She was a grey goat of mature age, and time had but more strongly developed her unbending peculiarities. There were certain roads that were distasteful to her. Much coaxing, and a stout chain, would get her well started upon the objectionable highway; but, like the immortalised lover, "trifles light as air were confirmation strong" that her dislikes were reasonably founded. A butcher's dog, school children with hoops, a solitary rider, or an everyday tax-cart would substantiate her worst fears; and with a bleat of conscious triumph, she would stop short, wheel, and bucket back, bells tinkling, pursuer shrieking, until her reiterated plaint died out in the distance. Ill-advised indeed was the unfortunate one who teased or obstructed Nelly. Attempt to thwart her, and with leaps of rage she rose upon her hind legs, her wiry person sloping at an alarming angle of forty-five, her wicked head and pointed beard another acute angle set transversely, and in this fell guise she would advance upon her foe, and often succeed in butting her adversary into the nearest ditch. There was a curious resemblance in Nelly to a bearded gentleman in a jocund state of inebriation, and the evil glint in her eyes suggested the traditional depravity of her kind. To Nora she was a source of constant terror; and the cunning old creature, conscious of her power, was ever on the watch to pay off old scores at unexpected moments.

When Ivy had suggested that the Mudsbury road on the Horston side was less windy, Nora had averred that in the Houndsley-cum-Sentum direction it was certainly less muddy; so over iron ground that rung under their feet they walked towards Houndsley-cum-Sentum.   Perhaps the irritating gusts of tearing wind prevented much conversation, or the constant stoppages to haul on the obdurate Nelly, but the two girls have little to say to each other, and Cyril has the conversation all to himself.   Nelly being beyond the range from which she will attempt a bolt homewards, waddles sullenly behind.   As they reach a turn in the road, they perceive coming towards them, waving letters gleefully, Fane.

"What a bother!" Nora breaks out; but as Cyril cries suddenly—"Oh, here are Teddy, Billy, and Archie coming up behind us!" she smiles instinctively, and flourishes her stick at Fane.   Now, Nora's actions are often misinterpreted, and this one causes Nelly a deadly misgiving.   With a quick, angry shuffle, she hastens after her supposed enemy, and only the tinkling bells warn Nora of her nearness.   With a yell that sent Teddy flying to the rescue, Nora flew towards Fane, while the evil-minded Nelly galloped aggressively behind.

Teddy is near now.   "Nora," he shouts, "dodge her, or she will be on you."   As he speaks, he seizes Nelly's tail and partially arrests her.   It would be so easy for Nora to dart across the road.   As it is, before Teddy's fingers can grasp the collar he is fumbling for, Nelly edges Nora nearer and nearer to the ditch, and with a sudden thrust pushes her in!   Perfectly dry and not very deep, it could scarcely be called dangerous; but when Nora scrambles out, refusing Teddy's aid, her glove is split, and the palm of her hand bleeding.

"Why on earth didn't you dodge to the middle of the road as I asked you?" Teddy says shortly.

"I have no wish to be indebted to you for anything, thank you," Nora replies coldly, giving her hand to Fane to bandage up for her. Teddy does not speak, but lays by no means gentle grasp upon the triumphant Nelly, and his whole nature seems warped by one vengeful longing that cries in the words of the prophet of old—"I would there were a sword in mine hand, for now would I kill thee;" and Nelly, conscious of his evil meditations, hies her to Ivy's further side.

Poor Ivy, nearly distracted by Nora's perplexing tactics, talks to Billy behind a barrier of hardly won firmness, and keeps him safely discussing his ball. It is his first attempt at anything of the kind, and its rumoured preparations afford scope for sufficient conversation.

"Miss Nora told me," Billy remarks abruptly, "Horston was the most hideous place she had ever seen. Do you think it is as bad as that? I know it isn't beautiful"—regretfully—"but it has never had much of a chance. It has always been so deserted, and that makes it look melancholy. Now the rooms that are really inhabited seem to me alive enough"—smiling.

"Yes, indeed!" Ivy says, with a little laugh, as visions of the herd of dogs flit before her. "In noise and liveliness those few rooms should make up for the silence of the rest. But I think Horston isn't really hideous—it is only that the rooms want soft colouring and light, to get rid of their heavy stiffness and crowded oppressiveness."

Billy's face radiates with satisfaction. "Do you think there is anything more you could think of?" he asks eagerly.

Ivy feels aggrieved. It does seem hard that he should consult her about ideas that Nora's hasty remarks have suggested. She is truthful, however, and her memory shall help him. "Yes," she says slowly, "as you ask, I will tell you what I think it wants. We (Nora and I) noticed it only the other day. The upper terrace and the wide gravel sweep you cannot alter, but you might have more shrubberies, and all those stone vases filled, and on the second terrace I should make a narrow bed running the whole length for roses, and have them along all the shrubbery walks winding away to the park. The flower gardens by the tennis courts are lovely, and all the 'old' garden, only perhaps the front does want lightening, and roses on the second terrace behind the old fountains and sun-dial would make a wonderful difference, and break the very stiff lines."

Billy is listening with most absorbed attention. "Would you break up the second slope into flower-beds, as well as having the background of roses?" he says anxiously.

"No; I love the grass, and—and Nora never thought of that "—hastily.

"You would not have flower beds there at all?"

"I think "—hesitatingly—" no, I don't think that was thought of."

"But would *you*?"—shortly.

"I! Oh, no—I—should not advise it "—blankly.

"That's enough then "—briefly.

Nelly takes advantage of the pause that follows to carry out a strategical movement dear to her vitiated intelligence. With an upward thrust, planting her head just about the bend of Ivy's knee, she butts her young mistress with a bang against Billy's arm almost full length on to the road! Billy's quick grasp saves Ivy from falling, and supports her rather longer than absolutely necessary. He is conscious of a feeling of satisfaction, and yet to judge by his glare at Nelly, one would augur that her hours were numbered.

"Nelly is rather put out," Ivy remarks apologetically; "she does so dislike the dogs! We started without them, and now she is angry at their appearance; she is really so good generally."

Billy smiles. "Are you as lenient to the rest of the world as you are to Nelly?" he says. Then adds softly—"Will you be?" and looks down at her gravely waiting.

Poor Ivy! all the blood in her body rushes in one sweep to bang against her heart. Possibly those gifted in a thorough knowledge of anatomy might question this statement, but their objections cannot be considered worthy of notice, as the evidence of the senses settles the fact! It is possible to keep her fingers twisted in Nelly's collar and so adhere somehow to the moving group; it is also possible to place successively feet that are carrying a hundred pounds weight in each boot upon a road that comes swimming towards her; but it is *not* possible to answer Billy. In the first place, he cannot be meaning what—what it almost seemed he did mean. He cannot care for lenient judgment for himself—*he* does not ask for gentleness from her, it must be of course for—for Nora! He thinks she is not sympathetic enough; he thinks she does not try to lighten Nora's perplexities as a kindly elder girl should. With stiff lips and struggling determination Ivy tries to answer. Billy watches her rather glumly, poor dear, her long hesitation is scarcely reassuring.

"Will you?" he repeats.

"I will try to," comes in choked tones; and he is humbly content.

Nora, walking between Teddy and Fane, turns round abruptly. "Mr. Dare, your period of probation is over; I may ask anything I like, mayn't I? Teddy says the wind has changed; it will rain to-night, and you will hunt to-morrow. For once, only for once, will you mount me? *Do* grant me what I ask."

Billy smiles good-naturedly. "Of course," he says, "with the greatest pleasure. Which will you have? I fancy they are all up to your weight! Skyrocket or Skittles would suit you down to the ground."

"May I have any one I like?"

"Certainly."

"Then I want Tebasco."

Billy whistles dubiously. "Tebasco has never carried a lady. I am afraid you could hardly hold him."

"You said I might have any I liked," Nora cries sharply. "I choose Tebasco; it is surely my own look out. Or"—rather scornfully—"are you afraid for—your horse?"

Billy politely assures her he is solely anxious about her safety. His thoughts are his own. He is decidedly surprised at the request, and the others are certain that there must be some understanding between the two, or such an unblushing demand could not have been made.

Little do they know that Nora, half maddened

by Teddy's silence, which seems to her incomprehensible indifference, meditates a severe measure as a final test of his feelings.

Horston is to be filled with Billy's friends. A big shoot and hunting will engross Teddy. Whatever is to be done must be done at once. It is promptly arranged, and, of course, no one can object. Mrs. Peyton is surprised, and consents most unwillingly to Billy's reiterated pleadings that for *once* he may be allowed to again mount Miss Ivy. It is extremely puzzling. Why should he be so eager about Ivy if there is anything between him and Nora? Surely, even if they are waiting for Sir Noel Templeton's consent to the engagement, they might confide in her. He wishes to assure them perhaps of his good friendship for Ivy. Well, as the Vicar has consented to the arrangement, and the Master's wife will chaperon them, there is no more to be said; and Ivy, enraged at being made a sandwich of to screen Nora's enormities, finds herself, silent with mortification, riding one of Billy's best known hunters along the soaking grass-bordered roads that led them, this spongy February morning, to the meet at Bolter's Barn.

How could discontent linger after that glorious burst? A short check brings them all together again, and delight has filled Ivy's eyes with gladness, and flung sadness to the winds. Billy is overjoyed. For the first time for years Ivy is her old bright self again. Nothing like a good run to smooth the wrinkles out of life. The homeward ride shall settle everything. He passes his hand lovingly down Vagabond's neck, and watches Ivy in proud content.

Teddy pushes closer to Tebasco's side, his brown face bright with pleasure.

"I soon saw there was no cause for uneasiness; you were riding right well. My goodness! how he took that big wall out of plough. Our party forged pretty well ahead after those first three fields, didn't it?" gleefully.

Nora is indignant at his good temper. Teddy ought to be miserable. The fact of her riding Tebasco should spoil his best day's hunting.

"I don't suppose you would notice anything but the satisfaction of such a run," she says shortly.

"Well, no; not much," Teddy answers, with an honest laugh. "It *is* true; a fellow doesn't care for anything else in the world when he's hunting, I think. His debts and his duns, and all the other fatal things, don't bother him any more than the fact of his daily shave. Seems all right, somehow, until he is jogging home!"

"Of course, perfect happiness means pure selfishness!"

"I don't think it's that," Teddy says less brightly, as he notices Nora's ill-humour. "I think it is more because you have forgotten yourself and everything else for the time. You owe everything to your horse, and feel in charity with all men. Even the silly fool who tried to jump on you has been left behind and forgiven long ago."

What *can* one do with a man in this blissful frame of mind! At this moment there are frantic yells of " Yoicks!" "Gone away!" from the further side of the copse, and the field sweep madly round, and find themselves compelled to choose an almost impossible jump, or the irritating alternative of waiting their turn at the gate. The field seem to unhesitatingly prefer the gate.

"Come quickly!" Teddy cried to Nora, plunging eagerly into the jostling mass. It was a simple thing to obey, but Nora had a longing to defy him, and to avenge herself upon him. Tebasco, she knew, would tolerate no bullying. The waiting at the covert side had taxed his patience, and he was chafing even now. In a moment, with a dexterous twist, she curbs the fretting animal, and edges him out of the struggling current; he plunges and rears, but with firm hands Nora keeps him back until the crowd have passed through, and the horse, irritated and held by dogged force, comes straining furiously after them. As they emerge through a short grass ride on to the ploughed field adjoining the copse, Nora, still holding Tebasco in viciously, sees Teddy about a dozen yards ahead. She does not give him the chance of making a single remark, but giving the horse a stinging cut with her whip, comes tearing past, scattering clods of earth in showers as the infuriated animal races down a furrow. The wall at the end of the field is the biggest Nora has yet encountered, but she makes no effort to steady Tebasco for the jump. He takes it nobly, and as he flings it behind him, seems to be bent only on redeeming his position with a rush; he thunders over grass, and leaps three succeeding walls in a sort of blind fury that hardly stays to shorten his stride; he crashes through a "bullfinch," and the drop on the off affects nothing but Nora's hat; he tears on, and Nora, knowing that when really horse or man take the bit between their teeth there is nothing to be done but sit tight and keep cool, acts accordingly; and righting her hat, bends her head down, and almost laughs at the whizzing of the wind in her ears. As Tebasco rises for a post and rails near a farm, Nora sees there are only about half-a-dozen of the field anywhere near. They are racing downhill now, and along the bottom of the valley runs the railway. Ah! and something else too, for here ahead, its eddying waters gleaming in the chill, clouded light, runs Longdale brook! It will stop the whole field, of course, for it is both deep and wide, and now swollen by recent rain, quite unjumpable. Nora looks behind her. The entire field are bearing off to the right to gain the Longdale road—fox and hounds alone have crossed the brook; and she would be idiotic were she to attempt to follow. Ivy, sailing along by Billy's side, is making for the road and bridge. Nora will follow; but before she has time to make her wisdom apparent, Teddy gallops up.

"Come on!" he shouts. "What are you playing the fool with Tebasco for? You can't be mad enough to dream of putting him at a thing like *that!* unless you want to break your neck."

"I wish I *could!*" she calls back defiantly, as she holds Tebasco steady, and puts him straight for the brook.

The spongy field flashes into jets of muddy water as Tebasco races over it. Nora holds him straight, and as the width of water lies before her, gives him his head, and a sharp cut as he takes off. A sensation of being entirely hollow, and an odd catch in her breath, and then that awful grey water lies behind them, and with a scrambling second plunge, and deluged with the splash of landing, they are on the other side. She will cross the railway embankment and be absolutely alone with the hounds. As she casts one look back before making for the low wall, she reins in Tebasco with sudden terror Teddy is following her! Hot Coppers slips as he takes off. There is a blur of black, white, and chestnut, a great rolling splash, and horse and rider have disappeared. At any other time Nora would have shouted with laughter—now she turns very white, and feels sick and faint. Teddy will be dragged out *dead*, and she has killed him. She is positive—certain—it is the punishment she has brought upon herself, the just retribution that sometimes overtakes us in this life.

Tebasco has three heads, and his beautiful action is exactly like a channel steamer. One more minute, and then Teddy, dripping and hatless, is standing on the bank, and trying to effect a landing for Hot Coppers. With help the horse is hauled out, and Teddy rejoins Nora, smiling good-naturedly.

"We can soon pick them up, Nora; sorry you waited and lost your lead. Good heavens! what is the matter? Were you frightened?"—anxiously. Nora bursts into tears. Teddy comes closer. "What did you do it for, Nora?" he says; "Tebasco didn't bolt. What is the matter with you? Have you quarrelled with—Dare?"—hopelessly.

"Oh, *what* a fool you are!" she sobs. "I am sick to death of Mr. Dare. What is he to *me*? What have I been but the peacemaker between him and Ivy? Oh, go away; here they are coming back to look for us."

"I don't care if they are," Teddy retorts, dripping

but determined. " You shall answer me one thing first. Then if you don't care for Dare, you can for me, Nora, for "——

" Oh, stupid ! Isn't it because I *do* care that I am so miserable ? " she answers, smiling through her tears ; and then Ivy and Billy are upon them.

Billy runs his eyes anxiously over his horses and their riders. " All right ? " he questions quickly. " We heard there had been an accident, and—she—was so frightened, we came back. Did Tebasco bolt ? "

Nora fumbles with her reins. She looks rather upset, and yet she is smiling. " I was stupid," she says, " but I think it's all right now," with a nervous laugh.

" Yes," Teddy adds promptly, " we've made it all right now."

And rather wondering at their brightness, Ivy turned her horse's head and rode by Nora's side, for as Teddy was soaking, and they were all by this time " out of it," they moved homewards. It was trying to lose the end of the fun, for now that no accident justified their recall Ivy could not help regretting her lost minutes of absolute happiness.

" How I adore hunting," Nora cried suddenly, looking across Ivy to where Billy rides on her near side. " Mr. Dare, you don't know the good Tebasco has done me. When I am savage, I can only ride my rage down."

" I would not mount you for such a purpose," Billy replies, " or you'd break your neck for mere want of thought. Not that I don't think girls can ride just as well as men," he adds hastily, " and I like to see them out. If I had a wife she should hunt whenever she liked," with a swift glance at Ivy.

" And if *I* had a wife," Teddy supplements shortly, "she should never hunt at all !"

"*Indeed* I shall !" Nora bursts out passionately. Then an agony of shamed confusion floods the tell-tale crimson to the very roots of her hair. Ivy stared at her in speechless amazement, her brown eyes glancing in frightened bewilderment past Nora's bent head to Teddy's brown face. The stern firmness vanishes in his quick uncontrollable smile. Bending down to Nora he whispers tenderly—

" So you shall, darling. I did not mean it. Of course you shall !"

A great rushing rings in Ivy's ears—a mist rises and hides everything from her. Perfection's dainty little ears have vanished, and the saddle is soaring upwards. She catches at the reins aimlessly, and sits quite silently, swaying to the kingly creature's tread, though she can neither see nor hear for some time. Billy's voice comes to her presently like a clear whisper heard amid a surrounding storm. "We are almost at home, Ivy—speak to me just once—and give me the answer I have waited for all these years."

She can speak no word, she cannot even *see* him, but stretching out her left hand put it into his strong right one, and hears above Fane's and Archie's boisterous welcome his soft " *At last, darling.*"

" Billy !" Fane shouts, " we will be down to dinner. Several fellows have come already. Glad you are all alive, but what a fit of the blues you are all in. Not a word, and we've been yelling at you ever since you turned in at the gate. Is that Teddy behind with Nora? Come on in and tell us all about it, or must you be off, Billy? Don't dismount, I can lift Ivy down."

Billy is at Ivy's side before Fane has finished speaking, and takes the small lady down without a word. He holds her hand a moment as he says good-bye, and then shouting a cheery farewell, rides away into the darkness.

CHAPTER XXIV.

"Was never true love loved in vain,
  For truest love is highest gain."
—George Eliot.

It is the day of Billy's ball. All the boys are at Horston for the big shoot. Ivy and Nora chattering as they sit together over the schoolroom fire. Long, indeed, does it take Nora to sew the buttons on her gloves. She breaks her fourth needle, and flings its fragments into the fire absently, as she remarks thoughtfully—

"Humility like Teddy's is maddening. Imagine his believing, first, that I cared for Sir Silvergilt, and when I came down here, for Mr. Dare! It was all I could do to propose to him with becoming hesitation. You see, Ivy," colouring suddenly, "I have known for more than a year that he *did* care, although he was so selfishly silent. What do I care about his being poor? Aunt Julia may delude Sir Silvergilt in the vain hope that I will consent at last. I don't mind a bit about India—I like hot days, and love cotton frocks. Such nonsense of Teddy thinking he must leave the regiment, I won't hear of it. I have told him I am only desirous of marrying the uniform, and should not have cared an atom about him if it hadn't been for the boots! but he is too conceited to pay any attention to what I say, and really believes I'd marry him if he exchanged into the line! Now nothing would induce me to! Imagine expecting a man who has ridden always to dismount and walk through life with a wife! He is so darling he thinks he could do it; being human, he couldn't; he would be footsore at the first milestone, and lay his head in the dust at the second."

"I think you misjudge Teddy there," Ivy answers earnestly; "he is too manly to moan when once his mind is made up. He wanted long ago to share the three hundred a-year Uncle Percy left him, with Fane, but father would not hear of it, and now Fane seems not to want it—he never is in debt now, and finds his allowance ample. I hope he will when he is in the army. Archie, of course, is no anxiety, and "——

"I do think it is the oddest thing," Nora breaks in, "sending a boy who is to be a clergyman to walk a London hospital, attend lectures, study physiology with a young physician, and metaphysics with an old philosopher."

Ivy smiles as she answers, "Father knows best. If Archie is to teach others what is the purpose of life, he must understand something of humanity and its needs—at least, so father says; and Archie must learn that religion means principle, and the thousand hard and fast lines of wrong and right are wiped out often by circumstance—so father says."

"How delightful!" Nora answers lightly, for the Peyton theology often puzzled her. "Always put down the wrong you or others do to circumstance! I like that; it's cheering; circumstances are often too strong for me."

"You are pretending to misunderstand, Nora; you know it is the hardest, fastest line of all, not a question of some trifling immaterial matter, but the unswerving testimony of your own conscience. You know what father is always saying—'Happy is he that judgeth not himself in that which he approveth.' We may pretend we don't know when we have been doing wrong, but we *do*; we are bitter, and selfish, and cross, all the while knowing we are paining our poor little good angel, who sits without a moan after a while, and suffers silently." Ivy is smiling, but her eyes are dim with tears.

Nora's arms are round her in a minute, while her work tumbles into the fireplace. "Ivy, don't!" she says tremulously. "I didn't mean it. I didn't mean anything. I could bite my tongue out because I say *vile* things, and then you get heartaches for Teddy. You goose, as if I didn't know. But I am not really as awful as I seem. There's a brake inside me that jams down and stops me rushing at a bit of mischief that does seem so desirable. Oh, Ivy, if I've often said horrid things, you understand *now* I never meant them. I wanted to make it all right, and the only way seemed to make general hay, and scratch every one up a bit. I daresay it was not pleasant, but I never believe in 'let sleeping dogs lie.' I think one should stir them up with a dangling bone to see if they will bite. It *is* all right, isn't it, darling? You are not choking in silence any more at the greatness of your sacrifice. Don't, oh, *please*, don't, Ivy. I won't say a word, oh, I won't even open my lips. Oh, I *am* so sorry!"

Her words are addressed to the empty room. Ivy has flown. Her feelings are too overwrought for the merest remark to be made about them at all, and she sobs away in her own room in a state of nervous excitement that threatens to culminate in a severe headache. Like a true woman, she refuses to recognise that her sorrow has spent itself in storms of doubting tears, and that joy is even now lighting in the poor little tired eyes a fitful wistful gladness.

When Mrs. Peyton looks down upon the two girls in their white gowns, and glances from Nora's dazzling beauty to Ivy's sweet downcast eyes and quivering lips, she smiles gravely. She does not know that the very sight of her inspires Ivy with strength. The simply severe folds of the heavy velvet, and the soft lace gathered to the full smooth throat, make her grand beauty almost sublime. The girls gaze up at her speechlessly. Ordinary expressions are all too commonplace. There is a nobility that overawes until the calm smile in the clear eyes kindles reverence to speech.

"How beautiful you are!" they cry simultaneously. "Mother, I must kiss you, you are so lovely."

Mrs. Peyton smiles and kisses both girls. "I want to see my children," she says. "Nora, if your aunt and uncle will give you to us, you are to be

my child too. So let me see how both my daughters
look." Mrs. Peyton stands with her arm round
Ivy. Nora is silent before her. She is so radiantly
beautiful, so utterly glad, that the mother, looking
at her crowned with life's richest gifts—beauty, and
youth, and love—could only breathe a blessing over
so exquisite a piece of God's creation.

"Aunt Mary," Nora says suddenly, "tell me to
be good, and I will be good—I feel I can be, if
you say it quick—this minute."

"Very well, Nora darling," as she smiles into
the sweet blue eyes, "then remember that as there
can be no engagement between you and Teddy until
your uncle and aunt consent, you must not dance
too much with him to-night or "——

"Oh! but I *must*. I—oh! you would never say
that if you knew! I assure you solemnly, it will be
the only time I will have a chance of feeling good—
really and truly, I won't answer for myself if I
may not be with Teddy. I shall be horribly rude to
every one else, or else flirt with them madly out of
pure rage," Nora concludes desperately.

"No, dear child, you will respect, not lower yourself, and all the more now for Teddy's sake."

"I did not mean it," Nora mutters.

"I know it, but there are some things we should
not allow our tongues even to say," Mrs. Peyton
answers gently.

Nora puts her arms round her aunt's neck and
kisses her. "I am going to be a perfect saint," she
says. "I can do it if I keep one eye fixed on you
all the time, so you must be always where I can
keep revolving around, or remember, auntie, if you
go to the wall, so do I!"

Here the Vicar enters, muffled up in his wraps, and after a proud glance at his wife and the two girls, suggests that as Rat Trap is waiting, they had better be off. Ivy sits as near to her mother as possible. Mrs. Peyton has only spoken to her once, when Nora was shouting through the little front window to her uncle—" I like some lines I found to-day of Mrs. Browning's; I know my child will too—

> "'And I smiled to think God's greatness
> Flowed around our incompleteness,
> Round our restlessness—His rest.'"

That waggonette, mounted upon most incomprehensible springs, had always a tendency to rock Now rendered all the more top-heavy by its roofing apparatus, it lurches like a little lugger in a storm. The occupants sit tight, and the Vicar, perched beside the invaluable " Abel," bellows encouragement or timely warnings through the canvas covering. As they turn in at Horston they are perforce obliged to unhook sundry fastenings to get a view of the effect the Vicar shouts is " quite inspiriting." All up the winding drive are fixed open braziers full of tar or pitch or some brightly burning compound, that illumines the dark leafless avenue with great wavering flashes of light, and gleams through all the upward circling roadway, like giant fire-flies flitting behind the black trunks of the trees. Nearer the effect is much more brilliant. The old-fashioned west garden is bright as day, great tongues of coloured flame bringing curiously cut yews, prim hedges, and stiff stone fountains fauns and weather-beaten " Floras," into vivid glowing distinctness. All round the house, on the lower terraces, in the east garden, and away to the tennis courts and the great shadow of the park, flare and flicker and blaze innumerable tongues of leaping light. The men moving among them look weird and uncanny, like black flitting bats against the white full disc of the moon.

Horston is the Horston of old no longer. The huge hall, with its dim oaken walls, dark backgrounds for rusty armour, and moth-eaten banners, is aglow with light, and rich in subtle colouring from heavy *portières* over the many doors, from curious peeps of colour from the galleries above, from screens and cushioned window-seats, and warm rugs and the bright glint of steel. Vistas of fairy-like rooms lie behind the open doors, and half-dazed the girls follow Mrs. Peyton to divest themselves of their wraps. Cyril meets them as they emerge again into the hall.

"Billy has been dying for you to come, mother," he shouts. "I mayn't tell you anything, only I think it's like fairyland. Don't you, mother? All these men"—indicating the obsequious footmen—"are rather a bore"—whisperingly—"they're the only things that look grave. I *wish*"—regretfully—"they could dance too, then perhaps they would like it better. I *love* it!"

A group of men—the majority in hunt coats—come across the hall to meet them, Billy the brightest of them all, and smiling with a great content that made Ivy shrink into nervous silence. He just looked at her as they shook hands, and then giving his arm to her mother walked on, saying—"So very good of you to be early; I wanted to show you round myself before any one came."

Then introducing several of his friends, they all passed on together.

Where are the impressive, wholly respectable, and rather mouldy reception rooms? Where is that bleak *chef d'œuvre*, the white and gold drawing-room, with its crude curtains and furniture whose startling blues had been so lamentably preserved neath holland covers? Where are the massed multitude of pictures crowding the walls like an auctioneer's show-room? Where the vast gaps of staring glass and coldly un-backgrounded statuary standing on very excellent marble pedestals, planted at regular intervals, with their *chevaux de frise* of spindle-legged chairs at their base? Gone. The place that groaned at the knowing of them knows them and groans no more. Against soft-toned backgrounds beautiful pictures breathe and expand before one—not jammed into repulsive contact with a crowd of jarring mediocrity. Rare old cabinets have crept into a fuller existence, and tables no longer creak beneath a medley of curios, but exhibit a sense of arrangement that enhances the merit of all. Palms and flowers are everywhere in profusion, and delicate china, moderate mirrors, and modern lighting have made the old house unrecognisable. The ballroom, with its old gallery at one end, has been very tastefully decorated; and the musicians, already ensconced among a blaze of lights and flowers, are playing odd variations, testing strings, while others tune. Ivy is so unaccountably nervous at the very sight of Billy that it is a great relief to her to have his friends to talk to. And gradually the rooms fill, and dancing begins, Billy opening the ball with the

Duchess of Demarkation, who with her daughters, Lady Edith and Enid, and Lady Gwenneth Flyer, are among the earliest arrivals. The Duke and his eldest son, Lord Longstop, are as keen about treading the measure in question as any lads in their teens, and the quadrille is not merely a duty dance, for all are in bright spirits, and all are good neighbours, and the gay scene is invigorating and gladness catching.

Billy, in his character of host, has been unceasingly on duty, and Ivy has now begun to long for the sound of his voice, as much as in the earlier part of the evening she had nervously dreaded it. She lets her partner fan and talk to her, but her thoughts are roaming in the direction of a tall, red-coated man who stands waiting by Lady Gwenneth Flyer. This small lady takes a reef in her dress rather ruthlessly, and remarks, as she puts her hand on Billy's arm—

"Who, oh, who is the man who mows off frills and even *shoes* with that dexterous sweep of his very long off-leg? Do let us steer clear of him!"

Billy's laughing answer is given as they whirl away, and Ivy's partner promptly launches again in their wake.

Walking through the rooms after the dance, Ivy comes upon Nora and Teddy. It is refreshing to meet after so prolonged an absence, and Ivy smiles as she is passing them.

"Wait," Nora cries; "there is Fane, and as he is sure to stay, you may as well."

Ivy's partner looks rather amused, and in another moment Fane joins them.

There are several minutes of chattering, and then

Nora remarks—"There's the next dance. Go, Fane! Ivy, wait. Let Mr. Hardup seek his next partner. We will look after you."

"Don't let me keep you," Ivy says, dismissing her cavalier easily. "Now, Nora, what is it?"

"Nothing. Only to tell you you are looking lovely, and that you are breaking hearts by scores. Sit here for a minute. Doesn't auntie look perfect? I heard the Duchess say to her, 'Mary, you are like one star above myriad fire-flies, or the Venus of Milo among wax-works.' I thought it was so appropriate; there's such a restraining power about her, any one would feel saintly in her presence."

"So you have fled from it!" Ivy laughs, as she watches the swaying motion of her fan; but Nora, whose curiosity is boundless, and whose interest is stretched to its last strand, knows that it is a forced one, and that Ivy is almost too nervous to know what she is talking about. Her partner for this dance is vainly searching for her, and for the next one it is Billy. There is everything to make Nora curious, everything to make Ivy nervous. How is she to speak or dance, when the very sight of her tall host makes her heart bang thickly like a muffled bell? She has not spoken a dozen words to Billy since the sudden *dénouement* effected by Nora had cleared the air of misunderstandings in one flash of perception. She knows that his handshake and his every glance, that are so steady and tender, instead of comforting her, make her feel inclined to tear off and rush straight home. The ball so far has not been an unmixed joy to her. Nora and Teddy are possibly aware of this, certainly not Fane.

"Ted," Fane begins, trying to pull Nora's programme from his brother's hands, "I think we might come to some sort of an arrangement. Let me have one in every five, will you, Nora? or say every fourth dance."

"Certainly," Nora says.

"Well, let me have your card then. Give it up, Ted. What a grasping, jealous fellow you are! There *was* a time " —— pointedly.

"There *was* a time," Nora repeats lightly, "when I had to put up with *you!* Mercifully times have changed. Let him have it "—to Teddy—"he is quite deluded enough to imagine anything if you don't."

"Well," Fane retorts, "your ingratitude is revolting. Think of my faithful services. Why, this very day two years ago you simply would not move one yard without me! Stuck to me like a leech the whole evening." His face is perfectly grave as he looks at Nora while he speaks.

She leans back with a little grimace at him. "You are wrong," she says; "this was the Veglione, and to-morrow was the ball. I am not likely to forget it—it was the most horrible evening of my life—so your society is naturally a bitter experience! Oh!"—with a laugh—"what tortures we endured!"

"And the best of it was, Ted," Fane continues, "that when our fears were set at rest, then she was furious because she could not see the great collapse of Contarini! Certainly, to watch our worthy host walking into him was worth something, and didn't the "——

"What *are* you talking about? What do you mean about—Contarini?" Ivy asks, with suddenly arrested attention.

"Only the drubbing Billy gave him at the ball," Fane answers, with guileless forgetfulness; "for which he would have scored off him pretty freely at their duel next morning, had not the earthquake benevolently interfered."

Ivy looks with puzzled questioning at each of the three in turn. The ball—Contarini—Billy—duel— what *can* it all mean? Laughing and chaffing, they are mixing up fact and fiction for fun. She can see that Fane is blandly unconscious of having uttered anything startling; but when Nora's blue eyes are raised from Teddy's cuff, at which she has been vacantly staring, Ivy knows she is face to face with some facts long hidden, some concealed matter that surely is a mystery. Her hands hold her fan very quietly, and her voice is sufficiently callous as she remarks— "I did not remember having seen Mr. Dare at that ball. Are you sure about his being there, Fane?"

"You duffer! Just as sure as that he is here, and coming this way now. Why, don't you re- member? Oh, what's that for, Teddy?"—sharply. "Great ——!" as a sudden inspiration follows Teddy's kick, and promptly cuts short his retrospec- tive ramblings.

"Our dance, I think," Billy says, smiling, as he looks down at Ivy.

Nora is glad of her fan. Teddy and Fane are both very interested in their programmes.

"I'm off," Fane says, rising. "I think if all the dances you give me, Nora, are to be like this, Teddy is welcome to them. I have the red-haired girl in green all to myself anyhow, and she is rare sport."

"She is horrid!" Nora retorts. "I'm sure ten

years ago her hair was black; and her youth was passed among the sugar-canes."

"Accounts for her sweetness!" and Fane saunters off.

Ivy rises and walks away by Billy's side. This red coat sleeve and white glove belong to him. Her hand rests lightly on his arm, but she is miles and miles away from him. What are these facts that wrap a mystery round his past, involving him in the miserable experience that seemed to haunt her like a nightmare. What had he to do with Contarini? It was horrible! Billy had always seemed so strong and independent and aloof, like the poplar near Little Grumble, a beacon for miles round. What had he to do with masks and mummeries—those days of hopeless love and cruel hate—the wretchedness, the hypocrisies, the deception of it all? What possible power had drawn his simple direct interests into such a mesh of misunderstanding?

Billy walks on slowly—apparently they are not to dance.

"Here's a good place," he says, turning into a large conservatory, which, being heated well within and matted well without, is really warm. "On the other side there is a nicer place, and pretty, isn't it, under these palms?"

"Don't," Ivy says, with a curious contraction about her lips. "Palms frame all the terrible pictures of my life, I think. Would you mind if"——

"I don't mind anything," Billy says, standing still before her. "It does not matter if we are in a conservatory or a coal cellar; I only want to know—have I waited long enough—*now?*"

Ivy looks up with a swift glance, then the eye-lids fall heavily, and her lips grow white.

"Have I?" Billy repeats, taking her hands in his. "I had begun to hope there was a chance for me; if there—is not—just tell me as soon as you can."

His hands hold Ivy's quietly and firmly, but his voice is too full of keen vibration not to betray his emotion.

Ivy tries to speak once or twice, but the words will not come. Nothing matters now—nothing—Billy is here, and—he loves her—and the palms wave overhead, and the air is heavy with the scent of mingled flowers. Myriad coloured lights gleam, weaving shimmering webs as they flash across rich varied foliage; and far away the music of the "Dorothy" valse seems to set all the surroundings to the rhythm of the song.

Billy bends down until his blue eyes are more on a level with Ivy's.

"I have loved you so long, darling, can you love me a little—at last?"

She raises her eyes to his face—rather a stern face, strong in its self-repression, but full now of tender pleading. No words will come, but the brown eyes speak plainly enough, and he loosens her hands only to hold her more closely, while the little clinging fingers clasp as high as they can up to the summit of his collar.

There is silence while the fuller revelation comes to these two, that though to be loved is earth's greatest happiness, to love is Heaven.

"When once one *knows*, how easy all puzzles

seem," Ivy says softly, after a while, as they sit together, very little visible to any curious passers-by but a huge fan, a pair of very long legs, and a wisp of cloudy skirt. " And so it was *Nora* who sent for you, and you came at once, and then —oh, I am glad I never knew, it must have seemed so—*cruel.*"

Billy does not speak for a minute. Perhaps the memory of what had awaited him after that hurried journey was an experience not easily talked about. He holds Ivy's hand and smooths the small fingers with wondering pre-occupation, as if ruminating over their marvellous power to wound. For years, with one gesture they could have granted him the happiness he craved, and now that it is his, and they are confidingly clasped in his own strong grasp, have they brought him what he wanted, have they given him all he desired? He is no boy lover, blinded by his own infatuation, but a man to whom time has taught some of its severest lessons ere bestowing calm patience and clear sight. Surely he knows that what he has now is not the same as what he sought. Yes, he knows it; and it seems to him that had he been given all he asked in that first supreme struggle of boyish longing, life would never have made clear to him its meaning. It is the seeming loss that is often our highest gain, and Billy knows full well that the manly resolution taught by trial is the sole means whereby he has attained success. He has not been granted everything he asked so blindly then, but yet he seems to have gained infinitely more now. Waked from a dream of love to learn the duty of life, but to be given a deeper, truer happiness at last, was it not well to have endured? He bent down and kissed the little soft palm, and then says, with a satisfied sigh—

"When you are past the post, darling, you don't much care what the course has been. I have won my prize now; I don't want to look back on a time when I didn't draw away and retain the lead. It is the hardest race I was ever entered for, but—why, Ivy—oh, darling, don't make me feel such a brute—why, yes, it's true, you poor little darling, I wouldn't alter my place, the course, or pace, if I had the whole thing over again; it is worth everything—to win."

"I wonder you could go on caring"—humbly.

"Do you?"—pointedly. "Well, I don't know. I think men take longer making up their minds; but when they do, they don't change them."

"I suppose," Ivy replies solemnly, "that accounts for their general unsettled condition. Even *a man* says of them—'To one thing constant never.'" The words are regretted as soon as uttered.

There is a pause. Then Billy speaks calmly—"Judging by the back of your head, I should imagine you are inclined to retract that statement, or have you any further remarks to make about—er—*women?* What! poor things, have you nothing to say for them?"

"They are"——

"Yes," Billy assents promptly, "they *are*. Does that mean much more than—they exist? I should like to know more about them; doubtless you have much to say on the subject."

"They are not so easy to *talk about*"—loftily. "They are extremely difficult to understand."

"They *are*"—cheerfully; "but perhaps if you

would turn round and explain a little, I might be less hopelessly ignorant upon the subject. Now, supposing we keep to the matter in question—er—*constancy*—how would you place them there?" Leaning forward, he is criticising the contour of Ivy's cheek with amused deliberation.

"*My* opinion would hardly be worth much; you had better have a man's on such a subject"—craftily. "Of course, constancy and love are the same thing —*with women*—and you know what *a man* says about it—

> 'Love is of man's life a thing apart,
> 'Tis woman's *whole existence!*' "

"Well, I never knew that," Billy remarks musingly; "so a woman is always constant to whatever she has loved. I suppose they run the whole concern upon such a much larger scale than we do, they don't get mixed up at all. To keep things— er—separate—and—er—clearly defined—is a bit difficult sometimes, isn't it?" He is smoothing his moustache to cover a curious little smile, which perhaps Ivy feels, though she cannot see it.

"Where there is real love, nothing is difficult," she replies, still on the defensive.

"Takes a lot, doesn't it?" Billy goes on in an earnest, inquiring tone, "to keep half-a-dozen devotions at equal white heat! Can't run to that somehow. Can only make rather a poor show though I concentrate all mine into *one.*"

Ivy's face is buried in her bouquet. There is a suppressed choke, and on the petals of an unbending camelia gleams something suspiciously like a tear. Then the bouquet is tumbled on to the floor, and the tears that follow that one course cheerfully after each other down the silk facings of Billy's evening hunt coat.

"It's just that!" Ivy sobs; "I will never be able to—to show you that I love you. You are so strong and—and *everything;* and years ago I used to think you just nothing—only—only a boy!"—with a sob—"and now I have been so—so uncertain, and you have been so quiet, and so unswervingly *strong,* that—that I can't possibly *ever* make you know how I care."

"Can't you, darling? I am not so sure. Suppose you try? I think if you say, 'I love you more than any one,' that ought to square it, you know."

The brown eyes, all bright with tears, look lovingly into his. "I do—oh, you *know* I do! More —oh, a thousand times more than any one. More even"—in an awed, quiet tone—"and I can't understand it—but do you know you seem to have come *in front* of mother! I couldn't love any one more than mother, but you do seem to come in front. When I think of you, and mother, and Teddy, and father, and all, mother stands with all the group behind her, and then you come and slip—in front. Is that telling you how much I love you?"— anxiously.

Billy has no words for a few moments. "You have told me," he says at last, not quite as calmly as usual. "I daresay I shall want you to tell me over and over again. It will be because I dare scarcely believe it, not because I do not understand. No, never mind those people; they are going on and don't see us. Oh, my darling, just "——

"You *are* believing I love you?"—whisperingly.

"I am believing"—equally softly. "Ah, now, why

imperil the faith; it was growing so beautifully strong?"

"Strong faith doesn't require too constant proving," Ivy says, pushing her hair into order, as she stands before him smiling.

Billy shakes his head rather dubiously. "I'm afraid, after all, mine is lamentably weak," he says, as he puts her hand on his arm and walks off to the ballroom.

Mrs. Peyton is the centre of an interested group, who are beguiling the hours by conversation never spiteful or petty. The dear little Duchess had been the Mainwarings' friend before they married, and found in the quiet Vicar's wife her dearest companion. She had always gone to her for sympathy; and when Gwenneth insisted on marrying that great awkward Joey Flyer, had found comfort, and wisdom since proved correct; for his pretty wife improved his manners, and turned the rough country squire into the most popular M.F.H. in the whole shire. Mary Peyton's gifted nature and greater intellect never overawed her grace's smaller soul, and the two were laughing together now.

"Mary," the merry little Duchess begins, "where is the merit of great example? *My* girls are most desirably conspicuous, *where* are yours? Nora has dazzled the room, simply to vanish like the captivating Cinderella, stealing the hearts of all, and not leaving even a slipper behind; and Ivy, who seemed to be a most pattern daughter very much *en evidence,* has for the last half-hour been conspicuous by her absence!"

Alas for those innocents who dream of eluding the vigilance of chaperons!

"One of my delinquents is coming now," Mrs. Peyton answers, smiling leniently, as Ivy's tell-tale eyes are lifted up to hers.

Billy looks down calmly. "I believe I am guilty," he says easily. "I inveigled her into an argument until I made her see the question in my light—at last." He smiles as he lays a little stress upon the concluding words, then turns to the Duchess, with a profound bow—"The supper-room doors are being opened, I am half-a-minute late; will your grace pardon me?"

She smiles as she places her hand upon his arm. "You would not care if I withheld my forgiveness; you are too happy to care for anything. I congratulate you, I *am* so glad. I knew "—heartily—"it would come all right some day."

Billy is more convinced than ever that he really had always loved their Duchess.

In the grey of the early morning carriages roll continuously through the brown and quiet woods. Billy's ball is over, and there could be no dissentient voices to Nora's verdict that it has certainly been "a proper one." The drive home is a silent one. Perhaps they are sleepy, or maybe they have too much to say.

Only once, when Nora is expatiating upon her exemplary behaviour, remarking—"I have been simply angelic," Mrs. Peyton suggests softly—

"I thought, dear child, you were going to be so good, and not dance too much with Teddy."

"Well—I *didn't !*" Nora retorts firmly.

A benevolent smile from her aunt; a deprecating gesture from Ivy.

"I didn't," Nora reiterates, closing her eyes with

a pretence of sleepiness, though the lips twitch suspiciously. "I promised not to, and I didn't—so"—mildly—"*I sat out !*"

*　　*　　*　　*　　*　　*

*　　*　　*　　*　　*　　*

Down upon Horston blazes a September sun ; no breath sweeps over the languid flowers ; roses droop in the still heat; the terraces are silent; the deep verandah scorching. A tiny toy terrier and insolent looking bull-dog push their way through hanging venetians and survey the scene. A moment later and the venetians are pushed outwards, and several ladies step on to the terrace.

"Shall we try it?" Ivy asks, looking round at the others. "Shade about equal, with the chance of a breath of air. Don't you think if we crept across to that thick patch and had tea, we might feel more able to talk"—smiling.

"I'm not snubbed," Nora retorts; "my eloquence was spent in a good cause. Sybil has promised to come and stay with us. Such a blessing Lord Egerton's last craze is the poor Hindoo. While he raves about zenanas, Sib and I will 'run' a recreation room for lonely young Englishmen away from their clubs, and pining for culture."

"Zenanas! Nora, you should really think," Sybil says, opening her parasol, and preparing to follow Ivy; "you know men are not allowed"——

"That's just why they are interested," Nora continues recklessly. "If we made washing babies a mystery like freemasonry, every man would be wrapped in flannel aprons, with his sleeves rolled up, soaping anything he could lay his hands on, and

Lord Egerton would be the first to give you lessons
in the art, with your wee Sybil for his victim!"

Mrs. Cleveland is with Ivy, and Gwendoline
saunters after them, with the toy terrier in her
arms, and Snob at her heels. Horston is lively
enough now, and merry voices and laughter echo
everywhere. The Squire is a different man since
his marriage, and Ivy wonders how she could ever
have thought her big sunny-hearted husband silent
or morose. He has insisted on Nora and Teddy
coming to Horston directly after their honeymoon,
and crowded together his friends to slaughter
partridges and do him honour before he sails for
India. This is the only cloud that darkens their
clear sky, and as later Mrs. Peyton walks across the
glowing garden, and sees all the bright faces, and
her happy Teddy stretched lazily at Nora's feet,
she whispers—"It is so true, que la vie ne peut
jamais être tout à fait heureuse, parce qu'elle n'est
pas le ciel, ni tout à fait malheureuse, parce qu'elle
en est le chemin."

Billy places a chair for her. All rise to greet her.
"Your mother," Mrs. Cleveland whispers to Fane,
"is like a grand snow mountain. I always feel
that though on earth, her head is up in heaven.
I want to kneel down as she passes."

"My mother," Fane replies softly, "is to me the
incarnation of goodness, an angel of God."

"Ivy!" Cyril shouts suddenly, "I hope you
don't mind. Looking for stamps in your desk, I
found this. I want it. I don't believe you knew
it was there. It is only an old horse-shoe pin, and
it was stuck through some dried leaves. I threw
them away. Can I have it? It is not a new one,

you see, all bent, but it will do for me." The small boy puts it into her hand as he speaks. Billy bends forward, and looking first at the pin and then at his wife, laughs as she flushes beneath his gaze.

"So you did not 'pass it on,'" he says, smiling. "Would you like to now?"

"Only to you," Ivy answers, sticking it into his coat; "now that your luck is mine, you may have it back."

"Oh, Ivy," Gwennie gasps, "Billy did give it after all."

"So I told you, dear, but you didn't understand. How the sunbeams chase us. Mother, darling, do you mind, or shall we all stay where we are, in the sunlight? It is just enjoyable at this hour."

"Let us all stay 'in the sunlight,'" Mrs. Peyton answers softly.

Mrs. Cleveland looks up quickly. The words bring back another picture—a strange, still scene, a dying prayer. She looks from Ivy's sweet glad face, to the big man bending over her, with the light streaming down upon them; and sees that prayer's fulfilment. Then memory recalls the quiet Mentone Churchyard high above the purple sea, and a tall grey cross that marks a soldier's grave, and that, too, is "in the sunlight."

PRINTED BY BALLANTYNE, HANSON AND CO.
EDINBURGH AND LONDON.